ALSO BY AYŞE KULIN

Aylin

Rose of Sarajevo

Last Train to Istanbul

Farewell: A Mansion in Occupied Istanbul

Love in Exile

AYŞE KULIN

Translated by Kenneth Dakan

Text copyright © 2008 Ayşe Kulin
Translation copyright © 2016 Kenneth Dakan

Previously published as *Umut* by Everest in Turkey in 2008. Translated from Turkish by Kenneth Dakan. First published in English by AmazonCrossing in 2016.

Published by AmazonCrossing, Seattle

www.apub.com

Amazon, the Amazon logo, and AmazonCrossing are trademarks of Amazon.com, Inc., or its affiliates.

ISBN-13: 9781503934955
ISBN-10: 1503934950

Cover design by David Drummond

Printed in the United States of America

With love they touched me always,
now and forever I miss their faces.

Foreword

In 1903, my father was born in the capital of an empire stretching from Bosnia to the Persian Gulf, and from Tripoli to Mecca.

In 1941, I was born in the biggest city of a republic founded in 1923.

My father and I were born into different worlds in the same city: Istanbul.

Love in Exile is set in Istanbul in the years between my father's birth and mine.

After some six hundred years of dominion over a vast swath of territory, the Ottoman Empire lost most of its lands in Europe, Africa, and the Middle East following defeats in the Balkan Wars of 1912–13 and in World War I. British, French, Italian, and Greek troops occupied and partitioned much of what was left of Anatolia at the end of the war.

Under Allied pressure, the sultan agreed to a treaty relinquishing not only all non-Turkish lands, but some Turkish land as well, prompting Mustafa Kemal Atatürk and a handful of rebel officers to launch the popular national movement that would culminate in the Turkish War of Liberation, the abolition of the sultanate, and the establishment, in 1923, of the Republic of Turkey.

In 1897, my paternal grandfather and his family migrated from the prized Ottoman province of Bosnia to Istanbul, where they adapted to a new language, set of customs, and lifestyle. My maternal great-grandfather and his family faced similar challenges as they adapted to life under a new regime in the 1920s.

Love in Exile is also the story of a forbidden and inspiring love.

An Armenian boy whose family moved to Istanbul in 1915 during what the Armenians call "Meds Yeghern," or "the Great Calamity," meets and falls in love with my great aunt, the daughter of a Muslim family, at the American school where they are both students.

Portrayed as well are the lives of three generations of women living together under a single roof as their government embarks on an ambitious project of modernization that upends traditional values as it adopts, and in some ways surpasses, Western reforms governing the equality of the sexes, universal suffrage, the right to work, and the nightlife that allows men and women the opportunity to mingle freely.

In this novel, a new generation that looks to the future with hope replaces a generation that has known heartbreak, homesickness, and disappointment.

Part One

Love in Exile

The Yediç Family
(1928)

Aunt Saraylıhanım

Aunt Neyir

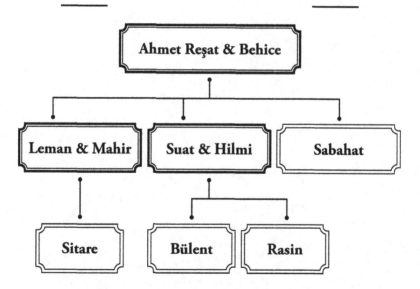

Ahmet Reşat & Behice

Leman & Mahir   **Suat & Hilmi**   **Sabahat**

Sitare   **Bülent**   **Rasin**

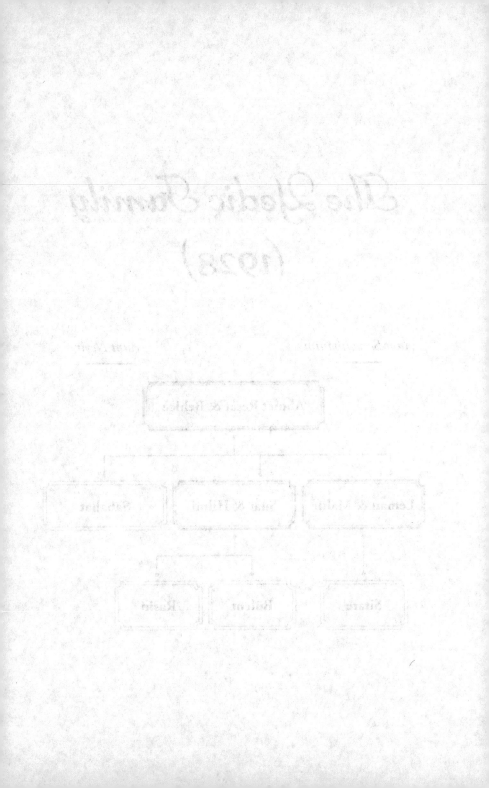

1

The Diary

1928
Beyazit, Istanbul

Leman put on her slippers, threw a shawl around her shoulders, quietly opened the door so as not to awaken her daughter, Sitare, and stole out onto the landing. Grumbling to herself, she climbed the stairs to the top floor. Even a simple afternoon nap was too much to expect in this house!

She and her husband Mahir had been up all night. Or rather, once Mahir had wrapped their daughter Sitare's arms and legs in strips of damp muslin and waited for her fever to fall, if only slightly, he had nodded off in a chair pulled up to the girl's sickbed. Leman, who had opposed from the start this business with the muslin strips, immediately removed them all and settled in for a bedside vigil in case her daughter took a turn for the worse. Left to her own devices, Leman would have placed a heavy blanket over Sitare to sweat out the fever. When Mahir woke up a few hours later, he rewrapped Sitare's limbs in damp cloth, ignoring the protestations of his wife and trying to hide how cross he was with her for trusting the old ways above those of modern medicine. By morning, Sitare's temperature had returned to normal, although she remained quite weak.

After lunch, Leman stretched out next to Sitare to ensure her daughter stayed in bed, and was looking at the illustrations in a stack of periodicals when she drifted off to sleep. But who could nap in peace with that racket upstairs?

When Leman flung open the door, Sabahat and Suat straightened up from the chest of drawers and looked at their furious sister.

"Why are you making so much noise?" Leman demanded. "I thought the house was about to crash down on our heads. What are you two doing up here anyway?"

"Sabahat is moving into her new bedroom," replied the middle sister, Suat. "She's trying to get that chest of drawers and its mirror to the opposite wall, but the blasted thing is so heavy she can barely budge it."

"Are you out of your mind, Sabahat?" Leman asked, as the baby of the family set to shoving the piece of furniture again. "Who would give up a spacious room on the middle floor for a cramped one up here?"

"I would," Sabahat said, puffing and red-faced.

"But it makes no sense. Your room is so bright and airy."

"I'm taking precautions."

"Precautions? Against what?"

"Well, they'll invite Grandmother Neyir to move up here from downstairs because of her bickering with Saraylıhanım, but she'll get winded climbing up and down the stairs, so they'll make up an extra bed in my room. I don't want to share my bedroom. I'm moving in here now so I don't have to hurt grandmother's feelings later."

"You're really too much."

"Leman, every time we have an overnight guest they're always put in my room."

"Don't talk nonsense, Sabahat. That's what the guestroom is for."

6

"Somehow, the guestroom always seems to be occupied. From Fazilet and Hüviyet, to Aunt Dilruba. Every time a visitor spends the night in this house, they do it in my room. Mother always says, 'Make up a bed in Sabahat's room!' Don't look at me like that. It's true, isn't it?"

Leman was peeved at Sabahat for dragging Mahir's nieces, Fazilet and Hüviyet, into this. "Has Fazilet ever complained about putting you up in her room when you stay over at their house?"

"Those two are always welcome; it's the old ladies I mind."

"Well, you do have a big room," Suat said. "And you could hardly expect the guests to stay in the rooms where we sleep with our husbands."

"I may not be married, but it's high time I had a room that nobody barges into and where nobody pokes around in my things."

"She must be talking about our children," Suat said to Leman.

"How could you get upset at your own niece and nephew? Shame on you!" Leman scolded.

"Say what you will, I'm moving into this room, and I'm going to put a lock on the door. Nobody will enter without my permission."

"Does Mother know about this?" Suat asked.

"Yes."

"Do whatever you want, but for goodness' sake, stop making so much noise. Sitare had just fallen asleep and you woke her up," Leman said.

"Then give me a hand with this chest of drawers, and we'll get it over with before you know it," Sabahat said.

"Are you mad? What business do women have moving heavy furniture?" Leman exclaimed. "You'll strain yourself and end up wetting your bed at night." She was about to leave the room when Sabahat's excited cries stopped her.

"Look! You'll never guess what I just found!" Sabahat was saying, as she leaned over to pick up a notebook. "Mehpare spent weeks searching for this notebook. Do you remember? It must have slipped behind the chest of drawers and been squeezed against the wall all this time. I heard a little thud just now as it hit the floor."

"Is it really that famous diary? Mehpare made such a fuss, even going so far as to accuse my little Sitare, and Bülent, of taking it. Are you certain?"

"It had a red tulip on the cover, didn't it? And look at the marbling on the inner cover! This must be it, the notebook we hunted for all those months." Sabahat started flipping through the pages. Suat reached over and took the notebook from her. She blew the dust off the cover and studied it.

"Mehpare, you goose! She was so certain my Bülent had taken it," Suat said.

Leman changed her mind about going back downstairs to Sitare. "You have to admit that your Bülent was a little terror back then," she said. "He'd squirrel away whatever he could get his hands on."

Leman had always felt a twinge of envy over Suat's son's blue eyes and yellow hair. Sitare's honey skin and hazel eyes had been a disappointment for fair-skinned, green-eyed Leman, whose ideal of feminine beauty was an alabaster complexion, blond hair, and blue or green eyes.

"Dust it off and let me have a look," the eldest daughter said.

Sabahat took the book from Suat and shook out its pages through the open window. She wiped the cover with the edge of the curtain she had taken down that morning and held the notebook out to her elder sister.

"Ugh! That old curtain's even dustier than the notebook," Leman said, jerking back her hand as though from a flame.

"Give it back to me!" Suat snatched the notebook from Sabahat and read aloud a few random lines in a low voice. Leman looked over Sabahat's shoulder to see what she was reading.

"That notebook belongs to Mehpare," Sabahat said. "Please don't read it . . . it's wrong." Met by the indifference of her sisters, Sabahat appealed directly to the middle one, the sister to whom she'd always been closest. "Suat, please don't. I'm begging you. I wish I'd never found it. Give the notebook to me and let me take it to its owner."

"There's no harm in having a quick look," Suat said.

Sabahat lunged at the notebook, but Suat held it aloft. Sabahat jumped a few times but was too short to reach it.

"Suat, please don't read it!" Sabahat pleaded.

Suat tossed the notebook to Leman, who, forgetting all about the dust, caught it in midair. Sabahat raced over to Leman.

"Shame on you both!"

"You've turned into such a prig. How lucky for us that you're going to that American school!" Leman tossed the notebook to Suat, who threw it back to her. When Sabahat realized she would never get the notebook back from her sisters, she stormed out of the room, slamming the door behind her.

Suat flipped through the pages, scanning each one. "Just look at what she wrote here!"

"Suat, perhaps we shouldn't?" Leman said.

"Sister! Look! Look what she wrote here!"

Leman's curiosity got the better of her. "What does it say?"

"It's about Beyba's return to Istanbul."

"You mean the day Father got off the ship and they took him to Ankara?"

"Yes! She writes about how overjoyed we were at the prospect of greeting Father and—hang on, I'm reading, stop tugging—how we all returned home in despair, how Mother fainted, everything. Look, it's all here."

"Read it aloud," Leman said. Her eyes had filled with tears.

"Her handwriting is barely legible. Let's read it together."

Sitting side by side in the room that had once belonged to Mehpare and her son Halim, the two sisters began reading aloud from the notebook balanced on Suat's lap:

9

Ayşe Kulin

September 11, 1924
This morning, at the sound of the call to prayer,
Saraylıhanım awakened us one by one. We, the entire
household, including the three children, performed our
prayers together in the common room on the second floor.
After two days of steady rain, the skies cleared as the sun
came up. It was so pleasant! As mild as a summer morn-
ing. We agreed it was a good omen. After prayers, we sat
down to breakfast but couldn't swallow a morsel. Behice
and I had nothing but a few sips of tea. We hurriedly
prepared. The children were dressed in their best clothes.
The previous night, Hilmi had arranged a pair of chauf-
feur-driven automobiles. He, Suat, and Bülent, along
with Sabahat, got into one. I squeezed into the other
one with Halim, Behice, Leman, and Mahir. Behice was
trembling. We were all terribly anxious but did our best
to conceal it. During the drive to the quay, we silently
prayed that this time the Almighty would not dash our
hopes. How many times had we traveled to the quay since
the blacklist was published in the Official Gazette? And
each time we had returned home in silence, our heads
bowed, after having waited for a steamship to dock or
a train to pull into Sirkeci Station. An inner voice told
me today would be different, that a ship carrying Reşat
Bey would steam into port and our beloved father would
be home at last. I believed this with all my heart. Hilmi
Bey is not one to speculate, and it was he who delivered
the joyous news last week of a telegraph from Bucharest.
Not once did I shut my eyes last night. I prayed until
dawn that God would reunite me with the truest friend
I had ever known. Oh, Lord! You took my mother and
my father, and the husband I loved more than my own

*life; please have mercy on me, and bring Reşat Bey, the
man I have always known and loved as a father, safely
to his home. That was the prayer I repeated all through
the night . . .*

"Really, Mehpare?" Leman said. "You'd think she was the only one
who prayed that night! We're his daughters! We were the ones that most
wanted him to come back. We wept for months, rejoiced time and again
at the news he was coming, and then wept again when he didn't. I didn't
sleep until he reached Istanbul, either! I also prayed until dawn."

"If you prayed, you did it reclining in bed. Are you telling me you
knelt on your prayer rug all night long, like Mehpare?" Suat asked.

"What exactly are you implying?"

Suat shrugged and resumed reading.

"Read it to yourself!" Leman snapped.

"But you asked me to read aloud."

"Read it in silence, and hand it over when you're done."

Her lips mouthing the words on the pages, Suat read for a time.
Leman did not need a diary to remember that terrible day. She could
still picture every detail.

After breakfast, she had stood in the doorway of this very room,
holding Sitare in her arms.

"I woke her up early today, and she won't stop fussing. Would you mind
distracting her for a while, Mehpare?"

Mehpare stopped buttoning Halim's shirt and said, "Certainly,
Leman."

Leman noticed Mehpare's red-rimmed eyes but decided there was
not enough time to find out why she had been crying. She rushed off
to her room and pinned her hair into a chignon, fingers trembling
with excitement. At the last moment, she rejected the blouse she had

laid out the night before with her new two-piece suit. After trying on several blouses in various colors, she settled on the cream one. The tailored skirt and jacket were gifts from her mother, who had insisted on having new clothes made for all the girls as soon as the family dared to hope their father might be rejoining them. Behice was adamant that her daughters and Mehpare not appear before their father in old clothes, laying bare the family's reduced circumstances. A visit to their old dress shop, Fegaro's, was out of the question, of course, so the seamstress Katina, who had been doing regular work for the family for years, was summoned to the house.

The rent from the apartment building in Pera would cover the cost of the cloth and the services of the seamstress, but there would be nothing left for Behice, who brightly assured the girls that her lightweight beige coat was as good as new, since she so rarely ventured out of doors these days. The girls saw through this, and if Leman's new suit the color of unripe almonds had not brought out the green of her eyes to such delightful effect, she might have worn her old one. Leman knew the sacrifice her mother was making, but she so wanted her father to find her as fresh and lovely as the day he had gone into exile. While Suat had her winning ways and sharp tongue, and Sabahat had her intelligence and drive, Leman was simply Daddy's prettiest girl; it was her one distinction. When she heard Mahir calling, she adjusted the angle of her little hat and hastily applied a bit more rouge to her cheeks.

"Leman, what's taking you so long? We're going to be late. The automobiles arrived long ago and everyone's waiting for you," her husband, Mahir, shouted from the ground floor.

The other members of the family had assembled in the entrance hall. Her mother had been sitting in an armchair by the front door for nearly half an hour with an odd expression on her face. Sitare and Halim were zipping about, but Behice Hanım was oblivious to their chatter. Suat, Hilmi, and Bülent had already taken their places in one of the automobiles idling in front of the garden gate.

"Shall we go now?" Mahir Bey asked his mother-in-law.

Behice Hanım was suffering a last-minute case of nerves over her appearance. She had neglected her looks even as the tears of separation had deepened the lines around her eyes. Now she was finding excuses not to leave the house.

"Keep a low flame under the food so it doesn't get cold," Behice told the housekeeper. "Be certain the rice is perfectly steamed; Reşat Bey particularly misses buttery rice pilaf. The windows are open. You'll need to take a feather duster to the sitting room again. And remember to comb out Saraylıhanım's hair."

"Come on then, quickly please, or we'll be late," Mahir Bey said, taking his mother-in-law by the arm and guiding her toward the gate.

As Mehpare would write in her diary later that day, they traveled to the quay in Tophane in silence, hearts pounding as they prayed that this time would be different. Leman pulled a cardigan out of her bag and tried to slip it around her daughter's shoulders. Sitare fretted and squirmed, saying the day was warm and she did not want it, at which Mahir scolded them both.

Everyone was on edge that day, and the casual observer would be forgiven for thinking they were in danger of missing a ship, rather than rushing to meet one that would drop anchor and await them in the harbor. The occupants of the two automobiles knew, however, that this day would alter forever the course of their lives, for better or worse.

It was with great difficulty that Ahmet Reşat found a place on the upper deck among the passengers leaning on the rail and waving to their loved ones. His eyes scanned the dock, quickly identifying his family in the crowd. There was Behice in the beige coat he knew so well. The young lady in the pale-green suit and hat must be Leman, and the one standing next to her in white was Suat. Even from a distance Suat looked decidedly plump. Perhaps she was in a family way?

The girl perched on Mahir Bey's shoulders must be Sitare, and the little boy in Hilmi Bey's arms would be Bülent. The boy in the sailor suit standing between Mehpare and Sabahat, and holding their hands, was Halim. Sabahat was shielding her eyes against the sun with her free hand as she searched for her father. As always, her blond hair was coiled on her head in two plaits.

As the steamer slowly maneuvered into position, Ahmet Reşat wished he could take wing like a gull; alight on his wife's shoulder; clasp his daughters in his arms; nuzzle his grandchildren's necks, delighting in that scent of innocence particular to young children; and embrace Mehpare and kiss her on the forehead. Now that the reunion was so near, his longing was unbearable. They were so close. He could not hear what they were saying, but he could see their excitement reflected in their every gesture. They were all looking up at the deck, but nobody had spotted him yet, even though he was waving to them. He saw Leman pull binoculars out of her purse. They had belonged to Kemal before he went off to fight and die in Anatolia. Ahmet Reşat had then given them to his eldest daughter when he went off into exile. He felt a pang in his heart and swallowed hard. He had ridiculed Kemal for his political views, but this land to which Ahmet Reşat was returning had been saved and rebuilt by men who shared Kemal's convictions. This new republic was strange to him, and he would have to adapt. The world of the Ottomans, the only world he had ever known, had been relegated to the history books. Those who had fled for their lives, leaving behind all their worldly possessions to come to Anatolia from "overseas"—that is, from the Ottoman lands of Rumelia in Eastern Europe—had clamored to become not subjects of an empire, but citizens of a nation. The same was true of the refugees from Crimea and the Caucasus. Life had drummed into these refugees from the far reaches of the empire a lesson they would never forget: only in unity, as one people and one nation, could they hope to be safe. If God blessed Ahmet Reşat with the opportunity to disembark from this ship and join his family, he, too, would become a citizen of the Republic of Turkey.

As he pondered his future, he felt a pain in his heart as sharp as the sting produced by salt rubbed into a fresh wound. In order for him to adapt to a world that had neither sultan nor caliph, this wound in his heart would have to heal. Over time, a scab would form and fall off, leaving behind a scar that perhaps, eventually, would fade to nothing. And it was then, and only then, that he would be able to declare: "Kemal, how right you were! I thank you for this nation to which you made the ultimate sacrifice. For the rest of my life, with each breath I take, I will remember you and pray for God to have mercy on your soul. And to you and your memory, I hereby pledge that I will ensure your only son grows up to become the patriot you were."

When Ahmet Reşat saw that Leman had failed to spot him even with the aid of the binoculars, he overcame his disinclination to disturb his neighbors and began frantically waving his fez in the air.

"Oh! There he is! Beyba!"

"Where, where? Show me."

"Let me have those binoculars, my girl."

"It really is him! Look, he's taken off his fez and he's waving it, right behind the woman in red . . ."

Behice finally saw her husband. "Ah! Thank you, God, for bringing him back to me!" she exclaimed. Then she burst into tears, though moments earlier she had warned her daughters and Mehpare that it would upset Father to see them crying. Ahmet Reşat saw that they were all dabbing at their eyes and that Mahir had taken the binoculars from Behice.

Amid the creaking protests of the hawsers as they were drawn taut, the ship arrived quayside. A group of police officers leapt onto the gangplank while it was still dangling in midair, and nimbly climbed aboard the ship. A few moments later, the narrow gangplank touched the dock, and the passengers began descending in single file.

When the steamer had disgorged its passengers, there was still no sign of Ahmet Reşat. Behice had gone chalk white and was twisting her handkerchief into knots. To avoid giving voice to their fears, nobody spoke. The family waited, all eyes on the gangplank over which the last passenger had descended at least ten minutes ago. There were two other families waiting on the dock. At first, they nodded at each other from a distance; then they came together and began speaking in low voices. One of the families was non-Muslim; the other one had come to meet Faik Bey, a deputy in the last Ottoman Parliament. Behice Hanım unburdened herself as though to old friends. Where could Faik Bey, Reşat Bey, and Monsieur Andros be? Did they have no idea what was causing the delay? None? Nobody knew anything. While the women anxiously conversed, the men murmured among themselves. Perhaps an interrogation was under way on the ship?

"I wonder if they're being detained and questioned. The least the authorities could do is tell us if they are on the ship or not," Faik Bey's wife said.

"Rest assured that your husband is on that ship. I saw mine up on the deck. He waved to us, but for some reason he still hasn't disembarked," Behice said.

Half an hour later, Mahir and Hilmi, along with the men from the two other families, decided to board the ship. A uniformed official blocked them at the gangplank. When Leman and Suat started crying, Mehpare discreetly directed the sisters' attention to their mother, who was leaning against the wall, tearfully uttering prayers. "For goodness' sake, Leman, dear, you're only worrying your mother further. We really must compose ourselves."

After exchanging a few words with Mahir Bey and Hilmi Bey, the uniformed official climbed up the gangway. He returned a short time later and headed in the direction of the port authority building without saying a word. Just then, two men dressed as civil servants came up and invited all three families to visit the harbor master. The three families followed the civil servants into the building and were ushered to three separate rooms on an upper floor. The harbor master spoke to Behice and her family first. Ahmet Reşat, as well as the other newly returned exiles, would be ferried across the Bosphorus to Haydarpaşa Station and put aboard a train to Ankara, where they would appear in court. Mahir and Hilmi propped Behice up by the arms.

The harbor master pointed to a chair and said, "Have her sit down there." Sabahat was no more aware of digging her nails into Mehpare's hand than Mehpare was aware of how tightly she was gripping Sabahat's arm. Suat gave Bülent a pinch to stop him from fidgeting, at which he started wailing. Hilmi Bey asked Mehpare to take the children out of the room, and Sitare and Halim began running circles around each other in the corridor. Bülent in her arms, Mehpare leaned back against the wall and slowly sank down into a crouch.

Back in the harbor master's office, Behice plucked up the courage to speak. "Sir, I would like to see my husband."

"I'm afraid there's nothing I can do."

"I respectfully ask that you find something you can do. I have been apart from my husband for years. Allow me this, at least. Do you understand? Please. I implore you."

The harbor master slowly got up and left the room. Behice turned to her daughters, who had started crying again. "Cry when you get home, but don't surrender to your tears in front of a man who treats your father like a common criminal!" she told her girls.

A few minutes later, the harbor master returned. "The gentlemen will be brought here before they are taken to Ankara. A brief meeting will be arranged." Looking at Behice, he said, "Not all of you can see him, however. I have been told that only two family members will be permitted."

"My daughters and I all need to see him. He would want to see his children."

"Those are my orders. Two of you." A clerk came in and whispered something into the harbor master's ear. "Your husband is waiting in the interview room. Decide who will see him."

Suat and Leman started arguing.

"I've decided who will meet with your father," Behice said.

"His wife and his firstborn, of course," Leman said.

"I'm afraid not, my dear. I'd like Mahir Bey to accompany me. Your father might have some instructions for your husband, issues of a masculine nature."

"But Mother—"

"I have decided!" Behice stood up. "Are you ready, Mahir Bey?"

Stunned and disappointed, Leman watched as her mother walked down the corridor with Mahir. She could not believe that the malleable, coddled woman who had always let her daughters run the household as they saw fit, down to choosing which dishes to cook every day, had made a decision of such magnitude completely on her own—and so quickly. Pouting, she turned to her brother-in-law. "Mother didn't want me!"

"It's for the best, Leman," Hilmi Bey said. "You'd have fallen out with your sisters if she had chosen you."

"But I'm the eldest!"

They could hear Bülent screaming in the corridor as Mehpare scolded Halim.

"Sabahat, why don't you take the children and go home with Mehpare," Suat said. "They're hungry. They should have had lunch hours ago."

"I'm staying here until Mother comes back." Sabahat sounded determined. The youngest sister was considered to have the sweetest disposition of the three, but Suat knew that once Sabahat had made up her mind there was no dissuading her.

It was agreed that Hilmi Bey would accompany Mehpare and the children home. The three sisters anxiously waited in the office of the harbor master for their mother and Mahir Bey to return.

Behice appeared a short time later. Suat noticed she was clutching something in her left hand, but chose not to ask about it in front of the harbor master.

"Girls, your father looked well," she said. "He is in good health, and his spirits are high. Our years apart seem to have taken more of a toll on me than on him."

"What did you talk about?"

"There was so little time. He asked about each of you and wanted so much to see you."

"Why hasn't Mahir come back with you?" Leman asked.

"There were some things he needed to discuss with your father. He'll be along shortly."

Mahir Bey rejoined the others ten minutes later.

"There's nothing to worry about. Your father has no complaints. He'll be back with us soon. Now let's go home," he said.

Behice did not say a word as she descended the stairs on Leman's arm. She walked out of the building, head held high and back straight. However, when her son-in-law motioned to an approaching streetcar, she said, "Perhaps we could arrange an automobile, Mahir Bey. I'm afraid I'm in no condition to stand."

Blushing red to the tips of his ears, Mahir said, "I gave everything I had to Reşat Bey. He refused, of course, but I insisted. Leman, are you carrying any money?"

Leman was not accustomed to carrying money while in the company of her husband. Among them, they scraped together enough coins for the streetcar home.

The moment the heavy garden gate swung shut behind them, Behice collapsed to the ground.

"Mother's fallen. Mahir, come quickly! Do something!" Leman screamed.

"It must be her blood pressure. Get some water and cologne," Mahir said, racing to the house to get his doctor's bag.

Suat was kneeling on the grass chafing her mother's wrists when she noticed the little bundle clutched in her mother's left hand. She gently pried open her fingers and unwrapped the silk handkerchief covering . . . ah, the diamond bird brooch Father gave Mother when he lifted her veil and saw her face for the first time!

"Silly mother," she said to herself. "If you were going to take your brooch all the way to the quay, why not pin it to your collar?" She slipped the brooch into the pocket of her mother's coat.

Mehpare ran up with a glass of water and a bottle of lemon cologne. "What's wrong? Was there bad news? Tell me what happened."

Nobody knew what to say to Mehpare. Mahir splashed some water on Behice's face and held the bottle under her nose. The moment Behice came around, she dissolved into tears.

"They took him away, and I don't know if I'll ever see him again." She sobbed. "I wish he'd never come back. If he were in exile, at least I'd know he was alive. At least I could hope to see him again. Now I don't know what they'll do; they could hang him, shoot him, throw him into prison to rot. He's gone. My Reşat is gone."

"Heaven forbid, Mother. Don't say that!" Suat exclaimed, tears streaming down her face.

"Your fears are completely unfounded," Mahir told Behice. "Please, you must believe me. Reşat Bey will be home in a month at the latest. I received assurances at the quay."

Too weak to stand, Behice was half-carried into the entrance hall and made comfortable in the armchair.

The sisters were crying on each other's shoulders in the kitchen. Mehpare was crying in the hall, along with the housekeeper and Nesime. Shut into his room on the floor above, Bülent was howling. Ahmet

Reşat's faithful manservant, Hüsnü Efendi, was pacing the length of the hall, bewildered but too timid to ask what had happened. Hilmi came downstairs and shot a quizzical look at Mahir, who sighed helplessly and shrugged.

"He's gone," Behice moaned. "They took my husband! Just as we were reunited, I've lost him forever!"

Into the hall padded a ghostly creature trailing a veil of white silk.

"Why all the weeping?" Saraylıhanım grinned toothlessly. "Did you not know that heads must roll in service to the state? The higher the head, the farther it rolls."

Everyone froze. Was God speaking the truth through this madwoman? Goose bumps broke out on Behice's arms before she collected herself, stiffened, and, for the first time ever in her married life, snapped at her husband's aged aunt. "Take this fool to her room. I will not abide her nonsense."

Mehpare took Saraylıhanım's arm and gently tugged her toward the stairs. "Where on earth did you find all this tulle? Oh! It's Suat's bridal veil! She'll be furious if she sees you. Come on, let's go to your room and take it off."

"It's my right to be a bride, too," Saraylıhanım said, dragging her feet. "And I want a present from my bridegroom."

"My brooch!" Behice cried. "Where's my diamond bird brooch? It was in my hand. I must have dropped it!"

Suat came running into the hall. "I took it when you fainted. Look, here it is in the pocket of your coat. Anyway, Mother, why in the world were you carrying it in your hand in the first place?"

"I slipped this brooch into your father's pocket just before he went into exile, thinking he could sell it if he fell on hard times. He returned it to me today; it was the first thing he did." Clutching the brooch, she bowed her head and said, "What am I without you? What do any of these trinkets mean if you are not here beside me?"

***

Memories of that day had haunted Leman's dreams for years. How could she possibly forget a single detail?

Suat put down Mehpare's diary and wiped away a tear with the back of her hand. "Do you remember how wretched we all were? I feel as though I've just relived that entire day. I wish I hadn't read this diary."

"Neither good fortune nor misfortune lasts for long, thank God," Leman said. "Remember how Mother's hair went gray as we waited in vain for news of Father? After six weeks, when she had nearly given up on life, suddenly there he was. We'd feared the worst, but they hadn't tortured him or thrown him into prison. He'd been acquitted. My, how we celebrated! The rams and sheep we sacrificed; halvah and friedcake were distributed to everyone in the neighborhood."

At that moment, lost in their shared memories, the two sisters were bonded by a new intimacy; faces somber, eyes shining with love for each other.

Suat closed the notebook and held it out to Leman. "Would you like to read it?"

"Not on your life. I'm not touching that dusty thing."

"All right then. After I've helped Sabahat settle into her new room, she can take it to Mehpare," Suat said.

"Don't make any more noise, Suat. I'll be furious if you do! Sitare isn't well. She needs her rest."

The spell was broken. The mysterious bond had dissolved. Leman went downstairs, tapped on the door of Sabahat's room, and poked her head inside.

"We're through with the notebook. You can go up and get it from Suat."

"Good. I've got half a mind to tell Mehpare you were reading her diary."

"Oh, I'm so scared," Leman said. "I do hope she doesn't thrash us."

"Just keep mocking me. God sees all. How could you, Leman? Don't you two know it's wrong to read someone's diary without permission?"

Leman stepped into the room and looked into her sister's eyes.

"Sabahat, if I were you, I wouldn't act like a little know-it-all to your big sisters. If Father ever finds out you've been at the cinema with a man, he'll cut you down to size."

"I haven't been to the cinema with a man."

"Yes you have, Sabahat. Celadet Hanım saw you there just the other day."

"There was a group of us, five girls and two boys. To hear you tell it, I was there on my own with a man."

"Who were those boys?"

"Friends from school. You already know one of them. Remember when you visited the school last week to talk about Sitare, and I introduced you to Aram?"

"That Armenian boy!"

"Is it a crime to be Armenian?"

"You know what I mean. This isn't about being Armenian. What were you doing at the cinema with boys?"

"They were already there. They happened to have gone to the same film as me and my girlfriends."

"Then you should have turned around and come home at once."

"Why? We'd gone all the way there, and besides, it was a Lillian Gish film."

"Don't ever let me hear again that you were spotted at the cinema with a man."

"One of those 'men' was a friend from school; the other was his big brother."

"He might be a boy, but they'll gossip about him as though he were a man. Don't ever do that again."

"If you say so, mother dearest," Sabahat whined in the singsong tones of a child.

"How apt that you mimic the voice of a child when you've been acting like one, and when you've forced me to offer you some motherly advice."

Sabahat bit her tongue. Her cheeks were flushed with anger, and she was particularly cross with her sister for implying that Aram was a mere boy. Having attended a French school before transferring to an American junior high, Sabahat was older than her classmates. As a petite girl, though, she looked younger than her years, and her classmates treated her as an equal. When Leman left the room, Sabahat seized one of the lace pillows on her bed and flung it at the door.

2

Ahmet Reşat's New Life

Not long after Mehmet VI, the last sultan, sailed out of Istanbul on an English warship in November 1922, Ahmet Reşat, the last Ottoman chancellor of the exchequer and an eyewitness to the death throes of an empire that had been in decline for centuries, fled into exile along with several other blacklisted cabinet members.

Ahmet Reşat found refuge first in Italy, the country of choice for many of his fellow exiles. Then, low on funds, he traveled to Romania, where he settled into a modest *pensiune* in Bucharest, paid for with the money his family occasionally managed to send.

The household of women he had left behind busied themselves with the stuff of daily life, largely sealed off from the wider world. By day, they waited for news and letters from Reşat Bey; by night, they prayed for his safe return. The absence of the family patriarch had drawn them closer. Petty jealousies and bickering were replaced by a sense of solidarity and self-sacrifice, even between Leman and Suat. The women did all they could to comfort and care for one another, displaying a new maturity marked by sensitivity, modesty, and frugality. Extravagances were out of the question. In any case, the family had already learned to live on less while Ahmet Reşat was still chancellor of the exchequer, during an era when the salaries of civil servants and soldiers were often paid months behind schedule. The regime may have changed, but life in the mansion was much the same, if duller and more isolated. Behice's father still sent stores of food from his farm in Beypazarı. Fortunately, Behice was a descendant of the Circassian line of the wealthy Söylemezzade family, and İbrahim Bey's only child. Now that Ahmet Reşat was in exile, İbrahim Bey no longer had to worry about embarrassing his son-in-law with his generosity, and he signed over all the revenue from his Istanbul properties to his daughter. Behice sent the lion's share of this revenue to her husband, although much of it was pocketed by middlemen before it ever reached him.

Behice and her daughters led a life that was self-contained, self-reliant, and utterly cheerless. There were no more visits to friends and relatives, no more excursions through the city streets, no more amusements of any kind. The few guests that still came rarely stayed overnight. Music was no longer heard. When Leman sat down at the piano one day to play a nursery rhyme for Sitare, her mother promptly asked her to stop making noise. Sabahat's violin lessons with Mr. Berger were suspended, and she stopped practicing in her room for fear she would upset Mother, who could not bear the sound of music while her husband was still in exile. The girls felt as though an evil fairy had waved a wand over the house, dooming its inhabitants to a life of gloom until their father returned to break the spell.

Ahmet Reşat was coping as best he could in Bucharest. He was frugal with food and drink but allowed himself the luxury of tobacco. Even so, he was forced to swallow his pride and move to a humbler pensiune in an undesirable neighborhood. Fortunately, two close friends in similar straits were there to keep him company. Drawing strength from the spiritual grace of his faith and, perhaps, from a stubborn sense of hope, he put himself in God's hands, wrote the occasional financial article for a small fee, found comfort in letters from family and friends, and gave thanks for being more fortunate than so many others.

Fearful that his son-in-law's military salary would be insufficient to support the household of women he had left behind, Ahmet Reşat insisted in letter after letter that he was able to cover his own expenses. His wife and daughters were equally adamant that he would receive everything they could spare.

Ahmet Reşat had been right to go west rather than to Egypt. In Romania, he could at least sup on boiled beef, avail himself of a privy with a door, sleep on relatively unsoiled sheets, and when the occasion demanded, as it sometimes did, find solace in a bottle of fiery plum brandy. He could bear the pinch of poverty, but a gnawing homesickness plagued him. The warmth of his wife's embrace, his girls' sweet prattle, the simple pleasures of being at home surrounded by family— this was what he missed most. He also longed to inhale the richness of a foaming cup of freshly ground coffee; to feel the steaming heat of a tulip-shaped glass of bright-red tea; to savor buttery rice pilaf, apricot compote, bluefish with lemon-dressed rocket; to behold the massed clusters of purple blossoms in his garden and the thousand glowing tones of a city sunset. He missed bundling up against the icy bite of the *poyraz* and yielding to the stupefying sultriness of the *lodos*, the warm wind from the south. He yearned for the colors, the smells, the sensations and flavors of his beloved Istanbul, even in a recurring dream in which he wandered among the sighing pines of the Princes' Islands. Night and day, his thoughts were with his country and his family.

He followed world events as best he could in the English and French newspapers but devoured the rare Turkish newspaper sent from home. He learned that the newly stateless sultan, Mehmet VI, had traveled to the Hejaz at the invitation of its newly declared king, Hussein bin Ali. The sultan had been bitterly disappointed to find that the grand sharif of Mecca had designs on the title of caliph, the spiritual leadership role assumed by the Ottoman sultans since 1362. Having angered bin Ali and with no offers of refuge or support from any other Arab leaders, the poor sultan retired to the city of San Remo on the Italian Riviera. Ahmet Reşat sympathized deeply.

It was also from the newspapers that Ahmet Reşat learned one rainy day in late autumn that the city where he and his ancestors had been born, blessed Istanbul, had lost its status as capital when the bland provincial town of Ankara was declared the new administrative center. *Whoever has done this has to be mad,* he thought. That evening, as the rain beat against the window of his lonely room, he allowed his tears to pour forth.

Two weeks later, he learned that Turkey would be a republic.

As Ahmet Reşat was eking out an existence in a strange land, his homeland was being utterly transformed. Were his wife, his daughters, his aunt, his sons-in-law, and Mehpare adapting? Or were they being buffeted by the winds of change? Homesickness and anxiety weighed on his heart.

Fortunately, Ahmet Reşat's exile would not last much longer. The list of leading "traitors and collaborators" had been whittled down from six hundred names to what was dubbed "The List of 150." That list, compiled by the Interior Ministry and published in the *Official Gazette* in June 1924, contained the names of five former members of the sultan's cabinet. Ahmet Reşat's was not among them.

He pictured his family offering ritual prayers of thanks, sacrificing rams, and cooking up cauldrons of halvah to distribute to the neighbors. A week later, there was a flood of letters and postcards confirming the happy news and congratulating him. Separate envelopes from Mahir and Leman arrived, as did a single envelope containing letters from

Behice and Suat. Mehpare sent her best wishes in scrawled handwriting and had painstakingly recorded Saraylıhanım's greetings as well.

His family assured him they were exploring ways to send money. For the first time, he did not object. All he asked was for the fare to return home, and the sooner the better.

Ahmet Reşat had been one of the few ministers in the cabinet of the last grand vizier, Tevfik Pasha, to support the nationalist movement. He had never openly admitted to arranging munitions and funds for the irregular army battling the occupying forces on the western front of Anatolia, but those in the know had later informed the new Republican government of the clandestine aid he had provided at such a critical juncture for their movement. Among those who would speak out on Ahmet Reşat's behalf was İsmail Hakkı Bey, a friend of Kemal's.

Acquitted of any crimes at a tribunal in Ankara, Ahmet Reşat was able to rejoin his family in Istanbul after less than two months of detention. Back in his own bed, he tossed and turned for many nights, wondering what he could have done to alter the course of history. Grand Vizier Tevfik Pasha had been an intermediary in efforts to improve relations between the sultan and the shadow government the nationalists had formed in Ankara. Unfortunately, the sultan had stubbornly closed his ears to any talk of an alliance between his Constantinople government and the rogue Ankara government, believing that his authority would eventually be reasserted in every corner of his empire. Had it been a missed opportunity? Could a few well-chosen words have persuaded the sultan to find common cause with the rival government in Ankara, thus saving his throne and altering the destiny of a nation?

For the first few months after his return to Istanbul, Ahmet Reşat stayed at home, resting, becoming reacquainted with his family and welcoming visitors. When the welcome home visits came to an end, he began to feel restless. He was too young to retire. From among the many job proposals the former chancellor of the exchequer received, he accepted a position as general manager of a large bank, both to keep himself occupied and to replenish the family finances.

As Ahmet Reşat had written in every letter sent from Romania, God seemed to be watching over his humble servant. His reputation was intact, he was dependent on no one, and together with his sons-in-law; his beloved daughters; his grandchildren; his senile aunt; his aunt's daughter-in-law, Mehpare; and Mehpare's son, Halim; he was still able to winter in the mansion in Beyazit and to summer in the large wooden house on the island of Burgazada.

There was no denying, though, that with his outmoded suits, his tall collars, his pocket watch and chain, his pointy English shoes, his gaiters, and his overly ornate Turkish tongue, he was still an Ottoman through and through—dignified and deserving of respect, but hopelessly behind the times. He was the proud picture of a traditional Istanbul gentleman: his back ramrod straight, a silver-knobbed walking stick at the ready, his graying hair close-cropped, his fine-boned Circassian features composed and gracious. Yet he felt, on occasion, like an antiquated machine cast aside to rust. Perhaps he belonged to another time, to the once upon a time of his grandchildren's bedtime stories—except those characters had not all lived happily ever after. He had battled venality, sycophancy, willful ignorance, and gross negligence. He had seen the state besieged from without until it finally collapsed from within. He had shame-facedly extracted new terms from creditors as war and mismanagement drained the imperial coffers. He had survived truly desperate times, so why did he, a man who had witnessed the collapse of a six-hundred-year-old empire, tremble in trepidation as he pondered the future of his family and his nation? He felt as though he were trapped in a maze or caught in a vicious circle, and there was no way out until he learned to keep up with the times and to adapt to the dizzying pace of a country in flux. Perhaps he was a product of a bygone age and would, in any case, not be long for this world, but he had his grandchildren to consider. It was his duty as the family patriarch to ensure that they flourished long after he was gone. He vowed to do his utmost to prepare his loved ones for a future he himself would not see, and, by considering the future of his loved ones, perhaps he would learn to embrace the present and make peace with the past.

Sabahat, Halim, Sitare, and Bülent would receive a modern education, not only in the languages of the occupiers who had humbled the Ottomans, but in the occupiers' schools of thought, the inner workings of their minds, their ethos, and their psyche. "Best someone at his own game" went the English expression. And nobody was more cunning at the game of divide and conquer than the English!

To avoid submitting again to the West, the Ottomans—ah, there he went again! There were no Ottomans anymore; they were all Turks now. Turks would have to learn the ways of the West.

Ahmet Reşat was eternally grateful to Mustafa Kemal for having saved the homeland and established a republic, but why this animus against the House of Osman? Why hadn't the new republic adopted a constitutional monarchy similar to Great Britain's, thereby accommodating the dynasty that had ruled over these lands since 1299? Could they not have preserved the pomp and glory of their ancient traditions?

In this new republic, the splendid palaces would be haunted by ghosts, the royal procession to Friday prayers would become a memory, and the imams' sermons would make no reference to His Sacred and Imperial Majesty. The sultan had been the Defender of the Faith. In a country without a sultan, who would defend Islam?

Ahmet Reşat seemed to be the only person in his immediate circle troubled by these questions. When he finally unburdened himself to his son-in-law, Mahir dismissed his concerns with a wave of the hand. "The sultan should have sent a letter not to the English but to the Ankara government," replied Mahir. "How could we have permitted a man so terrified of his own people to remain on the throne, I ask you?"

"In a dynasty so large, his successor could have taken the throne."

"What we need today is not an heir to the Ottoman throne but a leader who unites our people as never before."

My God! If this was the view even his closest family members held, was there anyone to whom he could pour out his doubts and worries?

As the days passed, he saw that his fears were largely groundless. The foreign reports of religious bans he had read about in exile had proven false. The mosques still filled for Friday prayers. The populace still fasted during Ramadan. During the first week of his return, his family had summoned a hodja to the house to recite prayers of thanks, even throwing the windows open so the entire neighborhood could hear, and they had gone door-to-door with celebratory halvah afterward. Ahmet Reşat had braced himself for the worst, but relaxed when the local watchman happily joined in the festivities.

When he visited the tombs of his mother and father in Eyüp, the Muslim cemetery was as tranquil as ever. Headscarved women still raised their cupped palms to the heavens and recited the al-Fatiha in front of modest tombstones shaded by mournful cypresses; gypsies still solicited tips for carrying tin pails to water the graves; hodjas still walked in front of coffins draped in the green of Islam.

It all looked the same. So had nothing changed?

"Everything is changing at an incredible pace," Mahir said. "Reforms slated for implementation in thirty years have been adopted in thirty days. It's astonishing. The Ottoman subjects must have been thirsty for change. We are undergoing a great transformation, top to bottom. This is a revolution, and we haven't spilled so much as a drop of blood."

"Oh? You overthrew a dynasty!"

"In times of revolution, royal heads roll. Consider the French Revolution, and the one in Russia. Our royal family was banished without a nosebleed. Is that not in itself revolutionary?"

Ahmet Reşat had no ready response. Perhaps he was being reactionary.

In this time of sweeping reforms and great social upheaval, Ahmet Reşat soon settled into a routine as humdrum as any he had known. Off he would go to his job in the morning, like any civil servant, returning in the evening after a full day's work. His house was still full of women, but, in theory at least, he also had sons-in-law to engage him on subjects suitable for men.

After dinner, the entire family would gather in the upstairs room with the long divan lining its walls, at which point he would find himself sorely missing the room downstairs that in less enlightened times had been reserved for the men of the house and their male guests. In his absence, that masculine sanctuary had been converted into an examination room for Mahir. In the old days, the women had settled onto the divan to discuss matters dear to their feminine hearts while the men congregated downstairs to debate affairs of state. Now, no sooner would he and his sons-in-law begin discussing current events than they would be interrupted as the thread of conversation was snipped by questions from the girls, the women, or Saraylıhanım, the last of whom had taken to wearing outlandish costumes and was barely coherent. He didn't dare propose that they enjoy a postdinner smoke in the exam room for fear the lingering odor would disturb Mahir's patients.

There were so many things Reşat Bey wished to learn. For example, Mahir had written that his resignation from the army had been hastened by an expedition he had undertaken in the vicinity of Edremit, but he had provided no details. Now, every time Reşat Bey tried to raise the subject, Mahir would silence him with a cocked brow and a covert glance at the women in the room. One weekend, while Behice and the girls were out shopping, Reşat Bey finally got some answers.

"Why are you so reluctant to talk about your trip to Edremit? Is there something you wish to keep from the women?" he asked.

"Were Leman to learn of that trip's true purpose, I fear it would upset her greatly, even today."

"You've succeeded in further whetting my curiosity."

"In February of 1923, following an outbreak of typhoid, I was sent on an investigatory expedition that was to take me from Edremit all the way to İzmir. There are no words to describe the conditions under which we traveled. My only consolation was the company of Doctor Hayim. Although we had set out with numerous crates of laudanum, morphine, boric acid, bismuth salts, calomel, and other medical supplies, we encountered so much disease in the villages along the way that our supplies soon ran out. It was snowing incessantly. There was a bitter northeast wind. Some of our wagons slid off the mountain roads, breaking axles and wheels. We were forced, on more than one occasion, to proceed on foot, and there were nights when we slept in wagon beds under our greatcoats, our limbs stiff with cold. The stench in those wretched homes . . . every family seemed to have one or two cases. We did what we could, and many times that meant ensuring the bodies were disinfected with lime before burial.

"One day, a blizzard struck as we were nearing a mountain village. We started walking, but the shrapnel wound in my heel reopened, making it impossible for me to continue. We eventually found shelter in a house, but, would you believe it, one of its inhabitants vomited on Hayim!"

"My God!" Reşat Bey exclaimed. "And there I was, wallowing in self-pity in Bucharest. What happened after that? Don't tell me you came down with typhoid fever!"

"No, God was watching over both of us. We sent a villager into town to enlist the aid of the military police. We limed and fumigated Hayim's soiled clothing. My wound became infected, and I grew feverish. We had no choice but to remain in that house until the weather cleared. Hayim Efendi—I mean, Hayim Bey; as you know, we no longer use the term 'efendi'—stayed with me and dressed my wound, but we had long since run out of medicine. By chance, Hilmi Bey was on leave at the time. He came immediately. Naturally, he didn't tell Leman or Behice what had happened. By the time Hilmi Bey reached us, the snow had stopped. They put me on a stretcher in an oxcart and later hoisted me onto a ferryboat bound for Istanbul. I spent a week at the army hospital before going home. Leman got wind that something had happened and was frantic with worry. At her insistence, I decided to stop treating pestilential diseases, resigning my position in the army."

"Mahir Bey, you didn't relate any of this in your letters."

"I expect you had enough worries of your own."

"I had no idea of the extent of your suffering here! All we can do is pray that the worst of our troubles are behind us."

"I fervently hope that is true for our family," Mahir said. "But troubled times are ahead for our country, I'm afraid."

"Why do you say that?"

"Sir, what I just described was the situation in Thessaly and the Aegean region. Things are far worse out in the East. The scourge of war has left behind pestilence and poverty; the peasants drive their primitive plows through that barren land, barely able to feed their families. The swamplands of Adana are breeding grounds for cholera. Further north, there have been outbreaks of trachoma, pox, and tuberculosis. There have been cases of leprosy as well. The government is trying to eradicate these diseases, but they don't know where to start. Making matters even worse, some of the tribal clans in the East have grown restive; they're powder kegs. The British are supplying them with arms and making empty promises. The intent, of course, is to foment rebellion among the Kurds in order to weaken our hand in Mosul. Hilmi Bey has served in the East and seen the conditions there with his own eyes. The tribal and religious leaders rule their peasants with an iron fist and prefer to keep them impoverished and ignorant. They resist all our efforts at modernization. We won the War of Independence, but our work has just begun."

Reşat Bey stroked his chin and was about to respond when the bell at the front gate rang. He walked over to the window and saw someone getting out of a cab with a great many packages in her hands.

"Ah, that must be Fazilet and Hüviyet. I can see Şahber Hanım getting out of a cab!" Reşat Bey said.

"Didn't Leman tell you she'd invited my sister and her daughters to spend the weekend with us?"

"Well then, where is Leman?" Reşat Bey said. "Her guests have arrived, but she's still out in the streets!" The men went down to the ground floor landing and found that the housekeeper had opened the door.

"We were not expecting you this early," she said. "I'm afraid the ladies have not yet returned." Reşat Bey raced over to the door to smooth over the housekeeper's blunder.

"My, my, look who it is! Welcome. How wonderful to see you. Come right in, ladies."

"We'd planned to come toward evening, but Naci had some business in the area, so we asked him to drop us off. That's why we're early," Şahber Hanım volunteered.

"And how delightful for us to spend the extra time with you. Our home is your home. I only wish Naci had been able to come in for a chat."

While the girls were smothering their uncle Mahir with kisses, Reşat Bey leaned close and gave Gülfidan, the housekeeper, an earful. "Guests must never be forced to explain why they are early. Where are your manners?"

He was climbing the stairs to the second floor when his thoughts returned to what Mahir had been telling him. Yes, his country's trials were far from over, but, praise God, contentment now reigned in his little world. He checked to see no one was looking before he knocked three times on the wooden railing and uttered a little prayer for the Republic of Turkey.

3

A Modern Education

So firm was Ahmet Reşat's tone as he informed his wife that their daughter Sabahat would be enrolled at the American school in Gedikpaşa once she had completed her studies at the French middle school, that Behice, who had been poised to object to her daughter's being bounced from school to school, held her tongue. She knew she was outnumbered. Mahir Bey and Hilmi Bey were in agreement with their father-in-law: all of the family's children were to receive a modern education and learn multiple languages. Ahmet Reşat intended to enroll Halim at Galatasaray Sultanîsi, the venerable high school renamed Galatasaray Lisesi after the revolution, but the boy had his heart set on Kuleli Military High School. Mehpare adamantly opposed both plans. She would not agree to send her son to Kuleli or any other boarding school, preferring for him to attend whichever school was nearest and to come straight home every day. Who did she have but her Halim?

Mehpare did not realize that as Halim grew older, he felt more and more smothered by his mother. Halim was irritated both by the continued mourning for a father he had never seen and by what he considered to be the burden of his mother's love. Slowly but surely, Mehpare's excessive devotion was causing its object to distance himself. The two people in the house Halim absolutely adored were Reşat Bey, whom he considered his grandfather, and Sabahat, who was his best friend. He and Sabahat were the same age. They had grown up together, played together, and skipped off to school together, hand-in-hand. Once Sabahat had learned to read and write at the local primary school, she had been sent to the French middle school, while Halim had bowed to his mother's wishes and attended a nearby middle school. Sitare and Bülent, for their part, had gone on to the American school in nearby Gedikpaşa.

Ahmet Reşat also hired a hodja to teach his youngest daughter and his grandchildren, all of whom were being instructed at school in the Latin script, to read and write Ottoman calligraphy. Hakkı Hodja came to the house three times a week at the end of the school day. He gave Sabahat lessons from the Koran, after which he tried to teach Sitare and Bülent the old Ottoman script. Sabahat was diligent and studious, while Sitare and Bülent drove the hodja to distraction with their antics. The children simply would not learn the old script. Sitare's crabbed, crooked calligraphy was a disgrace. Bülent would sit next to the window and keep peeking out at the children playing in the street. Every time the hodja arrived, Sitare and Bülent would play the same trick on him: the poor man's scarf, cane, or prayer cap would be tossed on top of the mirrored closet in the entrance hall as soon as he wasn't looking. After the lesson, he'd spend half an hour searching for the missing article before one of the children whispered its location into Sabahat's ear. Hüsnü Efendi would be sent to the cellar to fetch a ladder, the article would be retrieved, and the women of the house would apologize profusely. The hodja would mutter under his breath and continue to endure these indignities week after week for the sake of Reşat Bey, whom he greatly respected. Then came the last straw.

The children had noticed that, at intervals spaced roughly a month apart, their aunt Sabahat would inform the hodja that she was unable to attend her lesson. They were too young, however, to realize why he would release her at once and without question. One day, Bülent mimicked what he had seen Sabahat doing. Head bowed, hands meekly clasped, he said, "Hodja, forgive me, but I am indisposed this week and will not be able to study the Koran," at which the hodja's patience suddenly came to an end. He gave Bülent a clip over the ear and a severe scolding before writing a letter to Reşat Bey kindly requesting that he be relieved of his obligations to his young charges. He would gladly continue Koran lessons with Sabahat Hanım, but the time and money spent on Sitare and Bülent were a waste for all concerned.

Reşat Bey did not speak to his grandchildren for several weeks. The hodja never gave them another lesson, and they remained as ignorant of Ottoman calligraphy as ever.

As planned, Sabahat transferred from the French school to the American school in Gedikpaşa. After the strict discipline of the French nuns, she enjoyed the comparatively relaxed atmosphere of her new school and soon became fast friends with a number of her Russian, Bulgarian, Greek, and Armenian classmates.

As Sabahat's social circle expanded, Halim's loneliness grew. Sabahat no longer played chess and backgammon with him after school or told funny stories about her day. Either she would go straight to her room, put a record on the gramophone, and listen to songs in French and English, or she would bring home classmates.

Having lost Sabahat's interest, Halim turned to his other friend, Reşat, the grandfather who was only too happy to play backgammon, talk about school, and provide a sympathetic ear. Halim did not realize that his growing intimacy with Reşat was making his mother jealous and that it would bring about the end of their stay in the house.

4

Mehpare's New Life

One spring day, all the women of the house were chatting under the arbor in the back garden as the children frolicked. The men of the house were out, so talk turned, as it often did, to love and relationships. Mehpare was bemoaning the long-ago decision of their neighbor, Azra, not to follow the love of her life, a French officer, to his homeland.

"If you had been in Azra's place, would you have gone?" Behice asked Mehpare.

"Without hesitation," Mehpare replied. "I'd have followed Kemal to the ends of the earth."

"But Mehpare, Kemal wasn't French. You shared the same religion, and you were from the same country. On top of that, you were related."

"It wouldn't have mattered," Mehpare insisted. "Love comes first."

"I would rather give up a man than hurt Beyba," Leman contributed. She turned to her younger sister and asked, "What about you, Sabahat? Would you follow your heart against Father's wishes?"

"What kind of a question is that? I've never been in love. How would I know?"

"I'm curious. Come on, what about the rest of you?"

Halim, who had pricked up his ears at a safe distance, chimed in. "I wouldn't hurt Granddad Reşat for anything in the world."

"What about me?" Mehpare asked.

Halim pretended not to hear.

"What about me, Halim?"

"I wouldn't hurt you, either, Mother."

"Halim, who do you love more than anyone else in the world?"

"Granddad Reşat . . . and you, of course."

"Now that stings," Mehpare whispered.

"Oh, Mehpare! You're so touchy!" Leman scolded. "Of course Halim loves you best. You're his mother. But it's only natural for Halim to be devoted to Beyba, the closest thing he's ever had to a father."

"Beyba? What on earth is that supposed to mean? Behice, tell your daughters to stop calling their father Beyba. If they are ill-bred, you are to blame." Spreading her fingers wide, Saraylıhanım waved a hand in Leman's face. "If the five sisters of my right hand had become better acquainted with the left side of your head, you'd have learned to address your father as Bey Baba. A well-timed slap is heaven sent, they say, but I was unable to make Reşat see that. If only they had turned me loose, I'd have whipped you girls into shape in the space of a week."

Behice sprang to the defense of her brood. "My goodness, Saraylıhanım, the things you say! You think my daughters are still children. Why, they've got children of their own now. And what difference does it make if they call their father Beyba; it's short for Bey Baba, as you know, and what's wrong with that?"

"What! When did they get married and have children? Why didn't you consult me? Shame on you!"

Behice and her daughters stifled their giggles. Mehpare looked wistful. She slowly rose from the wicker chair and collected the empty dishes on the table so she would have an excuse to go inside. Nobody but Halim noticed her misery. The suffering that had clouded her face cast its gloom over her son, and his heart grew heavy.

Mehpare went up to the window in her room and looked out at the branches of the apple tree. How many seasons had she watched it bloom, shed its blossoms, and put forth fruit? It had grown old, thick, and graceless; most of its branches were now bare. Soon, it would die.

The many suitors Mehpare had attracted in her widowed youth had all gone home empty-handed. Their numbers had dwindled until there were none, not even aged widowers. Society had come to accept that Kemal's widow would spurn all proposals of marriage. When the occasional gentleman did express interest, the marriage brokers did not bother to pass the information along. They were tired of being refused. But then, just a few weeks earlier, and completely out of the blue, Behice had surprised Mehpare.

"We refused a proposal without troubling you over it," she had said. "A civil servant at the Sirkeci Post Office, nearly fifty. A widower. I didn't ask about his temperament or salary, on the assumption you wouldn't—"

"I'm not interested, Behice."

Mehpare looked out at the apple tree and considered her life. Were she to take Halim and leave this house, would he love her most of all? Here, living with this extended family, her son had Sabahat to confide in, his Granddad Reşat for help with his lessons, and an army of devoted women standing by to give him all the motherly love he could handle. In this house, he had five mothers, not one. Behice was the mother he respected; Leman and Suat were the pretty, young mothers; Saraylıhanım spoiled him terribly and, for all her faults, was always there to comfort and reassure him. Halim's own mother could claim only a one-fifth share of her son, and, adding insult to injury, he loved his Granddad Reşat more than he loved her. He'd admitted as much;

it had slipped right out. It was she, Halim's real mother, who enforced rules, who made sure he did not catch a chill, who nagged him, and who criticized his choice of friends for his own good. Perhaps she had not coddled him enough? Perhaps, if they lived in a less crowded house, just the two of them—and her new husband, of course—and she had Halim all to herself and he had only her, he would love her best of all . . .

That night, Mehpare nurtured this seed of an idea until dawn. At the morning call of the muezzin, she got out of bed and performed her prayers. Kneeling on her prayer rug, she fingered the beads of her rosary and thought long and hard. She was pensive for the rest of the day. That evening, during the toing and froing of dinner preparations, she found herself alone in the kitchen with Behice and decided to reveal her decision. Behice was astonished. Could it be that Mehpare, who had spurned scores of eligible young men from wealthy families, was interested in a middle-aged post office employee?

"Have I heard you right? Mehpare, are you saying you would encourage this man's interest?"

"Behice, I think the time has come for me to be the mistress of my own home."

"Have the girls been tactless?" Behice asked. "Listen to me, Mehpare. You've been like their elder sister; you helped bring them up. If they've said something to annoy you, don't hesitate to put them in their place."

"Nobody has offended me. Please don't blame the girls. It's just that . . . I . . . were I to marry . . . that is, before I go to seed . . ."

"Go to seed indeed! You're a young woman. If that's how you see yourself, imagine how I must feel! Mehpare, you're in your prime and you can still have children. It was Celadet Hanım who brought word of the gentleman's proposal. I'll ring her up." She paused and looked Mehpare directly in the eye. "Are you certain? Do you honestly want to go through with this? Don't disgrace me by changing your mind later."

"Call Celadet Hanım," Mehpare said.

"If it was your intention to remarry, there was that good-looking young nephew of İsmail Pasha's last year—"

"A young man would be too much of a bother. The gentleman in question sounds like a good match."

"Then I'll call Celadet Hanım. Let's meet your suitor first, though. Will you take a liking to him, I wonder? We can decide later."

"All right," Mehpare said, her face already smoothed by the peace of mind ushered in by a momentous decision no longer delayed.

After dinner that same evening, Suat tapped on Mehpare's door.

"You know what I'm like, Mehpare. Sometimes I shoot my mouth off without thinking, and I wanted to tell you I'm sorry if I've hurt your feelings in any way."

"Did your mother send you?"

"Yes. She's convinced I've upset you. I swear I have no idea what I did."

"You're my dear, beloved Suat. How could I ever be cross with you?" Mehpare cried, throwing her arms around Suat.

"Why do you want to leave us, then? Is it something Leman said?"

"Nobody has ever done or said anything to offend me. I simply think it's time I set out on my own. If I wait any longer, it will be too late."

"I had no idea you wanted to marry. We all thought you were dead set against it."

"I thought so, too, Suat. I suppose I've had second thoughts. And I don't want to be a burden anymore."

"How can you say that? Beyba would be so upset if he heard. You're a daughter to him, no different than the rest of us."

"Then don't tell him! Just tell him I've decided I would like to set up a home of my own. Halim should know what it is to have a home and a mother he can call his own and to live within his means."

"Father will do what he can to put Halim through school and help set him up later."

"That's not what I meant. Your father has so many mouths to feed as it is. You and your sister live here with your husbands and children. He's been supporting Saraylıhanım—may God bless her with a long life—for as long as I can remember. After İbrahim Bey died last year, Neyir Hanım came to live here. If my suitor agrees to look after Halim and cover his expenses, I should consider myself blessed, and accept him."

Suat tried one last tactic. "As soon as Hilmi returns from his service in the East, we plan to move into our own house. Don't breathe a word of this to Mother, but that is what we've decided. What I mean to say is, there will be fewer people in the house, and Father's burden will be lightened. The only reason I'm telling you my little secret is that it might dissuade you."

"Dearest Suat, do you not see? You want a home of your own; allow me to have mine."

"No, that's not it at all. I want to get away from Leman. She's becoming more fastidious by the day. No longer satisfied with ruling over her own room and the kitchen, she's begun meddling everywhere. Yesterday, she handed me a bottle of Lysol and ordered me to clean the lavatory in the entrance hall. Bülent splatters when he uses the toilet, she says. As though a little boy's pee could contain germs!"

"Don't mind her, Suat. She doesn't do it out of malice. I suppose she takes after Saraylıhanım. Before the poor woman reached her dotage, she'd scour everything three times."

"Please don't go. What will I do without you, Mehpare?" Suat's eyes brimmed with tears.

"Even if I marry and move away, I'll always be there for you. We'll visit each other as often as we can." Mehpare was getting a little moist-eyed herself, but the arrow had already left the bow.

Celadet Hanım informed Galip Bey that Mehpare would consider his proposal provided that he agree to assume responsibility for her son, a condition Mehpare had made Celadet Hanım swear repeatedly not to reveal just yet. Galip Bey responded in the affirmative. All that remained was to set a date for a visit from the prospective bridegroom.

Reşat Bey told Mehpare he would like to have a word in private before Galip was invited to the house. He and Mehpare sat side by side on the examination table in Mahir's exam room. Reşat Bey took one of her hands in his and looked into her eyes.

"You've always been a daughter to me, Mehpare. You know that this is your home, don't you?"

"I do, sir."

"Have you given sufficient consideration to this matter? Why, after all these years, have you suddenly decided to marry?"

"I'll soon be too old, sir."

"Naturally, I'll consent to whatever you want. Please know, how-ever, that you can change your mind at any time. If, even after you are married, you regret your choice, a home awaits you here. Always."

"I hope there will be no cause for me to return. And I am grateful for all you have done for me."

"I have done nothing to deserve your gratitude. Have you spoken with Halim?"

"I told him I wanted my own home. He did not object." Mehpare went a little pink in the face.

It was true that Halim hadn't objected, but she had also told him that Reşat Bey was finding it difficult to support his household and that she did not wish to be an additional strain on his finances.

"In order to immerse yourself in your new life with your husband, would you like to leave your son here with us?" Reşat Bey asked in all sincerity.

Mehpare leapt to her feet. "No, sir! I can't leave my son. I would never leave him."

"Why are you so agitated, Mehpare? Nobody will take him from you against your will. I was only offering to help if I could."

Mehpare took her seat again.

"I implore you, sir, make no mention of this to Halim. He would choose to stay here. I could not bear to leave without him. Please, don't ask him."

"I've always respected your wishes," he said. "I'll say nothing. As far as his school expenses—"

"Galip Bey has agreed to put him through school."

"But why, Mehpare! Halim is part of our family. Why should Galip Bey educate our child?"

"If we are to become a family, Galip Bey must treat Halim like his own son. He is sufficiently well-to-do, sir."

"Be that as it may, I would like to pay for Halim's education."

"If Galip Bey assumes full responsibility for Halim, the boy is more likely to respect and love him as a father. That is the only way we can become a true family. Please allow Galip Bey that opportunity."

Reşat Bey was at a loss for words. This could only mean that Mehpare wished to make a clean break, and it was her right to do so.

Bowing his head, he said, "As you wish. But remember what I told you. You and Halim are always welcome here."

Mehpare brushed away a tear.

Reşat Bey clenched his jaw and thought, *Why are tears allowed only to the fairer sex?* She was leaving his home forever, this young woman he had loved as a daughter, his beloved Kemal's widow, the mother of Kemal's son, both of them entrusted to his care, neither of them ever a burden in any way. He could have sobbed.

He folded his hands in his lap and looked at Mehpare, missing her already. Her husband had gone off to fight for his country on the third day of their marriage. She had been widowed the day she gave birth to his son. Her face had never worn a smile. Despite all Reşat Bey's heartfelt efforts to make her feel loved and welcome, she must have felt unwanted in his house. She was still young, and she wished to marry. All he had to do now was to give his blessing.

"I agree to whatever you want, my dear." He sighed. "I won't allow anything to stand in your way. It is your life. And your decision."

They continued sitting side by side for a time, silent and sad. Then Mehpare respectfully kissed Ahmet Reşat's hand, took her leave, and went up to her room.

Despite Mehpare's apparent eagerness to marry and the favorable reports on Galip Bey that had arrived after multiple discreet inquiries, a general cheerlessness descended on the house. Nobody rejoiced on Mehpare's behalf. As for her son, though sorry to be leaving the family he had grown up with, Halim was secretly pleased his mother would finally be directing her affections elsewhere. A new life might do them both good, he decided.

It was at Behice's insistence that the prospective bridegroom came calling even though Mehpare had seen no reason to meet him before the wedding.

Eyes on the floor, Mehpare brought a cup of coffee to Galip Bey, who had arrived with a big box of Hacı Bekir *lokum* tucked under his arm just as night was falling. Not once did she lift her eyes to her husband-to-be, even when she was seated across from him. Halim crept into the sitting room, kissed the visitor's hand without a word, and stole out again. The women chatted among themselves as Reşat Bey gravely listened to the guest, trying not to let on how distracted he was by Sitare and Bülent, who kept darting in and out of the room. Finally,

Reşat Bey cleared his throat and spoke, emphasizing how important Mehpare and Halim's happiness was to the rest of the family. Mehpare had always been dear to their hearts and held in the highest esteem. She was entitled to respect and tenderness wherever she lived. Meanwhile, Leman, Suat, and Behice studied every last pore and stray whisker on Galip Bey's face so that they would later be able to paint an accurate picture of him for Mehpare. He was of medium height and had a receding hairline. Other than a peculiar twitching of his recently trimmed almond-shaped moustache, he had no distinguishing features of any kind. He was neither handsome nor ugly, and his general demeanor lent credence to the earlier reports of a respectable life with no vices; no fondness for either visiting *meyhane* or drinking *rakı*, which he was said to imbibe only at weddings and other social functions; and no reputation as a skirt-chaser. Through marriage, the poor man hoped to fill the void left by his late wife and his newly married daughter; that much was clear.

"Our Mehpare is extraordinarily skilled and nimble fingered," Behice offered during a lull in the conversation. "There's nothing she can't do."

"You're a lucky man, Galip Bey," enthused Celadet Hanım right on cue, confident she had engineered yet another match.

Head tilted slightly to one side, the suitor kept a pleasant smile on his lips as he stole glances at Mehpare. Other than Saraylıhanım's having mistaken the suitor for the next-door gardener, all went smoothly. As the visit was drawing to a satisfactory conclusion, Behice got up, turned to Galip Bey, and said, "I imagine the two of you would enjoy a moment of privacy. We'll be leaving now." Reşat Bey concealed his astonishment as best he could as Behice led her husband and their daughters out of the room. A moment later, Leman stepped back inside, pried Saraylıhanım out of her armchair, and winked at Mehpare as she removed her great aunt from the room.

"Was that necessary?" Reşat Bey asked his wife the moment they reached the hall. "We've left them in there all alone. Whatever will he think of us?"

"What age are we living in, Reşat Bey?" Behice asked, raising her needle-thin eyebrows and pursing her bow lips. "Have we become a republic for nothing? Unmarried men and women have been speaking to each other for years now, and they even dance together. What harm is there in talking? Perhaps, left on their own, they'll find they're not suited for each other and call the thing off. Let's give them a chance to become acquainted."

Less than ten minutes later, Mehpare showed Galip Bey to the door and returned to the sitting room, which the family had reoccupied.

"How did you find him? What did you talk about?" Behice asked breathlessly.

"He seems like a good man," Mehpare replied. "As long he shows affection to Halim, I'll be happy enough."

"Are you certain?"

"I am."

"There's no regretting the thing once it's done."

"I know."

"Well then, I wish you both every happiness."

After everyone had retired to their rooms that night, Behice made a proposal of her own.

"I've been thinking," she said to her husband. "When Mehpare and Kemal were married, we were unable to provide the dowry she deserved. The nation was at war, and there was only so much we could do. We'll be unable to put together a proper trousseau this time as well. Why don't we give them my father's ground-floor apartment in Pera? Mehpare has done so much for this family; she brought up our children and suckled Sabahat at her own breast. She won't be beholden to her husband if we provide for her. Galip Bey will realize how precious she is to us and will treat her accordingly."

"Mehpare isn't a blood relation of your father's. Would it be right? Is that what he would have wanted?"

"We won't sign over the title deed. She can live there for the rest of her life. We'll tell the girls that the flat is to remain Mehpare's even after we've passed away."

Ahmet Reşat was filled with a burst of love for his wife. As she grew older, she was turning into a kinder and more considerate woman. He seized her hands and kissed them.

"Bless your heart, my dear," he said. "I can't tell you how happy you've made me."

The nuptials, attended only by close friends and relatives, were held at the registry office in Beyoğlu. Nothing could have been more different than Mehpare's first wedding ceremony, which had been hosted in the family mansion and presided over by a hodja.

Mehpare was dressed in her indigo-blue suit and white gloves. She wore the little hat with the veil concealing her almond eyes at the girls' insistence; the fur stole draping her shoulders was on forced loan from Behice. The smooth skin of her sober face was free of makeup. As the registrar solicited the couple's confirmation that they were accepting each other of their own free will, the bride was thinking about someone else.

Dearest Kemal, do not think I am betraying you. I have loved only you and will love only you forever. I do this for our son, whose love is all I have on this earth and whose love is all I will ever need.

After the ceremony, Mehpare nodded good-bye to her unsmiling, dry-eyed well-wishers and, accompanied by Halim and her husband, went off to the ground-floor flat of the İbrahim Bey Apartments in Pera, where views of the Golden Horn and a brand-new life awaited her.

***

Back in the mansion, Mehpare and Halim were sorely missed for the first few weeks. Nesime had assumed responsibility for the breakfast table but kept forgetting the salt-free cheese bought at the Spice Market for Reşat Bey, the honey spoons, the linen napkins, or one of the many other special touches Mehpare had quietly provided. It was Neyir Hanım who stepped into Mehpare's former role as family fortune-teller, squinting into the ladies' white porcelain coffee cups to divine from the brown sludge and runic smears an inevitably eventful future, news of which she delivered in an impassive and halting drone. Mehpare was no longer there to listen patiently while Suat aired her grievances against Leman, Behice found fault with Saraylıhanım, and Leman decried Nesime. They had lost a smoothing presence, a sympathetic ear, and a confidant. Sabahat, for her part, missed Halim, even if she had been neglecting him in recent months. But it was Reşat Bey who most keenly felt the absence of his adopted daughter and her son, an aching throb, as though he had lost Kemal all over again. He kept asking his wife and daughters to pay Mehpare a visit and find out if she was happy.

"It would be inappropriate to burst in on the newlyweds," Behice protested.

"Send Sabahat. She can drop by after school on the pretext of visiting Halim. How will we know if she's happy if you don't go and see her?"

Sabahat came home with good news. Mehpare had seemed content with her new life. Her only complaint was that she missed her family. The days passed, and Mehpare settled into a routine of weekly visits, with particular care paid to ensuring Reşat Bey was at home when she stopped by.

Mehpare gradually grew accustomed to her new home and husband, and the family gradually grew accustomed to her absence. The separation was most difficult for Halim. He had been plucked from the only home he knew and cast into strange waters, to sink or swim. Without Sabahat and Granddad Reşat, he had lost his best friends. Still, although he no longer belonged to the mansion, and knew it, at each visit he was greeted with love, had some spending money slipped into his pocket by Granddad Reşat, and was generally fussed over. The only thing missing on his visits was, more often than not, Sabahat. As it turned out, she, too, was navigating uncharted waters.

5

Uncharted Waters

Seated on a taboret in front of the mirror, Sabahat brushed out her ankle-length hair and rested her arms for a few moments before proceeding with the finger-numbing process of weaving her blond hair into the two long plaits she always pinned atop either side of her head in coiled mounds. She removed a few garments from her closet, studied them, and put on her favorite lacy white blouse and blue skirt before softly descending to the floor below, where she tapped on the door of the bedroom she had vacated a few months earlier.

"Have you done your homework, Sitare?" she asked, taking a seat in her niece's room.

"I've finished reading but not arithmetic."

"Why not?"

"I can't solve the figures."

"Bring me your notebook."

Sitare handed her notebook to her aunt.

"What's so difficult about this? Look, I'll do one for you, as an example. Promise me you'll do the rest, okay?" Sitare peered over Sabahat's shoulder as she solved the first problem.

"Now it's your turn. Do the next one."

Sitare sat in front of her notebook, diligently scribbling away. Then she gave up.

"I can't do it. I don't understand. Please do them all, Aunt Sabahat. I'm begging you."

"I can't do that. It's your homework, Sitare. And anyway, I'm on my way out. I'll have a look when I get back."

"But I don't understand."

"If you concentrate, you will. Now get back to it. Good luck."

Ignoring Sitare's pleas, Sabahat gave her a peck on the forehead and went down to the entrance hall, where she slipped into her navy-blue pelerine. Out in the garden, she turned and looked up at Sitare, who was tearfully waving good-bye in the window. Sabahat blew her a kiss, pulled open the garden gate, and tripped along the street toward the intersection where Aram was waiting to escort her to a classmate's tea party.

Behice and her two eldest daughters were shopping in Beyoğlu, after which they had arranged to call on Leman's sister-in-law, Şahber Hanım, in Pera; Şahber Hanım always expected them for five o'clock tea and never released them before seven in the evening. Reşat Bey would be joining the family at an even later hour, as Wednesday evenings were reserved for board meetings.

Sabahat was skipping along the street humming a popular tune when a stray bit of hair fell over her left eye. She tucked it back in place and bit her lips to make them redder.

When she got back home at around six that evening, her mother and sisters were still out. She changed her clothes and went down to Sitare's room. The young scholar was stretched out in bed with a book.

"Have you finished your arithmetic homework, Sitare?"

"No."

"Why not? I showed you how."

Sitare shrugged.

"You'll fail if you go on like this."

"I try, but I just don't understand."

Sabahat leafed through Sitare's notebook. She looked at the unsolved problems and shook her head. "Come on, we'll do it together."

"Not now. I just reached an exciting bit."

"What?"

"In *David Copperfield*."

Sabahat gave up and left the room. She resolved to have a little talk with the girl's parents. Sitare required a private tutor and some well-enforced discipline.

After dinner that evening, Sabahat made good on her plan. Leman and Mahir agreed that their daughter was a little unfocused even as they argued that her aptitude for languages proved she was bright. She was fluent in English and had learned the basics of French from looking through her aunts' old textbooks. Additionally, she had picked up Greek words from the servants, Armenian ones from the gardener, and German songs from Şahber Hanım's sons when they were in Turkey during their semester breaks. But she was lazy, hated doing homework, and had yet to meet an arithmetic problem she could solve.

"It would be wonderful if you could supervise her every day, just until she finishes her homework," Leman suggested to Sabahat.

"I'm doing what I can, but it's not enough. She doesn't take me seriously, and she gets bored so easily."

"Perhaps we should hire a tutor?" Mahir said.

"Do you remember what the children did to their last tutor?" Leman asked her husband.

"They were younger then, and Bülent and Sitare were always egging each other on. Private lessons might prove beneficial. I wonder if one of Sabahat's classmates would be interested. Would you mind asking around?"

"I'd be happy to," Sabahat said.

A few days later, Sabahat told her sister about a friend who was excellent at math, a courteous young man who had already taken on a few pupils to help support his family. Even better, his fees were half the normal rate. He would be available to teach Sitare three days a week, either in the school library or at her home.

"Have him come here," Leman said. "That way, I can keep an eye on them, and Sitare can have her after-school snack."

"Bülent's been having trouble with English spelling. Perhaps we should arrange lessons for him as well," Suat said.

"I'll ask," Sabahat promised.

After dinner that evening, the family gathered around the gramophone in the sitting room. The children wanted to listen to Sabahat's French records. Mahir decided to amuse his wife and sisters-in-law with a few of the dance moves he had picked up during his studies in Paris. Sabahat turned the crank, placed the record on the turntable, and gently lowered the needle to the record's outer rim.

"And here it is, the Charleston! I want everyone up on their feet and dancing!" she cried.

Mahir got between Leman and Suat to demonstrate the steps he knew. Sitare and Bülent joined in.

"My, that looks like fun!" Behice said. "I might have a go myself."

"You must be joking!" her husband protested. "God forbid, you'll fall and break your—"

A shriek cut him off. All eyes turned to the doorway, where a bug-eyed Neyir Hanım stood with her hand clapped over her mouth.

"What in the name of heaven are you doing? You'll fall and hurt yourselves."

"We're dancing," Sitare said, taking the elderly woman by the arm. "Come join us!"

Neyir Hanım hastily retrieved her arm. "I knew there was one lunatic in this house, but I didn't realize you'd all lost your minds," she said. "Mahir Bey, not you, too, my boy! You are thrashing about like an unhinged dervish!"

"It's called the Charleston, Grandma," Sabahat said. "It's all the rage. Sit down and enjoy the show."

"I shall do nothing of the kind! I fly from Saraylıhanım's ravings only to find myself in a lunatic asylum, as one would flee the rain only to be caught in a hailstorm! Might I ask that you at least keep the noise down?" was her parting shot as she closed the door to the sitting room.

So accustomed was the family to the intrusions and protestations of its eldest members that they continued dancing as though nothing had happened. When the song finished, the panting revelers sank onto their chairs. Sabahat was placing a new record on the turntable when her father peered at her over his spectacles and asked, "Before I forget, Sabahat, what's all this I hear about a tutor for Sitare? Do you know this person?"

"He's a friend of mine from school, Beyba. His name is Aram Balayan."

Leman and Suat exchanged glances.

"The Armenian boy? Is he to be our children's tutor?" Suat asked.

"Aram's extremely intelligent," Sabahat said. "Not only is he first in the class, he's on the student council. He also helps out in the library. He's good at everything. If you don't believe me, come to my school and ask our teachers."

"What's next?" Leman said. "Shall we launch an investigation?"

"Leman, there's nothing unreasonable about doing a little research on the boy. He'll be coming into our home, after all," Mahir said. "How can we learn more about him, Sabahat?"

"I told you, he's a friend of mine."

Mahir grew annoyed. "Are you telling me that the few hours a week you spend together in school makes you a good reference? Have you met his family? What do you know about his moral character?"

Sabahat had watched as her fun-loving uncle Mahir grew increasingly testy and tired these days. She blamed her big sister. Leman had converted the hall adjoining Mahir's exam room into a changing room, complete with a hammam-style basin and instructions for her husband to scrub off the millions of microbes spread by his patients, then put on a new suit of clothes, and then, and only then, join his family upstairs after work. Behice Hanım had steeled herself to try and talk some sense into her daughter when Mahir acquiesced, as always, saying, "If it will give Leman peace of mind, I'll do what she wants. A bit of bathing after work might be relaxing and refreshing." Behice had long ago decided that Mahir's immediate submission to all of his wife's demands, however ridiculous, was due to their age difference; Sabahat, however, interpreted it as his eagerness to still his wife's nagging tongue. She wondered what demands Leman had made on her husband today.

Sabahat ended the debate over the new tutor by suggesting he come to the house. "If Aram makes a good impression on you, great! And if he doesn't, I'll try to arrange lessons from one of the American teachers at my school, at twice the price. Don't expect a discount from them."

She knew she felt overprotective of Aram, but she did not know why. Fleeing the room before anyone could object to her plan, she started pulling pins out of her hair on the way to the door. Ahmet Reşat glimpsed the rope of yellow hair tumbling down his daughter's back, and the image of a similar braid, this one dark blond, flashed before his eyes. Some years back, Behice, whose hair was now streaked with gray, had opted for cropped curls. He looked at his wife now and was pleased to see she was wearing the diamond earrings he had given her upon the birth of their first daughter. He sighed deeply, returned to the here and now, and called out, "Don't forget to invite this young tutor of yours to the house. Let's see who and what this Aram Bey is."

59

6

Aram's New Life

1915
Merzifon, Anatolia

The Balayan family was just sitting down to dinner. From under the lid covering a pot of lentil soup, a plume of steam shot forth, hotly licking the expectant little face bent over it.

"Come on, my boy, take your seat," Nana said.

That evening would leave Aram Balayan with memories as hazy as fleeting shadows seen through a curtain of gauze. But certain details would stay with him for the rest of his life.

The little cubes of crunchy bread on the table, ready to be sprinkled onto his soup. The smell of sizzling butter making him hungry, making him reach for the bread. His big brother's soup spoon rapping his hand just at the moment a fist pounds on the door as his mother is ladling soup into his father's bowl. The ladle hanging in the air. Father pulling his soup bowl back. The knocking getting louder. Mother's arm still poised in the air. His hand still reaching for the bread. The footsteps of the servant running from the kitchen to the front door. Voices outside. Father pushing back his chair and getting up as five uniformed men burst into the dining room. Aram clapping his hands, thinking they are visitors, which always means presents, but his eleven-year-old brother, knowing better, coming over and squeezing Aram's hands tight. Father saying, "Shall we go into the sitting room, away from the children?" in a near whisper.

The uniformed men following Father out of the dining room, shutting the door behind them. Mother springing up and running after them. Nana, wordless and stock-still, staring with the eyes of an owl. Men tramping through the house. Mother running up the stairs, opening and closing drawers in the room overhead, rushing back downstairs. Aram following his big brother to the front door, to Father, and seeing those eyes. Father's mouth, nose, and cheeks a blur, but those eyes: sunken and black and defeated.

"Boys, I'm going on a trip," Father says in a ragged voice.

The uniformed men say something to Father.

"A business trip," Father says, this time in Turkish. He opens his arms wide and pulls the boys close.

"When are you coming back?" Aram asks. "Don't forget to get me a hoop this time. A red one."

"Look after your mother and your nana," Father says. "If I'm not back soon, look after them."

"Go back inside the house," Mother says.

The boys return to the dining room. They eat their soup, now cold.

"Nana, why aren't you eating your soup?" one of the boys asks. She says nothing. Low voices, tramping feet, the street gate closing with a clang; Mother coming into the dining room, alone, face pale, motioning for Nana to join her in the kitchen.

And that was when Nana stood up, and when Aram clapped his hands for the second time that evening and shouted, "Look! Nana peed herself! Nana peed herself!"

***

The night Father left on an unexpected business trip, Aram was an outgoing five-year-old with shining chestnut-colored eyes set in an open, pleasant face. Soon afterward, the shine would dim, and the face would become guarded. For the rest of his life, the smell of lentil soup and of bread cubes sizzling in butter, or the thud of a fist on a door, would fill him with dread and bring a lump to his throat. He never shared the secret behind this strange aversion to the smell of soup and to sudden knocks on the door, to those harbingers of a life of want and fatherlessness. His new life would be a life of hardship; a struggle to survive, to put himself through school, to know happiness, and to love.

The morning after Nana wet herself, Aram understood that his family's life had been turned upside down, even if nobody told him anything. He asked his mother about Father as soon as he woke up. When was Daddy coming home? Mother was getting ready to go out and in a big hurry. Aram kept pestering Nana. He was away on business, she told him. How was she supposed to know when he would be back? Aram was used to his father and uncles going off on long journeys. The men of the house frequently bought goods in distant places like Istanbul, Thessaloniki, and Damascus. But something was different that morning. Why wasn't his big brother going to school? Why was Mother hurrying out so early? She always made his breakfast and never left before he ate it. He grew scared and uneasy, even cried a little. Nana scolded him. "This is no time for bawling," she said. But when his mother came home from his aunt's house, he could see that she had been crying, too. Her eyes were swollen and red. His mother's tears would never end, not really, and their lives would never be the same.

Later in life, Aram never liked talking about or remembering the months that followed his father's abrupt departure. His mother and his aunt had waited, hoping against hope for their husbands' return for months, until, hope gone, their homes had been plunged into mourning and desperation. There was no more laughter, no more idle chatter, and no more joy. The women, overwhelmed and anxious, tried to run the family department store, and when they failed, as of course they did, what little income they had left was soon nearly gone.

The women put one of the houses up for sale and lived together for a time in the other one. They liquidated the department store, sold off their goods and their plots of land at cut-rate, wartime prices, stitched gold coins into the folds of their skirts, tucked a few jewels into their corsets, and, along with their children and their elders, boarded a steamer sailing the Black Sea from Samsun to Istanbul. Aram sometimes wondered if that journey was a memory or a long-ago nightmare, those three days huddled on the pitching deck, packed among hundreds of other families, vomiting and wretched. Were they going into exile, fleeing, or setting forth for a new life?

But Aram did remember sailing into Istanbul, city of domes and plane trees and minarets. The most beautiful city in the world. And in this most beautiful of cities, Aram would begin a new life.

While they were still in Merzifon, the women had contacted some Istanbul merchants who had done business with their husbands, but in the uncertainty and commotion of the Great War, nobody was able to offer much of a helping hand. They were advised to find shelter in one of the camps set up in churchyards for the displaced Armenians streaming into Istanbul from all over Anatolia. If they wished, the merchants could put in a good word with a priest at the Armenian Church in Gedikpaşa.

Aram's mother and aunt had no choice but to agree. It was no longer possible for them to live in Anatolia: there was too much pain, too much blood, too much ill will. They needed to go to a large, cosmopolitan city where perhaps things would be different.

Aram would later be able to recall a few scraps and fragments of those days in the churchyard in Gedikpaşa. He remembered the rows of narrow beds in the courtyard and how he felt like a king when he lay down on one of them in the shade of a giant plane tree. He didn't have to wrap his arms around his legs and pull his knees up against his belly like on the ship. Stretching out his legs, he wiggled his toes and clasped his hands behind his head. That moment of bliss ended when his big brother jumped into bed with him.

"The two of you won't fit like that. Sleep with your heads on opposite ends, or one of you will end up falling out of bed," Nana scolded.

Jirayir's toes were level with Aram's nose, and Aram's feet came up to his brother's chest. They giggled for a time, then they pushed and shoved each other a bit, before falling into a deep sleep.

How wonderful to be a boy in Istanbul!

Meanwhile, Aram's mother and aunt set about solving two problems straightaway: finding a place to live and a school for their sons.

While Aunt Siranuş wandered the quarter of Samatya looking for a house, Aram's mother, Rebeka, headed down a nearby street in search of the American school in Gedikpaşa a priest had told her about. She herself was a graduate of the American high school in Merzifon. The coins and jewels would not be enough to pay for both a home and an expensive education, but her English was good, and she wondered if she could find work at the school as an accountant or a librarian.

Asking for directions along the way, she soon found the right street and pushed open the garden gate. Girls and boys were chasing each other around the courtyard. Older students were sitting on the grass with their notebooks, some chatting, and others skipping rope and playing kickball. She looked at the girls, so carefree, so certain of a bright future, so much like herself at their age. If someone had told her that one day she would be sleeping on a camp bed in a churchyard and wandering the streets very nearly a beggar, she would have laughed out loud.

Beautiful young Rebeka, an American high school graduate from a prosperous family, and handsome young Agop, a French school graduate, also from a prosperous family, had been married in a church ceremony straight out of a fairy tale. *Just look at me now, Agop,* she thought, wiping away a tear. *I'm about to beg for a job.*

What was her husband doing right now? Was he alive? Was he ill? Why hadn't they heard from him? He'd been given half an hour to pack. "You're going to Damascus," they'd said. Where was he? Had he started a new life, with a new family? Would he ever come back, or was he dead? Did she have the right to pity herself when she still had no idea what had happened to him? She cast these thoughts out of her mind, bit her lip, threw back her shoulders, and walked toward the administrative building.

"Rebeka!"

Rebeka stopped and turned around.

"Is that really you, Rebeka? Now, let me see, Rebeka . . . Ohannes! Yes, that's it! It was Rebeka Ohannes, wasn't it?"

For a moment, Rebeka thought she was seeing a ghost. The hair was grayer, and the face and lips more pinched, but that pointy nose and those black eyes, penetrating as a sparrow hawk's, could only belong to Miss Putney. Yes, Miss Putney, her former headmistress from the American high school in Merzifon, had just swooped down on her. Rebeka involuntarily held out her hands in disbelief. Miss Putney seized them.

"Come along, my girl. We'll go to my office, and you can tell me what brings you here," she said.

"An ill wind, Miss Putney. An ill wind."

Rebeka fell upon her old headmistress's neck and burst into tears, allowing herself to sob long and hard for the first time since the day they'd taken her husband away.

***

When the sisters-in-law met in the churchyard that evening, Şiranus reported that she had come up empty-handed in her search for a home, but Rebeka had wonderful news: the children had been enrolled at the American school in Gedikpaşa. Their classes would start in fifteen days.

"But how will we pay for it?" Siranuş asked.

"We won't. The children will be studying on a scholarship. They don't expect us to pay a thing. We don't even have to pay the registration fees, Siranuş. Can you believe it?"

"But how is that possible?"

"It was a miracle. I ran into my old headmistress. There's an American endowment to help displaced Armenians, and they will be funding our children's education."

"The Americans have always helped us," Şiranus said. "God bless them."

Later, when Aram's classmates asked him where he was from and who his family was, he asked Nana, who was always at home. She told him, in the same voice she used for bedtime stories.

"There used to be a big department store right on the main street of Merzifon. Men's clothing was sold on the ground floor, and women's and children's on the upper floors. Your grandfather had a fabric shop when he was young, and over time he expanded into the clothing trade until, just a few years later, he was the owner of that department store, the fanciest in town. Your grandfather would send bolts of the fine cotton woven in Merzifon to traders in Damascus, and from Istanbul and Thessaloniki, he would order readymade clothing and odds and ends to sell in his store. When he got old, he passed the business to his sons. Merzifon was a prosperous provincial city in those days. Greeks and Armenians and Turks all lived there. Shopkeepers and merchants of different religions made a comfortable living. When I was a girl, we lived in a big three-story house surrounded by gardens. Your mother was born in that house. She was my firstborn, and we doted on her. Your grandfather gave the house to your mother when she married your father, and you and your brother were born in that same house. Your uncle and his family had a house just down the street, and your aunt and her family had one on the street behind yours. Although we didn't live together, we saw our relatives every day. Brothers and sisters, nephews and nieces, cousins and grandparents. We were a big, happy family until the night those men came and took away your father and your uncles. After that, we came to Istanbul. That's what you should tell anyone who asks."

"Is Dad ever going to come back, Nana?"

"Who knows, Aram? Who knows?"

There was a strange disconnect between that terrible night and the present. A hole. A gap. So many things were unknown, or forgotten by choice or necessity. As Aram got older, he filled in some of those gaps, but his past always felt like a jigsaw puzzle with certain essential pieces missing. Years later, those pieces would fall into place. The day would come when things he had never been told, things that had never been discussed at home in front of the children, things he had never learned in school, would be told and retold—sometimes in sorrow; sometimes loudly, insistently, angrily, aiming to touch his heart with hate. They would open his eyes to the past, his past, but his heart was closed forever to others' hatred and hunger for vengeance. Aram's heart would know only love. And no matter what they told him, that love would be his for the rest of his life, bringing him both torment and elation.

7

Smitten by a Fair Face

As always, Aram arrived earlier than the other students, unlocked the library door with the key in his pocket, put the key in the top drawer of the desk to his right, and opened the windows wide to air the room. The skies had cleared and a bright day beckoned. He gathered a few books left on the table, placed them on the shelf, dusted a few surfaces, straightened a chair, and cast an appraising look around the room, satisfied he could hand over responsibility for the library to his Bulgarian friend, Tessa.

There was still no sign of Tessa, even though students and teachers had begun arriving for the classes due to start in twenty minutes. Aram grew fidgety. He needed to be in his classroom when the bell rang. Before accepting this job, he had assured Miss Putney he would not neglect his schoolwork. Feeling a little edgy, he walked over to an open window and poked his head outside in hopes of catching a glimpse of Tessa coming through the schoolyard gate. What he saw there transfixed him: a young lady dressed in a navy-blue pelerine, holding the hand of a little blond boy in her right hand and the hand of a skinny girl a few years older than the boy in her left one. The young lady wore her blond hair in two thick braids coiled on top of her head. *A crown of hair,* he thought. As for her face, he had never seen one like it. Perhaps he had seen more beautiful faces, but never had he seen one so radiant. He wondered for a moment if she was the children's governess, quickly discarding the idea. No, she was too young, and far too poised, too exquisite, too superior, and too serene to be anything but a fairy-tale princess. As he stood at the window, staring, something miraculous happened: the young lady lifted her eyes, met his gaze, and smiled. He felt the heat rush to his cheeks, felt his heart pound and his stomach flutter. He slammed the window shut and fled from view.

For the rest of the day, Aram kept an eye out for the young lady every time he hustled through the crowded school hallways, but she was nowhere to be seen. The next morning, he was back at the window when she appeared at the gate in her navy-blue pelerine, the same two children in tow. *She comes here every day,* he said to himself. *She might even be a student.*

Aram arrived extra early the following morning and was there to open the gate when he saw her approaching. Before he could say anything, she nodded a greeting and hurried off to the building housing the nursery school. Now he wondered if she was a teacher.

He restrained himself over the next two weeks. He did not want to stalk her. Besides, the semester had just begun; he had a long list of books to order for the library and dozens of other tasks to complete.

The next time he saw her was at the first student council meeting. Miss Griffith, the chairwoman, began introducing the council members from the different grades. When it came time to introduce the girls, Aram pricked up his ears.

"Let me begin with our new members," Miss Griffith said. "Although she enrolled here only this year, one of our young ladies has become such an immediate success with her classmates that they elected her to represent them. Miss Sabahat Reşat."

Sabahat stood and nodded to the assembled students. Aram imagined that her eyes lingered on his for a split second as she acknowledged the applause, but he quickly pushed the thought and its implications from his mind. Her name was Sabahat Reşat. She must be a Muslim. He had assumed she was a Bulgarian or a Russian; her fair hair and white skin, and that blue-eyed towheaded little boy at her side, in particular, had misled him. She was a Muslim. He was crestfallen.

At the conclusion of the meeting, the first of three held annually to discuss complaints and plan events, the students went off to their separate classrooms to get their coats. Confident that he could now be considered an acquaintance, if not yet a friend, Aram caught up to Sabahat as she was walking across the schoolyard. "Aren't you forgetting your brother and sister?" he asked.

"They're my niece and nephew," she said. "The children of my two elder sisters. Hüsnü Efendi stopped at the school to take them home today because of the student council meeting. They're long gone."

"They're both cute."

"Aren't they? The boy, Bülent, started nursery school this year. Sitare goes to elementary school."

"A warm welcome to all three of you."

"Thank you." She hesitated before saying, "Actually, I should be attending high school. I'm the oldest person in my class." She blushed, as though embarrassed. By now, Aram had walked with her through the gate and into the street.

"Did you fail a grade? Don't worry, you'll graduate soon enough."

"No, that's not it. I'll let you in on a little secret: I finished middle school with the nuns, then transferred here."

"You mean at Saint-Benoît?"

"Yes."

"That's great. Your French must be excellent."

"I wanted to continue my studies there, but my father insisted I come here to learn English. He said I would be too old to master English if I left it until after junior high."

"I'm glad he insisted."

"I protested, but Father got his way. You know what fathers are like."

Actually, Aram did not know what fathers were like. He said nothing.

"So here I am. Even though we had English classes at Saint-Benoît and I took extra lessons all summer long, I got placed in the middle school here. Worse, I have to admit I'm finding it difficult at times. Mathematics is easy enough, but literature is a challenge."

"I can help you with your lessons any time you like, Sabahat Hanım. I'm good at English."

"Please don't call me hanım. I'm the oldest in my class as it is, and you're making me feel even older."

"I know the girls in your class. You're more petite than any of them," Aram said, in all honesty.

"My aunt's a great one for proverbs. She always says, 'The smaller the chicken, the more tender the meat.' I suppose I do look young for my age."

They both laughed. Aram decided that not only was she beautiful, she was fun to be with. There were so many things he would ask her if he dared. In order to keep the conversation going, he moved on to himself.

"I'm the complete opposite, the youngest in my class. It bothers me sometimes to have classmates who are two or three years older than I am. Some of them resent me for getting better grades and for being on the student council."

"Did you already know English before you came here?"

"No, but I still skipped a grade."

"You must be clever and hardworking."

"I've got no choice but to study hard."

"Why is that? Are you so ambitious?"

"No, that's not it. I'll let you in on a little secret, too: I'm here on a scholarship."

Sabahat frowned, uncomprehending.

"We all came here on a scholarship, everyone in my family. My big brother, my cousins, and me."

"What exactly does that involve?"

"We don't have to pay any school fees, but we risk losing our scholarships if our grade point average falls below a certain level. That's why we have no choice but to study hard. My brother had to drop out."

"What's he doing now?"

"He went into business."

"Does he work with your father?"

Aram paused. He'd been speaking the truth and from the heart. Still, he didn't want to say anything that would scare her off.

"Father isn't around anymore."

"Oh. I'm so sorry for your loss."

Aram didn't say his father might be alive. He decided to leave it at, "We sold off Father's business. Our family had a big department store in Merzifon, where we used to live."

"Merzifon is near the Black Sea, isn't it? It must be beautiful out there."

"It is. I was young. I can't remember anything very clearly."

"And where do you live now?"

"On Kumbaracı Street. Near here. What about you?"

"We live in Beyazit. Hey, you're walking in the opposite direction of your house just because of me, Aram."

"So be it."

"No!" Sabahat stopped walking. "I'll go my way and you go yours. You're getting farther and farther from home."

Aram would have liked to blurt out, "Please let me walk you home." But he didn't. "See you at school tomorrow." He smiled. She nodded and was gone. Aram just stood there watching her stride off, the girl with the soft voice and the gentle, honey-colored eyes. Then he sighed, turned around, and headed for the nearby tram stop.

The friendship between Sabahat and Aram deepened that year, even though they were in different grades. Whenever she had trouble with her biology lessons or her English literature homework, he was there to help. For her part, she taught him how to pronounce French words properly. Sabahat soon became a member of Aram's little circle, preferring those students to her own classmates. At that time, few Turks studied at the American school, so Sabahat was surrounded by Greeks, Armenians, Bulgarians, and Russian of both sexes. While Behice did not fully approve, she knew children tended to make friends at school these days, and if her daughter was spending most of her free time with non-Muslims, well, her husband was at fault, not the girl, for it was at his insistence that their daughter was attending the American school in the first place. All Behice could do was invite Sabahat's friends to their house every weekend in order to get to know them and to keep her daughter away from strange houses and quarters, not to mention the cinema. If the price she paid for keeping an eye on her daughter was regularly playing hostess to a gaggle of girls, so be it.

Behice consoled herself with her daughter's rapid progress in English in her first academic year. Sabahat continued to improve over the summer, and by the second semester of her second year, her teachers decided she was ready to skip to the grade above.

Her parents were delighted. While Reşat Bey was proud of his daughter's academic achievements, Behice Hanım was already looking forward to the day when Sabahat, a well-bred beauty with a sweet disposition, a junior high diploma, and fluency in two languages, would make a brilliant match. She imagined the suitors that would come calling and had already begun stockpiling linen for Sabahat's trousseau.

8

The Visitor

Aram knew it would be socially unacceptable to arrive empty-handed at the door of a Turkish gentleman and his wife, but he could not decide between a box of chocolates and a bouquet of flowers. Consulted on her opinion, his mother advised chocolate. Rebeka pointed out that the family in question was of old Ottoman stock, and while the times had admittedly changed, certain conventions and traditions endured. Cut flowers they might find strange; chocolates or Hacı Bekir lokum they would most certainly appreciate.

"Why not present them with both flowers and chocolates?" Aram asked.

"Son, are you going there to discuss lessons or to ask for their daughter's hand?"

"They'd never give her to me even if I did ask." Aram laughed.

"You told me you were going to tutor little children." A note of unease had crept into Rebeka's voice.

"I am. Both of them are in elementary school."

"Then what's all this about a daughter?"

"She's their aunt."

"Son, listen to me. Don't invite trouble. Whatever you do, don't become overly familiar with the daughter of a Muslim family!"

"What are you talking about, Mayrik? You wouldn't say that if you knew her. I've never met anyone so well bred and sensible."

"Her breeding is of no interest to us," Rebeka said.

What was of interest to Rebeka was the money Aram would earn, not the girl or the choice of a gift for her parents. Her son was the most successful student in his school and at the top of his class, unlike his brother Jirayir, who had lost his scholarship and gone off to work for a leather merchant in the Grand Bazaar. While she was grateful her first-born had become the family breadwinner, she had greater ambitions for her younger son. Aram earned pocket money from his job at the library and had further supplemented his income over the summer by teaching mathematics to the grandson of the local grocer and algebra to the girl living across the street. Were her son to begin tutoring the grandchildren of Reşat Bey, a former chancellor of the exchequer, he would be able to contribute to his family's upkeep without compromising his studies. *I'm so proud of him,* she thought. *He's intelligent and enterprising, just like his grandfather.* Still, her son seemed overly enthusiastic about these lessons, and she wondered why. Call it a mother's intuition, but Rebeka's joy was tainted by apprehension.

"I think Hacı Bekir lokum is best, Mayrik."

Shaken out of her thoughts, Rebeka responded with, "I think it is best you watch your step, Aram."

"Have you ever seen me go wrong?"

"Of course not, son. It's just . . . I have a funny feeling about these lessons, and I don't know why."

"Stop worrying. The children's aunt goes to my school. She's much older than me, three or four years. I'm only telling you this to put you at ease."

"What's a girl that age doing at your school?"

"She finished middle school at Saint-Benoît but transferred to our school so she could improve her English. Feel better now, Madame Balayan?"

"Seeing that they're Francophiles, perhaps you should take them bonbons instead of lokum? You can take the funicular up to Beyoğlu and buy them at Markiz."

"Are you going to give me any money for that?"

"Sometimes you have to throw out a sprat to catch a mackerel," Rebeka said to herself. There might be other children in need of lessons in Reşat Bey's mansion. She went off to the bedroom to get her handbag.

Hüsnü Efendi swung open the front door of the mansion to admit Aram, who had never been in a Turkish home this imposing. He found himself in what appeared to be a spacious hall or anteroom and surreptitiously shot a look to the left and then to the right. In the center of the hall, a magnificent gilded table stood directly beneath the glittering twelve-arm crystal chandelier suspended in the stairwell.

"Please follow me upstairs," intoned the butler, having eyed the visitor head to toe and apparently found him wanting. Aram hesitated, uncertain whether to leave the box of bonbons on the table or hand it to the butler. He was saved by Sabahat, who called out to him as she descended the stairs.

"Welcome, Aram Bey." Sabahat turned to the butler and said, "This young gentleman is the children's new tutor."

"God help him."

Puzzled by the butler's words, Aram handed the package to Sabahat.

"You shouldn't have, Aram."

Sabahat led him to the hall on the floor above. To one side was a piano, and to the other a mirror and table console on which a collection of globed lamps was grouped. Sabahat snatched a hand towel off one of the lamps and hid it away in the console drawer. Opening onto the hall were a great many rooms, and through a half-open door Aram caught a glimpse of a richly furnished, dimly lit sitting room. He was shown, however, into a bright room with a pair of bow windows and a backless, cushion-strewn divan running the length of the walls. Two pretty blond women introduced as Sabahat's sisters greeted him; one of them was tall and slender, the other somewhat plump. He sat on the divan across from them. The women, who at first glance bore little resemblance to each other, became more similar as the moments passed, their gestures and airs oddly mirroring each other. Suat, the shorter of the two, was effusive and amiable, while Leman Hanım was more aloof, seemingly content to let her admittedly striking eyes do the talking. Aram's own eyes were drawn to the high ceiling where the plaster ornamentation beginning midway up the walls culminated in crown molding and fretwork worthy of a palace. Other than the upholstered cushions in tones of dusty rose lining the divan, the large circular brass tray resting on a mother-of-pearl inlaid wooden stand that served as a low table for refreshments, and the two enormous Aivazovsky seascapes on the wall, the room boasted no other adornments or furnishings.

"How do you take your coffee?" Suat Hanım was asking.

"No sugar, please. Thank you."

Instructions were issued to the maid waiting in the doorway. Once she was gone, Suat raised the matter at hand. "Sabahat has spoken very highly of you, Aram Bey. I am afraid our children can be a little unruly at times. I hope they won't rattle you."

"I've met them. We get along well."

"My father engaged a highly esteemed hodja to teach them the old alphabet. As you know, their schools teach only the Latin script. The poor man was driven to distraction."

"I'm certain the children and I will reach an understanding."

"I do hope so. We'll find out soon enough."

Leman spoke to Aram for the first time: "Sabahat tells me you're good at figures. My Sitare cannot get her mind around them, and I'm so worried she'll fail her class."

Aram turned to Leman Hanım, looked into her enchanting eyes, and cleared his throat. "I have examined Sitare's arithmetic book and her notebook. A few lessons will suffice for her to catch up to her classmates."

Leman asked the servant, who had resumed her post at the door, to tell Sitare and Bülent to come to their mothers. A few minutes later, the urchins raced into the room, pushing and tugging at each other to see who could reach their new tutor first. Bülent threw his arms around Aram's neck. Sitare gave him a kiss on the cheek.

"I see you are on familiar terms," Suat Hanım said.

"We see each other at school every day," Aram quickly explained, praying that the children would say nothing about their walks home together. At the sight of Sabahat coming into the room with a tray of coffee, he was able to breathe more easily.

When they finished their coffees, Sabahat passed round the bonbons Aram had brought. She could tell that her sisters were warming to the courteous young man. The revelation that his mother played the piano increased him another notch in Leman Hanım's estimation. Talk meandered through a variety of topics, touching on the vulgarity of the latest fashions, the virtues of the new regime, and the course of world events. When Sabahat excused herself to go and get her father, the palms of Aram's hands grew moist and his heart started beating faster. The heavyset, berobed, and glowering Ottoman of his imagination turned out, however, to be a smiling gentleman, dapper if dated.

Aram sprang to his feet as the man entered. The sisters also stood. Once formal introductions had been made, Leman said, "Let us leave so you can discuss your rates with my Bey Baba." Then she left the room, trailed by her sisters and the children. Aram felt his cheeks burning. He was too embarrassed to lift his eyes and look at the man sitting across from him. He had not envisioned any haggling over rates. He had immediately told the girl he so admired and wanted to spend more time with that he would be happy to tutor her niece and nephew, and had come running to her home without a second thought. Now what was he supposed to do?

"Aram Bey, perhaps it is best we begin on a trial basis."

"If that is your wish, sir."

"I fear you misunderstand me. It is not your competence that will be on trial, it is my grandchildren. They can be quite mischievous. There was an unfortunate incident with their old tutor. If, after a few lessons, you find that the children's boisterousness exhausts your stores of patience, please feel free to withdraw from our arrangement."

"I am not one to admit defeat, sir."

"I do hope so! Would you be so kind as to inform me of your rates?"

"I . . . well . . . I had no expectations of that nature, sir."

"I won't hear of such a thing! What is the amount you charge to your other students?"

"Sabahat Hanım and I are friends, sir. We both sit on the student council."

"Friendship is one thing, and business another! If you take your duties as a tutor seriously, you should receive compensation for your efforts, should you not?"

Aram's protestations were no match for Ahmet Reşat's straightforward logic. He pronounced a figure.

"That strikes me as reasonable and fair," Reşat Bey said. He held out his well-formed hand and shook Aram's. Having warmed to the older man, and knowing, as he did, that he was guilty of abusing his trust on the subject of Sabahat, Aram could not help but blush.

As the sisters chatted after Aram's departure, Suat teased Sabahat. "That Armenian boy of yours is quite good-looking. Even better, he looks old for his age. He was but a pup when I saw him last year."

"Boys are like that," Leman said. "They grow tall at a later age than girls, but when they do, they shoot up into men overnight. He made a good impression on Beyba. Now, let's see if he can handle our little terrors."

"If he can't, we'll find a different tutor."

"Might I suggest you teach your children some manners instead of expecting others to deal with them?" Sabahat said.

Leman was stunned. "What are you trying to say, Sabahat?" she gasped.

"I'm sorry to say this, Leman, but you're always finding an excuse for the children. Bülent's father is far away, and they're both heartbroken over Mehpare's leaving—there's always something! It's only when they're shouted at that they listen," Sabahat said. "What did you ever let me get away with when I was their age? I'll never forget being made to sit in front of a plate of okra for three hours, but if Sitare decides she'd rather not have meat, an omelet is whipped up for her. I was sent to my room directly after dinner every night; Bülent bounces on his granddad's knee for hours."

"Surely you're not jealous of the other children, not at your age?"

"Of course not! I simply hope that my niece and nephew will grow up well mannered. We've already lost one hodja; I'd hate to lose another."

"Ah, now I understand. You're afraid the children will exasperate your precious Aram, and it will then reflect badly on you," Suat said. "Listen, Sabahat, I know how devoted you are to your friends, but you're getting carried away here. Family comes first. And furthermore, I advise you against being seen out in public with him. People won't realize he's an Armenian boy several years your junior and a tutor for your niece and nephew. There will be talk."

"You have said all that already. And besides, I'm trying to tell you something important, but you're banging on about something completely unrelated," Sabahat said as she left the room to go check on her mother, who had been laid up in her room all day with shortness of breath.

When Sabahat was out of earshot, Leman looked at her other sister and asked, "Do you think we're spoiling our children, Suat? It's true we never spared the rod when it came to Sabahat. Perhaps she has a point."

"All of those years of discipline haven't done Sabahat any good. Just look at how she turns on us."

"I've decided to sit down and have a serious talk with Sitare before the new tutor comes. I'll ask Mahir Bey to stop indulging her. It's his fault she's turned out to be such a handful, not mine."

Suat had no such complaints about her own husband. Not only was Hilmi absent most of the time, when he was at home he was overly strict with Bülent, perhaps hoping to compensate for the overindulgence of the boy's grandparents.

"If I were you, I'd sit down for a talk with Sabahat first," Suat said. "It seems to me that this friendship of hers has gone too far."

"But she's always been like this. If she takes a liking to someone, she's all in. Remember how devoted she was to Halim? Now, she never even mentions his name. Don't come down hard on her; soon enough she'll have new friends and no time for Aram Efendi."

"What did you think of him, anyway?"

"He struck me as a clever boy, the kind who may well succeed in straightening out the children. All I ask of him is that Sitare makes headway with her arithmetic."

"You never think about anything but Sitare. I hope you're right."

"And you always think the worst," Leman muttered under breath as she ambled out into the hall, where she immediately caused a commotion.

"Where's my hand towel? Who took my hand towel?"

Suat ran out into the hall as Sabahat came bounding up the stairs.

"Where is the hand towel I draped over this lamp?" Leman screamed, eyes blazing. She turned on Neyir Hanım as the elderly woman shuffled into the hall. "Did you take it, Grandma?"

"What towel? I haven't seen any towels."

"I put it in the drawer," Sabahat said calmly.

"Why?"

"Because we had a guest! Towels belong in the bathroom, not in the hall." Sabahat pulled the towel out of the drawer and handed it to Leman.

"What business do you have meddling with my towels, Sabahat?"

"All I did was put it in the drawer. It was dry."

"Mahir keeps his boxes of medicine in that drawer. You put my towel right on top of them. Here, throw it away. I don't want it anymore."

"Why throw away a perfectly good towel?" Suat said. "We'll wash it, and it will be good as new."

"Mind your own business! I better not catch you touching my towel again!"

"Leman!" a voice rang out. "Towels are kept in the bathroom. I better not catch you draping yours on that lamp again."

Leman turned and looked at her mother, who was standing on the landing. "When I leave mine in the bathroom, everyone dries their hands with it," she said.

"We all have our own hand towels. Why would anyone use yours?"

"But what if they do?"

"I'm going to have a word with Mahir Bey and ask him to treat your morbid fear of germs. It will be the end of you yet, my girl."

"It's no surprise that none of you appreciates the dangers of microbes. That's because none of you is married to a doctor."

"If I had known you would become obsessed with germs, I would never have allowed you to marry a doctor."

Behice Hanım hitched up her dressing gown and headed for the stairs. Pinching a corner of the towel between her thumb and index finger, Leman held it at arm's length as she flounced off to her room under the half-mocking, half-pitying gaze of her sisters.

Part Two

The Mansion in Sultanahmet

The Kulin Family

(1934)

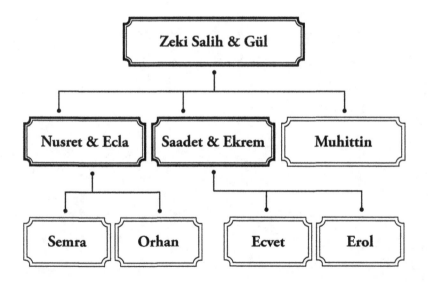

Zeki Salih & Gül

Nusret & Ecla   Saadet & Ekrem   Muhittin

Semra   Orhan   Ecvet   Erol

9

The Homeland Is Gone

October 5, 1908
Rami, Istanbul

The deep-gray clouds darkening the horizon late that morning had warned of the rain to come, and in the afternoon it poured. Nose pressed against the windowpane, Muhittin was watching the storm when he spotted the tall, thin figure of his father turning into the end of the road. By the time a great gust of wind had swept Zeki Salih to the front door amid a whirl of autumn leaves, Muhittin was there to open it. Zeki Salih stepped inside and, without taking off his sodden coat or greeting his son, kicked off his shoes, stomped up the stairs and into the bedroom, pulled a revolver out of the nightstand drawer, threw up the window sash, and fired every last bullet at the poplars lined up across the road.

At the sound of the terrifying salvo, Muhittin dashed from the bottom of the stairs to the kitchen, where his mother was rolling out pastry.

"Muho, stay in the kitchen. Bolt the door from the inside and don't open it until I tell you," she said, gathering her skirts and taking the stairs two and three at a time. When she opened the bedroom door, her husband had his back to her, shoulders wracked with sobs, oblivious to the rain pelting him through the open window.

First, Gül gently took the revolver dangling from her husband's right hand and tossed it onto the bed. Then she lowered the window and said, "Salih Bey! Salih Bey! What is it, my lamb?"

Zeki Salih slowly turned and gazed at her through bloodshot blue eyes.

"My country is gone! Our Bosnia is gone, Gül! We no longer have a homeland to which we can return," he cried. "The sultan is going to sign the treaty. Bosnia will be annexed by Austro-Hungary. It's official!"

Gül sank onto the end of the bed before her legs could give out, wishing she could blubber like her husband, but restraining herself nonetheless.

"This is our homeland now, Salih Bey," she said. "Bosnia was already lost. Hasn't it been controlled by Austro-Hungary for many years now?"

"They're surrendering our land without firing a single bullet or sending a single battalion. Just signing it away. My country is gone," Zeki Salih repeated. Tears rolled down his cheeks and onto his dripping-wet coat.

Zeki Salih sat down next to his wife on the bed and rested his head on her shoulder, then he put his head on her lap and started sobbing again. Gül stroked the light-brown hair matted to his head. After a moment, she spoke in soothing tones.

"Salih Bey, you're not happy in Istanbul, I know that. We have relatives in Bursa, in İnegöl. Would you like to move there? They say it's just like Bosnia, that it has the same rushing streams and green meadows as Travnik. Even the mosques, bathhouses, and markets are much the same. Let's sell our property and move to İnegöl. You could buy a farm, breed animals, and ride horses again. What do you say, Salih Bey?"

Zeki Salih slowly lifted his head from his wife's lap, straightened, and said, "We're staying here, Gül. I've got my children to consider, and I won't let them suffer what I have. Just as my name was known throughout my homeland, theirs will be known here. I'll educate my daughter and my two sons in the most prestigious schools in Istanbul so that my boys become accomplished men and make a name for themselves, that's what I'll—"

Gül touched her slender fingers to her husband's lips, silencing him.

"Nobody has ever questioned your good name, Salih Bey, you who come from the Kulinović bloodline. And fear not, your sons will carry on the family name when you are gone."

"Gül Hanım, I want to be worthy of my name. Neither your fortune nor my name stretching back eight centuries has proved beneficial here. The Kulinović name is known only as far as the garden gate, and we are renowned only among our relatives. Nevertheless, I'm not going anywhere. I'm staying right here. I'm going to bring up my children in the most illustrious city in the Ottoman Empire. I allowed myself to be called a migrant; I will not allow my children to be called provincials. May they be held in the highest esteem! May they grow up to become accomplished men!"

"Bring them up to be conscientious and respectful so that their accomplishments benefit others," Gül said. She picked up the revolver she had tossed onto the bed, wrapped it in a length of cloth, and placed it on the top shelf of the closet.

"Goodness, Salih Bey, what did the poplars do to you anyway? Instead of shooting at those who lost Bosnia, you shot up those poor trees."

"The poplars understand perfectly well what I did, Gül Hanım! My heart's bleeding. It's been torn out of my chest! Now, don't get cross with me when I say there's only one thing that can stanch the pain: a nice, ice-cold—"

"Salih Bey, you have every right to drink this evening. And just this once I won't send you off to a meyhane. Change your clothes, go downstairs, and make yourself comfortable on the divan. I'll be along well before evening with both your rakı and your *meze*, lovingly prepared with my own two hands." Gül sadly regarded her husband, who had curled up in the fetal position on the bed, and added, "Now, dry your tears so the children don't realize you've been crying." She went downstairs to the kitchen and called out, "Muho, open the door."

Muho timidly peered through a crack in the door. "Majka, is it bandits?"

"Don't be scared," Gül reassured her son. "There aren't any bandits here; they're somewhere else. Your father was firing his revolver upstairs so he could scare them all the way off in Bosnia. Perhaps someone heard and realized there is one man, at least, who is eager to put up a fight."

She sent her son to the sitting room, bolted the kitchen door, and, once she'd buried her face in the apron she'd left on the countertop, sobbed to her heart's content.

When Muhittin's big brother, Nusret, and big sister, Saadet, got home from school later that day, their little brother rushed up to them in a panic. "Dad's cross today so don't go anywhere near him or he might shoot you."

Nusret looked at Saadet, rolled his eyes, and said, "What in the world is he going on about?"

"He's just a child, spouting nonsense," Saadet said.

"I swear it's true," Muhittin insisted. "He lost something, and he's ever so cross about it."

"Mother, what's all this about Father being angry?" Saadet asked. "Silly Muho says he lost something. Did Father forget his walking stick at the coffeehouse again? Shall Nusret go and fetch it?"

"Your father lost his homeland today, Saadet. Today we lost our Bosnia forever!" Saadet was too young to be dismayed by the news, but her mother looked so miserable that the young girl ran up and flung her arms around her.

To Nusret and Saadet, it was more than their mother's failure to give each of them a glass of milk and to hover nearby until their homework was done that set that day apart from all the others: their father was home. On ordinary days, their mother would sit across from them until their homework was done and then check their notebooks. In fact, that is how the children had come to believe their mother could read and write. On ordinary days, their father would usually come home late, long after the evening call to prayer, when they were already in bed. As he staggered up the stairs, Father would ask, "Have the children done their homework?" and Mother would reply, "Yes, they have, Salih Bey." "And have they performed their evening prayers?" was always met with, "Yes, they have, Salih Bey." As the children nodded off to sleep, they would hear doors opening and closing, and the low murmur of their parents' voices as Father sipped a cup of coffee Mother prepared in a long-handled copper pot.

But on that particular day, Nusret and Saadet found their father in his cups, cross-legged on the divan in front of the window. When he motioned the children over, all three came running. "Sit down," their father said. Nusret and Saadet knelt in front of the divan, hands on their thighs. Zeki Salih scooped Muhittin up onto his lap, solemnly looked into his children's eyes, and said, "I want you to listen very carefully to what I am about to say. Your mother and I have two homelands. We were born in one and we will die in the other. You have one homeland. Love it with all your might, love its every stone and mountain, love it above all else, even more than you love yourself, and that way nobody will be able to come and take it away from you. One day, when you have grown old, God willing, may you close your eyes to this world in your homeland." It was not his words but the quaver in their father's voice—the conviction that one's homeland was precious and must never be lost—that resonated in the hearts of Nusret, Saadet, and even five-year-old Muhittin.

10

Leaving Behind Rami

1915
Istanbul

Zeki Salih offered up a prayer for divine blessing and turned his back on the horse-drawn wagons carrying the contents of his home in Rami to his newly acquired mansion in Sultanahmet. The sight of the departing drays provoked a visceral reaction in him, and he shuddered at the thought of having to resettle. Life had taught him that with each new move came new trauma. Gnawing at him now was a sense of fear, both insidious and pervasive, the fear of journeying from the familiar to the unknown.

In 1897, as he was being uprooted from his homeland in Bosnia, Zeki Salih had suppressed his sorrow but denied his fear, even to himself. This time, though, there was no dismissing the dread provoked by the prospect of a strange home in a strange neighborhood. There would be new rooms, new streets, new neighbors, and new coffeehouses.

He would have to prove himself and adapt all over again.

His new neighbors would never realize that Zeki Salih was no common immigrant but a man from a noble family. They would laugh at the accent he was helpless to smooth, ascribe to ignorance his unfamiliarity with Ottoman calligraphy, and mistake his lack of employment for indolence. They would never realize that he, a Bosnian *beg*, had always been accustomed to living on the revenues generated by his land; that the only employment he had ever known was the management of a vast estate that also provided livelihoods for the hundreds of villagers who plowed and tilled his fields; that the Bosnian gentry were not illiterate or ignorant, but read and wrote in a script they had developed among themselves, a script in which some of the Balkans' finest poetry and most heroic epics were chronicled. Perhaps, over time, his new neighbors in Sultanahmet would regard Salih Bey as a fine fellow of good character. That was all he hoped for.

Nearly two decades earlier, as he was preparing to leave his home in Sarajevo and move to the house in Istanbul he was now preparing to vacate, he had anticipated that the respect accorded him in his homeland would not be forthcoming in his new country. At that time, however, he did not think it would matter, for the Ottomans were still the masters of the Balkans.

11

Leaving Behind Bosnia

1897
Bosnia

It was Gül who had wanted to immigrate to Istanbul. Rose-scented, rosy-skinned Gül Hanım. His wife, his beloved, his blessing.

"Let's leave Bosnia, Salih Bey," she had said one day, giving voice, perhaps, to a sense of foreboding. "I know how reluctant you are to leave your land, but life in the shadow of the cross is no life for us. My elder sister just followed her husband to Istanbul. My brother-in-law has always kept an ear to the ground. If he wrote all those letters to my sister urging her to join him at once, there must have been a good reason for it."

Gül pestered her husband for the better part of a year.

"If we leave, I'll do whatever you want."

"Give me a son."

"Will we leave if I do?"

"I promise!"

When their son was conceived not long afterward, Zeki Salih kept his promise and took his wife to Istanbul even before their son was born. How did they know it would be a boy? Gül had seen a newborn in a dream, had rocked in her arms a white-skinned son fragrant as a rose. That is what Gül believed, and Zeki Salih believed Gül.

Entrusted to his steward and his closest relatives were the fields and orchards spreading across three-quarters of Travnik. A buyer was found for his mansion in Sarajevo. Zeki Salih got a lump in his throat as he watched their household goods being carted off to Travnik from the mansion in Sarajevo where he had spent his childhood and youth; where the vineyards and vegetable gardens were; where the bridge upon which he had first seen Gül and lost his heart was; where his father and mother rested for eternity in a graveyard. All of it, every last bit, would soon be a memory. The fear of being uprooted gripped him. For the briefest of moments, his tall figure leaned forward, as though poised to break into pursuit of the last oxcart rattling off to Travnik. But the moment passed. Zeki Salih straightened, ran his fingers through his thick hair, and said to himself, "This is our country, and we can always visit it when we get homesick. May the Lord keep and protect it!" There was ambivalence in the prayer, an uncertainty if he was praying for Bosnia, land of his birth, or for Istanbul, city of his future life.

Later, much later, Zeki Salih would thank God for allowing his family to get out of Bosnia in time, sparing them the suffering of the tens of thousands who were displaced by war, that great wave of refugees fleeing the Ottoman lands lost in the Balkan Wars of 1912 and 1913. He later heard tales of savagery from those who had witnessed the slaughter of children, the torching of homes, the laying waste of whole villages, the plundering of wagon trains. So graphic and vivid were these oft-repeated accounts of the disastrous war and its aftermath that their images would be seared forever into Zeki Salih's mind and into the memory of his community.

Some dismissed Gül Hanım's insistence that they leave for Istanbul as the caprice of a spoiled wife, but it was the reason they were able to travel in comfort, and Zeki Salih would be forever grateful for her foresight. He and his wife were able to bid farewell to their friends and relatives before they boarded a passenger train with their cloth-wrapped bundles of silver dishes and utensils, copper pitchers, platters, and salvers. They were able to load trunks filled with clothes and sables, dozens of silver brocade coverings, and lace-lined curtains. Installed in the first-class compartment reserved for their family, they would reach Istanbul after a long but uneventful journey.

Gül's elder sister, Fatma Paşe, had readied their new home in Rami, a peaceful district outside the ancient city walls of Istanbul. Fatma had even planted an ever-blooming rose shrub in the garden, so that the following year its perfume would waft in on the breeze and fill the rooms of the house where Gül, whose name meant "rose," after all, would be nursing their firstborn.

Running past their new home in Rami was a wide dirt road, and across from it a row of poplars stood along a stream that flowed as far as the eye could see.

"In the spring months the cottony hairs of those poplars will fly through the air," Gül griped, "getting into everything."

"I'll have screens put in the windows, my rose," Zeki Salih promised. He busied himself with finding solutions to all his pregnant wife's complaints and kept his homesickness in his heart.

Yes, they had been right to come to Istanbul. Yes, had they stayed in Bosnia, they would have known firsthand the ravages of war and been at the mercy of unbelievers. Yes, his son would be born and grow to manhood, praise God, under the green banner of the caliphate. All true, but Zeki Salih was troubled nonetheless, and had no one to whom he could pour out his sorrow. Zeki Salih yearned for the land where he was born and bred, for the streams where he had bathed, for the mountain pastures where his horse had galloped. He missed his mother tongue, missed perching on wooden chairs for intimate chats in the coffeehouse, missed the Rumelian songs ringing out in the meyhane. He missed the greenness of Bosnia, the crystal waters of the Milaç, the steep street winding up to the wooden latticework and bay windows of his old neighborhood, the cedar-scented storage cupboards of the mansion where he had played hide-and-seek with his future bride. He missed every last detail of the life and the land that had been his until he came to Istanbul. The pining for all he had lost consumed him, and he found little comfort even in the arms of his beloved Gül.

Zeki Salih patiently waited. In order to adapt to his new country, to get accustomed to his new life and stop missing Bosnia, he would wait for the birth of his son. Surely an occasion so joyous would ease the ache in his heart.

Some months later, that same year, he ceremoniously whispered into the ear of his newborn son a short prayer and the name Ahmet Nusret. Zeki Salih also added in a low, choked voice: "Son, may the One True God allow you to dwell in your birthplace, never knowing what it is to be torn apart, your body in one place, your soul in another. And may you never be derided for your traditions and your native tongue."

Gül noticed the tears in her husband's eyes when he lifted his lips from their son's ear, but she failed to notice the pain behind what she assumed were his tears of joy.

A Bosnian beg was expected to occupy himself solely with the management of his land and the revenues and produce it raised. A beg could hunt. He could devote himself to charity, such as the building of schools, public fountains, and mosques. He could distribute alms and provisions to the poor. He could assemble trousseaus and contribute to dowries for brides-to-be. He could preside over the evening fast-breaking meal in the month of Ramadan. What he accepted and expected in return was respect, nothing more. Zeki Salih, beg of the Lowlands of Travnik, had enjoyed sufficient resources to meet all of these obligations. Even wealthier was his wife, the daughter of Hajji Musta Bey of the Gümüşiç family, the owner of vast holdings in Banja Luka. Both husband and wife were distant descendants of the two families that established the first, albeit short-lived, Kingdom of Bosnia at the beginning of the eleventh century. Along with the other Balkan provinces, Bosnia was the Ottoman gateway to the West. Its social order was stable and structured; even the wealthiest and oldest families swore absolute fealty to their ruler and obeyed his laws. Wealthy families residing in the large towns and cities treated their sons and daughters equally. Polygamy and the strict segregation of the sexes were not local practices, and never had been. Muslim Bosnians sought to lead by example in their community. They were passionate about their dignity, their honor, their language, and their religion, and were the loyal servants of Islam and the sultan.

None of these qualities did Zeki Salih Kulinović a bit of good in Istanbul. He did not know what it was to work nor how to write in any script but the one used among Bosnian beg. In Istanbul, Zeki Salih amounted to nothing. In the streets of Travnik, Banja Luka, and Sarajevo, everyone had stepped aside and respectfully buttoned up their coats as he passed; in Istanbul, he was the invisible man. His heavy Rumelian accent made him dread even simple interactions. Shopping was a chore. He made no new friends outside of his circle of relatives, speaking little and growing more withdrawn. The only things that brought him joy were Bairam feasts and the month of Ramadan. Just as he had done in his homeland, he celebrated Bairam by inviting all of his neighbors, rich and poor, to gather at the long tables set up in front of his home. The tables were laden with a vast array of dishes, from traditional soups, roast lamb, saffron-scented pudding, and stewed fruits, to flavors less familiar to the Istanbul palate, like cheese dumplings, chicken stewed with rice, grilled sausages, and, of course, Bosnian-style baklava. That same ritual was repeated for the evening fast-breaking meals throughout the month of Ramadan. His mother and his wife repeatedly assured him that nobody in Istanbul expected such lavish hospitality, but Zeki Salih considered it his duty to fill his neighbors' bellies in that holiest of months, no matter where he was living.

Zeki Salih was not alone in leaving Bosnia. Among the relatives who had migrated to Istanbul prior to Zeki Salih were such influential personages as the children of Selimbey Şahinpasiç, cousins after whom the district of Alibey was named, and members of the Ottoman Parliament and the Assembly of Notables. Some relatives had become entrepreneurs by investing in property with money they brought with them from Bosnia. A brother-in-law, Şahin Paşazade Selim Bey, bought large tracts of land in Sirkeci and became the proprietor and manager of the Şahin Pasha Hotel, a modern and elegant facility without rival in all of the historical peninsula of Sultanahmet. Zeki Salih had no idea how to invest his money and was embarrassed to consult those who did. However, when his brother-in-law, Selim Bey, was dividing his Sirkeci holdings into parcels, Zeki Salih bought some lots of land adjacent to the hotel, as well as a large commercial building he later let out. Still, Zeki Salih would have preferred living on the revenues of his estate in Bosnia to becoming a landlord or a businessman.

Summers he spent mostly in the garden of the old house in Rami; winters, he could be found near his new home, in a coffeehouse in Kocamustafapaşa frequented by Bosnians. At night, he frequently chose to drown his homesickness at one of the meyhane where he had become a familiar face.

Gül Hanım adapted to this new country much more easily than her husband. She never once felt like a stranger in a city where so many of her relatives, including her elder sister, had already settled. Through constant communication with the household staff, her Turkish became fluent in no time. Shortly after becoming installed in her new home in Rami in 1897, she began nursing Nusret, her firstborn.

In 1900, the year Nusret turned three, Gül Hanım gave birth to a girl, Saadet, their new source of joy. Three years flew by, and in 1903, Gül found she had a toddler in her arms, Nusret tugging at her skirts, and a baby kicking in her womb. She was too distracted to pay much mind to her husband's struggles, his homesickness, and his growing attachment to rakı.

Salih Bey and Gül Hanım named their third child Muhittin. In contrast to restless Nusret and chatty Saadet, he was placid. Despite being the baby of the family, he was never spoiled by his parents, because Gül had a soft spot for her firstborn, and Salih Bey doted on his daughter. It was left to Grandmother Vasfiy'anım, or Hamma, as everyone called her, to pamper little Muho. Hamma nicknamed the youngest of her grandchildren, with eyes as blue as alpine lakes and with skin as white as snow, "Moj Beli," Bosnian for "My White One."

12

Death Throes

Muhittin turned five in 1908, the same year Austro-Hungary announced the annexation of Bosnia, and Bulgaria proclaimed independence from the Ottomans. Not to be outdone, the king of Greece began pressing for union with Crete, then a semiautonomous state under Ottoman suzerainty. Crete had been simmering with uprisings and revolts since the 1850s, and since the turn of the century, the star and crescent that had fluttered over the gate of Chania as a symbol of centuries of Ottoman sovereignty had been replaced by the royal crown and cross of the Greek flag. The Ottomans were powerless to stop the island's eventual union with the Kingdom of Greece in 1913, but that did not stop them from organizing various marches in the meantime to protest the inevitable.

One day, an official circular announcing a massive rally in the historical heart of the city was sent to all the schools in Istanbul. Nusret was instructed by his middle-school teachers to bring any brothers he might have to the event. Gül Hanım objected, saying Muho was far too young. As Nusret kept insisting and Muho threw temper tantrum after temper tantrum, Saadet chimed in with the suggestion that she accompany Muho to the rally and keep a protective eye on him, a proposal that nearly earned her a box on the ear from her father. Finally, it was decided that Muho would be allowed to go on the condition that Nusret and his cousins, Saim and Ramiz, promise to take Muho by the hand and never let him out of their sight. Donning their conical felt caps, the boys set off early in the morning. As a last-minute precaution, Zeki Salih decided to send his manservant, Raci Efendi, to follow the boys at a discreet distance, intervening only if absolutely necessary.

Under the watchful eye of Raci Efendi, the boys walked to Nusret's school, where carriages were waiting to convey them and their classmates to Beyazit, the starting point of the demonstration. Told he would not be allowed to travel with the students, Raci Efendi decided to make his own way there. The plan, which was to catch up to the boys at the students' meeting point, would indeed go astray: Raci Efendi found it impossible to cross the street, let alone locate the boys in the midst of the tremendous throng streaming from Beyazit to Sultanahmet Square. It looked like the entire populace of the city, young and old, rich and poor, had flocked to the demonstration. The occasional cries of "Allahuekber" gave way to a chant taken up by all of the marchers: "In defense of beloved Crete, spill our blood, we entreat."

That slogan roared from a thousand throats, echoing like the cascading waters of a mighty waterfall. Had the marchers been ordered at that moment to spill their blood for Crete, they would have laid down their lives in a heartbeat. The fate of Crete seemed to depend on the strength of the slogan these Ottoman subjects never tired of repeating. Even Raci Efendi shouted himself hoarse as he jostled his way through the crowd.

Flanked by Nusret and Ramiz, both of whom held him by the hand, Muho was being swept along in a torrent of trouser- and shalwar-clad legs when his felt cap fell off. Wresting a hand free, he bent over to pick it up. Several protestors tumbled over the little boy, and Muho's hand slipped out of Nusret's. Trampled and scared, he started crying. His big brother's cries of "Muho! Muho!" grew fainter. Mustering all his strength, Muho bawled "Nusret! Nusret!" but nobody could hear him over the deafening crowd. He tried and failed to get up. Feet stepped on top of him, one after another, dozens of them. He curled up like a pill bug, arms clasped around his head, and waited.

Nusret was fighting his way back to a shop sign he had noticed at the moment Muho's hand slipped from his. Working his way through this tide of humanity was akin to swimming against the current of a rushing river, but after what seemed like hours, he arrived at the shop sign. Frantically looking to the left and the right, he elbowed his way to the opposite side of the street.

By then, Muho had managed to drag himself to the curb. He was again curled up in a tight ball, convinced death was imminent. The words to every last prayer his mother had taught him were on his lips; his last wish was to be admitted to paradise.

A hand seized him by the scruff of the neck and pulled him heavenward. At the sight of his big brother, Muho opened his mouth to speak, emitting a series of weak wheezes. Nusret enfolded Muho in his arms and, paying no mind to the snot and tears streaking the grimy little face, smothered him with kisses. The brothers made it to the pavement and plunged into the first shop they found, an upholsterer's. Muho was placed atop the counter, where a quick examination failed to turn up any broken or dislocated bones. The shopkeeper fetched a glass of water. Nusret helped Muho drink it and wiped away his tears.

When Muho's sobs finally died down, he managed to croak, "My cap fell off. Father's going to be so cross with me!"

"No he won't, Muho," Nusret said. "You're a little hero. You nearly died for your country today."

"You nearly died for nothing, you mean!" said the shopkeeper. "If taking to the streets solved anything, the empire would never have been reduced to this state!"

Nusret glared at the man and said, "Well, we did what we could."

"You're still wet behind the ears. If you really want to do something for your country, wait until you grow up, then do it. If your generation turns out to be like ours, resting on its laurels, frittering away its savings, caring only about lining its pockets, there's no hope for the Ottomans, I fear."

Nusret tried to make sense of the man's words. Perhaps there were other things he could do for his country. If only he were older!

When Muho got home that afternoon, his voice was hoarse, his feet were swollen, his back was bruised, and he was so exhausted he could barely stand. Soaking his feet in a basin of warm salt water prepared by his mother, he regaled everyone in the household with the tale of his heroics, thoroughly convinced that he had helped save Crete. That night, as the little boy sank into a contented sleep, there was no way he could have known that the Ottoman defeat in the Balkan Wars would be followed by the loss of Crete in 1913. Unbeknownst to Muho, the empire would continue to crumble, bit by bit.

13

Zeki Salih's New Life

Sultanahmet, Istanbul

In the heart of historic Istanbul, not far from the former hippodrome now known as Sultanahmet Square, stood a pink, three-story mansion whose property extended as far as Sümbüllüçeşme Street, where it ended in a small garden shaded by an old plane tree. This was the home to which Zeki Salih and his family moved in 1915, many years before a certain family living in a mansion within walking distance in Beyazit would become their relatives.

The first thing Zeki Salih had done when he acquired the title deed was to plant cherry, plum, and apple trees in that garden. It took nearly a year to repaint all of the rooms, renew the marble in the hammam, and install additional toilets on the upper floors, so that by the time Gül Hanım moved into their new home, the plants were flourishing, and she was as pleased as a newly married bride at the sight of a garden in full bloom. She had believed from the start that a new home would mean a better life, even if she could not say why. As the years passed, she was proved right.

Gül Hanım loved her new home. Her sister and the numerous relatives who had emigrated from Sarajevo all lived within walking distance. The Grand Bazaar was five minutes away, Sultanahmet Mosque just two. If they turned right upon leaving the house, they reached Divanyolu, the main avenue of the city since Roman times and the scene of festivals and processions. Zeki Salih Bey had admired a house on Divanyolu, but it had slipped through his fingers as he was haggling over the price. Gül Hanım had been upset at the time but saw now that it had been a blessing in disguise. Their current home was on a peaceful side street, yet just a stone's throw from the bustling avenue. In their garden, Salih Bey could sit under the plane tree come evening and enjoy a quiet drink.

So huge was the house that each of the children and Hamma had their own bedrooms, with rooms to spare for the assorted cousins, nephews, nieces, and other relatives on extended visits. The room just off the main entrance facing the street became the *selamlık* reserved for men, whereas the more spacious one looking out over the garden was used as a formal drawing room. The other side of the long room opened onto a space that doubled as a sitting and dining room. The bedrooms were on the second floor, and guest rooms complete with large cupboards for storing bedding were located on the third floor.

Here in this new house, Gül Hanım and Salih Bey felt as though they would be able to recreate the carefree life they had enjoyed in Sarajevo and, now that they had grown accustomed to Istanbul, know true peace of mind.

Zeki Salih's Turkish had improved enough that he no longer shied away from speaking it. Living as they did in the heart of a vibrant city, the family never lacked for visitors, many of whom stopped by after a shopping excursion to the Grand Bazaar. A stock of *sljivovica*, the plum brandy from the old country, was kept on hand for the Bosnian men, and for the women, phyllo pastry was regularly rolled out for Balkan-style baklava—to the delight of Zeki Salih and his sweet tooth.

No sooner had Zeki Salih adapted to his new country than it was gone. In 1923, the empire was replaced by a republic bent on reform. Zeki Salih welcomed the greater mingling of the sexes, and he accepted the abolition of the sultanate, but when the Hat Law banned his beloved fez, he blew his top. At first, he refused to go out into the street without his tasseled hat of red felt. After a few days of fuming indoors, he realized his resistance was futile even if he swore to his God that never, under any circumstances, would he appear in public wearing the headgear of the infidel. When winter came, he braved the cold bareheaded until, having caught a chill and been laid up in bed for several days, he accepted a fedora gifted by his son Nusret. Soon afterward, Salih Bey finally stepped into the street in that fedora, scurrying along, his head bowed, his eyes avoiding the glances of passersby, every bit as ashamed as if he were stark naked. Over time, he would grow accustomed not only to his new hat but to the bare arms and heads of women. His tongue would cluck at the just-below-the-knee hemlines even as his eyes darted away from the sight of a shapely calf, only after lingering there for a few seconds. *Thank God,* he thought, *Gül Hanım still wears a scarf over her hair in the Bosnian style.* What would he do if she embraced modern fashions?

In contrast to his fellow Muslims, who never dined out in Istanbul during those years, Zeki Salih and his sons were regulars at the restaurant in Şahin Pasha Hotel, owned by his uncle. On special occasions, but never more than once or twice a year, the women and girls would dine with the rest of the family in the private room beside the main dining area.

In 1915, the year Zeki Salih Bey and his family moved to the new house in Sultanahmet, the children had all completed elementary school. He enrolled his sons in Vefa secondary school and his daughter in a local middle school.

At a very young age, the elder son, Nusret, had shown himself to be a quick learner. That he was a stroppy handful of a boy no one could deny, but his mother blamed it on an overabundance of brains. Bored by children his age, he was forever playing pranks at school and just as frequently getting a good caning from his teachers. As he matured, he remained both the most headstrong and the most successful student in his class.

Saadet also did well in school, particularly at reading and writing, and brought home a letter of commendation at the end of every year. Unlike her brothers, however, her academic pursuits would be cut short.

After school one day, Saadet and a group of her classmates went to a candy shop on Divanyolu. It was crowded. The girls giggled and chatted as they stood in line, then headed home with their purchases.

A couple of days later, Saadet arrived home from school to find her frowning father waiting for her. She had no idea why.

"Do you always come straight home after school?" her father asked.

"Of course I do, Father."

"You're telling a lie."

"It's the truth, Father."

"In that case, it must be Remzi Efendi, who claims to have seen you in a candy shop two days ago, who is telling a lie."

"Father, I did go to the candy shop with my friends."

"Didn't you just tell me you always come straight home from school?"

"The candy shop was on the way. You know, the place on the corner with the blue awning at the end of our street."

"I know where it is."

"Forgive me, sir."

"You were wrong to go to the candy shop, Saadet. As of today, I'm removing you from school."

"But why, Father?" Saadet's lower lip began to tremble.

"People are talking. Because of you, they're saying Salih Bey allows his daughter to go into candy shops on her own. And that is why I am forbidding you to attend school."

"But Father, that's not fair! All I did was buy a paper cone of boiled sweets, and then I left the shop. Cinnamon is Hamma's favorite flavor. I got it for her."

"From now on, you are not allowed to go outside alone. If you wish to go to the candy shop, you can go with your mother or your brothers."

"Father, I promise you, I'll never do it again. Please don't take me out of school."

"This matter is closed, Saadet."

Zeki Salih got up from his cross-legged position on the divan and left the room. In tears, Saadet ran to her mother, who had known what was about to happen and was not the least surprised.

"Mother, please persuade Father," she pleaded.

"Don't press him, Saadet," her mother advised. "Surely you know how stubborn he can be. Let some time pass, and we'll discuss it again."

"I'll have failed my lessons by then!"

"Your books alone won't prepare you for life, my girl. Let's make the most of this. Sit by my side and learn how to prepare your favorite dishes; watch Hamma as she rolls out dough. You haven't picked up a needle and thread for two years. Start embroidering linens for your dowry chest. A girl's time is better spent learning the domestic arts than with her nose in a book. What will all your studying get you? A post in the Imperial Council?"

Finding no sympathy from her mother, Saadet next went to Hamma, who had just performed her prayers and was rolling up her rug.

"Why all the tears, my lamb?" her grandmother asked in Bosnian.

"Father forbade me to go to school."

"You can stay here beside me, like your mother once did."

"If they won't let me go to school, I'll take my own life."

"Stop talking nonsense or you'll make your old grandma cross. Fury and bluster is for men, and we women have only our wits with which to manage men. Go and splash water on your face, calm yourself, and then come and sit down for a chat."

In the bathroom on the floor below, Saadet huddled over the running tap and sobbed for a time. She returned to Hamma with dry, if red-rimmed, eyes.

"Do you want to go to school so very much?" Hamma asked.

"I want to be a teacher."

"Saadet, the first thing you need to do is win over your big brother Nusret. Then he can persuade your mother. She wouldn't refuse her son. When your mother tells your father how repentant you are, you may be forgiven."

"But I haven't done anything wrong, Hamma."

"Do you want to assign blame or do you want to go to school? Use your head. Nobody ever got anywhere by defying fathers and husbands. If they say you have done wrong, you have."

"But I—"

"Just do what I say. Stop protesting and start arousing your brother's pity."

Hamma couldn't even speak Turkish, but Saadet always looked up to her as the wisest person in the house. Serene and soothing, Grandma had a solution for everything.

The three siblings' childhood and teen years coincided with massive territorial losses, the collapse of the empire, and the enemy occupation of Istanbul and much of Anatolia. Arising from the ashes of despair would be a new nation and a new people. Nusret, Saadet, and Muhittin were part of a fiercely patriotic and idealistic generation determined to protect the newly drawn boundaries of their land and to prove to the European powers that not only could they catch up, they could even surpass their former occupiers. The revolution was under way, and the enlightened youth of the day were asking what they could do for their country. Nusret and Muhittin had decided to join the army, but the endless series of wars and battles ended before they could take up arms. "Peace at home, peace in the world," the nation's founding father had just declared. The young Republic of Turkey was in need not of soldiers, but of doctors, engineers, architects, technicians, and teachers.

"I'm going to be an engineer," Nusret had said to his younger brother, "and you should become a doctor."

"Absolutely not!" Hamma cried. "I know my Moj Beli. He can't bear the sight of blood."

"What makes you say that?" Gül Hanım asked.

"Have you never looked at Muho while a ram is being sacrificed? He runs off and hides for the next three days. If someone cuts her finger in the kitchen, he goes all pale and nearly faints."

"I'll be an engineer, too," Muho said. "I want to build roads and bridges and dams. They are what Anatolia needs most."

"What am I supposed to do while the two of you are roaming around Anatolia?" Saadet asked.

"You'll bring up clever, hardworking children for the homeland," her mother said, "just as I did."

"Mother, I want to study, not have children."

"Nothing becomes a girl like becoming the mistress of her home."

Saadet held her tongue. Grandma was right, there was no point in defying her elders. Besides, for the past few months she had spent far more time thinking about a certain young man than about her old school and her friends.

***

Bosnians celebrate spring with outdoor feasting and merrymaking they call *teferič*. As the festivities got under way that particular year, the Kulinović and Kulenović families, who, like so many Bosnian Muslims shared a common ancestor, however distant, had spread their tablecloths side by side on the grass. Salih Bey had not objected to the introduction of his daughter to young Ekrem, a grandson of the respected chief prosecutor of Istanbul, who was in turn a cousin of Salih Bey's father.

Saadet had not minded her headscarf slipping down to her shoulders as she laid out dishes for the picnic, perhaps because she was aware that the coppery highlights in the plaits of her auburn hair were glinting in the noon sun.

She caught the young man stealing glances at her. Later, both families, their youngest and oldest members alike, took turns on the swings and went for a walk along the banks of a brook. When the boys started playing with a ball, it kept coming to a bouncing stop somewhere near Saadet, and it was always Ekrem who came bounding up to retrieve it and whose eyes crinkled into a smile every time he looked at her.

When it came time to pack up their things and go home, Saadet found her palms were sweating as she shook hands with Ekrem.

The friendship that began at that picnic culminated two years later, when Saadet turned eighteen, in a springtime wedding. So in love was the bride with her husband that she had long since forgotten all about school.

Nusret went to Germany in the early years of the republic to study mechanical engineering at a university in Berlin. A brilliant student widely expected to graduate with the highest honors, he was also a devotee of the freewheeling bars and cabarets of the German capital. The heavy-drinking, fun-loving, free-spending Turk was a magnet for German women. Unable to finance his nocturnal activities, Nusret appealed to his father on multiple occasions for a supplement to his regular allowance, and each time Zeki Salih produced the requested amount, determined not to let his son fall on hard times in a foreign land. Once, Nusret wrote to his mother complaining of the winter chill. She immediately bundled up her husband's sable-lined dressing gown and posted it to Berlin, only for the renegade son to strip out the sable shortly afterward and present it to Helga, his latest girlfriend. When he later wired his family news of his engagement to an aristocratic young lady, his mother sent a family heirloom; the engagement was called off and the jewel never returned.

Nusret's profligate life was becoming a drain on the family finances, but every time Zeki Salih threatened to force his son to mend his ways by withholding his allowance, Gül Hanım would defend him by pointing out his academic prizes and awards. "He's a young man," she would say. "Let him sow his wild oats in his youth. If he must, let him have his fill of women and drink now rather than later!"

That reference to drink stabbed at Zeki Salih's heart every time his wife said it. His own libations she had tolerated without a word all these years. For her sake, he would keep sending money to their son.

It was only after Nusret had returned to Istanbul, diploma in hand, that he learned his father had been forced to sell the lot next to the Şahin Pasha Hotel to finance his carousing in Berlin. He was upset and ashamed of himself.

Just as his mother had predicted, Nusret came back to Turkey ready to find a job and settle down. Just as he had planned with his younger brother—except much closer to home than anticipated—Nusret became the chief engineer of the Municipality of Istanbul. It was not long before he found Ecla, the wife who would share his neatly ordered new life.

When it came to Muhittin's education, the family had lacked the resources to send him abroad. While Nusret was working toward his doctorate and living it up in Berlin, Muhittin was studying at the College of Civil Engineering in Taksim. It was only when Nusret visited during one of his semester breaks that Muhittin would go to clubs and bars, for which he was rewarded with a throbbing head and low marks. Some of his professors finally put two and two together, and when he did poorly on a project or a test, they would say, "Ah, I see your brother is back in town."

In 1929, Muhittin graduated with honors and a degree in civil engineering. Zeki Salih wanted to send his younger son to Germany for his postgraduate studies, but lacked the means. Nusret's expenses were still being paid, life in Istanbul was becoming less affordable, and the revenues from the family's properties in Bosnia were on the decline, in part because Zeki Salih was not there to manage his land. In the end, the family had to rely on a state scholarship to send their Muho to the School of Engineering at Berlin University.

The state had sent Muhittin to Germany to learn irrigation techniques, but there were no opportunities for field research in that rainy city. Muho, who hated wasting the state's resources, finally sat down and wrote a letter to his betters requesting that he be transferred to an institution in a more suitable climate for his studies.

The response he received astonished him.

> *Muhittin Efendi,*
> *Continue to benefit without complaint from the scholarship the ministry has provided, and do not be presumptuous.*

The letter was Muhittin's first exposure to the bloated, unwieldy, and unaccountable bureaucracy he would continuously battle throughout his long career.

14

The Quagmire

1934
Adana, Turkey

After Muhittin returned from Germany, the Ministry of Public Works
sent him to Adana to establish an irrigation system. At the train station
in Ankara, the young engineer boarded the Anatolian Express for the
long journey to his first posting.

Muhittin was traveling to Anatolia for the first time in his life.
Other than his studies in Berlin and some trips to a few Central
European cities, he had spent his entire life in Istanbul and its environs.

When he arrived in Adana, he was dismayed to find none of the
features that make a city a city and temperatures over a hundred degrees
in the shade. Unable to find a decent hotel, he decided to stay at the
building site where he would be working. It was a Sunday, and the
only person on site was a surly watchman who, annoyed at having been
roused by what he assumed was the arrival of an ordinary technician,
proceeded to ignore Muhittin until he realized he was speaking to the

new resident engineer. Groveling ensued, after which Muhittin was shown to his room and asked if he wished to issue any orders. Muhittin would not have known where to begin. He looked at the dirty room, the hundreds of mosquitos squashed on the walls, the primitive toilet outside, and the rust-colored water trickling from the tap.

Leaving his suitcase behind, he set off in search of Nazmi, an old classmate employed at city hall. He expected to find a watchman who would be able to provide him with Nazmi's address. After a night at a friend's house, he would find a house to rent for the rest of his stay. Things did not turn out as planned.

The news he received at city hall sent Muhittin rushing to the hospital. His friend, who was being treated for malaria and had gone blind in his right eye, was overjoyed to see Muhittin. After they finished talking about old times and catching up, Nazmi asked, "Are you taking quinine, Muhittin?"

"No. I haven't come down with malaria yet."

"Don't wait until you do. Take a dose every hour on the hour," Nazmi cautioned. "Otherwise, you could end up like me, blind and bedridden. It's a terrible disease; once you get it, you never fully recover. It can dog you for the rest of your life."

Muhittin went directly from his friend's hospital bed to the nearest pharmacy, and there he bought two boxes of quinine. Under a burning sun, he then walked the entire length of the district of Seyhan, thinking: *People are losing their sight, their health, and even their lives due to the conditions in this country. If I really intend to stay here, I will have to get used to hardship.*

His new life would have none of the comforts of the mansion in Sultanahmet, of that he was now certain.

Hours later, dripping with sweat, he walked back to the building site, took a chair up to a vantage point overlooking the Taurus Mountains, found some shade, and sat down. Across from him was a vast swampland. It would have to be drained and converted into farmland. It would not be easy, but it was his job to succeed. That is why he had been educated, why he had pored over books, sketched projects, and conducted experiments. He had done it to bring water, light, and life to Anatolia. To raise the standard of living in his country. To stop Christian Europe from belittling and scorning the people of Anatolia, and to prevent them from deciding one day to invade these lands yet again!

First thing tomorrow morning, he would assemble a team and assign the men their work. So much had been achieved with so little these past few years; surely he could get the better of a swamp! He considered the alphabet reforms, back in 1929. It had succeeded beyond anyone's wildest dreams. Up through his junior year of university, his class had been using the Perso-Arabic script; in the final year, over the course of just a few months, they had completely switched over to the Latin alphabet. The impossible had been achieved, again and again. Even his father had overcome his initial resistance, become literate in the new letters, and now eagerly awaited the delivery of the newspapers every morning.

Muhittin smiled. *Draining a swamp is child's play compared to reforming a language,* he thought, even as his heart sank at the sight of the quagmire stretching before him. He went to his room, stood in front of the small, round mirror nailed to the wall with a piece of wire, and stared into the clear, candid blue eyes of his reflection. "Come on, Muho," he said to himself. "Roll up your sleeves. You've got work to do. You'll make a success of this. Where there is hope, there is strength. Never lose hope!"

Part Three

The River of Life

15

Sticky Rice

1929

In the mansion in Beyazit, the young tutor was enjoying more success than his venerable predecessor. Thanks to Aram's stores of patience, Sitare, despite the occasional lapse, soon caught up to her classmates, advancing to the next grade on schedule and without having to take any makeup exams.

Despite being the younger of the two, Bülent was better than Sitare at concentrating for long periods of time. The mothers, Leman and Suat, were both pleased with the new tutor's amazing progress, as was Aram himself. Not least because every time he went to the mansion, Sabahat was there. At the conclusion of the separate lessons for the children, he would join her and her sisters on the divan for tea and a chat. When her elder sisters were out, Sabahat would have friends over from school. As she played the violin, the girls would sing along, or they would dance to the latest songs on the gramophone. Aram, the only male granted admission to the house, felt at times like a rooster in a henhouse—but who was he to complain? Besides seeing more of Sabahat than he had ever dared to hope, he was able at the beginning of each month to hand his mother the fees from his lessons, and he never spent a penny of it. Everyone was pleased. In fact, Mahir Bey was so happy with Sitare's progress that he proposed Aram continue the lessons over the summer. The family would be staying on the island of Burgazada, as they always did, and would Aram Bey care to join them there twice a week, with full reimbursement for his travel expenses, of course?

Aram had an even better idea. A customer had given his brother an old tent that had proven itself rainproof and comfortable during a camping trip with cousins in Çanakkale. Were Aram to find a suitable place on the island to pitch his tent, he could easily continue his lessons, saving the trouble and expense of travel.

Sabahat was delighted to hear of his plan. "We have a huge garden, Aram," she said. "Providing we get permission from Beyba, you couldn't find a more agreeable spot to stay."

Mahir Bey was pleased that the matter had been settled so easily. In any case, Aram had become like a member of the family. He was such a polite and proper boy and had worked miracles on those two little monsters, Sitare and Bülent.

Aram spent that summer in the empty lot next to Reşat Bey's house and continued to give Sitare arithmetic lessons three times a week. He also carried baskets and bags for Sabahat and her sisters when they ventured down to the beach for a swim, met Mahir Bey on the quay in the evenings to relieve him of any parcels, and occasionally served as a companion to Reşat Bey. He did not accept the constant invitations to join the family for dinner or use their kitchen and bathrooms. That summer, Reşat Bey took a true shine to this boy.

As the summer days began growing shorter, Sabahat, foreseeing her mother's protests, secretly completed her pre-application to the American High School for Girls in Arnavutköy. Once the family migrated back to their winter home in Beyazit at the start of September, she decided the time had come to raise the issue of her educational ambitions, which included obtaining a high school diploma. Schools would be opening their doors in a few weeks. While the school did not require uniforms and other preparations, registration fees and the first tuition installment would soon have to be paid. She decided to speak to her father first and deal with her mother later. Naturally, when she asked for her father's permission, she would neglect to mention that she had already begun the process. She was certain he would not refuse her, but if he did, she would withdraw her application without a word to anybody.

Sabahat arrived at the bank where her father worked and informed the clerk that the general manager's daughter was there to see him. She followed the clerk to an upper floor and knocked on an imposing door. At first, Father was none too pleased to see her. Had something terrible happened at home?

"Beyba, my only purpose in coming here was to talk with you in private," Sabahat assured him. "I'd prefer not to discuss this at home."

"What could be so important, and why couldn't you wait until I got home?"

"It's about my education."

"Why would we talk about that? Haven't you graduated with honors?"

"I have, sir, which is why I wish to pursue my education further. At the very least, I would like to earn a high school diploma in order to repay my debt of gratitude to the family and to contribute, one day, to its maintenance."

"My dear girl, all fathers strive to give their children the best possible upbringing. You owe me nothing, so there's no need for you to attend school in order to repay an imaginary debt."

"You misunderstand me, sir. I am eager to learn. Now that my English is satisfactory, would you not consider sending me to the American High School for Girls?"

"Why you have not mentioned this eagerness of yours before?"

"A number of my classmates are going on to high school this year. I wanted very much to join them, but was reluctant to ask you. I already know what Mother will say, and, hesitant as I am to become an additional burden on you, I said nothing. I have since learned that outstanding students will be offered reduced tuition."

"Sabahat, there's nothing to consider," Reşat Bey said. "If it is an education you want, it is my duty to educate you. Let's get you registered at once. I hope it's not too late."

"I wouldn't wish to inconvenience you, Father. I'll handle the registration procedure on my own this week. All I ask is for your mediation with Mother. Oh, and one more thing, would you mind being the one to inform her that I will continue on to high school?"

"But why should your mother object?"

"She wants me to marry."

"Sabahat, if a promising suitor appears, then we will consider marriage. You cannot be expected to sit at home and wait for a husband."

"That would be silly, wouldn't it? Beyba, I couldn't agree with you more." Sabahat curbed the impulse to throw her arms around her father; physical demonstrations of affection made him slightly uncomfortable.

"I'll be going now; you must have work to do," Sabahat said.

"Wait, and we'll leave together," her father said. "I'll be ready in a few minutes."

Outside, it was a golden September day. Arms linked, father and daughter walked across the Galata Bridge toward their home on the historic peninsula, discussing their strategy for dealing with Behice Hanım. They both knew it would not be easy to persuade her. As far as she was concerned, her daughter's education was finished. Sabahat had wanted to learn French; she had been enrolled at a French school.

Her father had wanted her to learn English: she had been enrolled at an American school. She was now fluent in both languages, an accomplished and knowledgeable young woman. The time had come for her to learn the domestic arts. Her rice pilaf was sticky, and except for a pair of pillowcases, the linens in her dowry chest had not been embroidered. Were an acceptable suitor to make his intentions known one day soon, the family would be disgraced.

Sabahat promised that on the weekends she would take up her needlework and learn to cook. And if her parents found an agreeable suitor, she would marry him after she graduated from high school.

"By then, you will be too old; nobody will want you," Behice said.

"The times have changed; nobody wants to marry a girl of sixteen," Reşat Bey assured his wife. "Why, I have even heard of girls attending university."

"Good gracious," Behice cried. "I can't imagine such a thing. Sabahat's education ends with high school!"

"Sabahat, which of your friends are going on to high school?" Suat asked.

"Armine, Sofya, and Fofo will all be in my class."

"What will Aram be doing?"

"He'll be studying at the high school for boys."

"Are you telling me your school admits boys?" Behice asked.

"Yes, but they're separate. He'll be going to Robert College, the prep school. The girls' campus is in Arnavutköy, and the boys' is way up the Bosphorus, in Bebek," Sabahat said.

"And how do you propose to go back and forth to Arnavutköy every day?

"I'll be a boarder, Mother," Sabahat said. "I'll come home on the weekends."

"I've heard quite enough!" Behice said. "What a ridiculous plan. I would like to have a word with your father later this evening. Alone."

The talk with Reşat Bey did not go as Behice had hoped. He was determined to send their daughter to the high school in Arnavutköy, the most prestigious institution of its kind in the city. Sabahat was an excellent student, and it would be wrong to thwart her desire for a modern education, he insisted. In this new age, the pursuit of science and scholarship was open to the fairer sex as well. And furthermore, a well-educated young woman would be more likely to find a suitable mate. The helpmeet of this new breed of man would have to bring more than just a pretty young face to married life.

"I see," Behice huffed, "that once again you pay me no heed. I am surprised, though, by your insouciance on the subject of your youngest daughter sleeping and eating far from home."

Reşat Bey patiently explained how difficult it would be for Sabahat to commute to Arnavutköy every day. In the winter, she would be leaving the house before sunrise and returning long after sundown. Would Behice prefer that their youngest daughter travel the dark city streets on her own?

"I can see I've been wasting my breath," Behice said. "Allow me to say one last thing, Reşat Bey: if anything happens to Sabahat, it is on your head."

The following day, Sabahat met her friends with the wonderful news that she would be joining them at high school.

16

Saraylıhanım Gets Crowned

Reşat Bey folded the newspaper and laid it on his desk. Taking off his tortoiseshell glasses, he rubbed his eyes and then closed them after leaning his head against the back of the armchair. It was what he always did when he was pondering something, in this case, the article that he had been reading. He knew of only one person he could discuss the article with: Ahmet Reşit Rey, a kindred spirit and former fellow minister in the Ottoman cabinet. He pulled a visiting card out of the top drawer, and on the back of it he jotted a message asking if his old friend would be able to receive him that afternoon. Hüsnü Efendi was summoned, given the card, now in its envelope, and instructed to deliver it to Reşit Bey's home in Nişantaşı.

Ahmet Reşat frowned at the music and childish laughter coming from the top floor. He climbed the stairs, still deep in thought, and knocked on Sabahat's door. When there was no response, he knocked again, harder this time. A moment later, he pushed open the door and peered inside. Wrapped in a long cape of some kind, Sitare was standing on the table jabbering away as she repeatedly whacked Bülent, who was wearing a dress, with the handle of a broom. Facedown on the floor lay a little girl. Sabahat was sitting in a chair reading aloud, and Armine was traipsing about the room. Reşat Bey rubbed his eyes.

"Look, it's Granddad!" Sitare had seen him.

Several pairs of eyes swiveled toward the doorway. "What on earth is going on here?" Reşat Bey asked. "Have you all lost your minds?"

Sitare jumped off the table and, feet tangled in the long cape, staggered over to her grandfather.

"We're staging a *pièce*," Sabahat informed him, calm as can be.

"A what?"

"A play, Father. You know, theater. Sitare is the queen, and Beraat is her lady-in-waiting."

The little girl sat up and screamed, "It was my turn to be queen. Sitare always gets to be the queen. It's not fair."

"That's because I'm taller than you, Beraat."

"Queens don't have to be tall. Queen Victoria was short, and fat, too, but she was still the queen of England!" the little girl said.

Reşat Bey remained in the doorway, gaping.

"Come in, Beyba," Sabahat said.

"What is the meaning of this?"

"Each of the classes is supposed to choose a play and act it out. Sitare's class is performing their play next week, and me and Armine are helping them rehearse. They're learning their parts."

"What is Bülent doing in that outlandish costume?"

"Bülent is filling in for the princess, just for now."

"In women's clothing, like a *zenne* at a wedding? Take that off at once! That's right, I'm talking to you," Reşat Bey roared. Bülent's eyes filled with tears. Why was Granddad shouting at him?

"Sabahat, it is outrageous to dress boys as girls. Don't ever let me see you do that again!"

"But at school we always—"

"Not in this house, you don't," Ahmet Reşat snapped as he closed the door and headed back down to his study.

Had he been wrong to enroll the children in American schools? Theater, boys dressing up as girls, gramophones, dancing! He was unaccustomed to such things, but he knew, deep in his heart, that they did not deserve censure. So why was he so angry? It was he who had chosen to send his children to those schools, so how could he justify scolding his grandchildren, who were blameless, and doing it in front of guests no less? He sighed. Try as he might, he would never catch up to the times. He was stuck in his ways and fast becoming a crotchety old man. Startled by the butler on the landing, he shouted, "Where are their mothers?"

"Whose mothers, sir?"

"The children's mothers! Where are Leman and Suat?"

"The young ladies and their mother are calling on Mehpare Hanım."

"Why wasn't I informed?"

"I believe they left while you were taking your morning walk, sir. Mehpare sent word. I believe she has taken ill, sir."

"Is it serious?" Reşat Bey asked anxiously.

"I'm afraid I can't answer that."

Reşat Bey walked down two flights of stairs and into his study. Gülfidan followed him.

"Shall I make you a strong cup of coffee, sir?" she asked.

"Go ahead," Reşat Bey said. He had just picked up the newspaper and begun scanning the article again when there was a knock on the door and Saraylıhanım stepped inside.

"Welcome, Aunt," he said.

"Son, that thieving woman stole my gold bracelets."

"What woman? What thief?"

"Who else, that hag you brought here from Beypazarı!"

"Ah! God forgive you! How can you say such a thing, Saraylıhanım?"

"I can't stop her. In the twinkle of an eye, she steals all I have."

"The gentlewoman you slander happens to be Behice's mother. Don't tell me you believe she would do a thing like that."

"I know she would."

"Never! She's a Circassian, just like you."

"I don't know what she is. All I know is that if you don't stop her from doing it again, I'm going straight to the municipal police at the end of our street."

"Good God! Please don't! I'll have a word with her."

"You do that. Right this instant."

In his haste, Reşat Bey very nearly bowled Neyir Hanım over as he strode out of his study. She was standing teary-eyed just outside the door and had obviously overheard every word of his conversation with Saraylıhanım.

"Won't you please join me in my study, Aunt," he said. "Let's have a little chat."

"Why are you addressing that thieving woman as 'aunt'? I'm your aunt."

Reşat Bey muttered a prayer under his breath and said, "Of course you are, my dear. Now, why don't you go up to your room so I can have a word with Neyir Hanım?"

"I want to listen."

Reşat led a sniffling Neyir Hanım into his study before going out onto the landing again and roaring at the top of his lungs.

"Sabahat!"

In a panic, Sabahat came rushing out onto the landing of her floor and peered down the stairwell at her father.

"Beyba, has something happened?"

"Come down here at once and get Saraylıhanım. Occupy her for a time. Quickly."

"I'm not going anywhere! I want to listen to the thief's testimony."

When Sabahat came running down the stairs, she found Neyir Hanım in tears, her father red-faced and fuming, and Saraylıhanım impatiently tapping her foot on the floor. *Oh no, the old girls have been at it again,* she thought, inwardly sighing.

"Saraylıhanım, come on up to my room. We're putting on a play, and you can watch."

"No!"

"Well then, don't watch. I know, we'll make you the queen. Come and play the queen of England for us."

"Will I get to wear a crown?" Saraylıhanım asked.

"Of course you will."

"Fine then."

As Saraylıhanım slowly crept up the stairs, Sabahat raced into the bathroom, rummaged through the closet, and came out carrying Bülent's old potty.

She returned to the study, where she found Reşat Bey pleading with Neyir Hanım. "I plead with you to be reasonable. Saraylıhanım is not in her right mind, you know that. You mustn't take offense at her nonsense. What do you mean, go back to Beypazarı? Behice would be so distraught."

They were interrupted by Hüsnü Efendi's return from Nişantaşı, which coincided with the arrival of the ladies of the house from Pera. Ahmet Reşat walked out onto the landing. His wife and daughters were chattering as they removed their coats and shoes.

"What's the matter with Mehpare?" he shouted down the stairs.

"We can talk about it when I come upstairs," Behice said.

Reşat Bey's heart sank. Could she be having marital problems? Mehpare had sent word instead of visiting; perhaps that husband of hers, Galip, wouldn't let her leave the house. He anxiously waited for his wife. When the door opened, he sprang to his feet, but it was Hüsnü Efendi.

"Reşit Bey sent you this," he said.

Reşat Bey opened the envelope and read the note saying Reşit Bey would be delighted to have him over for tea. If it turned out Mehpare was in serious trouble, however, how could he steal away to Nişantaşı? His wife finally joined him.

"What is it? Why did Mehpare have you round? Has something happened?"

"Well, something has happened, yes."

"Go on, tell me. Is it her husband?"

"Of all the things to say, Reşat Bey! It's a delicate matter, not suitable for—"

"What's that supposed to mean? Are you going to keep it from me?"

"I'll tell you if I must. Mehpare is with child."

"No!"

"We, too, were astonished when she told us."

Reşat Bey didn't try to hide the disappointment in his voice as he said, "I wish them the best. And here I was, worrying myself over nothing."

"The thing is, Mehpare doesn't want this baby."

"What are you saying?"

"You heard me. She wishes to induce a miscarriage. She cries and cries. I advised her to come for a visit this evening and talk to Mahir, if she feels well enough."

"What does her husband have to say about this?"

"He wants the child. Mehpare's decision pains him badly."

"Good grief!" Ahmet Reşat said. "Has she gone mad? Choosing to deliberately lose her baby! May God forgive her! I could understand if she was seriously ill, or if she thought her husband was too old. But to decide for no reason that she doesn't want her own child? I'd like to talk her when she comes this evening."

"Her husband is not at all old, Reşat Bey. It turns out that he was registered at the same time as his elder brother. You know how lax parents were back in the day. Anyway, the clerk mixed up their birth certificates. He's not a day over forty-five."

"I was planning to visit Reşit Bey this afternoon, but I'll send word that I have to cancel. I can't leave the house at a time like this."

"There's no need to change your plans, dear. If they come, it will be for dinner. Mahir is on duty at the hospital until six. You'll be back before any of them gets here," Behice said.

"Ah, I nearly forgot: Could you go up to your aunt's room and try to soothe her? She's been squabbling with Saraylıhanım again and is threatening to go back to Beypazarı."

"I tell you, Reşat Bey, I'm so fed up with their bickering. I've got half a mind to send them both packing to Beypazarı. That would show them," Behice said, forgetting that the house in Beypazari had been closed up after her father's death.

Reşat Bey shook his head and chuckled to himself. The national news that had preoccupied him since he'd read the morning newspaper had been completely eclipsed by domestic troubles. There had been a time when he thought only of governance and duty. Now, the slightest family disturbance commanded his undivided attention. Perhaps this is what it was to grow old!

An uncomfortable silence hovered over the dinner table that evening. Mehpare hung her head. Galip Bey seemed to be following her lead: he neither looked at anyone nor spoke. At one point, Mehpare lifted her gaze and asked how Saraylıhanım and Neyir Hanım were doing.

"Don't ask," Behice Hanım said.

Sabahat giggled. "They've been banished and have to eat their dinners in their rooms."

"I was worried they were ill."

"When my great aunt refused to take Bülent's chamber pot off her head, Mother wouldn't let her sit at the dinner table," Sabahat said. "And Neyir Hanım is cross with us all. She refused to leave her room."

"I'll go and see them before I leave," Mehpare said. Nobody laughed but the children. For what seemed an eternity, the awful silence was broken only by the clink of cutlery. When the butler was clearing the soup bowls, Reşat Bey asked, "How is Halim? Why haven't you brought him with you?"

Mehpare looked at Reşat Bey for a moment, eyes swimming, and clapped her hands over her face as she burst into sobs.

"Oh no! Has something happened to Halim?" Sabahat asked.

Mehpare excused herself and rushed off to the bathroom.

"What's wrong, Galip Bey?" Ahmet asked. He'd gone pale.

Galip Bey saw that the entire family was awaiting an answer. He cleared his throat. "Mehpare is a little overwrought. As you know, Halim is now a young man. He's been . . . pursuing certain activities. His mother had words with him just before we left the house this evening."

"She's in tears. It must have been serious."

"Mehpare is a little sensitive these days, and easily hurt."

"You are a member of our family, Galip Bey. If you don't mind, could I ask you to be more explicit?" Reşat Bey said.

"He's been coming home late at night. I tell her to go easy on him and point out that he's a young man. If he doesn't knock about now, when will he have the chance later in life? She won't listen to me. Mehpare asked Halim to come here with us this evening and he spurned her, saying he was busy. There was shouting on both sides, and he slammed the door on his way out, saying he wouldn't be back anytime soon and something about staying with a friend. Mehpare nearly cried her eyes out."

"That's too bad," Reşat Bey said.

"What's he going to do now?" Suat asked.

"I don't know. He'll probably be back in a few days."

"How's he doing in school?" Mahir asked.

"I'm afraid he's not applying himself."

"That's even worse," Reşat Bey said. He fell silent again when Mehpare returned to the table. It was not until fresh fruit was being served that someone spoke. "Mehpare would like to talk with you about something, Mahir Bey," Leman told her husband. "Why don't you go down to your exam room together?"

Mahir got up and said, "After you, Mehpare."

When they were seated across from each other downstairs, Mehpare looked around the room. Here, in what had been the room reserved for men, Kemal had stolen many a kiss before they were married. She could picture her late husband sitting at his desk over in the corner. The leather sofa she was sitting on now had replaced a pair of velvet armchairs. She thought back to the braziers she had kept aglow so her beloved wouldn't catch a chill. For a moment, she even imagined Kemal had come up behind her and stroked her hair. She shivered.

"I've been told you're with child," Mahir said. Mehpare forced her mind to return to the present, in all its unpleasantness.

"That's right."

"How far along are you?"

"Two months . . . perhaps a little less."

"Would you like me to examine you?"

"There's no need. I don't want the baby. Could you help me?" she asked, resting her eyes on his for the first time that evening.

"You don't want the baby?"

"It was never meant to happen. It was an accident. And it will never happen again. Never!"

"What do you mean, never happen again?"

"My husband and I do not have conjugal relations. It happened only once, by accident."

"Mehpare, weren't you the one who wanted to get married?"

"I was."

"Did you not realize that a wife has certain duties in regard to her husband?"

"That is not why I married."

"What was your reason for marrying? It was to secure an education for Halim, wasn't it? Even though there was no need. And to spend more time alone with your son."

Mehpare bowed her head.

"Did you not spare a thought for Galip Bey and his needs? Does this man who married you with the purest intentions, who agreed to look after your son, not deserve your respect and your heart?"

"You can't mean that! He should have known I could never love him. My heart belongs to my husband. I hold Galip Bey in the highest esteem."

"Your husband is Galip Bey. Kemal died many years ago. Galip could not have expected you to still be in mourning. You say you respect him, but you deny him his conjugal rights. And now, you wish to abort the baby he wants. Mehpare . . . why?"

"Because . . . Why do you rebuke me? I thought you were going to help me."

"I'm trying to help you. Why did you quarrel with Halim today?"

"Ah!" Mehpare moaned. "A woman has entered my son's life."

"Is that so bad? A young man needs the company of a woman."

"But she's older than him, and a terrible influence."

"In what way?"

"He comes home late. He shows no warmth for me and never confides in me. It's as if we are enemies, as though I'm not enduring this marriage for his sake. I thought, when we left this house, that we would become closer. I thought . . ." Mehpare started crying. Mahir stood up and sat down next to her. He put his arm around her shoulder and pulled her head onto his chest.

"Cry," he said. "Cry out all your foolishness. Pour your heart out, and then listen to me."

Mehpare sobbed for a time in Mahir's arms. When her tears were spent, he pulled a white handkerchief out of his pocket. She wiped her nose and dried her tears.

"Halim is a grown man now, not your baby boy," Mahir said. "He's neither an extension of Kemal nor the ghost of Kemal made flesh. He's no longer yours, Mehpare. The harder you come down on him, the further you push him away. He will come to hate you. Let him be. Let him spread his wings. He's young. There will be women; there will be mistakes. That's how life is learned. Think back to your own youth, to your own passion. Were you any different?"

"You're right."

"This baby is a godsend, Mehpare."

"At my age!"

"You've just turned forty! Bring this baby into the world and shower it with the love and attention you have reserved for Halim. For ten years or so, your child will be all yours. It will do you good, and your husband as well. Having a child together may bind you and your husband together, which is the natural state of a proper marriage. If you do decide you don't want the baby, I will help you on one condition: divorce your husband."

"But why?"

"Because it would not be right for you to continue to torment a man who has done you no wrong. Give him the opportunity to find a woman who loves him."

"He's pleased with me."

"I don't believe it. A man can only endure so much if he is not loved."

"Have I made Galip Bey miserable? I hadn't considered that."

"Have you made him happy?"

This time, Mehpare cried softly, overcome perhaps more with pity for another than for her herself.

"Mehpare, I'm going back upstairs. Stay here for a moment and compose yourself. Don't be hasty in making a decision. Think it over. Wait a week to tell me what you want to do. But let me make one thing clear: it's a terrible sin to end a life for no reason."

Mahir retrieved his handkerchief from Mehpare and walked over to the door. "We spoke in confidence," he said as he left.

When Mahir was gone, Mehpare clasped her head in her hands. *Ah, if it weren't for that dream! None of this would have happened.* For many years now, Kemal had stopped visiting her in her dreams. That is, until one night a couple of months ago when there he was again in her arms, his stubble tickling, his lips on the back of her neck, her throat, her breasts; his hands; her legs opening, entwining, wrapping around his waist, around Kemal; on her, in her, together; pulling him closer, holding him tight, moving together, longing for him . . . oh, how she'd missed him. She had moaned and opened her eyes only to see . . . Galip Bey! What was he doing? How dare he come into her room!

"You were crying out in your sleep. I wanted to see what was wrong . . ."

When Mahir joined the family in the room with the divan, all eyes were on him.

"Where's Mehpare?" Leman asked.

"She's in the bathroom. She'll be along in a bit."

Face freshly washed, trails of mascara wiped away, Mehpare stepped into the room a few minutes later. Leman opened her eyes wide and shot a meaningful look at Mehpare's belly. Ignoring her, Mehpare walked over to her husband.

"Galip Bey, I'm feeling quite tired. Shall we?"

Reşat Bey and Behice Hanım made their farewells. The girls accompanied Mehpare and her husband down to the entrance hall.

"Give Halim a kiss for me, Mehpare," Sabahat said. "Tell him to stop by next week and that I miss him."

"I will."

"Mehpare . . . did you?" Suat whispered.

"I'm thinking it over, Suat. I still have time to think."

Suat and Leman stared at each other.

Hüsnü Efendi opened the door. Galip Bey slipped his arm into Mehpare's and said, "Be careful. It's been drizzling, and the steps are slippery."

17

A Secret Love, Secret No More

Sabahat turned the iron skeleton key in the lock of the carved wooden door and stepped into the cool, dark hall. What a strange sensation it was to enter an empty house, alone. *I feel like a thief in my own home,* she thought. She had only ever knocked on the front door and waited for someone else to open it. With slatted shutters all the way down and heavy curtains drawn against the blinding heat, the entrance hall was chilly. She shivered. Walking over to the door to the back garden, she fumbled with the bolt, unable to slide it. Here, in her own home, she was unable even to open the back door.

I've lived like a guest in this house, she thought, *never touching anything, never getting my hands dirty, never venturing into its deeper recesses.* There was the cupboard under the stairs, for example: What was stored there? She'd asked once, only to be told by Saraylıhanım: "Silly girl, what are cupboards for? Bits and pieces, of course." Bits and pieces! Not once in all these years had she been curious enough to find out what, precisely, was meant by that term. A chest full of silk gowns? Deeds, letters, and diaries? The Ottoman medals of honor awarded to her grandfather and father? Sabahat felt cross with herself for taking so little interest in the everyday objects that underpinned her life and gave it meaning.

Now she stood in the entrance hall gazing with the eyes of a stranger at this house in which she had grown up, amazed by all the little details she had failed to notice. The chandelier hanging in the stairwell was missing five crystal pendants. The marble top of the gilded table had a cracked corner, which must have been the reason Mother always draped a Damascus table linen over it. Why hadn't she spotted these details? The carpet was faded in distinct bars, alternating patches from the decades of afternoon sun pouring through the slats of the blinds, and the years of dampness had mottled the northern wall with the ghostly outlines of wolves' heads and giant ferns. The brass handle on the drawer of the console table was askew.

The absolute silence struck her next, the hush of a house grown weary and lonely. The best and the worst moments of her life had been spent within the walls of this house, walls that echoed with the chatter of children, the animated laughter of young women, the strident complaints of old grannies. But what about her father? In this house of women, had her father been drowned out and overwhelmed, or had he chosen to remain silent? Sabahat had watched as he increasingly kept himself to himself, and she knew he now believed himself to be a man out of time. Father was always at his most loquacious and enthusiastic on the days he left this house to visit his old friend, Ahmet Reşit Rey. Perhaps the clamoring of Bülent and Sitare, the chanson played on her gramophone, the din of a large family, and modern life were too much for him? Why had she never considered any of this before? *Stupid, thoughtless girl!*

For a moment, melancholy washed over her, bringing tears to her eyes.

Sabahat sighed and reminded herself that time was short. Mindful of her mother's repeated warnings not to lose the key or forget it inside the house, she set it on the little table next to the kitchen door. Hüsnü Efendi was taking his annual holiday, and the rest of the servants were with the family on the island. On the way back to the island after visiting Armine, a friend living in Arnavutköy, Sabahat was to retrieve the woolen shawl Saraylıhanım had insisted she needed even in the August heat. Her mother had reluctantly handed over the key with strict orders to close the windows tight and switch off all the lights.

What her family did not know was that Sabahat had no intention of visiting her friend. Instead, Armine was coming to the house, along with Aram, so the three of them could prepare a surprise.

Three days from now, Şahber Hanım's son, Naci, was getting engaged. The entire family planned to decamp from the island and head into the city two days before the ceremony. While there, they would spend two nights in the mansion. Suat would go to her dentist appointment; Behice and Leman would have their hair done in Beyoğlu; an engagement gift would be selected at Angelidis, also in Beyoğlu. Nesime, the least competent of the servants, would accompany the family in order to prepare their meals and lend a hand when required. "We'll go hungry for those two days," Behice Hanım had groaned.

"Don't worry, nobody died of starvation in two days," her son-in-law, the doctor, assured her.

"We could ask the cook to make some cold stuffed vegetables and breaded meatballs and take it with us, like a picnic," Leman suggested.

"Not in this heat," Suat said.

When it was confirmed that Sabahat would be allowed to drop by the house for the shawl, she had an idea: she and her friends would prepare a few cold dishes and leave them there. That way, she would prove to her mother and sisters that educated girls could be just as efficient in the kitchen as anyone else.

"What are you going to make?" Armine had asked, propping her chin on her elbow and looking at Sabahat as they lay on a carpet under the island pines, Aram loafing at their feet until it was time to begin that day's lesson with Sitare.

"Kidney beans and rice pilaf. They won't spoil right away."

"I have an idea," Aram said. "We could put ice on the food and keep it somewhere cool."

"Where will we find ice?"

"I'll go and get some from the icehouse."

"Would you really do that for me?"

"I'm at your beck and call."

"Oh, Aram! You're a wonderful friend."

"If you like, I'll go shopping for all the ingredients, too. That way, you'll be able to go straight from the landing dock to your house. I'll be by soon after with beans, onions, tomatoes, and rice."

"We already have rice in the pantry."

"And I'll bring strawberries from Arnavutköy," Armine offered.

"I'll agree on one condition: that you let me reimburse you."

"You can't be serious," Armine said. "Do I pay anything when I stay overnight at your house?"

"It's not the same thing. Either you let me pay you back, or I do all the shopping—and the cooking—on my own."

"Agreed then. You can pay for everything," Aram said.

"Can you imagine the looks on their faces? They'll all troop into the house, moaning about how hungry and thirsty they are, and when they go into the kitchen to get some water, they'll see a bunch of readymade dishes."

"Let's cover everything with towels," Aram said. "They'll pull off the towels and see the ice, and then under the ice they'll find the food. 'Who did this?' they'll all scream."

"And I'll say, 'Hmm, was it a fairy?'"

"You'd better be quick to take credit, Sabahat, or the next thing you know Suat will claim to be the fairy."

"She'll do no such thing!" Sabahat said. "Father will know it was me, his youngest, most studious, cleverest girl. I can't wait. This is going to be great!" She clapped her hands in delight. Aram gazed into her dancing eyes and decided she should never know anything but joy. If only he could do more to make her happy!

"Girls, it's time for my lesson. The little miss is expecting me."

As Aram walked off, Sabahat said, "You know, Armine, he really is the best friend a girl could have."

"Friend?"

"What's that supposed to mean?"

"Nothing."

That day, the two girls had engineered an excuse for Sabahat to go into the city. It was easy to do because Armine's birthday happened to be the following day. She had asked Behice Hanım if Sabahat could attend her tea party and had even extended invitations to Leman and Suat.

"Armine, how ghastly if they had said yes," Sabahat said. "However did you dare to invite them?"

"But they're not coming, are they? Sometimes it pays to be bold, Sabahat."

"Are you really going to spend your birthday at my house helping me cook?"

"I'll come around noon with the strawberries, grate some onions for you, and go back home."

"I can't let you get onion juice on your hands, not on your birthday! I'll get Aram to do it," Sabahat said.

Telling her mother she needed an early start to get Armine a gift, Sabahat caught the first ferry into the city, and now here she was, standing in the entrance hall, sniffing at the camphor-scented air unique to closed-up houses and wondering if she had made a mistake.

By the time Aram arrived with an armful of brown paper-wrapped parcels, Sabahat had long since aired out the kitchen. A freshly washed pot was resting on the hob, and the rice had been picked through and rinsed. She had found the woolen shawl in the designated drawer and brought it downstairs. Burying her nose in it, she had breathed in a scent she associated with the stories her great aunt told: the vagabond with the gold coins sewn into his shirt, the Circassian princess lowering her two flaxen tresses from her prison tower; the heroes and heroines populating those childhood tales, all of them, smelled of rosewater, just like Saraylıhanım. She was just putting the shawl on the table next to the key when the doorbell rang. *Aram!*

Now she was in the dimly lit kitchen cooking with Aram, as though they had been doing it together for a thousand years, effortlessly, not getting in each other's way, not stepping on each other's feet, in perfect harmony as they diced tomatoes, grated onions, and chopped parsley. An arm would reach for the grater as a hand adjusted the flame. One of them would bend down to open a drawer as the other one stretched for a high shelf. They were dancing without touching each other, their movements slow and sure, communing in silence, radiating bliss, so that the kitchen seemed to glow with a strange light or heat, one that illuminated their souls as it warmed their young bodies.

Sabahat was giving the pot a final stir when the doorbell rang. She raced through the entrance hall to open it.

"The house smells like onions," Armine said, bounding inside with two baskets of strawberries on her arm.

"I'll air it out when everything's cooked."

"Why didn't you wait for me? Is Aram here?"

"If he weren't, I wouldn't have started."

"What do you know about cooking? Do you ever help make dinner?"

"I asked the cook for some recipes. Aram helped me. He knows how to make bean salad."

"Of course he does; he's Armenian!"

"Do Armenian men cook?"

"Armenians are great cooks, men and women," Armine proudly said.

Sabahat took the strawberries and led her friend to the kitchen. Aram was standing in front of the simmering rice.

"Sit down, Armine, and I'll make you a cup of coffee," Sabahat said. "That much I can do on my own."

"While you're at it, could you make me a cup, too?" Aram asked.

"I'll be going shortly after my coffee. I have a million things to do before my party. Are you coming?"

"Of course we are," Sabahat cried. "I haven't even given you your present yet."

"Perhaps you'd better give it to me now. You might change your mind about the party."

"Why would I do that?"

"Oh, I don't know."

Scowling, Sabahat went off to the entrance hall and returned with a packet wrapped in bright paper. "Take it," she said, "if you really can't wait any longer. Don't tear it open. I'll tell you what it is: Jane Austen's *Pride and Prejudice*."

"Sabahat! Thank you! I've wanted to read that book for ever so long."

"I know," Sabahat said. "That's why I got it for you. Now, even if we don't come . . ." Her voice trailed off as she considered the possibility that she wasn't wanted in her friend's house. It seemed unlikely, but perhaps Armine's grandmother, whom she had never met, preferred not to have a Turkish girl as a guest in her home. Armine was Armenian.

"Enjoy yourselves. I've got to run," Armine said.

Sabahat showed her friend to the door. "Thank you so much for the strawberries," she said. "What a wonderful surprise it will be, and I'll be certain to tell everyone that you brought them."

"Bon appétit in advance! Give my best regards to your family."

Returning to the kitchen, Sabahat unburdened herself to Aram. "I felt as though Armine didn't want me in her grandmother's house today. Did you notice that?"

"No, not at all."

"She practically insisted I not come. Perhaps we shouldn't go. Perhaps they don't want me there because I'm a Turk."

"I think Armine wanted to leave us here together."

"Aram, we see each other every day."

"Not on our own, Sabahat."

Sabahat sprang to her feet. Aram was standing on the other side of the table, looking into her eyes.

"Sabahat, don't you realize I'm in love with you?"

Her mouth went dry as her palms grew moist.

"Armine realizes it, but you don't."

Aram came around to her side of the table. In one swift movement, he lifted her up and seated her on the table. Placing his palms on the table, he leaned closer, close enough for her to feel his breath. "Are you telling me you don't know how much I love you?" he asked, looking deep into her eyes. "The lessons for the children, the tent next to your summer house, the way I do figure eights around your feet, like a cat: You never realized why?"

"What are we going do, Aram?" Sabahat whispered, her eyes brimming with tears.

"I don't know."

"I don't know, either."

"Perhaps I should avoid you, Sabahat."

"Why?"

"I've thought about it. I've considered going to a different school, moving to another neighborhood, applying for a scholarship to a university in America. I've thought about all those things, and more, but I've never done them."

"I'm glad you didn't, Aram, because if I was unable to see you again, I'd die."

Aram cupped the face he had dreamed of kissing all these years, leaned closer, and gently silenced her with his lips. A moment later, Sabahat pulled back. "What are we going to do, Aram?" There was no answer to that question, and they both knew it.

"You'll get married when you graduate from high school. They'd never allow a girl like you to remain unwed."

"I'll go to university after high school," Sabahat said. "You will, too, won't you?"

"Of course I will."

"See, I won't get married."

"The day will come when you graduate from university."

"We'll both find a job and start working."

"Are we going to spend the rest of our lives as nothing more than devoted neighbors?"

"What else can we do?"

"We can get married."

"My father would never allow that," Sabahat said. "Not because he doesn't like you and Armenians. Don't misunderstand."

"Couldn't we persuade him?"

"We could try."

"Before we do that, I'll have to complete university, do my military service, and become established in a profession. Will you wait for me, Sabahat?"

"Of course I will! Of course!"

"And if your father refuses us when the time comes, will you still marry me? We could go to America. We could find work there."

"Would you be willing to leave your mother on her own?"

"There's nothing I wouldn't do to be with you. My mother is used to living alone."

"How long has it been since your father died?" Sabahat asked.

"I don't know," Aram said.

"What do you mean you don't know?"

"My father didn't die. They took him away."

"Took him away? Where?"

"I don't know."

"So he's alive?"

"I don't think so, Sabahat. If he were alive, he would have found us. Most likely, he's dead. I have no idea how or when or where it happened."

"That's terrible!" Sabahat said. "Haven't you asked your mother about it?"

"I've never talked about this with my mother or anyone else. We forget so we can go on with our lives."

"Why are you talking in riddles, Aram? Perhaps Father could help you. He doesn't have the influence he once did, but he is the head of a bank."

"Never bring this up with your father. Never!"

"If you ask me not to, I won't. Shall we go to Armine's party?"

"She already has her present. Must we?"

"Of course! Particularly if she deliberately left us here alone."

"You mean, so we can prove we haven't done anything wrong?"

"We have nothing to prove to anyone. I told Mother I was going to a birthday party, and I don't like lying."

"I feel ashamed enough as it is when I see your parents, as though I'm taking advantage of their trust and kindness."

"Don't. We're not doing anything wrong. We love each other, Aram, and our love concerns only us," Sabahat said.

"Now, that's what I wanted to hear!" Aram said, throwing his arms around her. From her perch on the table, Sabahat nestled her head against Aram's chest, catlike. The young couple was motionless for a long moment, a moment Aram would treasure for the rest of his life, that would buoy him in his darkest days. Every night since his first glimpse of Sabahat at the gate of the American school, he had imagined holding her tight in his arms, just as he was doing now, and kissing her forehead, her cheeks, her chin; feeling her lips part, the wet heat of her tongue and mouth; running his fingers through her free-falling hair; nuzzling her breasts; savoring her; stroking her belly, her thighs . . .

He had imagined this thousands of times, but now, when they were finally alone in the dim kitchen, he could not even bring himself to kiss her properly. She was looking at him, and in her eyes he saw love, but he also recognized the complete trust she had in him. Either she was unaware of his desires, or she was confident he would not act on them, and this innocence of hers both restrained and inflamed him.

"I love you, Sabahat," he whispered.

"I love you, too. And I'll love you until the day I die, whether we're able to be together or not."

"We'll find a way," Aram said. He gave her a peck on the lips. She slipped free of his arms and hopped off the table.

The food had cooled. They wrapped the ice he'd brought in towels, placing makeshift ice packs over and around the pots. Over each basket of strawberries, they draped a linen napkin. Moving again in perfect harmony, they washed the cutlery, plates, and grater, and put them back in their places, then finally switched off the light and left the room not in the manner of a young couple who has just confessed their love but like a lovingly married couple who still enjoys washing the dishes together, even in their twilight years.

They had nearly reached the front door and the outer world when Aram threw his arms around Sabahat. She pressed her lightly curled hands against his chest, keeping him back, but perhaps in response to the heat of his breath and body, her arms slowly slid up and around his neck. He kissed her full on the lips this time, drawing her tight. For the first time, Sabahat felt a young man's body, urgent and strong, pressing close.

"Please, Aram . . . please don't." With a low groan, he released her.

"Could I ask you to do just one thing for me? Would you undo your plaits?" he said. "I want to run my fingers through your hair." Down came her hair, a heavy curtain falling to her ankles. Aram stroked it, kissed it, breathed in its lavender scent, and helped her braid it again.

"Sabahat, I'm waiting for the day when, for my eyes alone, you wear nothing but your hair," Aram said.

"That day will come."

They stepped into the street, cheeks flushed, eyes bright. Sabahat was thinking she had never been happier when Aram abruptly let go of her hand.

"Is anything wrong?" she asked.

"It's wrong for me to hold your hand in your neighborhood, dear," Aram said. "We can't tell the world of our love, not yet. I'll have to protect you until we're ready."

"Aram, it's enough that you've told me of your love. I'd been waiting for ever so long."

18

Muhittin's New Life

1935
Adana

Muhittin read the telegram for the third time. He stood up, paced the small room, sat down, and read it again. He was being summoned to Ankara by the ministry. His presence was requested in the office of the chairman of the Department of Agriculture—at ten thirty in the morning, in just two days.

Was he at fault in some way? That seemed impossible.

From the moment he'd arrived in Adana, he had, as the phrase goes, worked like a donkey, morning to night. His team had played a role in his success, of course. The students from the School of Agriculture spending their summer break here were keen to gain work experience and had pitched in to complete the project as quickly as possible. The foreman, Hüseyin, was a dynamo, spurring on his workers.

Getting up on a tractor to address the laborers at seven in the morning, Muhittin would roar, "Come on, men. This is war, a war as sacred as the War of Independence. We chased the enemy out of our lands. Now it's time to reconstruct and to build a better future. We'll drain this swamp, and then what will we do? We'll grow cotton in every part of these plains. We'll weave the cotton in our own factories. We'll ship our textiles all across Turkey on our own railroads, and we'll export to the world, too. You'll all get well-paying jobs in the new factories. You'll make money and prosper. But first we have to battle malaria. We have to drain this swamp! Come on! Let's see what you can do!"

While the laborers were eating their raw onions and bread for lunch, Muhittin would go to his corrugated steel hut to prepare reports for the ministry. His supervisor in Ankara had called several times to congratulate him. So what was the meaning of this telegram?

"Musa," he said when his foreman arrived at the site, "find out when the next train leaves for Ankara and what time it arrives there." Musa was heading for the cookstove to make a morning pot of tea. "That can wait. This is more important!"

When Musa ran outside, Muhittin began making calculations. Would he be able to make his farewells to Perihan and her family? What about Nazmi? If time was too short for visits, he would write them each a note, stopping by the post office on his way to the train.

Nazmi would understand his friend's having to leave in a hurry, but Perihan would be heartbroken. He grimaced. Perihan was his paternal aunt's granddaughter. Before he had set off for Adana, his father had thrust a scribbled address into his hand and admonished him to call on his relatives. Two years earlier, his aunt's son-in-law had been posted to the Adana branch of Ziraat Bank. Knowing his relatives would insist he stay with them, Muhittin had waited to contact them until he was settled into his new quarters. They had been thrilled to see him. He had refused their offers of a place to stay, but promised to visit regularly.

Sometimes he would go there for dinner, and he spent nearly every weekend with the family, chatting, playing bezique, and touring the local attractions. Over several spring weekends, however, the family was preoccupied with a serious matter that nevertheless proved to be a great deal of fun: the question of a suitable family name. The Surname Law of 1934 had decreed that, for the first time in history, every citizen of Turkey had to adopt a surname. Those who failed to choose a name would be prosecuted. While non-Muslims had long used family names, it was an alien concept for most Muslim Turks. The newspapers all ran page after page of potential names. Ayşe, the family servant, was furious. "What will they dream up next? We Turks have never had surnames," she said. "We all have nicknames."

"What's yours?" Muhittin asked her.

"Blue-eyed Ayşe."

"Ayşe, that's a description, not a name."

"Fine then. We all have 'descriptions.'"

"Why don't you choose Blue-eyed as your family name? That way, you won't be mistaken for a different Ayşe."

They'd all laughed, but the widespread use of nicknames, patronymics, and monikers was a constant source of confusion. The country had tens of thousands of men known simply as Tall Hasan, Fat Hüseyin, Ahmet Son-of-Murat, Black-Browed Mehmet, and Pilgrim Mustafa, yet entire regions were resisting the new law! Others happily chose a surname derived from the region, city, or village of their birth, or opted for a last name that reflected their professions. Muhittin's uncle had advised him to adopt a name that was "neither too long nor too short, that begins with a letter near the beginning of the alphabet." Muhittin and his relatives in Adana would spend entire weekends mulling over this choice of a surname.

It was on one such day that Muhittin received a letter from home written by his big brother but dictated by their father, Zeki Salih. The purpose of the letter was to remind Muhittin that his family had long used the name of their ancient ancestor, Kulin. The name was familiar to Muhittin. In fact, while he was studying in Germany, he had introduced himself as Kulin in place of his given name, which foreigners had difficulty pronouncing. Before he went to bed that night, Muhittin looked into the mirror and addressed himself by his new name: "Muhittin Kulin." *It has a certain ring to it,* he decided.

The following day, he stopped by his relatives' house to tell them of his decision. Perihan opened the door. She was wearing a stylish dress he'd never seen before, and her hair shimmered in loose waves that spilled down her shoulders. Was that a touch of rouge on her lips? He'd never noticed how pretty she was. This tall young woman was smiling at him with warm brown eyes.

Perihan had graduated from high school and wanted to attend a university in Istanbul. She had asked Muhittin to persuade her father to let her go. They'd spent hours planning her new life, and Muhittin had offered his brotherly advice. In the past week, however, their relationship had taken a strange turn. Perihan's subtle hints and inexplicable tears finally forced Muhittin to bring up the many disabled children across Anatolia whose parents were cousins.

"Muhittin, that only happens when first cousins marry. I've done research. It's different with second cousins," Perihan had said.

"Are you telling me you're absolutely determined to marry a relative, Perihan? I wouldn't advise it. Besides, you're still young. You might want a career when you finish university. The republic is in need of women like you. Why throw away a bright future by marrying too early?"

Perihan's eyes filled with tears, and she left the room. Her grandmother asked Muhittin, "What about you, my boy? You're long past marrying age. Why aren't you ready to settle down?"

"I've got years of work ahead of me. I could be posted at any moment to a mountain village in a remote corner of Anatolia. I wouldn't want my wife to suffer hardships, nor would I want to leave her behind."

"Are you saying you'll never get married?"

"It's kismet. If I meet someone one day who makes my heart race, and if, despite myself, I find I have eyes only for her, then I'll get married. But I haven't met anyone like that yet," he said with a shrug.

Relieved as he was at having made his lack of intentions clear, Muhittin became a less frequent visitor. Now he did not want it to seem like he had fled Adana without saying good-bye, especially since he had no idea if he would be returning.

He left the work site and began walking toward the swamp, wiping away the sweat pouring down his forehead even though the sun was still low on the horizon. Muhittin squatted on the ground and gazed at the wild grasses and the millions of glistening silver dewdrops refracting the sun's early rays. It was his favorite moment of the day: the early morning stillness of a world refreshed and stirring to life. He made a point of getting to work long before the laborers arrived, early enough to walk a mile or two through tall reeds under a blushing sky, collecting his thoughts and considering the life he had lived and the life that was to come. Despite—or perhaps because of—his reverence for nature, he dreamed of taming her, building dams to hold back her floods, blasting tunnels through mountain rock to bring the fruits of civilization to highland villages, planting electricity pylons across the windswept steppe.

In 1923, the year the republic was founded, Şuayip, a university classmate of his, had spent nearly a month traveling from Elazığ to Istanbul. There were barely more than eighty-five hundred miles of paved roads in all of Anatolia. The only other means of transport was the recently nationalized Anatolia-Baghdad railway, and the lines connecting İzmir to Afyon and Bandırma. Back when Muhittin was a high school student at Vefa, Istanbul imported its sugar from Austria, its vegetable oil from Siberia, and its rice from Egypt. Locally grown crops would rot before they reached the cities. As a civil engineer, he knew that the construction sector relied on imported iron and cement, as well as imported lumber, roof tiles, and even bricks. Never mind heavy machinery; even basic hand tools, nails, and spikes were purchased abroad. Outside of a handful of cities, there were no pressurized iron mains to carry water or grids to transmit electricity.

That they had accomplished so much in little more than a decade was a miracle. Sometimes all it took to achieve the impossible was a stroke of genius: for example, healthy men unable to pay the small annual tax of six lira earmarked for the laying of new railroad tracks were given the opportunity to pay off their debts by helping to lay rail for ten days a year. And that was how the railroads were built!

The buzz of a mosquito in his ear reminded Muhittin that he had forgotten to take his quinine that morning. When he got back to the site, Musa was waiting for him.

"There's a train tonight, Engineer Bey. It arrives in Ankara in the morning," he said. "I booked a seat."

Muhittin decided to visit his friend Nazmi first and then his relatives. He hoped Perihan's father would be at home so he could say goodbye to everyone. Perhaps his second cousin would give up on him. As it turned out, there was a silver lining to having to depart Adana.

Two days later, he was in the appointed place at the appointed time. Mahmut Bey, the chairman of the Department of Agriculture and a family friend, embraced him warmly before pointing to a leather armchair and saying, "Won't you please sit down, Muhittin Bey?"

"Sir, your telegram did not specify any reason for recalling me to Ankara. Perhaps I have overworked my team, but that swamp cannot be drained too quickly. Have you received any complaints concerning my performance?"

"You are also there to oversee the development of a dam."

"That is true. However, I am conducting that study completely on my own. The other engineers are all busy with their own projects."

"Have you requested monetary compensation for the study?"

"No, I have not. A ministerial delegation was visiting Adana. When the minister learned I was a civil engineer specializing in waterworks and irrigation, he wondered if I might conduct a study for a dam. Naturally, I said I would."

"And have you had enough time to do so?"

"Sir, there is little in Adana to occupy a man of my age and marital status. I have conducted some preliminary fieldwork in the evenings, when the light permits, and will be able to submit a final report this winter."

"Muhittin Bey, I am afraid we have no choice but to bring your study to a halt."

Muhittin's heart skipped a beat. Bring the study to a halt? Then why on earth was Mahmut Bey beaming at him? Who in his right mind would deliver such terrible news with a grin?

"The Municipality of Ankara wants you."

"What?"

"Let me explain. I was in a meeting with the minister a few days ago. We are developing some projects to build reservoirs near Ankara. He said he required the services of a hardworking, reliable, and capable engineer. You are not without your admirers. And your brother is much appreciated for his work in the Municipality of Istanbul."

Muhittin didn't know what to say. He squirmed in his seat.

"The governor of Ankara is expecting you in his office."

"Sir, what will happen to my work in Adana? Is it to remain unfinished?"

"Why would it? Engineers come and go, but the state is a permanent presence. Someone will be appointed to replace you."

"But I—"

"You were chief engineer in Adana; in Ankara, you will be the director of engineering for the State Hydraulic Works."

Mahmut Bey stood up. The conversation was over. Muhittin leapt to his feet, shook Mahmut Bey's hand, thanked him, and left the room.

He felt dizzy at this unexpected development: he had spent a sleepless night on the train wondering why he was being reprimanded, only to learn he had been promoted! Mahmut Bey must have smoothed his way, of that he had no doubt. He wondered if he should have kissed his benefactor's hand. No, in this day and age, it was only elderly family members whose hands were respectfully kissed. Anything else could be interpreted as a blatant attempt to curry favor with one's betters. He considered, and just as quickly rejected, stopping by the telegraph office to wire his family. No, better to wait until he met with the governor. Jogging down the steps of the ministry and hustling to his meeting, he noticed that the chestnut trees in the new capital had grown tall enough to shade the pavement.

19

I'm in Love

Sleep was evading Sabahat, even though she had been in bed for several hours. Every time she closed her eyes, she was back in the kitchen in Beyazit, sitting on the table with her cheek on Aram's chest, hearing the pounding of his heart. "I love you," he had said. He had finally said it, after all these years of waiting, and Sabahat knew many more years would pass before he would be able to say anything else. She would wait, no matter what, refusing suitors, one after another, unable to tell anyone why. Only Mehpare would have understood her, but Sabahat could not confide in someone so devoted to her parents and so averse to hurting them. Still, she wished she was a little girl again, her head in Mehpare's lap, pouring out her troubles to a sympathetic ear.

Sabahat screwed her eyes shut and willed herself to feel sleepy. She was just beginning to drift off when she sensed a presence in the room. Turning onto her left side, she opened her eyes and screamed.

"Hey! Who are you? What are you doing here?" She fumbled for the switch on the nightstand lamp.

"Shh! Shh! Sabahat, don't be scared, darling. It's me."

The light clicked on at last, illuminating a tiny woman in a long flannel nightgown, her straight gray hair falling past her waist.

"Grandma! It's almost three in the morning. What are you doing in my room? Were you unable to sleep?"

"Ah, my girl, Saraylı tried to strangle me. She mistook me for an enemy soldier."

Sabahat couldn't help but laugh.

"I didn't want to wake you, but I got cold on the divan and my back seized up. I tried to get back into the bedroom, but Saraylı had propped a chair against the door. Could you spare a blanket, my dear?"

Sabahat pulled back the quilt on her bed. "Get in next to me, Grandma. We'll sleep together tonight and deal with Saraylıhanım in the morning. She'll have to open the door to go to the toilet, don't you think?"

"You think she gets up and goes to the toilet? Nesime comes in to clean up after her."

"Come on, get in with me. Don't catch a chill."

"Will we both fit in that bed? I would hate to disturb you."

"Grandma, you're no bigger than a spoon. We'll fit. Hop in."

"Hoping for what?"

"Hop in," Sabahat said, louder this time.

"Why are you shouting? Do you think I'm hard of hearing?"

Sabahat turned her face to the side so her grandma wouldn't see her laughing. The old woman climbed up into the bed and curled into a ball.

"Your hands are like ice," Sabahat said, modulating her voice to what she hoped was the ideal volume. "I hope you don't catch a cold."

"I'll be fine. I'm made of sterner stuff than that. Look at me, have I gone all doddery?"

"Perish the thought," Sabahat said. "We already have one of those in the house."

"I can remember the events of seventy years ago as though they happened yesterday."

"Tell me about those times."

"What do you want to hear? You already know it all."

"Everything."

"Behice was my everything. I loved her, looked after her, brought her up. That's the story of my life!"

"Grandma, did you ever fall in love?"

"I was in love with my husband."

"Was it a love match?"

"My dear girl! There was no such thing in those days. His mother saw me somewhere, found me suitable for her son, and asked my parents for my hand. And so we were married."

"Why did you say you loved him, then?"

"It's the miracle of nuptials. My sainted husband was a handsome man. I took to him over time, and then I loved him very much indeed."

"And then what happened?"

"He went off to war like all the other young men and was martyred."

"Were you terribly upset?"

"I was so sick at heart I miscarried his child. My tears flowed. Your grandmother was there in my hour of need. She had just married İbrahim Bey. She arranged for me to live with them. She consoled me. I cried myself to sleep in her arms, night after night. Although she was a new bride, she put her sister first."

"Grandma, why didn't you remarry?"

"Ah, my child. I was in mourning, and my beloved sister was carrying Behice in her womb. The poor thing came down with a terrible fever after she gave birth. She was burning up, and there was nothing they could do. They call it childbed fever. Behice had not yet reached her first month when her mother passed. Ah! Why are you making me revisit those dark days?"

"And that's how you brought up my mother as your own daughter?"

"Yes. I had lost my husband and my beloved sister. Behice was the tiniest little thing, and so helpless. İbrahim Bey, your grandfather, was grieving something terrible. I would hear him in his room at night, howling, and in my own room, alone with my own grief, I would tear at my hair till dawn. One day, İbrahim Bey came to me and said, 'Neyir Hanım, you are my daughter's aunt, and the sister of her mother. Would you bring her up as your own daughter?' 'Would I?' I cried, 'Would I?' I looked after Behice until she was a young woman, and I married her father. She knew me as her mother and always called me Mother."

"I still don't understand why you never married outside of the family."

"When Behice was three years old, İbrahim Bey said to me, 'You will be my sister for all eternity in the next world, Neyir Hanım, but the tongues of this world are wagging. Will you permit me to silence the gossip by marrying you?'"

"And did you not object? Did you not tell him you wanted to set out for a life of your own?"

"No, my dear. Behice was my life. İbrahim Bey, may he rest bathed in divine radiance, told me that were I to lose my heart to someone and wish to marry, he would divorce me at once. That never happened. I was happy with my life. İbrahim Bey treated me with kindness and generosity. My hands never touched soap and water. He never made me do housework. I never wanted for anything. On my back, I wore the finest Bursa silks. He made much of both me and his daughter."

"But Grandmother, since you were married in the eyes of the law, did you not . . . do anything with my grandfather?"

"You impertinent girl! İbrahim Bey never laid a hand on me. I knew what it was to have a husband. I had known love. I had no need for a man. Behice was all that mattered."

"What about İbrahim Bey? He was still a young man back then. How did he manage without a woman?"

"What makes you think he had no women? While he was building the house in Tozkoparan, he made the acquaintance of a Greek madame and would visit her now and again. Don't busy your head with such things. It's time we slept."

"Grandma, do you believe in love?"

"What is love, my dear? I don't remember anymore."

"Love is everything. Love is what gives life meaning, love is the reason for our existence. I cannot imagine a life without love."

"Well then, I hope you know love when you grow up."

Several moments later, Sabahat whispered, "I've already grown up, and I'm in love." There was no response from her grandmother, whose breath she could hear rising and falling in her ear. Sabahat tried, yet again, to fall asleep.

"What's the matter with you?" Behice asked her youngest daughter early the next morning.

"I couldn't sleep last night."

"Of course you couldn't, not with an old woman in your arms."

"It's got nothing to do with her. She's tiny, and she slept quietly."

"I'm so tired of those two. Nothing but trouble," Behice said. "We had to force Saraylıhanım's door open. There was a puddle on the floor. Don't mention a word of this to Leman. I'll never hear the end of it."

"Where is Grandma going to sleep now?"

"How do I know, Sabahat? We don't have forty different rooms in this house. The bedrooms are all occupied. Your sisters naturally wouldn't want their children in their rooms at night. If I put Saraylıhanım in a room with Nesime, your father will get upset. I have no idea what to do."

"It wouldn't be fair to make someone else share a room with Saraylıhanım. It's best for everyone if she sleeps alone," Sabahat said.

"What about putting Bülent and Sitare in the same room?"

"They'd be up all night, every night."

Behice was nearly in tears.

"Grandma can sleep with me," Sabahat offered.

"Night after night, sharing your bed?"

"We'll put a mattress on the floor, and I'll sleep there."

"I won't hear of it! No daughter of mine sleeps on the floor. We'll have to put a simple bedstead in your room."

"Weren't you the one who gave up your spacious room back in the day, Sabahat?" Suat teased.

"I was," Sabahat said, "but I couldn't bear for Grandma to feel as though she's causing us trouble. She'll be staying in my room from now on. And that's that!"

That afternoon, Behice, Leman, and Suat went to Pera to call on Mehpare and find out what she had decided after her consultation with Mahir. Galip Bey and Halim were not at home. Mehpare greeted them warmly but looked as though she, too, had suffered a sleepless night. There were dark circles under her eyes. When the girls asked after Halim, Mehpare said he had been staying with a friend for a few days. Having seated her guests, the hostess went off to the kitchen to make coffee. Behice followed her.

"Mehpare, if you are certain you don't want this baby, act quickly. But I think it best you carry it to term."

"At my age, I don't know what's best! You could be right, Behice. I need something to bind me to life. When I lost Kemal, I had my son at my breast. I lived for him. Now that my son has abandoned me, I don't feel like living anymore. If I go on like this, I fear I may take my own life."

"What are you saying, Mehpare? What do you mean, take your own life? Are you so unfortunate as that? Is Galip so cruel to you? Why have you never said anything? Pack your bags and come back to us immediately. We'll look after both you and your baby. Don't hesitate for even a moment."

Mehpare grasped Behice's hands. "That poor man has done nothing wrong. He shows me only respect and endures my caprices."

"Well then, why do you talk of killing yourself?"

"I'm so upset over Halim. He doesn't love me, Behice. He doesn't love his own mother, even though he is everything to me."

"I have never heard such nonsense, Mehpare. He loves you, but you smother him."

"Oh no!" Mehpare yelled as the coffee boiled over. "Please go back to the sitting room. I'll clean up here and make another pot."

"You need to hear me out while you wipe up that mess. Listen, you say your husband is kind. God has planted a new life in your womb to make your marriage happier. You're not the only person in the world who has lost a loved one. What about my aunt? She was younger than you when her husband was martyred. What about my father? So many people have put their pain behind them and turned their faces to the future. And what are you doing? All I hear from you is Kemal, Kemal! Halim, Halim! You are showing ingratitude to God, Mehpare."

"Halim abandoned us, Behice. He's living with a wicked woman."

"It's your nagging he fled. Don't worry, he'll be back when he needs fresh laundry."

Behice joined her daughters in the sitting room.

"How long does it take to make coffee?" Leman asked. She went over to the window and looked out over the red-tiled rooftops and stands of cypresses to the opposite shore of the Golden Horn. The sun shimmered on the waters rippling in the wake of colorful fishing boats, bright and beautiful. Mehpare soon came in with a tray of steaming cups of coffee.

"Have you got a cigarette?" Behice asked her. "I forgot my case at home."

Mehpare was rummaging through a drawer for cigarettes when Leman asked, "So, have you made your decision? Are you going to have the baby? Mahir hasn't told us anything. I'm dying of curiosity."

"I've decided. I'm having the baby."

Leman and Suat screeched in unison as they ran over and embraced Mehpare, covering her cheeks with kisses.

"You've made the right choice, my girl," Behice said. "May God watch over you both, and may this child bring joy and good fortune to your home."

There was a knock on the door. Mehpare was leaning over to light Behice's cigarette, so Suat offered to open it. "Ah, it's Halim," she announced. Mehpare's hands trembled.

"Halim, your timing couldn't be better. If I didn't know better, I'd think you'd come home to see us. Mother and Leman are in the sitting room," Suat said. Halim walked in and kissed Behice's hand before he kissed Leman on both cheeks. Not making eye contact with Mehpare, he said, "How are you, Mother?"

"I'm fine, son. I feel better now that I've seen you. Are you hungry?"

"Yes."

Mehpare went back to the kitchen. Halim asked how Sabahat was and said he missed her.

"If you miss her so much, why don't you come for a visit?" Leman said. "You're neglecting Beyba as well. They both keep asking after you. Come over for dinner this week."

Mehpare came into the room with a breakfast tray. "We'll visit together," she said. "I want to thank Mahir in person."

"What did Mahir do for you?" Leman asked.

"He opened my eyes."

"Very well then, I'll expect the three of you for dinner. It's only fitting that Galip Bey also attend our little celebration."

"What are we celebrating?" Halim asked.

"Mehpare! Does this mean you haven't told your son yet?"

"Told me what, Behice Hanım?"

Behice looked at Mehpare, who was blushing.

"Halim," Behice said, "you're going to be a big brother soon. Now, would you prefer a little sister or a little brother?"

"You must be joking." Halim laughed.

"It's no joke," Behice said. "Now, is it too much to ask that you not upset your mother in her delicate condition?"

20

Prying Sisters

The mansion in Beyazit began buzzing with activity once Mehpare decided to keep her baby. Grandmother and Behice began knitting undershirts, booties, and blankets, while Leman and Suat compiled lists of potential names and set to embroidering the edges of the calico sheets reserved for the newborn. Saraylıhanım joined in by gathering up scraps of fabric and wool, which she fashioned into bizarre necklaces and crowns. The family showed her the tolerance and patience normally accorded to a two-year-old, interfering with the senile woman's amusements only when it endangered her safety. Saraylıhanım was dimly aware that a baby was on the way, but she thought it was Halim.

One sunny November day, Leman and Suat were sprawled on cushions in the bay window, needles at work as they chatted. "Sabahat has received a letter nearly every single day. Have you noticed?" Suat asked her elder sister.

"No," Leman said. "Who are they from?"

"I recognized Aram's handwriting on the envelopes."

"Has Aram gone somewhere?"

"You don't care about or notice anything, do you? He's off on a class trip. I'm certain I mentioned it the other day."

"I suppose I paid you no mind. We haven't required his services as a tutor for some time. Can you believe it, Suat? My Sitare is doing wonderfully now, not a single low mark."

"Leman, I'm trying to talk about something more important."

"So Aram is off on a school trip. What's so important about that?"

"Don't you find it strange that he writes to Sabahat every blessed day?"

"Every day? Aram does?"

"Finally!"

"Are you certain, Suat?"

"I wish you'd pay more attention. Every time the postman drops a letter in the mailbox, she comes running out of her room and pounces on it. She's supposed to be on holiday. Some holiday! She never goes anywhere; she's too busy waiting in front of the window for the postman."

"Are you suggesting she has feelings for Aram?"

"I'm not suggesting anything. I'm flat out telling you."

"It can't be true. It's impossible!"

"Don't say I didn't tell you."

"Father would keel over if he learned of this, but he'd kill that little rascal first."

"And that is why I think we should talk this over with Sabahat, before it's too late and before Father and Mother get wind of it."

"But what if it's not true, Suat? What if you're imagining things?"

"Have you been listening to anything I've said? Something is going on between Sabahat and Aram. We have to confront her and put an end to it."

"We need to make certain first. I'd hate to get tangled up in this for no reason."

"Let's read the letters. It's the only way to find out."

"Wait until Sabahat is back in school. Then we'll do it."

"The letters are written in English."

"How do you know that?"

"I went in to see Grandma one day, and Sabahat happened to be reading something. Poor Grandma suffered a coughing fit, and while Sabahat was getting her a glass of water, I glanced at the letter she'd left on the desk. And that's how I found out they're corresponding in English."

"Good gracious. Isn't English similar to French? Perhaps we'll understand enough to make a decision."

"No, we need to find someone who speaks English. What about Sitare?"

"Sitare would go straight to Sabahat and tattle."

"We could make her swear not to say anything."

"I'm not getting my daughter involved in what could turn out to be a scandal. Sabahat is our sister. Just imagine if it became public knowledge that she had fallen in love with an Armenian boy. The fewer people that know about this the better, even within the family."

"What about using a dictionary?"

"Don't be silly! Hold on a minute . . . I just had an idea. Why don't we get Bülent to read it? He's learned enough English, hasn't he? He's your son, and he's always been an obedient boy. We'll scare him into keeping this a secret."

"Brilliant! Bülent's our best and only hope!" Suat said.

"All right then. We'll do it as soon as the schools reopen. Is it Wednesday that Bülent has a half day?"

"There's another snag. Sabahat locks her letters away in a drawer."

"Are you certain?"

"Yes. I checked. The top drawer is full of her underthings. The letters are locked in the drawer below."

"She keeps her underthings in the top drawer?"

"Yes."

"That foolish girl! Secrets should always be hidden away in the uppermost drawer. All we have to do is remove it, and we'll expose everything in the drawer below."

"We also have to find a way to get Grandma out of the room. She'd tell Sabahat we were going through her things."

"Why don't we simply explain we're doing it for Sabahat's own good?"

"By the time we made ourselves clear, everyone would find out. You know how hard of hearing Grandma is."

"I have another idea, Suat. Grandma has been coughing all night. I'll ask Mahir to arrange an x-ray."

"And we can get Sabahat to take Grandma to the doctor. While she's gone, we'll get Bülent to read the letters," Suat said. "It'll all be out in the open before Aram gets back from that school trip."

On the day Mahir had arranged for the x-ray, Sabahat said she had urgent business at school. The elder sisters, too, claimed to be busy that day. Leman exchanged glances with Suat as they both wondered if Aram was back in Istanbul, and if that was the reason Sabahat so uncharacteristically refused to help Grandma.

"If Sabahat can't accompany your grandmother, one of you girls will have to," Behice said. "Don't leave me alone out on the streets with a deaf old woman."

"I'll do it," Suat said.

Leman, who loathed hospitals, heaved a sigh of relief and rushed off to Sabahat's room to help her grandmother get dressed. Half an hour later, Behice Hanım and Suat got into a cab with Neyir Hanım.

21

Bülent the Translator

Bülent was astonished to find his aunt in his room when he got home from school. Normally, she only came into his room to nurse him when he was ill.

"Is something wrong?" he asked.

"Darling Bülent," Leman said, "remember how I went to Beyoğlu yesterday? Well, I got you a box of your favorite chocolates at Markiz."

Bülent eyed the box resting on his desk. "Thank you," he said.

"I need you to do something for me."

"What?"

"Bülent! The correct response is, 'How can I help you?'"

"How can I help you, Auntie?"

"I'd like you to read a few letters."

Bülent stared in puzzlement.

"The letters are written in English. You've done well in your English classes, haven't you?"

"Yes."

"Then read the letters and translate them for me."

"Why don't you ask Sitare?"

"That's the most important part. Let me explain. The letters are to remain a secret. Nobody will know about it but us and your mother. Now, swear on your honor as a man that you will never tell anyone else about these letters. Sitare can't make a promise like that, can she? That's why I've asked you to read them for me. Because you're a man of your word, and I know you'll keep your promise."

Bülent was intrigued and not a little proud that his auntie had such faith in him.

"Do you promise not to tell anyone?"

"Let me see the letters first."

"You have to promise first, on your honor as a man."

"I do," Bülent said.

"Swear it on your life."

"I swear it on my life."

"Now, Bülent, you've made both a promise and a solemn vow. If you don't keep your word, your mother will punish you for the former, and God will punish you for the latter. I can tell you your mother won't take you to the cinema next week if you've lied. As for what God would do, well, I won't presume to second-guess Him."

"What will He do, Auntie?"

"He'll blind you! But if you keep your word, nothing bad will happen. Do you understand?"

"I do," the boy said, wide-eyed. Leman pulled a letter out of the stack in her hand. She and Bülent sat side by side on the bed, and he began to read.

"*Dear Sabahat* . . . Oh, these letters are to my auntie!"

"Keep reading."

"*It has been five days since I left Istanbul, and I already wish I were back. The woods here are beautiful and the weather is fine, yet I am—*"

Leman cut him off. "What does it say?"

"*I've been away from Istanbul for five days, and I want to come home.* I mean, whoever wrote this letter does! *The woods are nice and so is the weather.* That's as far as I got before you stopped me."

"Read it a line at a time, translating as you go."

Bülent followed his auntie's instructions. The first letter was a friendly account of a school trip. The second letter was written in the same spirit, but in more detail. Bülent handed over the second letter when he was finished and moved on to the third. He stopped in the middle, bored.

"Auntie Leman, why are we reading Auntie Sabahat's letters?

"Your mother and I are curious."

"Why?"

"You wouldn't understand. You're not old enough."

"Tell me what you're curious about."

"We hope to get to the heart of the matter concerning the letter writer and Sabahat."

"What?"

"See! You're too young to understand."

"I'm bored."

"I'll take those chocolates back then."

"Go ahead."

"All right, Bülent. Just finish the letter in your hand, that's a good boy."

Bülent translated the third letter all the way to the end. Leman gathered up the letters and warned Bülent one last time not to tell anyone.

"Not even Mother?"

"Your mother, but nobody else. It's wrong to keep secrets from mothers," Leman said, kissing Bülent on the cheek before hustling off to the floor above.

The top drawer was still on Sabahat's bed, just as Leman had left it. After putting the letters back into the blue box in the second drawer and making sure it was sealed tight, Leman managed, with a great deal of huffing and puffing, to slide the top drawer back into place. She took a step back and looked over the room. Nothing was out of the ordinary; Sabahat would never realize her letters had been read. That is, unless Bülent snitched.

Leman went down to the room with the bay windows and settled onto the divan to await Suat's return. About an hour later, Behice and Suat helped Neyir Hanım out of a cab and supported her on either side as they walked to the house. Leman ran downstairs to greet them at the front door.

"Leman, this is the first time your worrying amounted to anything," Behice said. "Fluid has collected in the poor thing's left lung. That is why she's been coughing so badly."

"Oh no! Is it tuberculosis?"

"You're the wife of a doctor! Of course it's not tuberculosis. The doctor prescribed some medication." Behice leaned down and shouted into Neyir Hanım's ear, "You'll be fine as long as you give up smoking, isn't that right, Mother?"

"I'll give up smoking, but only if you give me up," Neyir Hanım said. "It's time you let me go."

"Go where, Mother? You'll be here to see Sabahat get married, God willing." Suat and Leman raced up the stairs while the other women were removing their coats in the entrance hall.

"Have you read them?" Suat asked.

"Most of them. There was nothing in them."

"What do you mean? What was he writing about, page after page?"

"What didn't he write about, you mean. The places he went, the mountains, the meadows, the forests, the wildlife, even the birds and bees!"

"What kind of lovers are they?"

"Suat, you're the only one claiming they're lovers."

"But if they're not in love, why do they write to each other every day?"

"How am I supposed to know?" Leman said. "Perhaps they've become pen pals. Perhaps they'll both become newspaper correspondents one day. Who knows? Stop obsessing over their supposed love! You've wound me up for no reason."

Leman spun on her heel and walked off to her room. In a low voice, Suat said to herself, "The only thing you ever notice is invisible germs." *If only I could read English*, she thought as she marched off to Bülent's room to get a firsthand account of the letters' contents.

22

Germs Won't Kill You

With a few fashion magazines tucked under her arm, Sabahat poked her head through the half-open door of Leman's room. "Hey! What are you two doing in there? Sitare! Bülent!"

Sitare stepped off of a pillow and, red-faced, pleaded with her aunt. "Please don't tell my mother. I'm begging you."

Sabahat glanced at the articles strewn across the floor: Leman's nightgown, her house robe, her scarf, and the blue blanket Bülent had been gleefully jumping up and down on when she entered the room.

"What is the meaning of this?"

Sitare picked up the pillow, plumped it, and put it back on the bed. She pulled the blanket out from under Bülent's feet, folded it, and began picking up the other things.

"I'm talking to you. Why did you throw those things on the floor, and why were you jumping up and down on them?"

Sitare shrugged.

"I'm about to lose my temper with you," Sabahat warned.

"I'm picking everything up."

"Why did you throw those things on the floor in the first place? That's what I'm asking you."

"To prove something to Mother."

"What?"

"To prove germs don't kill people or make them sick!"

"We're conducting an experiment, Auntie," Bülent chimed in. "You know, like what they do in the laboratory at school."

"If your aunt sees you stepping on her things, she'll wring your neck, you scamp."

"Maybe she'll die before she gets the chance," Bülent said. "From germs!"

"She won't die, Bülent! I told you, she won't die," Sitare said. "Remember how when we rubbed her pillow on the cat's bottom you kept insisting she would die, but she didn't, did she?"

"Tell me this instant what you're trying to do here, or I won't be responsible for what happens next," Sabahat said.

Sitare slipped the folded nightgown under her mother's pillow and hung the house robe on the hook behind the door.

"Auntie, you know how terrified my mother is of microbes. All we're trying to do is demonstrate that microbes aren't deadly. When I accidentally dropped my sweater on the ground the other day, she made me throw it away—and it was new. 'Don't, Mother, we can wash it,' I told her. She wouldn't listen to me. She won't listen to Father, either, and he's a doctor. So I jumped on her pillow with my shoes on and dragged her nightie on the floor. Let's see if anything happens. Will she get sick or die?"

"If she does die, we'll both be murderers," Bülent said, his lower lip trembling.

Sitare smacked Bülent on the bottom. "I told you, she won't die! Nothing will happen to her!"

Sabahat seized Sitare by the arm and sat her down on the upholstered bench at the foot of the bed. Taking a seat next to her, she said,

"Sitare, sweetie, your mother has a phobia, an irrational fear. You need to be more understanding. When she was growing up, germs were far more deadly and widespread. In fact, our Uncle Kemal, Halim's father, came down with tuberculosis. Everyone was afraid of catching his disease. That is why your mother is terrified of microbes to this day."

"Then why doesn't Auntie Suat worry about germs all the time?"

"People are different. We all have our own fears and ways. Be more understanding, Sitare. I won't tell your mother what you did today because you're right, ordinary germs won't kill you or make you sick, but if she found out what you've done, it would break her heart. Promise me you'll never do anything like this again."

"But I can't stand it anymore, Auntie. Hygiene is all she ever thinks about!"

"Promise me, Sitare. And don't you ever make Bülent your partner in crime again. All right?"

"I promise."

Sabahat opened one of the magazines she'd been carrying and pointed to a page of white dresses. "Which of these do you like best? I'm having a dress made for my graduation."

"Oh, that one is really pretty. Are you going to wear it to the ball?"

"Yes, to the graduation ball at the end of June."

"Armine, Piraye, Aram . . . will you all graduate together?"

"I hope so. My friends are all good students."

"If I go to high school, will I get to wear a fluttery white dress like that one when I graduate?"

"Of course you will. If you study hard and you pass all your tests, Father will send you to high school, too."

"Really? Are you sure, Auntie?"

"Listen, Sitare. High school is expensive. They won't be able to hire a private tutor for you. You'll only get to go to high school if you're a hardworking student."

Sitare pointed to a long gown with a tulle skirt embroidered with daisies and said, "Look at that one, Auntie. If you don't pick this one, maybe I'll wear it to my graduation ball. What do you think?"

"That won't happen for many years. Who knows what the fashions will be then."

"Can I go to high school, too?" Bülent asked.

"Of course. Just like Aram. But you'll never get to wear a nice dress like this, Bülent, because you're a boy," Sitare said. "I'll get all dressed up, and you'll have to carry my bag for me."

Bülent snatched the pillow Sitare had so carefully plumped up and threw it at his cousin's head. Then he ran out of the room. A moment later, Suat's voice could be heard shouting, "Sitare, what have you done now to upset my boy?"

23

A Run of Bad Luck

Muhittin paused on the steps in front of the dignitaries' box and gazed down on the milling crowd below, his eye lingering on the ladies' gaily colored dresses and hats, that rippling field of summer flowers. *What a remarkable sight,* he thought as he carefully positioned his new camera and captured the scene forever—in black and white, unfortunately—for his parents.

Before he sent the photograph, he would write on the back: *Weekend at the Ankara Hippodrome.* He wished he could take a self-portrait for his big brother, who was quite a sharp dresser and would appreciate the dapper figure Muhittin cut that day in one of the custom-tailored white linen suits and straw-colored silk shirts, complete with a hand-embroidered *MK* monogram on the left breast, his mother had shipped to Ankara at great expense. It was understood that Muhittin would have to look his best as he accompanied Ankara's overbearing governor on various tours of inspection and official business.

Muhittin had only recently come to realize why the governor seemed to require his constant company: in addition to the daily demands of his new post, lately he had been expected to perform certain duties that were well outside of his job description.

First, the governor had barged into his office two months ago, demanded to know if he spoke German and, without waiting for an answer, as usual, said, "You must be fluent, you studied in Berlin. Report to the Ministry of Education at two o'clock on the dot this afternoon, Muhittin Bey!"

"But sir, today I am—"

"Change your plans. It is absolutely critical that you be there. Give them your name at the door, and you will be taken straight into the meeting room to act as the interpreter for the minister himself. Why are you looking at me like that? The minister's interpreter has taken ill. They needed a replacement, and I suggested you."

"What does this meeting concern?"

"As you know, Hitler's Civil Service Law has resulted in the dismissal of thousands of Jewish civil servants, from professors to judges. The representatives of an organization formed to help Jewish scholars and scientists secure employment in other countries is meeting with representatives of the government today. The president wishes to appoint some of these highly qualified émigrés to our new professorships and hospitals. The minister of education is chairing a meeting today to negotiate the details. Muhittin Bey, we cannot rely on just any interpreter. Be there." The governor was just leaving the room when he turned, threw Muhittin a meaningful look, and said, "Don't forget, you're acting on the express wishes of the president."

Directly after lunch, a slightly resentful Muhittin walked to the ministry building. He was shown a place at a long table headed by the minister of education, Dr. Reşit Galip, immediately to the right of whom sat an elderly professor by the name of Malche and the renowned pathologist Herr Schwartz. Seated around the table were various high-ranking bureaucrats, academics, and members of the Reform Commission. Muhittin sat down and started interpreting. An undersecretary announced that negotiations would begin with economics and commercial sciences, at which a gentleman Muhittin had not yet met took the floor and said, "Is there a professor of applied economics you could recommend?"

Herr Schwartz glanced at his list, found three suitable candidates, and read aloud a brief résumé for each. Next on the agenda were professorships in finance, law, chemistry, business administration, and every department in the School of Medicine. "Could you recommend a specialist in the field of microbiology?" "Could you recommend a specialist in the field of orthopedics?" Variations of this question were repeated, each time with the same sense of urgency and enthusiasm. The men gathered around the table that day knew they were making history and that the persecution in Germany would contribute to the flowering of science and the creative arts in other countries, including their own. Salaries and the broad outlines of the contracts for the new state employees were agreed upon, and the meeting was adjourned while the minutes were being drawn up. Muhittin gratefully reached for a glass of tea from the tray being handed around in the corridor. His throat was dry. He had been reluctant to attend the meeting but was now proud to have been a participant. At one point, Herr Schwartz came up to him and said, "We have exhausted you with our endless negotiations. I would like to thank you and to say how thrilled I am to have discovered that your wonderful country will be a safe harbor." Muhittin could feel his chest swelling with pride.

A few minutes later, they were all seated around the table again. The minutes of the meeting were read out and approved. Then the minister of education stood up and made a speech Muhittin would never forget.

"This has been a truly extraordinary day," the minister said. "We have achieved something without parallel anywhere in the world. When Constantinople was conquered five hundred years ago, many of the scientists of Byzantium migrated to Italy, becoming the impetus for what we would later call the Renaissance. Today, as a result of this meeting, some of the greatest minds in the world will be migrating in the opposite direction, to Istanbul. Gentlemen, you bring us your science and your knowledge and contribute to the advancement of our youth. I would like to express my gratitude and appreciation to each of you."

As Muhittin translated the minister's words, his voice shook with emotion. Minister Galip and the German guests signed the official report, bringing to an end the seven-hour meeting. Although it was nine o'clock, it was not yet dark outside. Muhittin walked home with a light step, overjoyed that Turkey had welcomed thirty leading scientists in a single day, with many more likely to arrive later.

Two weeks later, the German professor appointed to the newly opened Hydraulics Institute of the Department of Agriculture offered Muhittin a proposal. On the phone was a Professor Stüwe asking for Muhittin's assistance both as a translator and for lab work and engineering applications. If Muhittin accepted, the professor would ask the administration to pay his consulting fee.

"That won't be necessary," Muhittin said. "Hydraulics is my area of expertise. I would be happy to help."

During his lunch breaks, he now rushed to the institute to translate for Professor Stüwe, but one hour was not enough time to get much lab work done. Muhittin was a civil servant with regular work hours and had only his lunch hours and his weekends to spare. Professor Stüwe suggested shifting the three o'clock class on Wednesdays to five o'clock to enable Muhittin to lecture once a week.

"I'll have to discuss that with the governor," Muhittin said. Although the managing director of the municipality was responsible for such decisions, Muhittin knew the governor interfered in everything and always had the last word. He decided to go directly to the top in order to save time.

"Why do you want to teach, Muhittin Bey? Are we not paying you enough?" was the governor's response.

"Sir, I don't need more money, but the students need what I can teach them."

"Are there no other professors in Ankara?"

"No one has conducted the studies I have."

"And what is so important about these studies?"

Using the simplest language possible, Muhittin explained the use of glass canals and modeling in the laboratory to test projects before they were constructed in the field.

"Is that not a waste of time and money?" the governor asked.

"With all due respect, sir, spending millions on a project whose feasibility has not been properly tested is a waste of money."

"Are you telling me I'm wrong, Engineer Bey?"

"No sir, I am merely pointing out that I am right. But if you object, the weekly lectures won't happen, of course."

The governor was unaccustomed to being challenged, and certainly not by a young upstart and subordinate like this blue-eyed engineer. He considered for a moment and said, "Very well then, you can lecture on Wednesdays."

A few weeks later, the governor's invitation to a racing meet popular with Ankara society coincided with a critical lab experiment scheduled for the same weekend.

"Are you telling me you are refusing my invitation, Muhittin Bey?" the governor asked in disbelief.

"The project team has been developing this for weeks. I have to be there. Had I known you would honor me with this invitation, I would have rescheduled the lab work. Would the governor be so kind as to consider extending me an invitation to the races next week?"

"Fine, Muhittin Bey. Next week it is."

Now, as Muhittin stood near the governor's box in his linen suit taking photographs to send to his family, he marveled at his extraordinary run of luck.

He had neither appealed to friends in high places nor cringed and fawned before his superiors, and yet he had been plucked from the swamps of Adana and deposited in the middle of Ankara society. Unable to believe it, he had written to his elder brother to ask if he had pulled any strings.

"Are you mad, Muho? I'm an engineer and a civil servant just like you. What influence do I have?" Nusret had replied. "If I were you, I'd sit back and enjoy it."

There was one thing Muhittin had learned about lucky streaks: they were bound to come to an abrupt end.

At the races that day, the governor introduced Muhittin to his niece, a most pleasant and genial young lady. He and the niece sat together three rows behind the governor, betting on the same horses and losing every time. As Semiha was leaving the track, she requested and received Muhittin's telephone number.

"We occasionally have tea parties and a little dancing at home. I would like to invite you to the next gathering," she said. "I understand you to be newly arrived from Adana and without a friend in the city. My uncle says your loneliness has driven you to create extra work to fill the long hours. Lessons in a laboratory, I believe he said."

"Your esteemed uncle appears to have neglected to mention that I take great pleasure in my work," Muhittin said.

That was the last he saw or heard of Semiha until the governor sent him a note ten days later requesting his presence at the Ankara Cinema for the screening of a new American film at eight o'clock in the evening. Muhittin was standing in front of the cinema at a quarter to eight. Press photographers had staked out their positions nearby. He was waiting in an inconspicuous corner when the governor arrived twenty minutes late. The press swarmed the automobile, firing off questions amid the popping bulbs. Waving to Muhittin was a member of the governor's entourage: Semiha. Muhittin ventured out of his corner and nodded a greeting to the governor. Semiha came up to him and entered the cinema on his arm, whereupon he insisted they sit two rows behind her uncle. During the intermission, Muhittin went to the lobby to get Semiha a bottle of fizzy lemonade and a chocolate bar, avoiding the many hangers-on there. When the film was over, the governor swept off with his entourage—leaving Semiha behind!

"I'll take you home," Muhittin offered. He hailed a cab and gave the driver an address on Menekşe Street. When they pulled up in front of the apartment building, Muhittin asked the driver to wait while he walked the young lady to her front door.

"Won't you come up, Muhittin Bey?" Semiha asked. "I'd like to introduce you to my mother."

Muhittin was flabbergasted. "Semiha Hanım, isn't it rather late for that?" he said. "I do hope I'll have the opportunity to make your mother's acquaintance at a more reasonable hour one day soon. And in any case, the cab is waiting."

They shook hands in front of the door, and she stepped inside her building. Muhittin went over to the driver, paid the fare, and set off into the night with his hands plunged in his pockets, deep in thought. His life was changing at a dizzying pace. Since moving away from the relative serenity and order of his childhood home, he had lived in Berlin, Adana, and Ankara, locked into a hectic schedule in each city. He had worked hard developing projects and ideas, smoothing the way for his rapid rise. However, trailing a governor to races, cinemas, and cocktail parties was something new and unpleasant. Had his brother been there, he would have said, "Don't be such a blockhead, Muho. Stop your bellyaching and make the most of it! Young men are lining up for the chance to escort the governor's niece!"

Perhaps Semiha had hit a nerve. Other than a couple of engineers, it was true he had no friends in Ankara. Muammer was just about to get engaged and wasn't available very often, and his roommate spent all his free time gambling. He supposed there were days when he felt a little lonely. Is that what was bothering him? Actually, deep down, he knew that was it. His career was going well, but his personal life was going absolutely nowhere! The clock struck midnight as Muhittin walked along the deserted streets, listening to the echo of his footsteps and the nagging voice in his head.

Arriving at work early the following Monday, Muhittin was scanning the newspapers delivered daily to his desk when he spotted some photographs of the governor and his entourage at the Ankara Cinema. The caption for one read: *Among the audience members were the governor's lovely niece, Semiha Hanım, and Muhittin Bey, director of engineering for the State Hydraulic Works.* That's all he needed. Thank God it was an Ankara paper. Had his family seen it, the questioning would have been relentless.

He wondered how Semiha would react to the photograph of the two of them seated together. He felt bad for her. The gossips would be out in full force.

The phone rang. The governor's personal secretary asked him to hold the line for a moment.

"Muhittin Bey, have you seen your photo in the newspaper today?"

"I have, sir."

"I'm hosting a dinner at Ankara Palace this evening. Be there at eight o'clock."

The conversation ended with a click. Muhittin sighed. Semiha would probably be there.

He finally realized that the governor wished for him to court his niece and was even prepared to shepherd him along.

Semiha was a sweet girl, and blameless. He had seen how upset she was when her uncle forgot her at the cinema. Muhittin had only himself to blame for his loathing of traps and pressure of any kind. Had he not been relieved to leave Perihan behind in Adana? *What's wrong with me?*

he thought. *Mother's right: I don't appreciate kindness, and I don't fall for nice girls.*

The party gathered for dinner that evening at Ankara Palace was more intimate than he had expected: a few close friends of the governor; Semiha, naturally; and the mother he had declined to meet. He was seated between the mother and Semiha. The latter seldom spoke, but Feride Hanım and the woman sitting next to her more than made up for that. Feride Hanım, he learned, had moved to Ankara with her daughter when she was widowed. Having decided it would be unseemly to remain in the provinces, she now resided with her daughter on one of the floors of the small apartment building he had seen the night they'd gone to the cinema.

When the dinner was over and everyone was making their farewells, he noticed that Semiha was downcast, and felt a twinge of regret. Not wanting to encourage gossip, he had neglected her, inadvertently hurting her feelings. Hoping to make amends, he went over to bid her a warm goodnight. He had barely opened his mouth when Feride Hanım cut him off by inviting him in a booming voice to a tea party the following Saturday. The other members of the party lingered in the doorway, waiting to hear his reply.

"Thank you for your kind invitation," he said. "What time would you like me to come?" They agreed on four o'clock. There would be other young people. It would be so much fun. She was an old woman, but she adored spending time with young people. Feride Hanım would have gone on in this vein had Semiha not taken her by the elbow and said, rather sharply, "Come on, Mother, let's not detain Muhittin Bey any longer. It's late." Semiha propelled her mother through the doorway without a goodnight or a backward glance.

Muhittin couldn't sleep that night. How could he slip free of their clutches without breaking the girl's heart? Having accepted the invitation, it would be disgraceful to cancel. He had no choice but to arrive with a box of chocolates, and he would repay their hospitality by inviting both daughter and mother to either the cinema or the theater. Having discharged his obligations, he would then avoid them both.

The tea party that Saturday turned out to be as "fun" as the mother had promised. Also in attendance were several unattached young people, as well as a few married couples. They listened to music, chatted, and played a few hands of bezique. He tried to explain to Semiha that he had neglected her at dinner only to protect her name. He was expressing his concern that the photograph was likely to be misinterpreted when she interrupted him.

"Is ignoring me the only way to stop people gossiping?"

"Perhaps not, but forgive me if I am unable to consider any other way," Muhittin said.

"I had not taken you for a man whose only aim in life was amusement and carousing."

"I am no devotee of amusement."

"That is the impression you have left."

"Perhaps, through no fault of my own, I have made the wrong impression. If that is the case, I am truly sorry. In the future, I will be more careful." Semiha walked off, and Muhittin begged his hostesses' leave after a decent interval had passed. It was late, and the other guests were preparing to leave in ones and twos. Feride Hanım showed Muhittin to the door; Semiha waved to him from the living room. With a wink, the mother exclaimed, "You young people! Silly misunderstandings can happen. We expect you again soon. Our door is open to you, anytime you wish."

Muhittin saw that the mother, too, had been under the impression that he was courting her daughter. He discarded the idea of inviting them anywhere. A note thanking them for having invited him to their home would be his last communication.

***

Muhittin threw himself into his work over the coming days and weeks. Much of his time was spent outside the city conducting research at the Porsuk River and the Çubuk Reservoir.

At city hall one day, his path crossed that of the governor.

"How are you doing, Engineer Bey? How is your social life going?"

"I'm too busy with work to have any kind of a social life, sir."

"Any kind?" the governor asked, raising an eyebrow.

"Any kind," Muhittin replied. The governor's face darkened.

A month later, Muhittin was invited to play bridge at an engineer's house. He had just learned the game and enjoyed it. When he arrived at the bridge party, he found Feride Hanım and Semiha seated in the living room. While Feride Hanım reproached him for having disappeared, Semiha greeted him warmly, simply saying she was sorry he had not contacted them. He explained how busy he had been, and the ice seemed to melt. They played bridge at the same table, and he was even paired with Feride Hanım for one hand. She was a most formidable player.

When the party broke up that evening, it was raining outside. Muhittin decided to invite the mother and daughter to share his cab. So insistent was Feride Hanım that he join them in their home for a coffee that he felt he couldn't refuse. As Semiha made coffee in the kitchen, Feride Hanım said, "Muhittin Bey, we'll be having our dinner soon. One of our neighbors is from the Balkans, and just this morning she sent us a tray of homemade Bosnian *börek*. As a Bosnian yourself, this is an invitation you cannot refuse." Without waiting for a response, she called out, "Semiha, don't make coffee yet. Muhittin Bey is staying for dinner. We'll have coffee afterward."

Muhittin wondered how Feride Hanım had learned he was Bosnian. The only time he could recall having mentioned his family background was when he encountered Ambassador Hüsrev Gerede in the governor's office. He had been asked by Hüsrev Bey, who was himself Bosnian, if the surname Kulin was connected in any way to the Kulins of Bosnia. So, the governor had been discussing Muhittin with his sister!

As he made his farewells at the door, he invited Feride Hanım and her daughter to accompany him to the theater the following weekend, saying he would arrange a cab and the tickets.

"You live very near the theater. Don't go through the trouble to pick us up. We can meet there," Feride Hanım said.

Perhaps I've treated them shabbily, he decided in the cab on the way home. He'd dined with them in their home, and they would be going out on the town together the following week. As for what happened after that, only God could know! In her letters, his mother always asked when he was going to find a suitable wife. Nusret's daughter, Semra, had turned three; his wife, Ecla, was pregnant with their second child. Saadet had given birth to two sons in two years, and they were growing up fast. And here Muhittin was, in his thirties, and not even engaged yet!

Muhittin took Semiha and her mother to the play, as planned, and then to Özen Patisserie for cream cake and tea on the only boulevard in Ankara. Feride Hanım said she expected to have Muhittin over for dinner soon and would ask the Bosnian neighbor to roll out dough for meat dumplings.

Bairam was fast approaching, and Muhittin missed his family. Nusret's wife had given birth to a boy they named Orhan, and he was anxious to see this new nephew as well. He decided to combine the religious holiday and a long weekend for an extended stay at the mansion in Sultanahmet.

Along with her husband and children, Saadet was now back in the family mansion in Sultanahmet. She pressured him to stay longer while they had the opportunity, after so many years, to gather as a family under one roof. In the evenings, he spent hours catching up with both his brother and his sister. Two days before he was due to return to

Ankara, Muhittin fell ill with fever. The doctor forbade him to board a sleeper car until he had made a full recovery.

Saadet told him that despite the magnificence of the in-laws' home on the Bosphorus, her mother-in-law had made her life hell, for which reason she had moved back to Sultanahmet. She also gossiped a great deal about Nusret's wife, Ecla, whom she had been unable to love. It wasn't long before the conversation turned to the question of Muhittin's prolonged bachelorhood. Were there no eligible girls in Ankara, Saadet wondered, for a handsome engineer? She promised to find a good match in Istanbul if he allowed her.

"Saadet, you talk about finding a wife the way you talk about finding a house," Muhittin said. "Even as a woman, you chose your own spouse. Let me do the same."

"I'm worried about you, Muho. You're all alone. You were in bed with a fever for four days. Who would have nursed you if you had been in Ankara? Everyone needs a life companion. Solitude is unique to God."

"I'll let you in on a secret," Muhittin mock whispered. "There is a girl—"

Saadet screamed. "Is she pretty? Is she clever? Are you deeply in love? Whose daughter is she?"

"Hold on, Saadet. Catch your breath. I'm not in love, but she's a nice, suitable, pretty girl. The niece of the governor—"

Saadet cut her brother off a second time. "Oh no, Muho! Lord help us! Watch your step! Get out while you can. The governor is your boss; don't make him your uncle as well. I've heard he's got a terrible temper. What if his niece takes after him?"

"She's soft spoken and sweet tempered. I tried to tell you, nothing has happened yet."

"I suggest you find a girl who isn't related to the governor. That is, if you haven't fallen in love with this girl already!"

"Had I fallen in love, we would have been engaged long ago," Muhittin said. "Did Nusret waste any time after he met Ecla?"

Ten days later, fully recovered and with a doctor's report in his pocket, Muhittin returned to the office a little paler and much thinner than when he'd last been there. Work had accumulated in his absence, and he was immediately buried in paperwork. Toward the weekend, he received a phone call from the governor's secretary informing him that his boss was expecting him immediately.

Taking his doctor's report out of the top drawer of his desk and slipping his latest report on the reservoir into a binder, Muhittin left his office.

The governor was seated behind his desk, frowning and sullen. He pointed to the usual chair and growled, "Sit down!"

Muhittin put the binder on the desk.

"What's that?"

"It's a report on the Çubuk Reservoir."

"Pick it up! Now's not the time for that!" The governor gave the binder a push, sending it sliding across the desk and onto the floor. Muhittin picked it up, set it on an end table, and sat down.

"You've been absent for some time."

"I was visiting my family. There's a flu epidemic in Istanbul, and I'm afraid I caught it. I submitted the doctor's report to the administrative center, but if you would like to see it . . ." He pulled the folded report out of his pocket.

The governor waved his hand impatiently. "I don't need it."

Before he had started working for the municipality, Muhittin had been told that the governor was snappish, overbearing, and downright rude to anyone he disliked. To date, though, he had always been courteous to Muhittin.

For the first time, the governor had addressed Muhittin using *sen*, the familiar form of "you."

"You wished to see me, sir?"

"You say you went to visit your family. Did you discuss a personal matter with them?"

"I'm not following you," Muhittin said, genuinely puzzled.

"Engineer Efendi, don't you think it's time you settled down? Don't your mother and your father want to see their son married?"

"They don't interfere in my personal life, sir."

"Well, I do."

Muhittin flushed red.

"And I'm telling you the time has come for a decision."

"Concerning what, sir?" Muhittin asked.

"Marriage."

"I'm the only one who can make that decision, sir."

"Then make up your mind already! My niece is not the kind of girl you can toss aside. She's from a good family."

"I can assure you that there has been nothing in my conduct toward your niece that would disturb you or hasten a decision to marry."

"You don't say! Well, am I meant to be relieved? You gallivanted with her all winter long. Your photograph even appeared in the press."

"Sir, our meetings were nearly always arranged at your invitation. And whenever we did meet separately, we always had a chaperone."

"I don't care! For what reason is a young lady introduced to a young gentleman? So they can go to the cinema and theater together every weekend? If your intentions were not honorable, why in the devil did you keep seeing her?"

When the governor began opening a desk drawer, perhaps reaching for a gun, Muhittin reflexively snatched the heavy crystal ashtray from the end table.

"Sort this out, Engineer Efendi. Or face the consequences."

"If you'll excuse me, sir," Muhittin said as he stood up and walked to the door.

Heart pounding in his ears, knees quaking, he marched to his office, closed the door, opened it again, and called out to the clerk standing in the hallway, "I'm busy. Don't let anyone into my office." Slamming the door, he went over to his desk and sat down. It was only then that he realized he was still clutching the ashtray and that he had forgotten the binder on the end table.

Muhittin rolled a sheet of paper into his typewriter and began pounding on the keys.

```
February 2, 1936

To the Mayoralty and Governorship of
Ankara,

For reasons I deem appropriate, I am
tendering my resignation as director
of engineering for the State Hydraulic
Works, a post I have held since September
2, 1935.

Muhittin Kulin, Chief Engineer MSc
```

24

A Toast to Sabahat

Sabahat, a member of the student council, the president of the book club, and the production designer for the drama club, as well as a participant in nearly every other school function, graduated from high school with honors. Rather than honoring her promise to her mother to stay at home on weekends, she had busied herself with friends from school. So hardworking and successful a student was she, though, that Reşat Bey believed she deserved to spend her free time as she chose. To his mind, his youngest daughter was a role model he could hold up to the younger members of the family. Halim had dropped out of school, Sitare had to take makeup tests, and Bülent, who was still young, was a quick learner but quite naughty in the classroom. There were days Reşat Bey would sigh and wonder why he did not have a son as intelligent and accomplished as his daughter, but then, at the breakfast table, he would see her sweet face and blond ankle-length hair, and feel grateful for what he did have.

Behice Hanım, on the other hand, firmly believed that the sole benefit of a high school diploma was the enhancement of a girl's marriage prospects. She had long since decided that fluency in two languages and a diploma should more than suffice for her daughter, a view she shared with Suat, who had been encouraging her mother to keep Sabahat at home more often. All Behice asked was that Sabahat sit at her mother's side, do a little housework, play her violin and—this was the part that seemed to be eluding her daughter—wait for a husband!

"What's so bad about waiting for a husband, my girl? Or shall a girl as pretty and educated as yourself wind up a spinster?"

"Mother, my education was obtained at great trouble and expense. I would like to finish it."

"Finish it how? There isn't a school in the city you haven't attended."

"There's university."

"God forbid! Boys go to university. If only Halim had been willing, your father would have spared no expense to send him."

"Let me do what Halim won't."

"What will you do when you graduate from university? What good will it do you?"

"It will allow me to become a teacher. I'll teach literature at the American School for Girls."

And so it went, round and round, all through Sabahat's final year of high school and the summer after her graduation. Hidden behind his newspaper just a few feet away, Reşat Bey would listen to every word, gradually becoming convinced that nothing would deter Sabahat from her ambitions. His two elder daughters were married and had not only given him a grandchild each, they continued living in the family mansion. What more could Behice want, he thought, at a time when so many wives were following their husbands from one provincial posting to another. If God had given him a clever daughter instead of a son, and if she was set on earning her own bread and butter by leading a life completely different from her sisters', then by God, he would fully support her.

One rare evening, the entire family was having dinner in the summer house: Mahir was not on duty at the hospital; Hilmi was not at his posting in the East; Sabahat was not at boarding school. Reşat Bey had seated himself between Saraylıhanım and Neyir Hanım to forestall any bickering.

"I can't remember the last time I had the pleasure of seeing you all gathered around the same dinner table. I would like to propose a toast to mark this auspicious occasion. Would anyone care to join me?" Reşat Bey said.

"If you had told me you were drinking rakı, I would have had some meze prepared," Behice said.

"I want to celebrate the sight of so many beloved faces in one place," Reşat Bey said, his eyes on a large canvas resting on the floor. The oil painting Hilmi had been working on for days—a pine-dotted island landscape under a summer sun—was finally finished and leaning against the wall next to the sideboard.

"Just look at this work of art my son-in-law has created. Let's raise a glass to him."

"Get some rakı glasses from the sideboard. You'll find a carafe in there as well," Behice instructed Nesime, who was standing by with a pitcher of water. "And tell the cook to break up a little ice."

A rakı glass was placed in front of each of the adults, with the exception of Sabahat. Back in the kitchen, Nesime opened the zinc-lined wooden cupboard, inside of which, nestled among blocks of ice, were bottles of water, a bottle of rakı, and a large bottle of sour cherry sherbet. She pulled out the rakı and asked the cook to help her chip off some ice. The rakı was decanted and borne with great ceremony into the dining room, where two fingers' worth were to be poured into the gentlemen's glasses, and half that measure into the ladies'. Saraylıhanım tugged at Nesime's arm to get more rakı as Neyir Hanım and Suat covered their glasses with their hands to signal they did not want any. Reşat Bey raised his glass.

"Let's drink to Hilmi Bey's art, and to the health and happiness of my family." He beamed, waiting for the others to join him. When Suat raised a water glass, he turned to her and said, "What's the matter, my girl? Why aren't you joining us?"

"Beyba, it would be inadvisable . . . this is not a good time," Suat stammered.

"Seeing as we are toasting the family, I would like to share some good news," Hilmi said. All eyes turned to him.

"Suat and I are expecting our second child. We wanted to wait until we were certain to tell you," Hilmi said. "Mahir Bey brought us the test results today, bless him."

Everyone jumped up and raced over to kiss Suat.

"What happened? Are we at war again?" Saraylıhanım asked.

"She's going to have a baby!" Reşat Bey shouted.

"A baby? Who? Sabahat?"

"She's not even married, you goose," Behice said.

"Married or not, has that stopped me?" Saraylıhanım persisted. "Or is it you who is having a baby?"

Neyir Hanım drew Behice aside. "Let's send Saraylıhanım to her room before she disgraces herself. This could get ugly."

"Sit down and pay her no mind, Mother. Just for tonight, let's all sit together in peace."

When the women of the family had returned to their seats, Reşat Bey raised his glass again with the words, "To my next grandchild. May this child be blessed, healthy, and of service to our nation."

The family continued the meal in a festive atmosphere, despite some bickering between its two eldest members. After the cook brought in dessert, Reşat Bey raised his glass a third time.

"You're getting tipsy," Behice objected from the opposite end of the table.

"This is the last one," Reşat Bey assured her. Rising to his feet, he said, "And this, the last of our toasts tonight, is to the university education of our youngest daughter. As her mother rejoices at the news of our new grandchild, I am certain she will consent to Sabahat's ambitions."

Silence fell over the table. Behice glared at her husband.

"Were Sabahat to earn a university diploma, she would represent the sixth generation of our family to achieve that distinction. Shall we drink to that, Behice Hanım?" he said, raising his glass in her direction.

"Reşat Bey, yet again you have acted as you see fit. Go on, down your drink," Behice said.

"Do you not consider your daughters' husbands to be your sons, Beyba?" Suat softly said, but in the commotion at the table nobody heard her.

25

Games and Deceits

In the summer following her high school graduation, Sabahat was enrolled in the School of Literature at Istanbul University in time for the upcoming academic year. She had already studied many of the great works of English literature, from Chaucer through Henry James. A bookworm, she had always devoured contemporary fiction, in both French and English, and had become acquainted with the classics of the Divan tradition under the tutelage of her sisters, benefitting greatly from the family's extensive library. University she found easy, and had she chosen to skip her classes, her grades would not have suffered. Even so, Sabahat never missed a class, not with Aram waiting at the end of her street every morning to walk with her as far as the main gate of the university.

After a few months, however, when her coursework entered particularly well-trodden ground, she began to attend the occasional lecture at the School of Chemistry, where, incidentally, she always sat next to Aram. While women comprised the majority of the students in Sabahat's department, the opposite was true in Aram's. The blond girl who sometimes sat in on lectures next to the Armenian boy did not go unnoticed. Who was this girl, also seen taking walks through the campus with Aram Balayan?

Meanwhile, Behice Hanım had not only warmed to Sabahat's university enrollment, she had begun to take pride in her daughter's academic achievements. Some female relatives had also begun attending university, and her cousin Mesure had gone so far as to gain employment at a company. Society's admiration, though grudging at first, was building toward these young women striding the streets in padded jackets and matching skirts, briefcase in hand. In any case, Behice was preoccupied with more pressing matters these days. Suat was expecting, and her mother had thrown herself into assembling baby clothes and rearranging rooms. Suat's baby could sleep in a crib in the parents' room for the first few months, but it would then need a room of its own. She couldn't put a crying baby in with Bülent. Perhaps an extension could be built out into the garden?

As Behice considered these and other questions, Leman was cultivating a friendship with the mother of Beraat, one of Sitare's classmates. Merziy'anım came of old Ottoman stock and was a keen poker player. Leman took to spending her weekends at Merziy'anım's nearby home, where she became an instant success with the genteel circle of cardsharps eying each other over green felt. When it was Leman's turn to host the poker parties, vast quantities of sponge cake and tea scones were prepared for the guests, just like in the old days, and Hüsnü Efendi was sent by streetcar all the way to Lebon for chocolate cake.

Beraat was the youngest of Merziy'anım's five children. Her eldest son, Ekmel, was three years older than Sabahat. When Leman learned that Ekmel was single and had been educated in Germany, she sprang into action. A way had to be found to introduce Ekmel to Sabahat.

The first person to learn of Leman's plan was Suat, whose initial reaction was, "No matter who you find, Sabahat won't be interested. Instead of raising Mother's hopes, only to dash them later, why not approach Sabahat directly and ask her if she's willing to meet this Ekmel of yours?"

"She'll never agree. We'll have to orchestrate something."

"How? What will we say? 'Merziy'anım, our sister is terribly timid. Help us lure her into a meeting with your son'?"

"Merziy'anım thinks the world of Sabahat. They were introduced last year by her eldest daughter, Bedia, who, it turns out, was classmates with Sabahat. Ah, if only Halim would straighten himself out, we could introduce him to Bedia."

"One thing at a time, please. I know you don't believe me, but Sabahat's friendship with Aram is going to end badly. Mark my words, she'll bring disgrace on the family. Let's put our heads together before it's too late."

"We'll need Mother's help. There's strength in numbers. I've decided to tell her about Merziy'anım's son tonight."

"Good."

Behice had begun losing hope in her youngest daughter. Previously introduced and rejected in turn had been a string of eligible bachelors, including Münif Pasha's middle grandson, a few young officer friends of Hilmi's, the engineer Ferruh Bey, and two doctors rustled up by Mahir Bey. It was only natural that Behice would take a dim view of this latest candidate's prospects. Leman, however, remained determined as ever. This one was different, she claimed. A modern young man with a German education was certain to appeal to Sabahat.

Several hours of scheming resulted in what seemed like a sure-fire plan. They would hold a birthday party for Sitare, who had been clamoring for one anyway, having attended many for her non-Muslim school friends. Sabahat would want to be present at her niece's fifteenth birthday celebration. Sitare had been born in June, which meant the party could be held in the garden of the house on the island, starting at three in the afternoon! They'd plant violets on both sides of the pathway leading to the house. The wicker furniture was a bit worn, but the party would be a good excuse to renew it.

"What are you three getting so excited about?" Sabahat asked, silencing the three women, who were looking at her like children caught red-handed.

"We were thinking of arranging a birthday party for Sitare when she turns fifteen. Out on the island. What do you think, Sabahat?"

"Great. Whose idea was it?"

When the three women said, "Mine," in unison, Sabahat burst out laughing.

"Clearly, none of you came up with this wonderful idea. It was Sitare herself who asked for a party, wasn't it? She's been going to these kinds of occasions for years. It's high time she had one of her own."

"You found out us out; really, Sabahat, you're far too clever for us," Behice Hanım said. "Now, let's draw up a list of guests to invite."

"Mother, Sitare's birthday is still ages away," Sabahat said.

"The intervening months will pass in the blink of an eye," Behice Hanım said, secretly hoping that in the blink of an eye she would be presiding over an engagement ceremony for Sabahat and Ekmel.

26
Ambushed

It was early spring in Istanbul. The roses were budding, and the apple trees were flowering. The muddy palette peculiar to the winter months was yielding to the magenta of the Judas tree. Within two weeks, or three at the most, wildflowers would swarm the hillsides, and wisteria would drape the garden walls in clusters of amethyst. Ah, city of peony and lilac! On this fine morning, Sabahat, who was outside in the garden, musing on the miracle of spring, was going not to her lectures, but to a seminar given by a chemistry professor from Germany. Thanks to Aram, she had developed a passion for chemistry. Sometimes she wondered what her father would say if she decided to major in chemistry once she had earned a degree in literature. Sabahat breathed in the sweet-smelling air and skipped over to the garden gate, graceful as a gazelle.

Aram was waiting at their corner. As he took her textbooks and notepads, he said, "I thought you weren't going to your classes today."

"I'm going to the one after lunch. We're analyzing Jane Austen today. You know how much I love her. If you're free, why don't you come along?"

"I'll do that."

"Oh, Aram, before I forget to tell you. My family seems to be getting more and more modern. They've decided to throw a birthday party for Sitare. Can you believe it?"

"When? This weekend?"

"No, it's not until June, but they're so eager they've begun drawing up the guest list. Perhaps we could surprise them."

"What kind of surprise?"

"We could deck out the house in balloons, or buy some new records. I don't know, let's think of something different."

Chatting away, they had reached Divanyolu and were walking toward Laleli when several young men blocked their path before allowing them to pass.

"Do you think they'll invite me, too?" Aram asked.

Before Sabahat could answer, the same four young men were standing in front of them again.

"What are you doing?" Aram asked.

"You talking to me, monsieur?"

Aram was taken aback. This was the first time anyone had addressed him that way.

Tugging at Aram's arm, Sabahat led him to the pavement on the opposite side of the street. "Never mind. They probably saw my blond hair and thought I was a foreigner," Sabahat said. "That's probably why they called you 'monsieur.' Don't get mixed up with that pack of stray dogs."

They hadn't walked ten paces before their path was blocked again.

"Where are you off to, chatterboxes?" one of the men asked.

"Mind you own business," Sabahat said.

"We asked nice, give us a nice answer," the man said.

"My answer is this: it doesn't concern you," Sabahat said.

"Wait, stay out of this," Aram said, moving in front of Sabahat. "What is it, brother? What do you want to know?"

"Where you're going."

"To the School of Chemistry."

"Where's the girl going?"

"We're going to the same place."

The men were crowding Sabahat and Aram into the hall of an apartment building.

"What's it to you where I'm going?" Sabahat said.

"It's a lot to us! Aren't you, a Muslim girl, ashamed to be seen out with this germ of an Armenian?"

"You dog!" Sabahat cried.

"Sabahat, go home!" Aram yelled. She shoved one of the men, trying to reach Aram's side. The other three had him by the throat, both arms pinned behind his back.

"Let go of my friend this instant, you dogs!"

"I'm warning you, you keep talking like that, and I won't care if you're a Muslim or a girl."

"Let him go, I said!"

"I think *you* should let him go, pretty girl." One of the guys grinned.

"Brother, what do want you from me? She and I have been friends for years. We're neighbors. Let us go," Aram said, his patience wearing thin.

Sabahat began kicking one of the guys twisting Aram's arm. "You lowlifes! You dogs! What do you want from us?" One of the guys clamped a hand over Sabahat's mouth. A knife blade flashed silver.

"Run Sabahat," Aram yelled. "For God's sake, run!"

Sabahat rushed at the guy with the knife, but a different one grabbed her braid, which had fallen free, and threw her out of the apartment building. He closed the door. Sabahat pounded on it with her fists. She pressed her face against the frosted glass and tried to look inside. All she could see in the gloom were shifting shadows. She ran out onto the pavement and begged a few passersby to help her. Nobody was willing to risk being late to work or school. Hair in disarray, tears running down her cheeks, Sabahat began running toward the police station near her house. She stopped midway. They would take her statement and find out she was Ahmet Reşat Bey's daughter. The police would probably summon him. She changed her mind. She would go home and ask Hüsnü Efendi or one of her brothers-in-law to help. Would they be at home? Perhaps she could call Şahber Hanım's son, Naci? No, he lived all the way out in Beyoğlu.

A panic-stricken Sabahat slumped through the garden gate she had so joyously exited a short time earlier. She paused in the garden for a moment to catch her breath before ringing the doorbell. She could hear Nesime shuffling to the door. Nesime flung it open.

"Oh my goodness! What happened, young miss?"

Sabahat threw herself into Nesime's arms and began sobbing.

"Leman Hanım! Suat Hanım! Come quick!"

"Shh. Please don't shout, Nesime," Sabahat begged the servant. It was too late. The women of the house were all rushing headlong into the entrance hall.

"What happened to you, my dear?" Behice said, pulling Sabahat out of Nesime's arms and into her own.

"Let me wash my face, and I'll tell you," Sabahat said, walking over to the small bathroom of the entrance hall. She looked at her wretched face in the mirror. What should she tell them? She considered telling the truth, then decided that would lead to too many questions. She splashed water on her face and pinned up her plait. After smoothing her hair and drying her eyes, she left the bathroom.

Her mother and sisters, Saraylıhanım, Grandma, the housekeeper, and Hüsnü Efendi stood in a line, awaiting an explanation.

"They stole my money," she said.

"Where?"

"As I was walking to school."

"Those filthy purse snatchers!" Leman cried. "They didn't hurt you, did they? You should have given them whatever they wanted. It's worse if you resist."

"I knew something like this would happen!" her mother said. "Girls have no business going to university!"

"What happened?" Grandma asked.

"Purse snatchers. Purse snatchers, Mother. They robbed Sabahat."

"Purse what?" Grandma asked. Saraylıhanım was murmuring an Istanbul folk song. Lifting her arms, she danced a little jig.

"How much did they steal?" Suat asked.

"Not much."

"Well then, why are you crying?"

"The poor girl was scared!" Leman said. "Come on up to my room, and I'll put some rubbing alcohol on your hands and arms. Those thieves must have pawed you."

The army of women slowly headed for the stairs.

"Aren't you coming?" Behice asked Sabahat, who was still standing in the entrance hall. "You had quite a scare today. Stay in until evening. Don't go to any lessons."

"I'm going to make myself a nice cup of coffee. It will calm me down."

"Nesime will make it for you."

Ignoring her mother, Sabahat went into the kitchen and paced for a few moments without touching the tea housekeeper Gülfidan had forced on her. Her thoughts with Aram, she made a cup of coffee. He had gone back home, she supposed, and was stewing there in a terrible temper.

Suat was the only one to hear the front door shut with a soft click. "That girl's an absolute loon," she muttered to herself. "When is she going to shape up?"

Rebeka's astonished face appeared in the doorway of No. 7 Kumbaracı Street.

"Won't you come in, Sabahat Hanım?" she asked.

"Is Aram at home?"

Rebeka stepped aside and motioned for Sabahat to come in. Having been to the house several times before, Sabahat walked directly into the living room, followed by Rebeka.

"Sabahat Hanım, why have they done this to my son?"

"I don't know. Would you please tell Aram I'm here?"

"I will, but he shouldn't get up. He's recovering in bed."

"Oh no! Is he hurt?"

"Come and see for yourself," Rebeka said. They walked down a hallway. Rebeka opened a door and stepped aside. Aram was propped up against a few pillows, the right side of his face puffy, one eye closed. His left arm was resting on a pillow, the fingers swollen to the size of sausages.

"Aram, what have they done to you!" Sabahat screamed. He turned toward the door and tried to sit up straight, grimacing in pain.

"Are you all right, Sabahat?" he managed to ask.

"Are you in pain, Aram?"

"A bit. Don't worry. It'll pass."

"What do you mean, it'll pass? How will it pass? What if you have a broken nose or a cracked head?" Rebeka said, her face pale and grim.

"I'm fine, Mayrik. I'm fine."

"The doctor will decide if you're fine."

"Have you called a doctor?" Sabahat asked.

"He's on the way."

"Why, Mother?"

"Madame Rebeka, I can bring my brother-in-law over this evening. He can give Aram a full examination."

"We have a family doctor, a good one. Don't trouble yourself."

"Could I wait here until the doctor comes?" Sabahat asked. "Is anything broken? I need to know."

"There's nothing you can do," Rebeka said, coldly.

"Then I'll come back this evening." She went over to Aram and took his right hand, wanting to bring it to her lips, but, under the eagle eye of his mother, she settled for a gentle squeeze.

"I hope you get well soon, Aram. I'll be back." Leaning closer, Sabahat whispered, "I'll visit every day until you're better."

She followed Rebeka to the front door, now open. "Were you with Aram when he was attacked?"

Sabahat looked at Rebeka without saying a word.

"You'll pay dearly for this friendship of yours. Both of you," Rebeka said.

"I don't understand."

"You must understand. What happened to him today could happen to you tomorrow. Don't walk together anymore."

"But Aram and I have been friends for years, and nothing like this has ever happened."

"Our country is changing. Besides, you were just children."

"Will you let me visit him?"

"I'd rather you didn't."

Sabahat nearly gave in to the impulse to embrace Rebeka, whose eyes were swimming with tears, but Rebeka took a step backward and folded her arms.

"I'm sorry," Sabahat said. "I'm so sorry." She stepped outside. The door shut. Her own tears didn't come until several minutes later.

Rebeka returned to her son's bedroom and sat down next to him on the bed. "Aram," she said, "there are some things I need to tell you. I wish I had done it earlier, but you were a boy, and when you grew up, and I knew you would be living in this country, I decided it would be better if you didn't know. I see now that I made a mistake."

"Mayrik, please. I know, more or less, what you're about to say," Aram said. "My whole body aches . . . This isn't a good time."

"This is precisely the right time."

Perched on the edge of her son's bed, Rebeka talked for three hours as Aram listened, at times tearful, at times nauseous, at times recoiling from this long lament for the dead and the lost. It was a tale of horror, violence, and slaughter. Armenian men had been torn from their homes, never to see their wives, their children, and their mothers again. It was a story of wailing Armenian girls and children searching the roads for their missing families, many of them taken into the homes of Turkish families, adopted, and converted to Islam; scattered families, scorched homes, confiscated properties, broken hearts, and, yes, severed heads, rotting corpses, the Hamidiye cavalry, Ottoman soldiers, blood, tears, and pain. She talked until her mouth was dry, until no more tears could come, until she was drained. And now, having unburdened to her son the weight on her shoulders and the pain in her heart, she fell silent and felt devastated. For a few moments, neither mother nor son spoke, each of them turning inward, not to their thoughts but to the sound of their own hearts. Then Rebeka reached out, gently rested Aram's wounded hand on the palm of her own hand, and softly asked, "Now do you understand, Aram, why you should stay away from that girl?"

"Mother, what does any of that have to do with Sabahat?"

27

A Cracked Head

Taking advantage of a lull in the dinner table chatter, Behice carefully chose her words as she floated the idea of holding a banquet on the island to mark Sitare's fifteenth year.

"We already hold banquets every blessed summer day," Reşat Bey said. "All our relatives come to stay, feasts are prepared, we dine for hours on end, and music is played. What's the difference between your banquet and the ones we already have?"

"This one will be held in honor of Sitare, to celebrate her birthday. She's been attending parties for her friends for years now and always brings them presents. I thought it would be nice to hold a party for her, just this once."

"A birthday party! I don't want to hear anything about birthday parties. They're for infidels! We always give the children gifts on Bairam, new clothes and shoes for everyone, even the household staff. We don't need to invent new excuses for gift giving."

"But Beyba, Sitare has her heart set on a party," Leman said.

"It doesn't mat—" was as far as Sitare got before a pinch under the table silenced her.

"But everyone is doing it these days," Leman said. "I don't want my girl to feel left out. There's nothing wrong with having a party. We'll invite just a handful of her friends, Beraat and a few others, and some of the relatives we haven't seen in a long time. It would be a good occasion to have Hilmi's sister and his nephews over. We'll have a nice day, all together. And they'll bring Sitare lots of nice gifts. You'd like that, wouldn't you, dear?" Leman asked.

Sitare clapped her hands. "Yes, yes, I want to have a birthday party."

"You've already made up your minds. Why are you asking me?" Reşat Bey sighed. He turned to his youngest daughter, who hadn't spoken once, and asked, "Is anything the matter, Sabahat?"

"I'm a little upset. You know Aram, the children's tutor?"

"Yes?"

"He was attacked on the street. They beat him up badly."

"What?"

"He might have a cracked skull. I was going to ask Mahir if we could go and check on him after dinner. They live nearby."

"That's terrible! I wonder why they did it. Did he recognize his assailants?"

"I don't know."

"Find out and let me know. I'll have a word with the chief of police. We can't stand by as these bandits roam free."

Everyone began talking at once. Suat turned to Sabahat, who was seated next to her, and in a low voice asked, "Is there any connection between your purse snatcher and what happened to Aram?"

"Of course not," Sabahat said, just as Mahir rose from the table and said, "I'm finished with my dinner. Tell me where the boy's house is and I'll go straight there."

"I'm coming with you."

"You most certainly are not!" Suat told Sabahat. "Not at this time of night. Mahir Bey can go on his own."

"Your sister is right," Reşat Bey agreed.

"I'll go downstairs with you and give you directions," Sabahat said.

The garret windows in Sabahat's bedroom were too high to allow a view of the garden gate, so Sabahat stood on a chair in front of the window, ears near the rafters, listening. When she heard the clang of the garden gate, she rushed down to the entrance hall and sat on the stairs, waiting for Mahir to finish washing his hands in the small bathroom.

"You scared me," Mahir said when she stood up in the shadowy stairwell.

"How is he? Did he hurt his head? Is he in pain?"

"Aram is fine. There are no fractures in his skull. If anyone has a cracked head, it's you, Sabahat."

"Please tell me the truth. Is he really okay?"

"Their family doctor had already taken an x-ray. Other than some contusions and bruising, he's fine. He'll make a full recovery."

"Oh, thank God!

"Why are you so worried, Sabahat? Tell me what really happened. I won't repeat it to anyone."

"We were walking along the street on our way to the university when four or five men blocked our path. They pushed Aram into the hallway of an apartment building and beat him up. I ran away."

"They didn't say anything?"

"They said something about a Turkish girl walking with an Armenian."

"Don't walk with him anymore, Sabahat."

"But why? How can this happen in a civilized country?"

"Who told you this was a civilized country? Wise up, little sister. Next time, they'll rough you up, too. Give this up before it's too late."

"What's that supposed to mean?"

"I mean, stop being so obstinate. Please, Sabahat, listen to me. Don't ever go walking with him again."

Leaving Sabahat in the dark stairwell, Mahir began climbing the stairs. He stopped, turned, and said, "If I were you, I wouldn't visit his house, either. Don't worry, he'll be fine, but it's better you don't see his face right now."

Sabahat heaved a sigh of relief. Madame Rebeka must not have told Mahir Sabahat had been at their house that very day!

Ten days later, Aram was back in his classes, the swelling gone, the purple bruises faded to a brownish-yellow. For a time, Sabahat and Aram did not walk together.

One Saturday afternoon, they were waiting with a group of their friends for a streetcar to take them to the cinema in Beyoğlu. It was drizzling. Sabahat was about to unfurl her umbrella when she heard the streetcar approaching. Armine leaned forward and peered at the street. By the time she said, "It's the one that goes to Karaköy," Aram had already leapt onto the slowing car.

"Hey, that's the wrong one," Sabahat called out.

"What a pity!" a male voice said.

Sabahat turned to her right and recognized the face smirking at her. Without thinking, she raised her umbrella high into the air and brought it down with a whack on the head of one of Aram's assailants. Armine and everyone else gathered at the streetcar stop began screaming and shouting. Wide-eyed, the man clutched his head with both hands and lurched toward her.

"What the hell's going on?" he shouted.

"He assaulted me!" Sabahat screeched. "Help!"

"She's lying," the young man protested as the crowd closed in on him.

"Why would she lie?" an elderly gentleman demanded to know. "She wouldn't hit you with her umbrella unless you had done something. You shameless rascal! You impudent guttersnipe!"

As the young man fled the scene, he shouted, "You'll regret this, lady!"

"Of all the nerve, threatening the poor girl still!" the elderly gentleman said, shaking his head.

"Sir, you saw what happened. If he does try to harm me, might I rely on you to make a statement to the police?" Sabahat asked. "This is not the first time he has threatened me."

"I'll be of service any way I can," the man said, pulling a business card out of his wallet and handing it to Sabahat.

Sabahat and her friends waited in vain at the entrance to the cinema that day. When the gong sounded, they rushed into the theater, but she was far more conscious of the empty seat next to her than anything that was happening on the flickering screen.

On Monday, Sabahat waited in front of the School of Chemistry. When Aram saw her, he hunched slightly and looked around, only then coming up to her.

"I was worried about you, Aram. You never showed up at the cinema Saturday. Did something happen?"

"No," Aram said. "Perhaps it's best that we aren't seen together these days."

"Are we going to surrender to them? Who are they? What do they want from us? Why should we be more afraid of them than of our own families?"

"Because our families don't know anything."

"I think your mother knows, Aram. She wasn't at all friendly the day I visited you."

"She suspects something, nothing more. I keep denying it."

"Are we going to deny our love for the rest of our lives?"

"Remember what we decided? Until I'm able to stand on my own two feet, we'll deny our love. Once I'm making a living, we'll shout it from the rooftops. We won't care what they do or say. We'll go somewhere else if we have to. But what would you do if your father threw you out of the house now?"

"I'd go to Mehpare's house."

"Be patient, darling," Aram said. "Now, go to your classes, and let's be more careful."

"I don't care who sees us together."

"Sabahat, what would I do if they hit you? I couldn't bear it, and neither could you. Go on, off to your class you go. We'll be meeting at Piraye's tea party this weekend. We can talk there."

"Will we be meeting at the streetcar stop like always?"

"I can't put you in danger. We'll go separately."

Sabahat looked into Aram's eyes. They held hands for a brief moment before Aram gently pulled his away. Sabahat walked off with a drooping head and a heavy heart.

The following day she left home with the bag of heavy books Aram normally carried, and, as she was approaching their corner, she was astonished to see . . . Aram's mother!

"Madame Rebeka?"

"Sabahat Hanım, I'd like to walk with you to the university today."

"Has Aram sent you?"

"I came on my own initiative. They beat Aram up again yesterday. He's in the hospital."

Sabahat clutched Rebeka's arm for support. "Which hospital?" she whispered.

"I'm not telling you."

"I'll search every hospital in the city."

"You would be making a terrible mistake. Next time, they'll kill my son. I'm begging you, please give Aram up," Rebeka said, nearly in tears. "This can only end in tragedy. For now, they're content to batter him. Soon, they'll do the same to you. Both your people and mine."

"There's no such thing as 'your people and mine,' Madame Rebeka. We're not at war. We're one people. Please."

"We'll never be one people. Never!"

"How is Aram? What have they done?"

"He has a broken nose and a few broken fingers. Don't worry, he'll survive. He'll get better, but if you keep seeing each other, he will end up dead one day. As a mother, I'm begging you. If you love my son, have mercy on him."

"Even if I give him up, he'll never agree to give me up."

"You'll give each other up. You have no choice. Aram told me to tell you not to wait for him in front of his school building. Don't send your brother-in-law this time. We'll take care of this on our own."

"I have to see Aram. Please."

"If you keep persisting, I won't be responsible for what they do to you."

"They? Who are 'they'?"

"Aram has friends. He has relatives and a community who will protect him."

Rebeka pulled a folded sheet of paper out of her handbag and handed it to Sabahat. "Here, Aram wrote you this letter."

Sabahat began reading it. "Whose handwriting is this?"

"Mine. My son can't hold a pen right now."

Rebeka walked off. Sabahat folded the letter and slipped it into her blouse. When Rebeka had disappeared from view, she pulled it out and began reading.

> *Dear Sabahat,*
> *I'm in bad shape this time. I can't even write. Don't worry, I'll get better. Please don't try to see me again. I'm afraid of what they'll do to you. This can only end in tragedy. Let's treasure forever the sweet memories of our days together as we go our separate ways. I never wanted this to happen, but we have no choice. You deserve only*

the best. I wish you, from the bottom of my heart, a long
and happy life. May God watch over you.
Love,

Aram

Sabahat folded the letter and slipped it back into her blouse. The next time she met with Aram, she would read it aloud to him, and they would laugh together at Rebeka's attempt to pass off her own letter as her son's.

28

The Birthday Party

The south-facing main gate was festooned with colorful balloons, and, just as envisioned by Leman, violets lined both sides of the pathway leading up to the island house. String-drawn pouches containing little gifts for all the children dangled from the branches of the almond tree. Below a green canopy of vines, the banquet table looked out over the sea. On the table rested an enormous vase overflowing with hydrangea blossoms Sabahat had cut that morning. Pale purple napkins, starched and pressed, were neatly spaced on the white tablecloth. Leman and Suat's sisters-in-law—Şahber Hanım and Pakize Hanım, respectively— were there with their broods. Leman's dear friend, Sabiha Hanım, had brought her sons, Necdet and Sedat, and her newest dear friend, Merziy'anım, had brought her eldest son, Ekmel, and two of her daughters, Bedia and Beraat. A visibly pregnant Suat, assisted by Mehpare, raced here and there, busy with last-minute preparations. Feeling a little out of place, Halim had taken a chair to a quiet corner of the garden.

"Halim, what are you doing here all by yourself, son?" Reşat Bey asked.

"I don't know any of Leman's friends."

"How can you say that? You've met Şahber Hanım's children, haven't you?"

"I'm talking about the tall one."

"That gentlewoman is the mother of Sitare's classmate, Beraat. You never visit us anymore. It's no wonder you can't keep track of the family friends."

Halim glumly stared at the ground.

"What are you doing these days, son? I heard you quit school."

"I'm going to take a correspondence course."

"Why would you do that?"

"I don't like having my tuition paid by Galip Bey."

"Son, why didn't you tell me earlier?" Reşat Bey asked in all sincerity. "I would gladly have assumed the costs of your education and had been doing so until your mother insisted I stop. I wish I'd known."

"Don't let it upset you. I wasn't a very good student. I don't like going to school. I want to work and earn a living."

"In this day and age, what positions are available to a young man without a high school degree?

"I'm going to get a cab and medallion. A used cab, of course."

"Where will you get the money to buy a cab?"

"I'm saving up."

"How?"

"By working, sir."

"You've found a position somewhere? Where, Halim?"

"Behind the wheel of a cab."

"Hold on. Are you telling me you've become a driver?"

"Yes."

There was a long silence. Reşat Bey's shoulders visibly slumped. His beloved Halim, whose welfare Kemal had entrusted to him, and whom he had hoped to educate at one of the now-defunct imperial high schools, was driving a cab. A nephew of the chancellor of the exchequer was a cabdriver. They would think that he, Reşat Bey, had begrudged his nephew an education! An ironic smile played across his lips as he thought, *Who knows, perhaps Halim is making more as a cabdriver than I ever earned back in the days when civil servants, the military, and even top state officials went unpaid for months on end.* He cleared his throat before he spoke again. "Does your mother know?"

"No. She'd be upset if she found out."

Reşat Bey hesitated before he said, "Stop by the bank at the beginning of next week, and we'll discuss this further. I can secure you the funds to buy your own cab."

"I'll stop by on my lunch break Monday, sir."

"All right Halim, now off you go. Mingle a little with your relatives instead of hiding out behind the bushes." As Reşat Bey pointed with his chin in the direction of the guests, his eye landed on his granddaughter.

Fragile as a wildflower in her ruffled lilac party dress, Sitare was not quite a young woman, but certainly no child. She was tall for her age, and the short, girly hemline insisted on by her mother exposed her long legs, so that as she wandered about, her grandfather was reminded of a self-conscious stork.

A waltz began playing on the gramophone. Naci encircled Sabahat's waist with his arm and began twirling her around the paved courtyard in front of the dining room.

"May I have this dance, young lady?"

Sitare turned around and looked at her father. "But I don't know how to waltz," she said.

"Then I'll teach you." As Mahir lifted his daughter's right hand and clasped her waist, he was amazed at how tall she had grown. "When did my little girl get so big?"

"While I was sleeping, I suppose," Sitare said. And with a one-two-three, two-two-three, they were off, moving forward and backward. "Did I step on your foot?" Mahir asked.

"No!" Sitare said. She would have been happy to waltz with her father until dawn. Her dearest father, whom she loved more than anyone in the world, protected her from her germaphobic mother's worst excesses.

"Dad, can we do the Charleston next, just like old times?"

"Hey, Naci, play us something we can do the Charleston to," Mahir called out to his nephew, who was now lounging under a tree with his accordion. When the first notes rang out, Beraat, Fazilet, Hüviyet, Naci's fiancée, Melek, and all the other young men and women came rushing into the courtyard from the lawn. Mahir stood in the middle, a bit rusty perhaps, but still managing to cut quite a rug as everyone sang, "Waiter, bring me a beer," in place of "Yes sir, that's my baby."

"Leman," Mahir called out to his wife, "come join us!"

"You all can barely fit in that courtyard as it is," she said. She was clucking to herself and thinking her husband was likely to break his neck or have a heart attack when Bülent got tangled up in his own feet, fell to the ground, skinning his knee, and burst into tears.

"Kids shouldn't dance," Sitare sniffed.

"I'll show you," Bülent said. "Give me until evening." Hoping to make Sitare jealous, he began dancing with Betül, a girl her age.

When everyone had finally had enough of the Charleston and Naci's accordion playing, Suat put a tango on the gramophone. Ekmel wasted no time in approaching Sabahat to ask, "Would you care to dance with me, Sabahat Hanım?"

Suat held her breath. *Yes,* she thought, *Ekmel and Sabahat are dancing!* She found Leman's eyes, and the two sisters exchanged a knowing glance.

"*Sevdim bir genç kadını* . . . I loved a young woman . . ." As Sabahat danced with Ekmel, she sang along to the popular Turkish tango.

"Your voice is lovely," Ekmel said.

Sabahat leaned back slightly and looked at Ekmel. The young man she was dancing with was tall and good-looking.

"Please don't!" she said. "Insincerity leaves me cold."

"Are you telling me you don't think you have a lovely voice?"

"Don't push your luck, Ekmel. You know just as well as I do that our mothers arranged for us to meet."

"I didn't know that, but even if it is the case, do you object to having met me?"

"You don't need to pay me compliments."

"Had I met you somewhere, without the involvement of our mothers, I still would have asked you to dance, and I still would have complimented you."

"Why?"

"Because I like you. You're just the sort of young lady I was hoping to meet. Intelligent, full of personality, educated!"

"I like you, too. You're good-looking and outspoken. Can I tell you a secret so you'll stop wasting your time? Ekmel, will you keep my secret to yourself?"

"Of course I will."

"You have absolutely no chance of becoming my fiancé or my beau. If you wish, we could become good friends, though."

"That's better than nothing, but why must we remain just friends?"

"The answer to that question is the secret I asked you to keep: I'm in love with someone."

"Who?"

"Someone who isn't here today. Someone I have loved for years, and will love forever."

"I envy him. Where is he right now?"

Sabahat stopped dancing. Slipping her arm into Ekmel's, she said, "Ekmel, what I need right now is a friend, someone I can trust. Let's go sit down on those chairs over there, and I'll explain."

Arms cradled in front of her belly, Suat worked her way through the tangoing couples and darting children, reached Leman, tapped her sister's arm, and motioned with her eyes to Ekmel and Sabahat, who were walking toward the arbor. Leman tapped her fingers on the wooden table in front of her. Suat then pointed to another young couple. Over behind a fig tree, Mahir's nephew, twenty-year-old Necdet, was pulling something out of his pocket. He gave it to Sitare, who gave him a kiss on the cheek. Leman stared for a moment in disbelief before she rushed over. She shuddered to think what Mahir would do if he saw their little girl.

"What are you two doing here?"

Necdet blushed, but Sitare smiled nonchalantly and showed her mother the postcards in her hand: Jean Harlow, Ida Lupino, Claudette Colbert. "Necdet is selling me pictures of movie stars for a kiss apiece," Sitare said.

"What!"

"Each time he gives me a postcard, I give him a kiss. Mother, I can't wait to show the girls when school starts!"

"Necdet! You should be ashamed of yourself. You're old enough to know better."

Necdet was too embarrassed to look at her. "Auntie, it was just a peck on the cheek. I swear it!"

"If I catch you doing something like this again, I shall speak to your father. Now, take your postcards and get out of my sight."

"You mean I kissed him for nothing? I'm not giving my pictures back to him!" Sitare shouted. As Leman lunged for the postcards, scattering them on the ground, Necdet turned tail and ran.

"Sitare, you're no longer a child. You can't kiss boys like that."

"He's my cousin, and I only kissed him on the cheek. The pictures are wonderful, Mother. Beraat is collecting them, too. Now I have all the best ones."

"Are you listening to me? You've grown up. Even if he is your cousin, and it was only on the cheek . . . wait, what do you mean *only* on the cheek? Where else could you have kissed him?"

"On the lips. I've seen them kissing on the lips in the movies. Haven't you?"

"Sitare, don't make me give you a good smack on your birthday. From now on, you are forbidden to kiss boys."

"Even Bülent?"

"That's enough, Sitare! Yes, I'll make it easy for you. Yes, even Bülent. You've grown up!"

"If I've really grown up, Mother, stop dressing me in these short dresses. They make me feel like a little girl."

Ten days later, Ekmel and Sabahat were sitting across from each other in Patisserie Lebon drinking tea and talking when Sabahat burst out laughing.

"These low chairs are fine for me, Ekmel, but your knees are level with your ears," she said, at which he laughed, too.

"I'm glad we had a good laugh," he said, "because you're not going to like what I'm about to tell you."

"Tell me."

"I waited in front of the School of Chemistry, just like you said, looking at the photograph you gave me and checking the entrance. Aram never came. I went inside and found his lecture hall. I asked around and nobody had heard of him. Finally, someone told me that Aram Balayan had dropped out. I asked why, and the guy said he got sick or something. Oh, Sabahat! If I'd known you'd start crying, I wouldn't have told you."

"Now you'll have to go to his house."

"Where is it?"

"I'll show you. Have you got the letter with you?"

"Yes."

"Good. His mother will answer the door. Don't tell him you're from the university. Say you're an old friend from high school, that you're organizing a class reunion, or make something else up."

"What if she won't let me in?"

"She will. But remember to say you're a friend from high school. Come on, let's pay the bill and go." They tussled over the bill, and Ekmel ended up paying for them both. After taking the funicular to Karaköy, they boarded a streetcar that stopped a short walk from Aram's house. When they reached the top of his street, Sabahat said, "Turn left; it's the eighth door, right next to the grocer's. I'll wait for you here. Take as long as you need. Don't worry about me."

"I must be mad," Ekmel said.

"No, you're not mad. You're the best, most understanding friend in the world."

Shaking his head in disbelief at what he was about to do, Ekmel reluctantly walked down the street and found the house next to the grocer's.

29

Red Fish

Holding a paper bag full of the personal items that had not fit into his briefcase, Muhittin walked from city hall to Kızılay Square, where he ended up on a park bench watching a school of fish, frenzied and flashing red in the ornamental pool. The fish darted here and there, suddenly, inexplicably, dashing back to where they had started. *Not unlike me and my career path,* he reflected. *Where do I go now?* He had defied the governor, who did not take kindly to being rebuffed. Muhittin repeatedly reviewed in his mind every word of the heated exchange that had just taken place, and each time, he decided he could not have acted differently.

Would Semiha learn what had transpired between Muhittin and her uncle? *Should I call her and explain?* He rejected the idea at once. She would feel humiliated. Semiha was a sweet-natured, well-bred young lady who had done nothing to deserve this. Muhittin felt a twinge of regret at the thought of never seeing her again. If the governor had not come down on him quite so hard, perhaps they would have been married one day, and his respect would have turned to love. "That fool-ish man!" he muttered to himself. "If only he hadn't threatened me!"

Or was he the foolish one? He began to think so as he walked to Çankaya, increasingly despondent and out of breath. An hour ago, he had been the municipality's chief engineer; now he was nothing. At the end of the month, Muhittin, "tall as a fence post," would have to borrow from his big brother to pay the rent. He had heard his mother use the term "tall as a fence post" so often that he couldn't help smiling. Well, he was not merely a big boy but a fully grown man, and one without a job. As he passed a shopwindow, he looked at his reflection and said, "All grown up and nothing to show for it."

How did one go about finding a job? By listing one's qualifications in the employment section of a newspaper? By distributing CVs to the various departments of the Ministry of Public Works? By knocking on the office doors of acquaintances? There was the distinct possibility that the spiteful governor would stymie his every effort. Well then, he would go to Istanbul and seek employment in the private sector. He would build apartment buildings and houses for the wealthy. He tried to swallow the lump in his throat. He hadn't studied engineering all those years in order to build houses for rich people! Had that been the case, he would never have left his family, his home, and his city, would never have come to Ankara and settled for a civil servant's salary. He had become an engineer to spread light, to bring water to the thirsty, to build housing for the homeless, to blaze roads to the most inhospitable and impoverished corners of his country. And what had he done? He had escorted the governor's niece to the cinema, squired her to the races, and visited her at her mother's home! And by doing so, he had unwit-tingly destroyed his future, his ideals, and his dreams. Muhittin turned on his heel and hurried back toward the square. Noon was approaching. He would walk to Ulus and have lunch at Karpiç. The money in his pocket today would be gone tomorrow, but after a nice meal and a glass of wine, he would be able to go home with a full belly and an improved outlook on life. It would be some time before he dined at a restaurant again, and so be it! And when he got home, he would have a nap, wake up refreshed, and ponder his future with a clear head.

Muhittin stepped into Karpiç, still clutching his paper bag and a little early for lunch. Patrons were seated at only a couple of the tables. He took a table and was about to signal to the waiter when a hand clapped him on the back.

"Ah, Muammer!" he said. "I didn't see you."

"I'm at a table in the back with friends. Come and join us, Muhittin."

"I'm afraid I'm in no mood for company. I'd hate to spoil your fun."

"Is something wrong? I hope you haven't received bad news from home."

"I resigned this morning."

"What?" Muammer said, gaping at his friend as though he couldn't imagine anything worse. "Let me guess: you had a row with the governor."

"You could call it that."

"Oh no, Muhittin! Just between us, that guy's trouble. Still, he doesn't normally interfere with the technical side of things."

"I'll fill you in on all the details later. You'd better get back to your friends."

"Come and visit me this evening."

"You know what, I'll do that."

"What are you going to do next?"

"Look for a job, I guess." Muhittin shrugged.

Muammar returned to his table. Muhittin found that he had lost his appetite. Everyone would be asking him why he had resigned. What would he tell them? He couldn't mention Semiha; it wouldn't be right to drag her name into this. He couldn't blame it on his colleagues, either. Perhaps it was best to hint at a falling-out with the governor and leave it at that. Yes, that's what he would do. Of course, he had no idea what the governor would say if pressed. If the governor slandered Muhittin in any way, he would file suit, and he would lose. The prime minister and president were the only men in Ankara with sufficient influence to win a court case against someone so powerful.

Muhittin realized a waiter was standing at his table.

"I am terribly sorry. I just realized I have some urgent business and will have to leave." As Muhittin walked out of the restaurant, Muammer looked on worriedly.

Outside, Muhittin breathed in the dry air of the Anatolian steppe and was sorry he had never taken up smoking. His brother would have gone through over a pack by now, finding solace in each inhalation. He decided to go the post office and phone Nusret, the only person to whom he could confide the details of his resignation—not that he would be able to speak freely within the echoing walls of the post office. The sound of his brother's voice would be comforting and so would any news from home. He could ask his brother to begin researching employment opportunities in Istanbul. When he got to the post office, he asked how long it would take to get a connection to Istanbul.

"Three hours," said the clerk.

"Never mind."

He left the post office and started walking home. Then, exhausted all of a sudden, he hailed a cab. When he got out in front of his house in Ulus, his roommate Tevfik, a fellow engineer, was not there. But why would he be? Tevfik had a job. Just before he fell into a deep but troubled sleep, Muhittin whispered to himself, "Don't give up hope; never give up hope."

30

Long Skirts for Sitare

It was at Sitare's birthday party that it dawned on Leman that her daughter was fast becoming a young woman. The leggy girl tumbling with the other children in a lilac dress that would have been appropriate party wear for any young woman if lengthened below the knee was the same girl she had caught bribing her cousin with a kiss. Yes, her daughter had grown long limbed and slim, with a fuller bosom and wider hips. Since she had taken to combing back her hair instead of wearing it over her forehead, her delicate face was undeniably more maiden than cherub. Even so, Leman could have sworn that Sitare, now fifteen, was as innocent and artless as a twelve-year-old.

"You keep telling me not to dress Sitare like a child, but if I send her out dressed as a young woman, she'll imagine she's all grown up. And so will others. Doesn't that worry you?"

"Leman, right now she's playing out in the garden with Bülent, who's five years her junior. When she starts going to high school this year with girls her own age, you'll notice the change," Mahir said. "She'll mature in less than a month, and she'll refuse to wear those short skirts."

"She already has." Leman sighed. "Well then, give me a little money, and I'll go to the market for some fabric. I'll have new clothes made before she starts school."

"Please take Sitare shopping with you, and ask her opinion as well."

"What will be next?"

"How can she grow up unless you treat her like an adult?"

"My mother decided what I wore until the day I married you."

"Unlike you, she may come out from under her mother's wing one day. We need to prepare her for a life of independence."

"Are you saying we'll throw her out of the house when she turns eighteen, like the Americans do?"

"Leman, am I American?"

Leman didn't stop quarreling with her husband, but as always, she took his advice. Both Sitare and Sabahat accompanied her to Beyoğlu, and they returned with arms full of boxes and packages. Katina, the seamstress, arrived with two assistants, and they set to work on pleated and bias-cut skirts, as well as double-breasted blazers. This time, the women of the house and Mehpare picked up their knitting needles not for babies but for Sitare, who, throughout this burst of activity, spent most of her time in the garden picking fruit from the uppermost branches of the trees and playing tag with Bülent.

September arrived, and the schools opened.

Before Leman and Nesime went off to help Sitare settle into her new room at the school, Mahir cautioned his wife not to investigate its previous occupant. But this time, Leman did not listen to her husband and refused to make up her daughter's bed until she had confirmed that the girl sleeping in it the previous year had not had tuberculosis or any other diseases. Leman was also relieved to see that Sitare's roommate, Azra, was the picture of good health, with plump, rosy cheeks.

Sitare was not scared in the slightest at the prospect of leaving home for the first time and sleeping in a dormitory, not after Aunt Sabahat's stories about the fun she had had in high school. Even though it was a warm day, Sitare walked out of the house for her first day of high school dressed in a plaid skirt, a green sweater her aunt knit, a treasured scarf Sabahat gave her, and the low-heeled shoes she had picked out with her father. It was terribly hot in the streetcar, but she felt so chic she did not loosen the scarf wrapped around her neck. As instructed, Sabahat and Leman were sitting two rows behind her, so that she could learn what it was like to travel unaccompanied.

One weekend, Mahir went to the school to pick up his daughter; it was his third time there, counting Sabahat's graduation ceremony and Sitare's registration day. He leaned against the trunk of a linden tree and waited for his daughter instead of walking up the flower-lined road to the imposing school building with its four stately columns. A group of high school girls was coming down the road, laughing and talking. One of them waved good-bye to the others and started coming toward him. He stood up straight. *Sitare?* My God, was this girl with the long hair in loose curls really his Sitare?

"Papa!" Sitare came running up and threw her arms around him.

"What have you done to your hair?"

"I curled it, father."

"How did you find rollers at school?"

"You don't need rollers! Look," she said, illustrating with her hands. "We cut brown parcel paper into thin strips, then twist a length of hair around it, and roll it all the way up, twisting the paper ends together. If you go to bed like that, you wake up with a headful of curls! Do you like it, Father?"

"You look beautiful, Sitare," Mahir said. "Your mother has lovely hair, too. You take after her."

"I hope I never have breasts like her." She laughed, gesturing with her hands again. "They're so big and floppy! Is Bülent at home? I miss him so much. I'm going to chase him to the top of the fig tree the second I see him."

Leman was right, Mahir thought, *this young lady will always be a child at heart!*

A lot was changing as summer turned to fall.

Sitare's appearance had been changed by the collective labor that went into making her new clothes, but inner changes had taken place as well. She fussed over her appearance and her hair now, something she'd never bothered with before, and she seemed a lot more inclined to daydreaming.

"Leman, go to the market and get your girl some proper rollers," Behice Hanım grumbled one morning. "Reşat Bey was just nodding off, and the rustling of paper coming from your daughter's head startled him, poor man."

"I'll get her rollers, but it's time you stopped letting her sleep with you," Leman said. As a little girl, Sitare had gotten into the habit, whenever she had a bad dream or it was storming outside, of creeping into her grandparents' bed and sleeping between them. She still did it from time to time.

"What should we do, throw the girl out?"

"She's not a girl anymore, Mother. Do whatever you would do if I tried to crawl into your bed," Leman said.

Sitare's family bought her a set of rollers, a clutch coat, and a purse that hung from a shoulder strap. A child at heart she may have been, but Sitare had begun to attract the attention of young Ahmet and the twins, Nazif and Mehmet Ali, from down the street, and also a small band of young men who would trot after her every time she and Bülent walked down to the ferry landing. Mahir was not amused.

31

The Phone Call

As it turned out, Muhittin did not have to look for a job for very long. He had already established himself as a highly qualified civil engineer and the leading expert in hydraulics.

In the hallway, the wall-mounted telephone that served the eight different apartments in Tevfik and Muhittin's building began ringing one morning as the two friends were having breakfast in the kitchen.

"Aren't you going to answer it?" Tevfik asked.

"It can't be for me," Muhittin said. Tevfik stood up.

"Don't bother. It's not for you, Tevfik. Calls are always for the chemist on the top floor."

"I'll check anyway." Tevfik came back a moment later and said, "It's for you."

Muhittin was more alarmed than pleased. Had something happened to his parents? As he was running to the phone, he bumped the table, knocking over a glass of tea. Muhittin ran down to the floor below and picked up the receiver dangling by a cord.

"Hello?" he asked, out of breath and expecting to hear his brother's voice.

"Am I speaking with the engineer, Muhittin Kulin?" a deep voice asked.

"You are. Yes?"

"I am calling from the General Directorate of Electrical Power. I would like to offer you a position. Can you come into our offices at nine thirty this morning?"

Suppressing his excitement, Muhittin said, "Just a moment." A few seconds later, he added, "Yes, sir. I am available at that time. To whom am I speaking?"

"The general manager, Avni Bey."

Muhittin flew up the stairs and into his flat. "God bless you, Tevfik," he said. "I'm so glad you went and answered the phone."

After he had wiped up the spilled tea, Muhittin took a quick shower, put on a suit, carefully selected a necktie, and set off for the General Directorate with a whistle on his lips.

By a quarter past eleven, he had been named chief engineer of hydraulic energy for surveys and development. And to top it off, once bonuses were factored in, he would be earning more than he had at his previous municipal job.

As he left his new workplace and walked along the main avenue toward Kızılay, he was thinking about the conversation he'd just had with Avni Bey.

"Are you married, Muhittin Bey?" the general manager had asked.

"I'm a bachelor, sir."

"I'm pleased to hear that. If we decide to give you the position, you are likely to spend a lot of time in Anatolia, for days and even weeks at a time. Some of our married employees have found that their home life suffers."

"You needn't concern yourself about me," Muhittin had assured him. "I've already grown accustomed to long stints in Anatolia."

"In that case, let me congratulate you on your new position."

"Thank you. May I ask you something?"

"Please do."

"Did someone recommend me?"

"We knew you were working for the municipality, where you were highly regarded. But we did get a ringing endorsement from Muammer Çavuşoğlu as well."

"That was kind of him," Muhittin said. "I won't let my friend down."

A bright, nicely appointed office awaited Muhittin on Monday morning. It looked out not onto the street but onto the back garden, and the fragrance of an acacia filled his room when he opened the window. After he dropped off his briefcase and thanked the clerk who had shown him to his room, he knocked on the general manager's door and stepped inside.

"Have a seat, Muhittin Bey. Let me get you a cup of coffee and introduce you to a few people," Avni Bey said. "First, I'll introduce you to Raif Bey, our senior manager. He'll give you all the information you need."

The office boy who brought the coffee was instructed to get Raif Bey, about whom Avni Bey continued to brief Muhittin. "Raif Bey is our pay clerk, our steward, our problem solver—call him what you will, but he is indispensable, and a good-natured and talented man." A few minutes later, a short, well-dressed middle-aged man trotted into the office.

"Muhittin Bey, let me introduce you to Raif Erçevik. I will be surrendering our new engineer, Muhittin Kulin, to your capable hands. It will be your duty to take him on a tour of the department, introduce him to the others, show him the archives, provide him with the new project dossier, and make certain he never regrets his decision to join us."

Muhittin stood up and shook Raif Bey's hand. Through the round spectacles perched on his nose, Raif Bey looked Muhittin up and down, and thought, *My, what a good-looking man.* Raif Bey admired beauty and elegance wherever he found it, in men and women, and he took an instant liking to this tall, blue-eyed, dapper, and courteous young man with the clear, frank gaze.

Muhittin was happy with his new workplace: the garden, the tower to one side, the red-tiled roof. He had often walked past this building and wondered why so few buildings with character were being constructed in the capital city.

Muhittin worked under Avni Bey and was responsible for three subordinates, all of them young engineers. Raif Bey was a retired officer, and Muhittin never figured out what his official position was, or if he even had one. Still, he appreciated the order and discipline Raif Bey, in his gleaming shoes and well-cut suits, always imposed.

Raif Bey always arrived first thing in the morning to supervise the cleaning ladies, so that by the time the rest of the employees arrived at eight thirty, their offices were swept and dusted, their dossiers neatly stacked, and their tea brewed.

As a former military officer, Raif Bey was familiar with every corner of Anatolia. For example, if a study was to be conducted in Van, he would know the name of the local headman, the best place to find breakfast, and whose home was available for lodgers. As the person responsible for the archives, Raif would instantly locate the requested file or paper.

Muhittin spent his first week studying project files. He gathered all the information he could about Turkey's reservoirs. He would soon be setting off for the Black Sea region. Raif Bey ticked off a long list of details about the area: weather conditions, hotels, local specialties, things to pack . . . Muhittin was thrilled. In Adana, a hot, arid region full of mosquito-infested swamps, he'd been responsible for irrigation projects in a land where he never saw so much as a raindrop. Now, he was being sent to a lush region, with mild, wet summers and cool winters. This time, he was in charge of developing hydraulic energy schemes for existing dams, as well as conducting preliminary studies for additional reservoirs. He was happy to gain expertise in a new field.

When he saw the misty mountainsides dotted with rhododendrons looming over the brilliant blue waters of the Black Sea, he cried to himself, "God really is watching over me!" From that day onward, the Black Sea region would be his favorite area of a country whose every region filled him with awe.

32

Sabahat Spills the Beans

Sabahat was in her bedroom reading the letter Ekmel had secretly brought her. Her hands were trembling and her heart was breaking. How she wished she was at Aram's side, pressing his head to her breast and comforting him. The letter told of his trials. His ribs had been broken, and now they ached not only when he coughed or sneezed, but every time he took a breath. They'd broken two of his fingers, fortunately on his left hand, so he was still able to write. Every so often as she read the letter, Sabahat would press it to her breast and cry. Why was he being made to suffer simply for loving her? Because he was Armenian? Why this injustice? How could they do this? If members of her own family had done this, she would have understood, even if she could never forgive them. But whoever had done this to Aram didn't even know him. A bunch of ruffians had taken it upon themselves to decide who could walk with whom, and who could love whom. What gave them the right? Who or what had encouraged them? How could they be so evil, so cruel, so misguided? How dare they!

. . . and that is why I dropped out of university. I decided
I would earn more with my foreign-language skills than
as a chemist. I'm doing translations at home and looking
for a job. I was interviewed by four different companies
last week. One of them, an American company, looks
promising. Hang in there, Sabahat. If they hire me, one
of the obstacles in our path will be eliminated. If nothing
else, I will be earning my own living. Keep studying hard.
One of us will have a university diploma, at least.

"No, Aram, I won't let you do that!" Sabahat said to herself. If he
dropped out of university on her account, she would never pass through
its gate again! She, too, had mastered foreign languages, and could teach
or translate, just like him.

Don't come to the house, Sabahat. After this last inci-
dent, my mother has little tolerance for our relationship,
and she might upset you. Don't give her the opportu-
nity. If there is any good news, I will find a way to share
it. Armine can give you my letters. We won't be able to
see each other this summer, but I will have found a job
by autumn. God willing, we can meet then to decide
together what to do next. I miss you so much. I have never
lost hope. Don't you, either. I know that one day we will
overcome every obstacle.
Aram

Sabahat wiped away her tears with the back of her hand, folded the
letter, put it in the blue box in the second drawer, locked the drawer,
and hid the key under her pillow. "Who's upset you now, sweetie?" her
grandmother asked, sitting up in bed. "Is it your sisters again?"

"No," Sabahat said. "It's fate, Grandma." She averted any more questions by saying, "I'm going downstairs. Father picked some grapes this morning. Would you like me to bring you some?"

"Bless you. If only I could manage those stairs more easily, I would save you the trouble."

"It's no trouble," Sabahat said, going over to her grandmother and kissing her on the cheeks. She ran down the stairs, through the entrance hall, and into the garden, where her sisters were sitting in the wicker chairs under the arbor having tea.

"I heard you met with Ekmel Bey again yesterday," Leman said. "Can we expect you to announce your engagement soon?"

"No."

"Why not?"

"Because I don't want to get married."

"But you said you liked Ekmel."

"I do, but not as a future husband."

"Are you afraid of marriage for some reason? You could speak to your brother-in-law about it. He could help you with your fears."

"I'm not afraid. I just don't want to get married."

"Why not?"

"I don't, that's all."

"Goodness gracious! You aren't a sapphic, are you?" Suat asked.

"Don't be disgusting, Suat!" Leman snapped.

"But there has to be a reason she insists she will never marry."

"Whether or not I marry is nobody's business but my own."

"We're not just anybody; we're your elder sisters."

"Fine then. If you really want to know, there's someone I've loved for years. If I marry, it will be to him."

"This person had better not be Aram," Suat said.

"It's him."

"I don't believe it! Like an idiot, I've been defending you all this time," Leman shouted. She stood and went over to Sabahat, screaming,

"May God give you what you deserve! You conniving runt! If Beyba gets wind of this, he'll kill you both."

"He'd have a heart attack before that happened," Suat said.

"Well then, don't tell him," Sabahat said.

"She's threatening us! What a wicked girl you are!"

"Father will never allow this marriage," Suat said.

"Why not? How is Aram any less desirable than your husbands? Is he immoral? Is he a thief? Is he a rapist? Has he ever done anything wrong?"

"What could be worse than seducing you?" Leman said.

"No, it was I who seduced him. When I set my heart on him, he was only seventeen, and younger than me. If I hadn't encouraged him, he wouldn't have dared to approach me. But I loved him, and I'll love him until the day I die. I'll marry him, or nobody."

"You can't marry him. He's an Armenian," Suat said.

"Who says Armenians can't get married? They're citizens of this country as much as anyone else."

"Armenians can get married, but not to Turkish girls."

"Muhip Bey's wife is Greek, isn't she? From what I've heard, Uncle Sadık once had an Armenian fiancée."

"That's not the same," Suat said. "Girls can't marry non-Muslims."

"Then I'll never get married. I mean it."

"Look here, missy! You can go through life a spinster for all I care, but Mother and Father must never know about this. Do you hear me?" Leman shouted, wagging her finger in front of her sister's nose.

Behice Hanım walked up, a smile on her face, a basket of freshly picked hydrangeas and roses on her arm. When she heard Leman shouting, she set the basket on the garden table.

"What is it now, Leman? Has someone used your towel again? Must you shout like a banshee at this time of night?"

Tears of resentment springing to her eyes, Leman said, "You should be thanking me, Behice Hanım. Go on, ask your youngest daughter what she's been up to. Let her tell you."

Sabahat ran off to her room. Leman stormed off and stomped her way up the stairs to her room, shattered both by her sister's betrayal and her mother's unfair scolding. *If only Mahir was here,* she thought. He would take her in his arms and comfort her. She would tell him what had happened. He was the only person she could tell. But he would be away until the weekend, visiting relatives. She had half a mind to get dressed and get on the first train that would take her to his side.

Down in the garden, Behice Hanım asked Suat, "What happened? Has Sabahat been ungracious to Ekmel Bey?"

"I wish that's all it was. Forgive me for saying this, Mother, but you were very unfair to Leman. You've spoiled your youngest daughter. Do you realize that? Both you and Beyba have pampered her and will never hear a word against her. I hope you don't live to regret it."

Behice watched Suat's teacup rattle on its saucer as she walked off, and wondered why, on this fine, peaceful night, her daughters seemed determined to squabble with each other. Perhaps Saraylıhanım was right. Had she not been strict enough with her girls?

33

Bosnian Börek

When the ball of dough had reached just the right consistency, Gül Hanım placed it on the wide kitchen counter and began rolling it out with a wooden pin nearly the size of a broomstick, pulling and stretching with her hands until it was paper-thin. She set the rolling pin on the counter and wiped her floury hands on her apron. She had wanted so badly to teach her daughter-in-law how to make Bosnian börek. As far as she was concerned, a bride who couldn't roll out wafer-thin phyllo and grate zucchini was no bride at all. But Ecla had no interest in being a proper Bosnian wife and daughter-in-law. No, she was an Istanbul wife. She was the granddaughter of a grand vizier. She spoke three foreign languages. These are the things on which she prided herself, the accomplishments she would recite in front of company and relatives. Gül Hanım had not uttered a word of complaint, not to her husband, Salih Bey, and not to her daughter, Saadet. But she knew that the all-knowing God could read her heart. It was true, she had never warmed to Nusret's wife.

Semra was her first granddaughter. *Well,* she had said to herself, *I will teach the girl what I could never teach the mother.* She would teach her granddaughter how to kneel on her prayer mat, how to say prayers, how to embroider, how to cook Bosnian dishes, how to sing Bosnian folk songs, and how to follow the old ways and traditions. But she had been horrified yet again. Her daughter-in-law had hired as a governess a lanky German in a navy-blue uniform. The girl had taken to calling her mother *mutti*. Semra was going to learn German! Well, if only she learned Turkish first! Finally, unable to bear it any longer, Gül Hanım had poured out her grievances to Saadet. It was as though Saadet had been waiting for a sign. The mother and daughter had put two chairs in the garden just outside the kitchen, where Salih Bey couldn't hear them, and had spent hours there—well, there was no other word for it—gossiping.

Nusret made a good living, and he spent every cent of it. They had an automobile when nobody else did. They had a German governess. They had a butler, a housemaid, and a cook. Even their breakfasts were prepared by a cook. If a woman couldn't prepare a meal for her own family, what good was she?

"And you know what else," Gül Hanım had said to her daughter, "Ecla looks down on us. There is no greater sin in our religion than pride. No greater sin than wastefulness. Shh, Saadet, Salih Bey is coming. Don't let your father hear us picking apart his daughter-in-law. Hush, girl."

Gül Hanım cut the phyllo into long strips with a knife and placed a spoonful of zucchini puree on each one before folding it up into a triangular pouch. She would serve Nusret, Semra, and little Orhan this börek for lunch. Ecla would probably never come again. *Then don't come!* Gül Hanım thought. She didn't touch börek. "Too fattening," she said. *Then don't eat it!* For a moment, Gül felt as though a lump of dough had got stuck in her throat. She swallowed several times. No, she wasn't going to cry, not after all she had been through, all she had overcome. She hadn't cried then, so why cry now just because she never got any respect from her daughter-in-law? She placed a pouch of dough on the baking tray, then another, then another. When she was done, she whisked an egg into some milk, added a bit of melted butter, and brushed the tops of the folded bundles of filled phyllo.

"Saadet, come here, my girl, and help me light the oven," she called out. Ecvet came running into the kitchen ahead of his mother. "Look, Nana used the biggest tray again," he tattled.

"Mother, you've made too many again! Semra eats like a bird, and Orhan can barely finish one of those. Who's going to eat all this börek?" Saadet asked.

"Münevver Hanım and her husband are coming over this evening. I'll send whatever is left over with them. Mücahit Bey is retired now, and they're a little hard up."

"Be careful not to offend them, Mother. You sent them some meat just yesterday. Don't fling their poverty into their faces."

"Don't you worry yourself, my dear, I know what I'm doing and how to do it," Gül said. She slid the baking tray into the oven, went out to the garden, and called to the other side of the wall, "Hello, Münevver Hanım!"

"Yes, Gül Hanım," her neighbor said. "Can I help you?"

"I wanted to ask you for a favor, Münevver Hanım. My grandson Ecvet has been eying your plums. He can see the branches over the wall and, well, he's just a boy, and his mouth waters at the sight. Would you mind terribly if he picked a few plums from your tree?"

"Mind? Why, of course not. Tell him he can pick all the plums he wants."

"Nana, I don't want any plums," Ecvet was saying, hopping up and down on one foot.

"Shh," Gül Hanım whispered. "Climb over that wall and get me a few plums. You can get a bowl from Münevver Hanım." She turned to her daughter with a knowing look and said, "We'll return the bowl full of börek. It's shameful to return a bowl empty. You see, Saadet Hanım, there's always a way for everything."

"Something tells me that's the Bosnian way," Saadet smiled.

"Well, seeing as the börek is Bosnian." It didn't matter what her daughter-in-law thought, Gül Hanım decided. She knew she was respected by the residents of Sümbüllüçeşme Street.

34

The Key of Time

Behice beamed at the babies sleeping side by side on her bed. First, she studied Suat's son, Rasin, whose lashes were so long they cast shadows onto his chubby cheeks. He was a strapping little fellow. Next, she looked at Mehpare's son, Ali, who was puny by comparison, and had a pale, thin face. They lay next to each other, these two babies, clueless about the life ahead. What sort of young men would they be? Behice, who had brought up three children of her own, two grandchildren, and Halim, knew that sturdy little Rasin might end up a man of short stature, while undersized Ali could grow up to become quite robust. A clever, well-behaved baby could turn into a shiftless and slow-witted teen. *The future is a sealed box only the key of time can open*, Behice thought. Mothers and fathers could speculate and presuppose, cooing and dreaming to their heart's content, but the weavers of fate might have other plans for their babies, and in the end, our destinies are written in the stars.

Reşat Bey had had such high hopes for Halim. When Behice had been unable to give her husband a son, the poor man had pinned all his hopes on Kemal's son, Halim, the little boy who would one day be educated in France. But what had happened? Halim was now driving a cab. For all Reşat Bey and Mehpare's protestations that Halim was "operating" a cab, it amounted to the same thing in Behice's eyes. And then there was Sabahat, their youngest, still unmarried and a university dropout. Behice bitterly regretted her initial opposition just one year earlier to her daughter's desire for a university diploma. Now, what right did she have to get angry at Sabahat for quitting? Well, at least Sabahat spent all her time reading books in bed and would learn in her own way.

Behice blamed the interruption of Sabahat's education on the purse-snatching incident. Sabahat hadn't said anything, but Behice was convinced the godless mugger had tried to molest her daughter. She'd never been the same after that day and had suddenly lost all interest in her studies. Having tried, and failed, to get her daughter to open up about that day, Behice had consulted Mahir, wondering if he would talk to Sabahat, only to be told that it was better not to pressure the girl, that everyone should back off. Well, she had backed off, and what was the result? Now Sabahat was wandering the house, a pale version of her former self, speaking only when spoken to, her nose buried in a book all the time.

Thank goodness Behice had these two bundles of joy to brighten her days and to make her smile despite herself. The hours just flew by, and she was grateful Mehpare so frequently brought little Ali to the house. Mehpare wanted nothing more than for Ali and Rasin to grow up playing with each other, and she now bitterly regretted having spirited Halim away from the house where he had grown up.

An unpleasant smell was coming from the bed. Behice was sniffing the air to determine which of the babies' mothers should be called to change nappies when she heard a series of thuds and an anguished scream. She ran out onto the landing, peered over the banister, and saw Neyir Hanım lying in a heap on the floor at the bottom of the stairs. She was hurrying down the stairs when Leman, Suat, and Mehpare all came flying out of the sitting room. Nesime had come running out of the kitchen and Mahir out of his exam room.

Kneeling on the floor, Mahir was asking, "Does it hurt here? What about here? Does it hurt when I press here?"

"Is anything broken, Mahir?" Behice asked as she reached the bottom step.

"I don't think so. However, she might have a concussion. She hit her head. We need to get her to the hospital for x-rays."

Mahir went into the garden in search of Hüsnü Efendi, who would arrange a cab.

"What happened?" Behice asked. "Did you slip? How did you fall, Mother?"

"Thieves will be punished!"

They all looked in the direction of the voice. Saraylıhanım was sitting at the top of the stairs, draped in tulle, glaring down at them like an evil phantom. Suat burst out laughing as Behice burst into tears.

"I'm sick to death of this," Behice sobbed. "I've run out of patience. First thing tomorrow, Saraylıhanım is going where she belongs. Lunatics live in asylums, and that's that. Oh! Nesime, run! I left the babies in my room. They'll turn over and fall off the bed. Run!"

"How did you fall, Grandma?" Leman asked as she helped the elderly woman take a sip of water.

"I wish I'd never left my room. I was walking down to the kitchen, holding the banister for support, when all of a sudden Saraylı came up behind me saying something about the jewels in her crown."

"That accursed crown!" Behice screamed. "How does she keep finding that chamber pot? 'Throw it out,' I said. 'We can always get a new one,' I said. She's gone completely off her rocker!"

Mahir returned and knelt at Neyir Hanım's side. "Don't be afraid. Stay still, and let me pick you up. I'll carry you to the cab and bring you straight home after your x-rays."

"Suat, please go with them," Behice said.

Suat was running upstairs to throw something on when she bumped into Saraylıhanım on the landing. "You've done it now, Saraylıhanım," Suat said. "Thank your lucky stars nothing is broken. And take that chamber pot off your head."

"That wicked crone stole my jewels!" Saraylıhanım sniveled.

When Hüsnü Efendi announced that the cab had arrived, Mahir carefully slipped his arms under Neyir Hanım.

"My chest hurts," she moaned.

"There's some bruising on your ribs, most likely," said Mahir. "You'll make a full recovery. Don't worry."

Leman opened the front door for her husband, and Suat followed him outside. Behice beat her breast in the doorway.

Behice, Leman, and Mehpare were sitting on the divan drinking the coffee Gülfidan had just brought them.

"We have to do something about Saraylıhanım," Behice was saying. "This can't go on. God forbid she does something to harm the babies one day."

"I don't believe she would ever harm the babies," Leman said. "It's Grandmother I worry about. Saraylıhanım has had it in for her since the day she moved here from Beypazarı. She's consumed with jealousy."

"She can't stay here any longer. She nearly killed my mother!"

"God forbid," Mehpare said.

"I'm going to speak with Mahir Bey," Behice decided. "He must know a nervous disorders specialist and a place where Saraylıhanım can receive treatment. He can arrange a room in Bakırköy. We'll hire someone to care for her. There's nothing else we can do."

"Mother! Bakırköy is for madmen! Saraylıhanım isn't mad, she's senile. There's not a house in the city that doesn't have a doddering old relative or two."

"That may be, but I can't go on like this. You saw how short of breath I got a moment ago."

"I understand, Mother, and I know your asthma has gotten worse, but Beyba would never allow it. We can't send Saraylıhanım to either a madhouse or a hospital."

"In that case, your father can stay here with his Saraylı. I'll take my mother and leave."

Leman shot her mother a skeptical look.

"Why are you looking at me like that? I'll move to Mehpare's! I can stay with her until the tenant upstairs is able to leave. Then my mother and I will move into a flat of our own."

"Behice Hanım, you'd always be welcome, you know that, but there's no need to quarrel with Reşat Bey over Saraylıhanım. You can send her to me. I'll look after her," Mehpare said.

"You'll do no such thing!"

"I would be happy to, believe me. Saraylıhanım has always loved me like a daughter. And I've always loved her as Kemal's mother. It would be no trouble at all. We have plenty of room now that Halim has moved out."

"What if she does something to little Ali? Doesn't that worry you, Mehpare?"

"She loves babies. It's your mother she doesn't love. Were she to get away from Neyir Hanım, she'd quiet down, I'm sure of it."

"What would Galip Bey say about this?"

"I had a child for his sake. What's more, and forgive me for saying this, it's my flat. I mean, the flat belongs to you, Behice Hanım."

"Don't ever say that again, Mehpare. We gave that flat to you."

"We are agreed then. Saraylıhanım will come and live with me and keep me company. Behice Hanım, please don't send her to Bakırköy."

"Mehpare, are you sure? Don't you want some time to think it over and consult with your husband?

"I've made up my mind. I don't need to ask my husband. He'll accept my decision, bless him."

"Well, since we managed to sort this out between ourselves, there's no need to upset Reşat Bey by telling him Saraylıhanım caused my mother to fall." Behice finished her coffee, placed her saucer on the cup, upside down, and then quickly flipped over the cup and saucer. "I don't believe in fortune-telling, but I do wonder about poor Mother," she said sheepishly. "Mehpare, would you mind? I do so hope brighter days are ahead."

"Let it cool first, and I'll be happy to read your fortune," Mehpare said. "By the way, where was Sabahat this morning?"

"She went off to Beyoğlu," Behice said. "To buy more books."

35

Confrontation

Determined not to miss a single precious second of Aram's lunch hour, Sabahat was at Haylayf twenty minutes before the appointed time. She took a seat in the back, facing the door. She had not seen Aram even once during the summer, their only communication being the letters Armine ferried between them. She had chosen Haylayf as a meeting place both to avoid Aram's attackers and to be far from the prying eyes and wagging tongues of family and neighbors. Trembling with excitement, she watched the traffic whizzing by. The pastry shop was empty except for two youngsters poking their forks at a single slice of cake.

Sabahat's heart started beating faster. Aram was walking through the door. *My God,* she thought, *he has lost so much weight.* The cheeks of his beautiful face were sunken, and he had dark circles under his eyes. She stood up. He took her outstretched hands in his. "Sabahat! At last! I missed you."

"I missed you, too," Sabahat said. She wanted to throw her arms around him but contented herself with squeezing his hand. They sat down. A waiter came straight over, and they ordered lemonade and börek.

"How are you?" Sabahat asked.

"I'm fine. I was sorry to hear you'd left university. Please go back, dear."

"Never. I'm never going there again, not after you dropped out because of me."

"Sabahat, I had other reasons for leaving. I could have complained to the police or found some other way to protect myself. Believe me, I'm making a lot more money working for Sokoni Oil than I would as a chemist. Why do people go to university? To get a good job, right? Well, I've got one. I'm still registered at the university so I won't get called up for military service. I'll manage that way for a year. Listen, I promised you that I would have a profession before the day came to talk to your father. Right now, I'm earning a good living, enough to support two. And I'll be getting a raise next year."

"Aram?" Sabahat hesitated, embarrassed to ask the question on the tip of her tongue.

Reading her thoughts, Aram said, "Sabahat, I'm going to ask your father for your hand."

"What about your mother? Your big brother? Your relatives?"

"They won't like it. Neither will your family. But we've decided to face the consequences, haven't we?"

"I've already told my sisters," Sabahat said. "I was fed up with their hunt for a suitable husband."

"What did they say?"

"They raised a ruckus, but they didn't say anything to my parents."

"It's time your mother and father found out, too."

"Aram, I should talk to my father on my own first."

"When are you going to talk to him?"

"At the first opportunity. I've been waiting for seven years. Isn't that long enough?"

They sat in the increasingly crowded café until it was time for Aram to go back to work, resting their hands on the marble-topped table, touching each other's fingers, gazing into each other's eyes, unafraid and unashamed of their love. They talked of the life they would live together, interrupting each other, completing each other's sentences. They were both weary of the deceptions, of the intermediaries, of hiding their true feelings and worrying what others would think. Yes, the time had come to face the consequences. Finally!

Unaware of what had happened at home, Sabahat was in no hurry to return. She and Aram walked together to the door of Sokoni. Then she walked from Harbiye to Tünel, dragging her feet as she decided what to say to her father. She loitered in front of the window of Lion Department Store and bought bonnets and bibs for the babies. At Lebon, she stopped in for a cup of tea and a boxed slice of cherry cake for Sitare, chocolate for Bülent. Now carrying the pastry box and the baby clothes, she decided nonetheless not to board the streetcar in Tünel, walking instead down Yüksekkaldırım, through Karaköy, across the Galata Bridge, and up the hill all the way to her home in Beyazit.

She was turning into her street when she saw her father, who was returning from work. His face lit up at the sight of her.

"What are you doing here? Did you decide to go to university today?" Reşat Bey asked.

"No, Father. I was doing some shopping in Beyoğlu," Sabahat said, holding up her parcels. "I'm done with university. I meant it."

"I never protested your enrollment, like your mother, nor insisted upon it," Reşat Bey said. "All I ask is that you tell me the reason you've dropped out. As your father, I have the right to know."

"Beyba, I'd like to have a talk with you, and I'll explain everything then."

"We can talk whenever you like, my dear. After dinner this evening, over breakfast tomorrow morning . . ."

"Let's talk as soon we get to the house," Sabahat said, eager to present her case while the lines she had rehearsed were still fresh in her mind and while she could still feel the warmth of Aram's hands.

"Is it urgent?"

"Yes, it is. I have been wanting to talk to you for a long time. Shall we go directly into Mahir's exam room, where nobody can disturb us? Please, Father."

"All right then, my girl."

Reşat Bey opened the front door with his key, and they crept into the exam room and sat down on the leather sofa.

"Tell me what's on your mind, Sabahat, my sultana," Reşat Bey said.

"Beloved Beyba," Sabahat began, at which Reşat Bey thought, *Oh no, this is serious.*

"I know you would like me to get married. I have refused a great many suitors. Mother worries that I will end up a spinster—"

Reşat Bey interrupted his daughter to say, "I would never force you to marry anyone against your wishes. I hope you know that. You will choose your husband yourself."

"Oh, Beyba, I knew you felt that way. I have the best father in the world, fair-minded and modern, the king of all fathers."

"Has your mother been pressuring you over that young man—now what was his name, the grandson of Tahir Pasha? If you don't wish to marry him, then you won't."

"Sir, I have chosen the man I wish to marry."

"That's wonderful! I have been waiting for so long for you to say that! And who is this lucky man?"

"Beloved Beyba, it is someone you hold in the highest regard. An honorable, studious, honest, trustworthy young man!"

"It sounds like you've made an excellent choice, my dear. Did you meet at university? Or was it at Robert College, before university? When did you meet? Wait, wait . . . let me guess, now who could it be?"

"He attended Robert College."

"Who is it?" Reşat Bey tried to remember the young men he had met at his daughter's graduation ceremony.

"Aram."

"Excuse me?"

"Aram Balayan. You remember him, Sitare and Bülent's tutor, my friend from the American school."

"What are you saying?"

"Beyba, I've loved Aram for many years."

"Silence! You shameless girl!"

"You misunderstand. Ours has been a platonic love, one that lives only in our hearts—"

"Not another word, Sabahat."

"Father, I am asking for your permission to marry Aram. We love each other with all our hearts. I will never consent to marry another. I'm begging you, I throw myself at your feet, please, Father. Aram is the best person in the world! The most honest and upright! When you get him to know him better, you will grow to love him. We won't be a burden on anyone, he's found a job, he's earning—"

"Silence, I said!"

Sabahat and her father sat in silence for a time, and as they sat, a wall arose between them, gray block by gray block.

"Daughter, you have destroyed me," Reşat Bey finally said. "Had you bashed my head with an ax, or carved out my heart with a knife, you would not have caused me such pain. You have trampled my honor, my reputation, and my good name. You have smashed my traditions and those of my ancestors. Get out, I don't want to see you."

Sabahat stood up across from Reşat Bey, her eyes of honey so beloved by her father flashing with rage.

"I do not deserve most of your accusations. I have injured neither your honor nor your reputation. Aram's hand has touched nothing but my own hand. I may be smashing your traditions, but it is high time they were smashed. If two people who love each other are unable to marry because of your traditions, then may they be smashed into a million pieces."

"Sabahat, I have never raised my hand in anger against you. Do not force me to do it now."

"Hit me, slap me. I won't feel a thing. It is your insensitivity that stings, Father. What has Aram done wrong? What makes him any less suitable a suitor than Ekmel? The only difference is that one will be buried by a priest, and the other by an imam."

"Shut up!"

"You are angry with me because I am appealing to your reason. Think about it, Father, and please understand that I speak the truth. I am going to marry the man I love, with or without your consent."

"If a daughter of mine marries someone from another religion, she is no longer my daughter. She leaves this house, and she does not attend my funeral."

"Is that your final word?"

"Yes!"

"Father, even if you disown me, I will be honored until my dying day to be your daughter, and I will always love you more than anyone in the world," Sabahat said. Running out into the anteroom so her father wouldn't see her tears, she gently closed the door behind her.

As Sabahat was rushing up the stairs to her room, she encountered Mehpare.

"Where have you been, Sabahat? If only you knew what happened today."

"I don't care what happened," Sabahat said, pushing Mehpare out of the way.

"You're crying! What's the matter?"

Sabahat went into her room and locked the door. Her grandmother wouldn't be able to get in, but Sabahat had no intention of letting anyone into her room until she had packed her bag. She pulled a valise off the top of the wardrobe and grabbed a few articles of clothing from the chest of drawers. There was a knock on the door. Ignoring it, she continued packing. There was another knock.

"Grandmother, please come back later. I'm busy right now. I can't open the door."

"Sabahat, it's me, Mehpare."

"Mehpare, please leave me alone."

"I will, but let me get your grandmother's cardigan and blanket first. The poor thing's shivering. She had an accident today, you know. Took a tumble down the stairs. She's resting right now. Sabahat! Open this door!" Mehpare's voice was getting more frantic. Sabahat turned the key. Mehpare entered the room to find Sabahat in tears, an open valise on her bed, and clothing strewn across the floor.

"What's going on here?"

"I'm leaving."

"You, too?"

"Who else is leaving?" Sabahat asked.

"Saraylıhanım is coming to live with me, or your mother says she will leave. Your grandmother nearly left and went to heaven. Everyone's leaving today."

Forgetting her own troubles for a moment, Sabahat asked, "What happened to Grandmother?"

"Saraylıhanım pushed her down the stairs. She's not well at all. Where are you going, dear?"

"I don't know, Mehpare." Sabahat fell on Mehpare's neck and burst into tears. They pushed the valise to one side and sat on the bed.

"Tell me what's happened," Mehpare said. Sabahat was too choked with sobs to speak. Mehpare softly stroked her head and let her cry for a time.

"Can I stay with you tonight?" Sabahat asked.

"I'm staying here tonight."

"No!"

"Someone has to stay with your grandmother and keep her from falling asleep. Suat was at the hospital all day, and Leman is terrible with patients. You've got troubles of your own. That leaves me."

"Can I live with you?"

"Sabahat, don't be such a child. Don't do the first thing that comes into your head, or you'll regret it later. Get a good night's sleep, and we'll talk about it tomorrow. If you want to stay at my house, you can. But spare a thought for your mother tonight. She had a terrible asthma attack, her eyes bulging out of her head, nearly choked to death, poor woman. Stay put for now."

Sabahat took the valise off the bed and put it on the floor. "We'll leave together tomorrow."

"That's better!"

"I'm not going down to dinner. Tell them I'm ill in bed, would you?"

"I will." Taking the cardigan and blanket with her, Mehpare left the room and went downstairs.

Everyone was in low spirits that night. Behice was propped up against several pillows on the divan, recovering from her attack. Suat had taken Ali to her room so Mehpare could spend the night with Grandmother. Perhaps dimly conscious of what she had done, Saraylıhanım was laying low. Only Mehpare knew Reşat Bey was down in the exam room, and she had decided it best to leave him alone and his family in ignorance. Leman and Mahir had just had one of their quarrels, as a result of which she was sitting cross-armed and pouting near her mother while he sat in the study with Grandmother, who was stretched out on the sofa there. Not only was the study near the toilet, Mehpare had insisted it was the best room in which to hold a vigil, because, unlike the room with the divan, there was nowhere else to lie down and risk falling asleep. Mahir had specifically said that Grandmother was to be kept awake and that they should take turns sitting with her.

Mehpare covered Neyir Hanım with the blanket and went to the room with the divan, where she sat at Behice Hanım's feet, next to Leman.

"What a terrible day!" Leman said. She now regretted the spat with Mahir, and the day's events had taken their toll, leaving her pale and worn.

"Hasn't Sabahat come home yet?" Behice asked.

"Yes, but she's having terrible cramps. She said she won't be down to dinner."

"The poor girl always suffers during her time of the month." Behice sighed.

"Why isn't Beyba home yet?" Leman asked.

"It's just as well he's late today. We won't have to worry about him in this pandemonium."

"Mother, try not to talk. You need to rest until you're breathing easily again."

At the sound of footsteps on the stairs, everyone's ears pricked up. "It must be Beyba," Leman said.

A haggard Reşat Bey walked into the room. Behice sat up. "Reşat Bey, what took you until this hour? If you had any idea what happened—"

"I know what happened," Reşat Bey said. "Our daughter's decided to marry an Armenian. From this day on, I no longer have a child named Sabahat!"

Behice leapt to her feet, stared at her husband's weary and wretched face, and in what must have been a split second saw, hovering before her mind's eye, the jagged pieces of the intuitions she had ignored, the gnawing unease she had suppressed, the suspicions she had cast from her mind, the doubts she had chased from her heart, the fears she had dismissed as the products of an overactive imagination. The edges of these pieces came together, forming a picture so glaringly, blindingly obvious that now she could no longer deny what she had so long refused to see. Behice gasped for breath, clutched at her throat, and crumpled to the floor.

"She can't breathe! She's going purple! Mahir! Mahir!" Leman screamed. "What have you done, Beyba? Mother had an asthma attack just today!"

Mahir came running in from the study and knelt next to Behice. Mehpare rushed to the study to be with Grandmother. Oblivious to them all, Reşat Bey dragged himself up the stairs, one heavy foot at a time.

36

Death Can Be a Solution

Mehpare dressed Grandmother in the cardigan and smoothed the blanket on top of her.

"Dear, let me sleep for just half an hour," Neyir Hanım said. "You're tired. You've talked yourself hoarse. Don't worry, nothing will happen. I'm made of sterner stuff. And just between us, if my time has come, so be it."

"You're forbidden to sleep tonight, Grandma," Mehpare said. "Mahir would be furious if I let you. He'll be coming in soon to take his turn. What would I say to him if he caught us sleeping?"

"You'd say we were exhausted. We're only human."

"Try to stay awake," Mehpare said. "Tomorrow, you can sleep all you want."

"But I'm tired now."

"I know, dear. I'm tired, too. I came here just to be with you. Would you want me to have left my house and husband for nothing? Morning will be here soon."

"I feel as though something is tugging down my eyelids."

"Just keep your eyes open a little longer."

"All right, but tell me more. What is my youngest granddaughter up to?"

"That's it! Ask me questions and I'll answer as best I can. Normally, I wouldn't keep talking about this, but I'll do anything I can right now to keep us both awake. Sabahat had a terrible row with her father. You remember Aram? Aram . . . Sitare's tutor. Well, she's gone and fallen in love with him. They've decided to get married. Reşat Bey won't give his consent. He says he'll disown her. Suat kept saying there was something between them, but Leman and I didn't believe her. It turns out Suat was right."

Despite having heard the story five times, Neyir Hanım posed the same question. "So what's going to happen now?"

"I don't know. When Behice Hanım found out, she had an asthma attack. Reşat Bey shut himself into his room. I found Sabahat in her room packing her bags. Morning will be here soon. It'll all work out in the morning."

"Does the girl not understand how serious this is?"

"Oh, Grandmother! The heart does what it must. Mine did. Why wouldn't Sabahat's? Oh, your eyes are closing again. Keep them open. Grandmother!"

Mehpare got up from the armchair and opened the window. "I'll tell you what, Grandmother. I'll go downstairs and make us each a nice cup of coffee. And when we've drunk it, I'll tell our fortunes."

"Can you tell the future?"

"I saw Suat's pregnancy, didn't I? I knew Sitare would pass and that Sabahat would skip a grade."

"All right then. Go down to the kitchen and make us some coffee."

"First, you have to promise not to fall asleep while I'm gone. I'll be back in three minutes. Do you promise?"

"Promise."

Mehpare looked for an illustrated book on the shelves. Unable to find one, she pulled out a photo album. "Here, you can look at this until I get back. No sleeping."

She ran downstairs, filled the long-handled pot with water, put in several spoonfuls of coffee, and set it on a low flame.

Reşat Bey crept down the stairs barefoot and went into the study. His mother-in-law was taken aback to see him, for the first time ever, in pajamas. Startled, she pretended to be asleep. Reşat Bey did not even look at her as he opened his desk drawer and started rummaging through its contents. Even when the photo album slid off Neyir Hanım's blanket and landed on the floor with a loud thud, he didn't look over. Finally, she called out to him, "Reşat Bey, son. I had a terrible accident today. Aren't you going to say anything?"

He said nothing, still searching through the drawer.

"I know you're upset, but if you don't wish me a speedy recovery, and I don't make it through the night, you'll feel guilty tomorrow. Son, there's a solution for every problem but death."

"Death can be a solution."

When Reşat Bey walked off without closing the drawer, Neyir Hanım caught a glimpse of the gun in his hand.

"Oh no!" Neyir Hanım screamed. Then she screamed again, as loud as she could, gasping in pain.

Leman was out cold, Suat was catnapping with the two babies at her side, and Mehpare was standing in front of the stove when they all heard their grandmother's piercing howls. Mehpare turned off the flame and had just reached the second floor when she heard the door to the exam room close on the floor below.

There must be a burglar, she thought. First, he frightened Grandma in the study, then he ran downstairs.

Leman poked her husband, who was still sleeping. "Mahir, something's happened to Grandmother. Don't you hear her? Get up." She switched on the lamp. Mahir sat up and rubbed his eyes.

Mehpare flew to Grandmother's side. "Reşat took his gun! Run! He's going to shoot her! Run!" Grandmother was screaming. As Mehpare was running up to Sabahat's room, Mahir was hustling down the stairs. It was only when they bumped into each other that Mehpare realized that there was no burglar in the house.

"Grandmother," Mahir said. "What happened to her? Did she fall?"

"Quick, let's go down to the exam room," Mehpare shouted. "Reşat Bey was carrying a gun!"

Scrambling over and around each other, they ran down the stairs, through the entrance hall, and to the door of the exam room, which wouldn't open. The door was locked, light seeping out from under it. Mahir pounded on it. Nothing. Mehpare dashed off to the kitchen to find something to break the lock. Mahir took a step back and kicked at the door with all his might. It still would not open. Taking several steps back, he lunged at the door, striking it with his shoulder, then tumbled into the room as the door gave way, landing on his father-in-law, who was sitting at the desk, gun to his temple. There was an explosion. Then the momentary, deathly silence was broken by women's screams and feet pounding on the stairs, in the entrance hall, in the doorway. And then, once again, deathly silence.

Hammer in hand, Mehpare was standing in the empty doorway. Behind her, pressed together, were all the women of the house, Hüsnü Efendi, and, in the very back, Saraylıhanım, wearing her crown no more. Each and every face wore an expression of sheer horror. Mahir and Reşat Bey were on the floor, one of them under the unhinged door, the other sprawled on top of it. Trickling out from under the door, a thin, red stream was feeding the growing stain on the carpet.

37

The Hospital

Leman and Suat were sitting on a bench together in the long, narrow corridor of the hospital. Balanced on Leman's knees was her handbag, and under her bottom was an open magazine. She sat erect, hiking up her skirt to keep the hem from touching the floor. Behice was behind the closed door of a nearby room, sitting at her husband's bedside. Mehpare was pacing the corridor.

"Mehpare, you're making me dizzy," Suat said.

"Do you think Nesime is having trouble minding the babies on her own?" Mehpare asked.

"Housekeeper Gülfidan is there."

"Yes, but she's looking after Grandmother."

"Mehpare, there's no need for anyone to look after Grandmother. She's in bed. But if you're worried, go on home. We'll stay here," Suat said.

"I'm not going anywhere until I see Reşat Bey."

"Fine then. Wait. When Mother comes out, you can go in next." Mehpare and Suat dashed down the corridor toward the doctor in white who had stepped out of a room. From the opposite end of the corridor came the rapid approach of footsteps. Leman turned, saw Sabahat, and looked away.

"Which room is father in?" Sabahat asked Leman, who did not answer or even look at her sister. "Which room is father in?" repeated Sabahat as she walked toward Mehpare and Suat.

"If I were you, I wouldn't stay here another second," Suat said. "If Mother sees you—"

A door opened, and Behice stepped out into the corridor. "How dare you come here," she hissed at Sabahat. "You father killer."

"Mother!" Leman cried, springing to her feet, spilling her purse and magazine onto the floor. "Don't say anything you'll regret. Please."

Sabahat winced and walked toward the open door.

"Look, Sabahat, we've been waiting our turn since morning," Suat said. "They're allowing only one visitor at a time, and Mehpare's next. She has to go back home."

Sabahat closed the door behind her.

Reşat Bey's arm was bandaged from the shoulder down. His face was bruised and scraped and splotched with an iodine tincture. Resting on his back between white sheets, eyes closed, he looked terrible, and if it weren't for the gentle rise and fall of his chest, he could have been mistaken for a corpse. Sabahat sat down on the bedside chair her mother had vacated moments earlier and whispered, "Beyba." There was no reaction. She timidly reached out her hand, thought better of it, and retracted it.

"Dearest Beyba, forgive me. I didn't realize I would upset you this much, enough for you to take your own life. I won't marry Aram. You can hear me, can't you? I won't get married. Not ever. I will be your girl until the day I die. Even if you throw me out of the house, don't cast me out of your heart. If you disown me, my life will have no meaning. I'll die. I stayed up all night, thinking about what happened. If you find a place for me in your heart, I will choose life over happiness."

There was no indication that Reşat Bey heard his daughter, nothing except for the tear that welled up out of the corner of his left eye and rolled down his cheek to the corner of his mouth. Sabahat reached out again, and this time she gently stroked her father's thick white hair. Then she stood up and walked out of the room. Without going over to the women watching her with a kind of hostile curiosity, she walked down the corridor. Mehpare came running up after her.

"Wait for me in the garden. After I wish your father a speedy recovery, I'll come down and meet you. Let's go to the house together."

"Are you not angry with me, Mehpare?"

"Sabahat, who could understand you better than me?"

38

The Evil Eye

Reşat Bey's bandages had been removed, and the bruises on his face had faded from a livid purple to a pale yellow. Physically, he had made a full recovery; emotionally, he was heartbroken and mortified. Along with the deep shame of having attempted suicide, there was the agonizing loss of faith in his beloved daughter and the remorse of having caused injury to his savior of a son-in-law. He was too humiliated to look anyone in the eye, but especially Mahir, who still winced in pain with each movement, sneeze, and cough, due to the two ribs broken by the door handle. Reşat Bey stayed in his study, not talking with anyone, not getting up from his desk, barely eating from the tray delivered to the study three times a day.

"If he doesn't die of sorrow, he'll die of starvation," Behice muttered to herself. "The evil eye has struck this family, the evil eye!"

And it really did seem that just when everything had been going well, an eye of malice or envy had turned on the family, throwing their lives into disarray. In a fit of madness, Saraylıhanım had pushed Grandmother down the stairs; the door had crashed down, injuring both Mahir and Reşat Bey; and if Mahir had arrived any later . . . Behice stopped herself. She couldn't bear to consider what might have happened. The bullet had hit his shoulder. God had spared the head of her household for the sake of his wife and children. At considerable expense, Behice had arranged for three rams to be sacrificed at Eyüpsultan. But even if she'd sacrificed a camel, what difference would it have made? The pleasure had gone out of life.

"Mahir Bey, what are we going to do? What will become of us?" she kept asking as she watched her husband recede from the world. She wasn't yet ready to think about Sabahat, nor had she any desire to see her daughter's face. She would wait for her husband to get well, and only then would she deal with her daughter.

Mahir came in with a bottle of the mysterious potion used to treat Reşat Bey's melancholia. Sometimes they would beg the patient to take it by the spoonful, at other times they mixed it into his coffee and tea when he wasn't looking.

"Time is the best medicine," Mahir was saying. "It really is."

Behice, who put little stock in platitudes, responded, "The sorrow I understand, but why does he feel so ashamed? Nobody knows about our daughter's foolishness, and nobody shall know. Why does he beat himself up so? Ah, Reşat Bey!"

Time passed. Reşat Bey's physical injuries healed, but he was as despondent as ever. Shut into another room of the house was Sabahat, as desperate and guilt-stricken as her father.

One evening, gathered in the study, the three men of the house discussed Sabahat. Hilmi wondered if it might be best to send her away. Perhaps she would forget that young man. They could write to their relatives in Ankara, informing them that the girl stood to benefit from a change of scenery. Perhaps a position as a secretary or translator could be found for Sabahat at an ambassadorship?

"Let's send a letter to Fatin," Reşat Bey said.

The following day, Mahir told Leman, who then told Behice, that a position was being sought for Sabahat in Ankara.

"Rather than sending Sabahat far from her home, let's dispatch that defiler. He knows English, too. He can work in Ankara," Behice Hanım said. How could she possibly allow her daughter to move to another city, especially when she would be going not as a bride but as some sort of working girl. Behice shuddered. Several days and buckets of tears later, she decided the time had come to make peace with Sabahat. Perhaps if her daughter presented a more cheerful face to the world, Reşat Bey would change his mind about sending her off to that provincial city. Ankara, the capital city! What nonsense! As far as Behice was concerned, any place beyond Istanbul was provincial.

She went down to the kitchen and found her daughter, her little girl, standing in front of the stove, her face pallid, her eyes red rimmed, her hair hanging like a horse's tail in a single braid down her back. Even her lovely hair had lost its shine. For nearly a month, Behice had not touched her daughter or looked her in the face. What if she left forever, and Behice never saw her again? The mother stood behind her daughter for a moment and then, in a soft whisper, said, "Sabahat . . . Sabahat, my girl . . ."

Suat, Hilmi, and Mahir were getting off the island ferry in Istanbul. For several days now, they had talked of nothing but Sabahat and Aram.

"Has he done his military service? He's long since reached the age of conscription. Now that he's dropped out of university, he should be called up, shouldn't he?" Suat asked her husband. Hilmi and Mahir exchanged glances.

"If Aram goes off to do his military service, Sabahat won't have to go anywhere, and Mother won't have to get so upset," Suat continued. "Do something."

"Shh! Not so loud, Suat," Hilmi said.

"Do you think we work at an induction center?" Mahir said in a low voice. "And anyway, I resigned from the army years ago."

"But you must know people in high places. What about you, Hilmi? Is there nothing you can do?"

"I can find out why he hasn't done his military service."

"The guy's already been beaten up twice. Do we really need to pile on?" Mahir said.

"All I'm going to do is make a few inquiries. What else can I do?"

"I think that man over there is listening to us. Let's talk about it at home," Suat whispered, forgetting she was the one who had raised the subject.

A week later, Hilmi had news for Mahir: "Just between us, I've taken care of it."

"Really? How?"

"I have a friend who works at the center."

"I wish you hadn't! What if he gets in trouble?" Mahir said.

"He'll have to do his military service sooner or later. Is there any way to avoid it? If he doesn't go today, he'll go tomorrow. In fact, it's better to do your service while you're young. Mahir, don't you remember? Isn't basic training easier the younger you are?"

"Hilmi, the next thing you know, you'll be telling me you did the guy a favor."

"By squelching this thing, we're doing them both a favor. There's no future for Sabahat and that Armenian!"

"When is he being inducted?"

"Any day now."

"Where will he be stationed?"

"Aşkale!"

"Oh, dear!" Mahir said, shaking his head.

"Well, where did you expect him to go? Florya? The young men from the West serve in the East, and those from the East are sent to the West. You know that."

"Are you going to tell Reşat Bey?"

"No. We're the only ones who need to know."

"Good. It would be one more thing he felt guilty about. Make certain he never finds out!"

"Now I can worry about my own posting," Hilmi said. "Pray I can get the post of my choosing as easily as I got his."

"You've requested a post in Istanbul, haven't you? You certainly deserve it, after all these years away."

"It's not Istanbul I requested," Hilmi said. "It's Ankara."

Mahir's jaw dropped.

39

Hilmi Dreams of a Home

When Hilmi completed the final details on the eastern border maps he was sketching and turned them in to his superiors, he requested to be transferred to the western part of the country. Petitions were submitted and reasons cited. Officers' preferences were not taken into account, not officially, but he had served in the rugged and underdeveloped East for a long time, and if his request reached a high-placed and sympathetic ear, his chances for a transfer looked good. He missed his home, his wife, and his family. Over the years, he had awaited leave as eagerly as any homesick boarding-school boy, counting down the days until the holidays. When he got home, Suat would be waiting in the window, and by the time he had rung the bell at the gate, his wife would have started running toward the garden, where she would be waiting for his embrace, for him to kiss her on the cheeks, mindful not to let his lips stray to her throat or her lips, both of them wary of the many eyes in the numerous windows, of his sisters-in-law, his mother-in-law, the children, the housekeeper, and the adopted woman. He would wave to them all, and they would rush up to him when he stepped through the front door, with hugs and kisses, chattering away in the entrance hall and around the dinner table while he waited patiently for night and the opportunity to love his wife as he had imagined so many times in his dreams and fantasies, only to find that just as they were being united body and soul, that little pest, his son, would crawl up onto the bed, wriggling in under the covers between man and wife, between mother and father. Suat would never agree to send the boy to his own bed. Hilmi knew that once he was back with his regiment, Bülent would reclaim his place in the marital bed, and the boy's bedroom on the second floor would be empty until the next time his father visited. So why couldn't Bülent stay in his own bed when Hilmi came home to be with his wife? Was it any wonder that Hilmi was sometimes gruff and bad tempered?

It was out in nature with his paints, brushes, and canvases that Hilmi knew true peace of mind. He would forget his troubles and himself as he painted for hours, expressing, perhaps, the thoughts to which he never gave voice or that he never allowed to fully form.

The one advantage of not living under his own roof was the company of his father-in-law, Reşat Bey, and his brother-in-law, Mahir. While he did not always agree with their views, they were well read, with their own take on life, and their conversation honed his own intellect. But when his male companions were not at home for one reason or another, the women reigned supreme, prattling over trifles, complaining, quarreling with each other, scolding the children. It was at these times that Hilmi would grab his easel and paint box, throw himself onto a streetcar and then a ferryboat, and sail to the far shores of the Bosphorus, alighting in the peaceful pastels of Göksu. Hours later, as evening fell, he would make his way home with a half-sketched landscape under his arm: a rowboat on Göksu Creek, the view from the footbridge of the ocher waterfront manor, cows grazing on grassy banks against the setting sun. Hilmi was a talented painter and a student of Şeker Ahmet Pasha. Had life permitted and had the empire not been engaged in constant battle, he would have become a painter or an architect instead of a soldier. Everyone has dreams and expectations of the future. He had not achieved his, not all of them, but he had come damn close. When wartime finally came to an end, Hilmi had been sent to a succession of border cities as a cartographer and topographer. As a professional soldier, what more could he have asked for? At least he was drawing and sketching; far from his family, but close to his pencils and paints. By the time he turned forty, the palaces and mansions he had imagined building for others had grown hazier and hazier, until his one distinct dream was a house of his own. What Hilmi wanted was a home where he could love his wife, horse around with her, chase her from room to room, and lie with her on the carpet wherever he caught her. It was his dream. It was his desire. A home for him, his wife, and— providing they slept in their own beds—his children.

Having never lived with Suat for any length of time, he had noticed, with the discerning eye of an artist, the subtle changes in her appearance. Each time he came to Istanbul on leave, at three-month intervals, he would find that his wife's face had grown a bit more worn. Unlike her elder sister, Suat never fussed in front of the mirror or agonized over clothes, perhaps because she did not have a husband to welcome home every evening. Over time, she let herself go, too busy with housework and children to care about primping and grooming. Unlike her elder sister, she looked after her children herself, feeding them, bathing them, putting them to sleep. When Mehpare left, it was Suat who diced onions in the kitchen with Nesime as Leman played the piano or listened to the gramophone, and it was Suat who cleared and set the table, brought Behice her aspirator, and sat with Grandmother. All that work and worry etched lines in her face and coarsened her complexion.

What a beauty Suat had been when she and Hilmi were introduced! After their first meeting, he had gone home and, while the image was still fresh in his mind, sketched her face. He had never seen such a beautiful nose, such a beautiful mouth, such perfect proportions. Her golden-brown hair had been gathered up at the neck. *I am going to wake up next to that face every day,* he had thought. *I must be the luckiest man alive!* But it was only for the first two months of their marriage that he was able to gaze at the face on the pillow next to his in the early morning light. Then came the years of duty, distance, homecomings, and separations, one after another.

Now, if Hilmi were transferred to Ankara, and if his beautiful wife agreed to move there, he and Suat would live in a house of their own, all on their own. Better late than never!

Bülent had grown too old to slip into his parents' bed at night, but Rasin had come into their lives. Away from his aunts and grannies, in a house where his father was the sole authority, his younger son would not grow up spoiled. He would sleep, play, and study in his own room. Or so Hilmi hoped.

Hilmi had been dreaming for a long time of moving to a house in Ankara. His castles in the air were gone, but he had scraped together some savings, enough, perhaps, that with prudence and economy, he would be able to buy one. That is, if Suat agreed to move!

40

Sabahat Writes to Aram

Dearest, dearest Aram,

I write this letter in the hope that it will find you one day soon. I'll forward it to Ekmel, who will visit your brother in the Grand Bazaar pretending to be an old Robert College friend who wants your address. Having already played this trick on your mother, I suggested we try it on Jirayir this time. When Ekmel learns your address, he will put my envelope into a larger one and post it to you.

We have both grown so accustomed to waiting that it makes little difference if a letter that would normally take ten days to be delivered takes a month. After all, we have vowed to wait a lifetime.

Again, Aram, we wait!

Up until my father's suicide attempt, we were waiting for the day we would be able to stand on our own two feet and set up a home. We thought the power of our love would be enough to overcome all of the world's follies, prejudice, and injustices. It turns out we were wrong! Speaking for myself, I realized I wasn't strong enough to risk losing my father, and I didn't want to cause his death. I retreated, and I thank you a thousand times, Aram, for forgiving me and understanding me.

The last time we met, you asked me to wait a little longer. At this time, I do not know precisely what it is that we are waiting for, nor do I feel like dwelling on it. I will continue to find strength in the hope that whatever it is we are waiting for will happen one day, while we still love and want each other.

Right now, I am sitting on a terrace in Cyprus, fragrant with that island's mimosa, filling my lungs with the Mediterranean air, and writing these lines with the expectation that, despite all that has happened, life is worth living.

Five days have passed since I began working as a translator at a bank in Nicosia, a position arranged by the general manager of the Istanbul branch of İş Bank, Selahattin. (I've never mentioned him before. He's the husband of one of our second cousins on my father's side of the family.) If anything good has come from the recent sad event, it is this: instead of trying to find me a husband, my family found me a job. The monthly salary I will earn here is not insignificant. But what good is money if I can't spend it with you, Aram?

I'll try to describe, in order, what has happened since we last met.

When Father came home from the hospital, we avoided each other whenever possible. I would have my breakfast early and return to my room, not venturing downstairs unless I had to, and never when he was there. Saraylıhanım went to live with Mehpare, and my grandmother moved into her room. I had my bedroom to myself again.

Mother seemed to regret her harsh words. One day, she embraced me in the kitchen and said she knew how much I loved my father. We made peace. My sisters and I have always fallen out and made up, and that's what we did this time, too. I spent my days in my room reading and would sometimes go out for tea with Armine, Mehpare, or Piraye. One thing that made life more bearable was Rasin, Suat's baby. He rarely cries, and he's got the most enormous eyes! Suat often left him in my room with me. There's something soothing about babies, and my most peaceful hours were spent with Rasin. Days passed this way, until one evening Mahir called me to his room and asked if I was content "to rot up in the attic," or if I would prefer to work. I told him I was eager to work. He said a family friend would arrange a suitable position, and that position turned out to be in Cyprus. Apparently, it was Father's wish that I be sent away from Istanbul for a time. I understand. Playing hide-and-seek in that house was a strain on us both.

And that is why I am writing to you from Cyprus.

What's strange is that, even after this tragedy, I don't feel at all guilty. I am sorry I am not the daughter my parents wished me to be, but I will never regret loving you, Aram.

Where are you? Where have you been stationed? It must be somewhere in the East. Please write to me the minute you get my letter. I think of you often and wonder how you are doing.

Love,
Sabahat

41

Aram Writes to Sabahat

My Sabahat,
Your letter reached me much more quickly than you had
anticipated. The moment Jirayir saw Ekmel, he figured
out what was happening, and said, "Give me the letter,
and I'll post it on the way home." Jirayir wrote to me
that the look on Ekmel's face was priceless. Anyway, now
that we have each other's addresses we can write as often
as we like, my dear.

I write this letter to you propped on my elbows in
a sea of poppies and daisies. Sometimes I turn onto my
back, look up at the sky, and say to myself, "Maybe we
cannot be together, in the same place, but she is looking
up at the same sky, seeing the same moon, and being
warmed by the same sun." At least we live on the same
planet, Sabahat. At least there is the possibility we could
meet again at any moment, anywhere. And even if we

cannot meet face-to-face, we can touch each other through our letters.

Sabahat, I discovered an ironworker in the town where I'm stationed. You know I'm good with my hands. I made a lamp with your initials on it. Today, I picked flowers for you. I'll press them and put some in my next letter so you can see how unusual the flora is here.

Never say you don't know what we are waiting for. We are waiting for each other. We are also waiting for the day our families finally understand us. I have never given up hope. If, despite the stories my mother told me, I don't hold any grudges, and if the sight of your face is enough to make me forget all the horrors of the past, then the Almighty must know what He is doing. Never lose hope. Never. I believe with all my heart that one day my mother and your father will have a change of heart.

Yours forever,
Aram

42

Sabahat Writes to Aram

Darling Aram,
I can finally say I have settled in. Up until a month ago,
your letters were my only source of pleasure. I would go
back and forth to work, not wanting to do anything else.
It is amazing how adaptable we humans can be. I never
wanted to come here. I knew full well that my family had
decided to send me into exile to keep us apart. But let me
say this: I am happy to have been exiled. I have made
friends, and we meet in the evening or bathe in the sea
on the weekends. They say it is sometimes warm enough to
swim even in November. You and I both like cold water.
It is a little chilly here now, but it is refreshing, and I
think of you every time I am in the sea. Being far from
home, alone and free, is a wonderful feeling. Another
advantage of my exile is that I am able to receive your
letters at home, without relying on Ekmel or another one
of our friends. Remember the ridiculous subterfuges they

forced on us! Even now, they still do not realize they will never prevent me from loving you.

Another good thing about my new life in Cyprus is that my sisters and mother, who rarely spoke to me at home, often write to me now that I am away. I even got letters from Sitare and Bülent the other day. So much has happened at home. My brother-in-law Hilmi is being posted to Ankara. They will be moving there in less than a month. Mother is distraught. Leman wrote that she is upset as well. Interesting. With Suat gone, Leman's list of suspects will have dropped from four to three, and she will have a much easier time catching whoever it is she suspects of using her hand towel. Joking aside, the house will be a much lonelier place now that Mehpare and Halim, Saraylıhanım, yours truly, and Suat and Hilmi and their children have all left. I wonder what Mother and Leman will do together all day long? Suat was always Mother's favorite. Poor Mother! And Sitare and Bülent are sad to be separated as well. My father even asked if they could leave Bülent in Istanbul, but Hilmi Bey refused. So, that's all my news from Cyprus and back home.

Did you get the cap and shorts I sent you? If you haven't, and you see your commander wearing a pair of pale-blue Bermuda shorts, you'll know what happened.

Write to me. Don't forget me. Love me always.

With much love,

Sabahat

43

Conversion

Hilmi and Reşat Bey were sitting on opposite ends of the leather sofa in the anteroom to Mahir's exam room. Mahir dragged up a chair and sat down opposite them. He had just measured their blood pressures and listened to their heartbeats and lungs.

"I can smoke here, can't I?" Hilmi asked.

"Of course you can, brother-in-law," Mahir responded. "That's why we came out here, so you could smoke. I can't allow anyone to smoke in the exam room, though. The women complain about the smell. I would ban smoking here, too, except that my patients seem to crave tobacco more than ever while they are waiting to be examined."

"Would you care for one, sir?" Hilmi asked, holding out his cigarette case. Reşat Bey took one, and Hilmi lit it.

"Mahir Bey, what can we do about Behice's cough?" Reşat Bey asked. "Along with shortness of breath, she now has bronchitis. She was coughing until dawn last night. Shall we have an x-ray of her lungs taken?"

"We had one done just last month. There is evidence that too much radiation can be hazardous," Mahir said. "Put several pillows behind her back and have her sleep sitting up."

"She is suffering so, the poor thing."

"Sir, I suspect that her discomfort can be attributed in large part to nerves," Mahir said. "Her world has been turned upside down. One of her daughters is far from home, the other is preparing to leave. She is about to lose her grandsons. Psychological factors can aggravate illnesses such as hers. I'm certain she will regain her health over time."

"She's already grown accustomed to Sabahat's absence," Hilmi said.

"That's what you think, my boy," Reşat Bey said. "I share my wife's bed. Neither of us has had a good night's rest for many weeks."

"Sir, while we are on the subject, I would like to point out that the measures we have taken are only temporary. We arranged for the young man to be sent to Aşkale, but we cannot keep him there forever, nor can Sabahat be expected to stay in Cyprus for the rest of her life."

"What do you suggest, Hilmi Bey?" Reşat Bey asked.

"Mahir Bey and I have discussed this at length."

"And?"

Hilmi looked to his brother-in-law, the more senior of the two, to take the lead.

"It is not our wish to be presumptuous or disrespectful in any way, sir, but we would like to express our opinion on this matter, if we may," Mahir said.

"I'm listening."

"The times have changed, sir. The principle of secularism has just been enshrined in the constitution. Restrictions on marriage between Muslim women and non-Muslim men have been abolished. What matters most to me is Sabahat's happiness. Her sisters have married and had children. Right now, we are all alive and able to take care of her, but only God knows what the future holds. Once our maker has claimed us one by one, is Sabahat to be all alone in this world? She is younger than the rest of us. If she enjoys a long life, like her grandmother, she would have no choice but to live with one of her nephews or nieces. Sir, Hilmi Bey and I have thought this over. We hope Sabahat might have a husband and children of her own."

"She refuses to marry. That is her decision," Reşat Bey said.

"Yes, but the person she wishes to marry is honest and upstanding. None of us chose to be Muslim. He was born Christian through no fault of his own."

"If Aram converted to Islam," Hilmi hastily added, "would you consent to their marriage?"

Reşat Bey said nothing. His right eyebrow was twitching. He looked at his sons-in-law for a moment, and then he slowly got up and walked to the door.

"I know how compassionate you are, sir." Mahir said. "Your heart would never allow hidebound traditions to ruin a girl's life, let alone the life of your own daughter."

Reşat Bey walked out without a word. Hilmi and Mahir looked at each other, uncertain if Reşat Bey, who was hard of hearing, had not heard them or if he was ignoring them.

44

The Ball

As Turkey continued to modernize, the upper and middle classes began attending a new form of entertainment, the *balo*, that was radically different from the wedding gatherings and religious feasts that had been central to their culture for centuries. The most eagerly anticipated and elegant of these dances was the Republican Ball held annually in every city and a good many of the large towns to celebrate the founding of the republic. Balls were also held to mark the New Year and to honor various professions: the Doctors' Ball, the Engineers' Ball, the Barristers' Ball, and so forth. These formal gatherings were staged not only for the purposes of entertainment, but to instruct the men of a patriarchal society on the finer points of polite society and the proper behavior for gentlemen when in the company of ladies. Gone were the centuries of rowdy all-male affairs revolving around free-flowing jugs of wine and bottles of rakı, pistols fired into the air, fistfights, and other forms of merrymaking that too often ended in grievous bodily harm or worse. Now, the men of this new nation were learning how to drink with women, how to dance with women, how to converse with women, how to compliment women, and even, within the boundaries of propriety, of course, how to let themselves go and have fun with women.

Every year, without fail, Mahir and Leman would attend at least two of these balls. One was the Doctors' Ball in April, the other the Republican Ball at the Pera Palace, also attended by many of their married friends.

Leman had for many years been the good-natured sartorial rival of Sabiha, the wife of Mahir's colleague and close friend, Ali Rıza Bey. Sabiha was an elegant woman, tall and slender, blond and blue-eyed, the belle of every ball. Leman was not a little envious. The two friends always sat together at the same table, basking in the admiring gazes of the entire ballroom.

Leman and Sabiha were discussing the upcoming Doctors' Ball of 1935 when the latter woman revealed that she was going to wear the same gown she had worn to the Republican Ball the previous year.

"I'll do the same," Leman had instantly said. "As you know, Suat is moving to Ankara and my mother has taken ill with asthma. At a time like this, I would derive no pleasure from poring over a dressmaker's patterns." Leman truly believed in the sincerity of her own words, but as she was strolling through Beyoğlu some days later, she happened to spot a bolt of fuchsia chiffon in the window of Lion Department Store. Shades of purple particularly suited Leman. She went into the store, leafed through the magazines in the fabrics section, found a dress pattern she liked, and was soon back on the street, this time with a length of chiffon under her arm.

Her preparations for the ball took nearly a month. A piece of dentelle would have to be found to rehabilitate her old handbag, and the same dentelle would be used to craft a corsage. Thankfully, Leman was skilled at delegating. Seamstress Katina was summoned to the house as an overnight guest, since there were, after all, plenty of vacant guestrooms those days. Mahir's tailcoat was sent to the cleaners, his wing-collar shirt was starched to within an inch of its life, and his japanned leather shoes were buffed to a high gloss.

On the morning of the ball, Leman stopped by the salon in Beyoğlu. As was the fashion in those days, she had her hair combed out and three curls were encouraged to grace her forehead.

That evening, Sitare gazed up in awe as her mother descended the stairs, regal in purple.

"Mother, you look gorgeous. That gown is perfect on you," she said, kissing Leman on the cheek.

Leman was unable to revel in the compliment. She had neglected to tell her friends that she was having a gown made and was already feeling the prick of a guilty conscience. Dear Sabiha would attend the ball in last year's gown, while Leman, a vision in fuchsia chiffon, would have to endure other guests' adulation. It was terrible, but it was too late.

Shrugging into her stole with Mahir's assistance, Leman walked with her husband to a waiting cab. They were finally off to the ball.

Waving them off, Sitare turned to Grandmother and proclaimed, "Mother is going to be the most beautiful woman at the ball tonight."

Sitare was sound asleep, having studied until the wee hours for her test the following morning. She had expected to learn all about the ball the following afternoon, since Mother would be sleeping in when Sitare got ready for school in the morning. Sitare would have to wait to find out how many times Father had led Mother onto the dance floor, what they had to eat and drink, and all the other little details Mother delighted in sharing.

So imagine Sitare's surprise when she heard her mother's voice late that night. Was that Mother sobbing and shouting? Sitare opened her eyes and rubbed them. She was in her bed and it was dark, but she could hear her mother. She switched on the lamp, leapt out of bed, and ran out onto the landing to see what had happened.

Everyone was in the entrance hall gathered around Mother, who was tearing at her fuchsia gown as Father and Nesime tried to undo the tiny buttons. Mother was weeping and screaming. It took a moment for her words to register: "He vomited! The filthy beast! He vomited!"

Grandma Behice and Grandpa Reşat fluttered and circled; everyone was talking at once. The gown was finally removed, leaving Mother in a bodice and petticoat. "Pour it there! There!" she shouted at Father, who was holding a bottle of rubbing alcohol. Sitare started coming down the stairs. When Mahir heard her, he turned and said, "Go to bed, Sitare. Don't worry, it's nothing serious. A drunk threw up on your mother's dress."

"That's not serious, Mahir?" Leman sobbed.

The queen who had descended the stairs just a few hours earlier was now a disheveled mess, her face smeared with rouge and black mascara trails. *She looks like a witch*, Sitare thought as she obediently climbed the stairs and got into bed. She was soon fast asleep.

45

That Big Black Door

"Mahir, I think Sitare has a fever."

Leman came back into the room and checked Sitare's forehead and throat again with her hand.

"I'm fine, Mother. Really. I'm fine."

"Does your throat hurt?"

"No."

"Your head?"

"My head doesn't hurt, either."

"Well then, why are your eyes glazed? You do have a fever!" Leman went out onto the landing a second time and shouted, "Mahir! Can you come up here for a minute?"

"I'll go down to Father," Sitare said, dashing out of the room and down the stairs before her mother could stop her.

"Come on in," Mahir said when he saw his daughter at the door to his exam room. He got up from behind his desk. "Sitare, it's true you're looking a little peaked." He pulled a thermometer out of a drawer, shook it, and handed it to his daughter. "Stick it under your tongue, and don't talk for three minutes."

"Mother would kill you if she knew I was putting a thermometer in my mouth."

"If you don't want her to kill me, don't tell her. This is the best way to check your temperature."

"But the inside of the mouth is so hot. Won't it show a higher temperature?"

"No talking for three minutes."

"Dad, I'll keep your secret if you keep mine. There's a concert at school this weekend. If you tell Mother I have a fever, she won't let me leave the house. I really want to go. Please give me some medicine to make me well as quickly as possible."

"All right. We have a deal. But if you're running a temperature, you'll have to stay in bed and rest until the weekend."

Sitare stayed quiet for three minutes. Mahir removed the thermometer.

"What does it say?"

"One hundred and one degrees. Have you caught a chill, I wonder?"

"How do I know? I'll get better by the weekend, won't I?"

"If you do exactly as I say, you will." Mahir took a couple of bottles out of the medicine cabinet and put them in his pocket. Father and daughter went upstairs.

"She has a fever, doesn't she?" Leman asked.

"Yes, but it's low-grade. Have Nesime make her some soup. I'll give her some medicine, and we'll send her to bed early tonight. She'll be fine in a couple of days. She must have caught a chill."

"That doesn't surprise me. She's more interested in looking chic than in wearing a jacket or sensible undergarments. And she throws her blanket on the floor, sleeping bare in the night air!"

"Mother, stop exaggerating."

"You're sleeping in my room tonight, Sitare. Your covers always slide off you when you're sleeping, and you know it. I'll keep you tucked in. And you might wake up parched and wanting a glass of water."

"The three of us in bed again, just like old times?" Sitare said, looking at her father.

"You're far too old for that. How would the three of us even fit in that bed? Your father will sleep in your room tonight."

"But Mother . . ."

"You promised," Mahir said. "Please. Sleep with your mother tonight. If your fever gets worse in the night, we'll figure something out."

"Are you going to keep your promise, too?"

"What promise?" Leman asked.

"That's between me and my daughter."

After dinner, Sitare took her medicine, went upstairs, and slid in under the billowy white eiderdown in her parents' room. *This is wonderful,* she thought, *so soft and so many pillows.* She switched on the nightstand lamp and was flicking through one of her mother's magazines when, due to either her fever or the pills, a little lead bird seemed to alight on each of her eyelids. She resisted, but was soon asleep. She was not conscious of Leman coming into the room and placing a hand on her forehead; her father pulling the eiderdown up to her nose and giving her a kiss on the cheek; the way he tiptoed out of the room, pajamas in hand; or her mother slipping into bed beside her. She was not even aware of Nesime coming in to wake up her mother, and the two of them leaving the room together. Sitare was in a deep sleep full of vivid dreams. She was wearing a tulle dress at her graduation, dancing with her father, her white skirt billowing as they waltzed. Everyone was clapping. "I'm proud of you," Father was saying. "You're at the top of your class." He was spinning her around, faster and faster, and then she was in someone else's arms, a young man who was not her father, her white skirt swelling, puffing up, turning into foam, obscuring her father's pale face, the foam rising and covering her father. She waved her arms to whisk away the puffy foam, the puffy clouds . . .

There was a terrible cry. A scream. More screams. Voices. People running. She kept her eyes shut, trying to return to her dream, to the waltz and the foam. Her mother was screaming. She sat up and switched on the lamp, scared. Stumbling out onto the landing, she looked down. Her mother was screaming in the entrance hall again. Everyone had gathered around her.

"Did someone throw up on you again?" Sitare called out crossly. Her mother fell silent and looked up. Everyone was looking at Sitare.

"Sitare! Go back to bed and go to sleep!" her mother said.

Grumbling, Sitare did as she was told. She wished her mother wouldn't scream like a crazy woman. Back in bed, she screwed her eyes shut, hoping to have the same dream, hoping he would be there again in her dream, her father, smiling at her, and the young man, holding her in his arms.

When Sitare opened her eyes, it was morning and Grandfather was sitting on the foot of the bed. She did a double take, unsure if she was fully awake. She looked around the room. Was she stuck somewhere between the dream world and the real world?

"Sitare? Are you awake, dear?"

"Grandpa?" She slowly remembered where she was, not in her own room, in her parents' room.

"How's your fever?"

"I'm better, Grandpa." What was he doing at the foot of the bed? Had she taken a turn for the worse in the middle of the night? She remembered the dream, and her mother screaming. Except—wait, that part wasn't a dream. *Oh no!*

"Sitare. My girl."

"I'm fine, Grandpa, really. The medicine Father gave me made me sweat. Look, my forehead's not hot anymore." She took hold of Reşat

Bey's hand and brought it to her forehead. "I can take another pill if you want. We can ask Father . . . Grandpa? What's wrong, Grandpa?"

"Sitare, sometimes, when we least expect it . . ." A tear rolled down Reşat Bey's cheek.

"What happened?" Sitare threw off the eiderdown and got out of bed.

"Has something happened to Grandma?"

"Sitare, don't go downstairs. Listen to me. You have to be strong. Your mother needs you now more than ever."

Sitare raced down stairs and hallways, opening doors, running from room to room, searching. *Grandma? She isn't in her room! Mother? Oh, there they are, Mother and Grandma, there on the divan.* They jumped up when they saw her, as off she ran to another room, to the study, to Great-Grandma's room. There she was, too, reading the Koran and swaying. Sitare ran down the last flight of stairs, through the entrance hall to the waiting room, empty! And the exam room, empty! The kitchen, empty! *Where is he? Where is Father!* Back she went, running up the stairs.

"Mother, where is he? Did he go to work? Where's Father?"

Nobody answered her. Sitare walked out of the room with the divan and found Grandfather sitting on the stairs. She sat down next to him and asked again, this time in a whisper: "Grandpa, where is my father?"

"He's gone, my girl. He's gone through that black door we all go through when our time comes, but his time came early."

"When?" Sitare didn't even realize she was still talking.

"Last night, toward morning."

As Sitare rose to her feet, something like tulle, something like foam, descended on her, making everything blurry, making her ears ring. A moment later, she was slumped sideways on the stairs. Reşat Bey, Leman, Behice, Nesime: She could hear them, but she didn't want to wake up. She could hear the doorbell ringing, could hear Galip Bey and Mehpare; she didn't want to wake up. Wouldn't wake up. No, she would dream.

46

Sabahat Writes to Aram

Dear Aram,

I am in tears as I write this. The ferryboat leaves in a few hours. I'm going home. Something terrible has happened. We lost Mahir. How can this be? Saraylıhanım is still running around with a chamber pot on her head. My grandmother is in her nineties. Mother and Father are alive—and may they live for many years to come, of course. It wasn't his turn, not Mahir, not someone so full of life, so good-hearted, so ready to help others. That house will seem empty now. He was the one I confided in, and I confess that I even told him about you. What will Sitare and Leman do now? How will they bear it? Aram, imagine, my sister is only thirty-eight. And what about my father? Mahir was his best friend from long before Mahir ever married Leman. How will my father bear it?

I've been homesick at times here, but I would stay on this island forever to avoid a homecoming like this.

Send your next letter with Armine. I'll write in more detail after I get to Istanbul.
   Yours, with love,
   Sabahat

47

The Mistress

After many months in the woods and alpine meadows of the Black Sea region, Muhittin was glad to see the humble poppies and daisies welcoming him back to the plains of central Anatolia. He had emerged victorious from his battle with the wild waters of the Yeşilırmak after spending many days navigating the river on a *kelek*, a type of raft kept afloat with inflated animal bladders. He returned to Ankara with a sense of achievement and peace of mind, knowing he'd done his job well.

Muhittin went straight to the office, then set off for the Çubuk Reservoir with Raif Bey to conduct a few studies and enjoy a few beers. On Saturday evening, he was finally at home and hoping to get some rest. Then he noticed the letter from Istanbul. The handwriting on the envelope belonged to . . . Nusret! He was thrilled to hear from his big brother. He opened the envelope and began reading. A shadow passed over his face. His sister's husband, Ekrem, had left home. Saadet and her husband had separated! How was that possible? They were crazy about each other, and theirs was a love match, not an arranged marriage.

The following day was a Sunday, Muhittin's one free day. He decided to go to Istanbul and sort this out. He put on a fresh suit of clothes and stuffed a pair of pajamas and a toothbrush into his leather briefcase, along with a few files he hoped to study on the train. Arriving at the station out of breath, he asked for a round-trip ticket to Istanbul. He would leave immediately and return on the overnight train the following day. The clerk handed over the ticket with a shrug and a smile that meant, "Well, I suppose you know what you're doing."

How had this happened? When had Saadet and Ekrem started growing apart? They had two young sons. What about them? Erol hadn't even finished primary school yet. Muhittin tried to quiet his mind and surrender himself to the arms of the rocking train, which normally lulled him to sleep, clickety-clack, clickety-clack. No, there would be no sleeping tonight! At one point in the letter, his big brother had admitted to being at fault in some way. Had Nusret quarreled with their brother-in-law? Had it turned into a terrible row, with Ekrem storming out of the house? No, that was ridiculous. Nusret didn't even live there! Perhaps Ekrem had fought with Salih Bey? That was impossible, too: Salih Bey loved Ekrem like a son, and Ekrem had always treated his elders with respect. So what happened? These were the questions that tormented Muhittin during the overnight journey to Istanbul.

When he reached the door of the house in Sultanahmet in the morning, Saadet called out, "Muho's here, boys. Your uncle's here. Run and tell Jijo." When he was about two, Ecvet had taken to calling Gül Hanım "Jijo," a Bosnian term of endearment meaning "cute and sweet." The name had stuck, and even Gül Hanım's husband and grown children used it from time to time. Now he could hear Ecvet and Erol running through the house yelling, "Jijo, Jijo!"

He stepped inside, and Saadet gave him a warm smile and a big hug just before she started crying in his arms. They went into the living room and sat down side by side, across from Gül Hanım. "Tell me all about it. What happened?" Muhittin said. "I'll talk to Ekrem, and we'll sort this out. I'm sure there's been a misunderstanding."

"No, there hasn't." Saadet wiped her eyes. "It's over with Ekrem."

"Could you get me a coffee, Saadet?" Muhittin said. "Let me wake up, and then we'll talk." As soon as she left the room, Gül Hanım told Muhittin that there was another woman in Ekrem's life, and Saadet had found out.

"Don't bother pushing her, son. Her nose is so out of joint it's reached Mount Qaf. She'll never forgive him." Gül Hanım got up, opened a drawer, and turned around holding something. "Look!" Cupped in her hand were two diamond earrings, one of them in several pieces, a necklace with a broken chain, and a couple of rings.

"Why are you showing me that?"

"I caught your sister with a mortar and pestle, smashing the jewels Ekrem gave her. These are the ones your father and I were able to save. Everything else is crushed and broken. Now, how you do talk sense into a woman who would do something like that?"

Nusret came over for lunch and a talk with Muhittin behind closed doors. Apparently, for many years Ekrem had been having an affair with the heiress to the Knapp family laundry chain.

"Aren't the Knapps Jewish?"

"Meaning?"

"Nothing. Whether she's Jewish or not, Ekrem should never have gotten involved with her. He's married with children! I would never have expected this of him."

"What world do you live in, Muho?"

"I try to live in a clean world."

"But the world's a dirty place."

"Unfortunately. How did Saadet find out?"

"Don't ask, Muho . . . I told her."

"What?"

***

Nusret had come to his parents' house for dinner one evening. He and Ekrem had a few glasses of rakı out in the garden. The family sat down to eat much later than usual. Ekrem scolded his hungry sons for lunging at the platters of food. Ekrem had been bad tempered of late, and he continued to drink rakı at the dinner table, along with Salih Bey and Nusret. That is, the men were all a bit drunk.

"Saadet, we need some salt," Ekrem said. Saadet ran to the kitchen and got some.

"Saadet, we're out of water," Ekrem said. Saadet ran to the kitchen with the empty pitcher.

"Saadet, get us some more bread," Ekrem said. Saadet ran off to the kitchen, sliced some more, and came back with a full basket.

"Pass the bread," Ecvet told his brother. Erol threw a slice at Ecvet, and it fell onto a platter of beans, splattering the table. Ekrem jumped to his feet, grabbed his son by the ear, and dragged him to the living room, smacking his bottom all the way and shouting, "You little donkey! Learn some table manners!" Erol, who in his nine years of life had never been slapped or beaten, sobbed so hard he could be heard in the dining room.

"Ekrem, it was an accident. Why are you being so hard on the boy? What's come over you lately?" Saadet shouted.

"Shut up!" Ekrem yelled from the other room. "Why are you always bugging me? I'm sick and tired of your questions and your nagging. Do you understand?" Saadet went deathly white. Her mother jumped up and stood behind her chair, fearing she was about to faint. When Nusret saw his sister trembling, he lost his temper and rushed out to the living room, saying, "You're the donkey, Ekrem! If you're really fed up with my sister, leave this house and go to your mistress!"

***

Muhittin, who had been listening calmly to the story, sprang to his feet.

"You told her! What business did you have telling her that? Ekrem had been covering his tracks. If you'd kept your trap shut, Saadet would never have found out, and this affair, like all affairs, would have ended one day," Muhittin said. "What were you thinking? What kind of idiot are you? You were drunk that night, weren't you? You wouldn't have done something that stupid otherwise. You've ruined Saadet's life!"

Muhittin leaned over his brother and pounded his fist on the end table; then he pounded it again and again. Nusret, who had never seen his little brother so furious, said, "You're going to break your hand, Muhittin. Why do you keep hitting the table?"

"So I don't hit you! So I don't bust your big mouth and break your nose. I know you're my elder brother, but this time I'm not holding my tongue out of respect for you, not this time! Someone's got to speak up. Otherwise, you'll never realize you've crossed a line. I'm telling you loud and clear: you made a terrible mistake!"

"You're right Muho. I shouldn't have said anything. I'd kept it a secret for such a long time, at least two years. But when I saw what he was doing to Saadet, I lost it. I mean, he was so clearly in the wrong and yet so indignant and abusive, as though she had done something wrong. It slipped out. I didn't think she'd hear, but she did. Now she knows, and it's all because of me."

"Did Ekrem leave that same night?" Muhittin asked.

"When we started shouting at each other, Mother sent the boys to their rooms and told us to stay in the living room with the door shut. We were going at it, and the door opened. It was Saadet. She could barely stand. 'Ekrem, do you have a mistress?' she asked. He didn't say a word. She repeated the question, and this time he said, 'What are you talking about?' 'That's what my brother said,' she told him. I denied having said it. She asked him a third time, studying his face to see if he was lying. 'You do have a mistress,' she said, and then she screamed, 'Get out! Get out of this house this minute! Go!' She screamed and screamed. Ekrem went out into the hall, took his hat off the coat stand, put on his jacket, and walked out. Mother started yelling, blaming it all on me. Please don't start in on me, too, Muhittin."

Saadet opened the door and came inside. "You're not fighting because of me, are you? Ekrem's done enough. I won't let him come between my brothers." She had washed her face and fixed her hair. "Muho, I'm fine," Saadet said. "Nobody can say my home was wrecked. This is my home, and I'm still here with my children. The only thing that's changed is that my husband is gone. He's never coming back, and I'll never forgive him. End of story, Muho!"

"What about the boys? Have they seen their father? What did you tell them?" Muhittin asked.

"The boys will continue to respect their father. That's our way, you know that. They can visit him every Sunday."

Muhittin regretted what he had said to his brother. His sister was right: what was done was done. There was no sense fighting among themselves. Still, as strong as Saadet looked, he was worried for her. Divorce was unheard of among Bosnians. This would be a first not only in their family but in their extensive circle of friends and acquaintances. The family would have to learn, all together, how to endure the shame and the sorrow.

48

The Still, Gray Lake

Muhittin was bouncing along in the passenger seat of a jeep, still thinking about the visit to his family. He wished there was something he could do to help Saadet. To take his mind off his family, he decided to strike up a conversation with the driver.

"How did you end up with the name Çapan? I've never heard it before. It is a kind of hoe, isn't it? Does it have a special meaning?"

"Well sir, it does and it doesn't," Çapan replied after giving the question a great deal of thought. "You see, my mother was out in the fields turning earth when she had me. All alone except for her hoe. When she felt the labor pains coming on, she held on tight to that hoe, to give her strength. And that's why she named me Çapan."

"You wouldn't believe the names out in Anatolia," Raif Bey said from the backseat. They drove another half hour in silence, Muhittin's brains scrambled from his thoughts and the violent shaking of the jeep.

"Stop here, Çapan," Raif Bey said. Muhittin and Raif Bey jumped out and walked over to the shore of a lake. Çapan followed with a picnic basket.

The lake was light gray and perfectly still. To Muhittin, who had recently splashed in the brilliant blue waves of the Black Sea, the body of water stretching before him had all the beauty of a tub of gray bathwater. If not for the hazy range of mountains way off in the distance, he would have felt as though he was walking across an enormous platter covered with gray-brown dust. Raif Bey took the picnic basket and bustled ahead to the desolate shoreline. He pulled a checkered tablecloth out of the hamper, then a bottle of beer wrapped in a towel. "I set it on the windowsill last night. I'm hoping the towel kept it cool," he remarked to Muhittin, who had caught up and was spreading the tablecloth on the ground. One by one, out came tin canisters of grilled meatballs, sliced bread and tomatoes, salt and pepper, tin plates, cloth napkins, and a bottle opener. Last of all, Raif Bey produced three tin cylinders that, lids removed, turned out to be drinking vessels.

Muhittin sat down on the tablecloth, impressed once again by his colleague's organizational skills. Raif Bey put some food on a plate and handed it, along with a bottle of sweetened soda water, to Çapan. "You're driving, son. No beer for you." Çapan took his plate and sat on a large rock a short distance away.

"I realize the lake here in Gölbaşı is something of a disappointment to you," Raif Bey said. "You can't please Istanbulis, no matter where you take them. Nothing compares to the Bosphorus. But I'd like to point out, Muhittin Bey, that the steppe has a stark beauty all its own. Once you've been here longer, you'll see what I'm talking about. The stillness, the silence, the nothingness: it's easier to think clearly out here. There's a reason most of the great mystics and dervishes came from the steppe. You'll grow to love it."

"I already like Ankara. I missed the greenness of the Black Sea when I first returned, but this city has such a sense of optimism and drive. You can feel it in the air."

"Do you live alone?" Raif Bey abruptly asked.

"I rented a place with a friend of mine, an engineer, but he went to Niğde two weeks ago to help build the Gebere Reservoir."

"So you're a bachelor, Muhittin Bey. Forgive me for asking, but why haven't you married?"

"I haven't met anyone I'd like to spend the rest of my life with."

"Believe me, I understand. I've reached middle age, and I'm still a bachelor. I never married, never could. About ten years ago, they took me to meet a prospective bride, who was widely praised for her breeding and beauty. Well, off we went to see her, and she was all they said and more. But her mother, I'm afraid, was rather large. I looked at the woman's double chin and imagined the daughter in five or ten years. I couldn't sleep a wink that night. The next day, I sent word that I was not interested after all. That was the last time anyone tried to make a match for me. After that, I accepted that I was a fussy middle-aged man who should remain a bachelor. My friend, I do hope you don't end up like me."

"Oh, me, too!" Muhittin agreed, perhaps a bit too heartily.

Over their picnic and beer, the conversation soon turned to Muhittin's family back in Istanbul, especially his elder brother Nusret.

"Nusret? How is it that I never made the connection? I know your brother," Raif Bey said.

"He rarely goes to Ankara on business. How did you meet him?"

"Not through work. We once placed poker at Cemal Bey's. He wears glasses, doesn't he?"

"Yes."

"I'm sure we're talking about the same Nusret. Isn't he married to the sister of Cemal Bey's wife, Leyla Hanım? Cemal Devrimel? Nusret was introduced to us as Cemal's brother-in-law."

"That's him." Muhittin laughed. "It's a small world!"

Muhittin's thoughts turned once again to his sister and to her new life all on her own. He was grateful to have so much work. As he sat on the shores of the still gray lake, not working, not reading, not writing, just looking out over the desolate landscape and listening to the silence, he realized how lonely he was.

On the drive back, Muhittin moved to the backseat and managed to doze off. As Muhittin was getting out of the car, near his apartment, Raif Bey said, "Muhittin Bey, I'm paying a visit to a close friend tonight. His wife and children are in Istanbul, and he's home alone. He's good company. Would you care to join me?"

"That's very kind of you, Raif Bey, but I'm a little worn out. I think I'd better stay home tonight."

Muhittin watched for a moment as Çapan drove away with Raif Bey, then he walked into his empty flat.

49

Sabahat Writes to Aram

Dear Aram,

I'm in Istanbul. Having arrived only yesterday, I was too late for my brother-in-law's funeral. The house is still full of relatives and neighbors. They say that on the day of the funeral the line of those wishing to offer their condolences extended out into the street. Mim Kemal, an old doctor friend of Mahir's, had sedated Leman and Sitare. They sat in the house, semiconscious, like zombies. Mother, Suat, Mehpare, and Şahber Hanım and her daughters all cried their eyes out. There was nothing anyone could say to comfort them. Father was so grief stricken they worried for his health. It was Naci who told me all about the funeral. There was such a large crowd that many of the mourners could not reach the gate, let alone the courtyard, of the Fatih Mosque. Naci said she's never seen such a well-attended funeral. Someone wanted to know whose funeral it was. An old man said, "Son, we're making our final farewells to a doctor who helped one and all. Everyone has come to pay their final respects. Say a prayer." All of Mahir's colleagues, his friends from the military academy, his patients, and half the neighborhood of Beyazit—and that's no exaggeration—were there. Everyone wanted a turn carrying the coffin on their shoulders, and they walked a long way with no need for a hearse. I went to the cemetery this morning with my family. We brought some roses from home. Sitare wouldn't leave her father's grave. Her grandfather Reşat has forbidden her and my sister from going to the cemetery again for a long time. Otherwise, they would go every day. "Excessive mourning only torments the soul of the deceased," Father says. I'm exhausted. I miss Mahir so much. How do we survive this? None of us knows. The house is crowded with people, but each of us is alone in her grief.

Keep sending your letters to Armine.

All my love,

Sabahat

50

Guilt and Mourning

The mansion in Beyazit had been the scene of many reunions and farewells in the month since Mahir's death. Suat had arrived with her husband and sons as soon as she received the terrible news. Hilmi went
back to his duties in Ankara after a month, and she remained in Istanbul
for another ten days with Bülent and Rasin, even though the older boy
would miss school. Suat would stay until after the traditional memo-
rial service, held forty days after a death. Sabahat had come, even if
she had missed the funeral. Mahir's elder sister, Şahber Hanım, along
with Hüviyet and Fazilet, had stayed at the mansion for ten days after
the funeral, and they still came every morning to spend their days in
the kitchen making lemonade, tea, and coffee for the steady stream of
visiting neighbors, close and distant relatives, and friends of Mahir's
from the military and from medical school. Mehpare was another pair
of helping hands, arriving every morning with her son and staying until
evening, when her husband stopped by after work to take her home
with him. Even after a month had passed, former patients and chari-
table cases, retired officers and long-lost friends were still coming to

the house to express their condolences, and the women were being run off their feet.

Leman was too exhausted to feel sorry for herself or to spend her nights not sleeping. Having lost eight pounds in four weeks, her cheekbones were sharper and her eyes seemed even larger, those green eyes that were once so vivacious now pools of pain. Reşat Bey felt a sting every time he looked at his daughter. Leman had taken to her bed after the funeral and risen from it to support her daughter. It was for Sitare that she stayed strong. For years, she had assumed responsibility for her daughter's diet, dress, and hairstyle, with her education and other serious matters being delegated to the girl's father. Mahir, who adored Sitare, had always been her confidant, friend, and playmate, and she was still too dazed to comprehend fully all she had lost.

The other person in the house struggling with a sense of guilt was Suat. Leman and her husband had rarely been apart after their wedding day, and when Mahir did have to leave the city, it was never for months on end. He was always at home, always there for her. Husband and wife would dress for dinners and balls, walk off into the night, Mahir's arm slipped through Leman's as Suat waved them off, missing her absent husband Hilmi more than ever. There had been evenings, too, when Mahir and Leman retired to their room early, and mornings when they emerged from it quite late. Suat had even envied them their quarrels. Married at seventeen, Suat had lived as a semiwidow except for the first years of her marriage. She and Bülent had accompanied Hilmi to his first posting, in İzmir, but their infant son had suffered diarrhea in the summer heat of that Aegean city. She had returned to her father's house with her baby and resolved never to follow her husband again. Accustomed as she was to the comforts of home, the support of an extended family, and a doctor under her own roof, she decided she had no business out in the provinces. And so she saw her husband only at holidays, except for a period when he was mapping parts of nearby Thrace and could come home more regularly. Now, every time the formerly envious sister saw the strain and bereavement on Leman's face, she felt the prick of a bad conscience and the need to pray at night for forgiveness. Hilmi, no matter where he was posted, was still alive and still her husband. Leman was a widow at thirty-eight.

After filling with visitors once again for the special service marking forty days since Mahir's death, the house grew calmer as the relatives went back to their homes, work, and lives. Hilmi Bey had taken the overnight train for the service and would return to Ankara that weekend, accompanied this time by Suat, Bülent, and Rasin.

The day after the service, the family was gathered on the divan in the sitting room. Sitare sat in the window seat, her back to the street, resting her chin on her knees as she stared with empty eyes at the door.

"Dear, perhaps you should return to school on Monday," Reşat Bey said. "Shutting yourself up at home will only make you feel worse. It will do you good to be with your school friends again."

"I'm not going to school, Grandfather."

"I know you're behind on your studies. Don't worry about failing this year. After what has happened, nobody is expecting anything of you. You can repeat a grade. All I ask is that you return to school."

"I'm not going."

"Fine then. You can go next year."

"I'm not going next year, either. I don't want to study anymore. I don't want to do anything."

Leman signaled with her eyes that her father should drop the subject. Reşat Bey fell silent. He hid his pain behind a newspaper.

"I have an idea," Hilmi Bey said. "Let's take Sitare with us to Ankara. A change of scenery."

"That's a wonderful idea," Reşat Bey said, lowering the newspaper.

"But what about Mother?" Sitare said. "I'm not leaving her."

"She can come, too," Suat quickly said. "Ankara is a small city, nothing like Istanbul. The neighborhood we live in is tidy and new, perfect for Leman. There's no litter; nobody spits on the pavement.

We live some distance from the city center, so it feels more like a town. What do you say, Sitare? Shall we all go to Ankara together? You can spend some time with your mother, and your grandparents can get some peace and quiet."

"Would you like to go?" Leman asked.

"Please come," Bülent pleaded.

They all held their breath and waited. Sitare sat up straight.

"I'll go."

One spring day, Reşat Bey, Behice Hanım, Sabahat, Mehpare, Halim, Şahber Hanım and her daughters, and Naci, waved their handkerchiefs, some of them damp with tears, as Leman and Sitare boarded the train to Ankara at Haydarpaşa Station. Behice Hanım was secretly hoping that her daughter would make a new life for herself in a new city. No one knew how to comfort the young widow, but they expected Sitare, the child huddled in a corner of the compartment, to move beyond mourning and return to the preoccupations of daily life. What nobody seemed to realize was that this "child" was now eighteen years old.

The whistle shrilly sounded as the train shuddered to life, creeping along the rails, faster and faster. Leman and Sitare were on their way.

51

The Eligible Bachelor

Just as she was about to put some fried meatballs onto a piece of newspaper, Suat hesitated: Leman might kick up a fuss if she came into the kitchen and saw the main course draining on yesterday's headlines. Her sister had been less fussy about hygiene since Mahir's death, but one could never be too careful. Old habits die hard. Suat closed and locked the kitchen door, opening it again only after she had transferred the meatballs to a platter and thrown the paper, now crumpled and greasy, into the trash. She began chopping tomatoes for a salad.

They were having dinner early that night because Raif Bey was coming to play poker. Suat was a little worried that Leman would think Raif Bey, a bachelor, had been invited specifically for her benefit. In fact, the poor man was an acquaintance of Hilmi's from the army, now retired and living in Ankara. As kind and as courteous as he was, Suat had never seen him as a possible replacement for Mahir.

The memory of her brother-in-law still brought tears to Suat's eyes. She recalled the time he had taken her and Leman to Romania, the two sisters dressed as nurses. The Great War had just ended, but the border crossings were open to doctors. The wooden tray inlaid with mother-of-pearl on the kitchen shelf was a memento of that trip. How they'd laughed at the prospect of Leman mistakenly being called on to perform the duties of a nurse! The family had always turned to Mahir, not only for medical attention but for practical, well-reasoned solutions to thorny questions. He had been their Luqman the Wise and their Marko Pasha, and he had brought joy to their lives. His relatives were as fun-loving as he was. She wiped her eyes with the back of her hand and went into the dining room to set the table.

"Go on, Sitare, help your aunt," Leman said.

"You, too, Bülent. Spread out that tablecloth, son. Your father will be home soon. Let's have dinner ready for him."

"Hey, fathead, aren't you going to help?" Bülent asked his little brother.

"Don't call your brother names."

"But he has a huge head!"

"Don't deprecate me," five-year-old Rasin piped up.

"Where on earth do you learn those words?" Leman laughed.

"That must be why his head is so swollen; it's full of weird words and useless facts."

"Leave the boy alone!" Suat yelled from inside the kitchen.

The table was set and everyone but Suat was seated around it when Hilmi's rich baritone rang out from the hallway. "Look who I brought home." Following Hilmi into the room was a short, spectacled man with a jolly face. Leman's eyes traveled to the bouquet of flowers in his hand.

"Leman, let me introduce you to my old friend, Raif Bey. And this young lady is her daughter, Sitare." Sitare stood up and shook hands with Raif Bey. "You remember how I mentioned Leman Hanım would be staying with us until the end of the month? Well, I can't think of a better person to keep her entertained and busy in Ankara. I have full faith in you, my friend." Leman extended a hand without getting up.

"Suat Hanım!" Leman called out. "Raif Bey has kindly brought you flowers. Come out of the kitchen and join us."

Suat looked in for a moment. "Welcome, Raif Bey. I've just finished frying some meatballs. Let me change for dinner while you get to know my sister. I'll join you in a few minutes."

Raif Bey was impressed both by Leman's melancholic beauty and by her daughter's loveliness. He skillfully navigated the conversation from one subject to another, avoiding any mention of death or funerals, as though the mother and daughter had traveled to Ankara for a holiday. After a brief description of the city's landmarks, he mentioned the fashionable gatherings at the horse track and wondered if they would do him the honor of accompanying him there the following weekend.

For the first time since Leman had arrived at her sister's house, nobody talked about Mahir during dinner. Afterward, the adults sat down to poker, and the children went for a walk.

During a tea break, Raif Bey asked Leman, "What school does your lovely daughter attend?"

"She was in high school, but she discontinued her studies after she lost her father," Leman said. "Perhaps she will resume them next year. The decision is hers. Our grief is still fresh."

"It must be difficult."

Sitare became accustomed to Raif Bey's frequent visits and began addressing him as Uncle Raif, as did Bülent and Rasin. She was making a slow recovery. Instead of staying in bed late, she now got up and had breakfast with Bülent before he went to school, and joined her aunt and mother on long walks. Ankara was doing wonders for Sitare. Leman was pleased.

A few more of Reşat Bey's relatives had recently settled in Ankara. There was the consul general, Uncle Nurullah, and his wife, and Uncle Fatin's daughters often stopped by for tea and coffee, held bezique and poker parties, and took Leman and her daughter to the races and for morning strolls on the boulevard. Mahir had been right: time heals all wounds.

During a break in another poker party one Saturday, Raif Bey drew Leman aside and asked if he could consult her on a certain matter.

"Yes?" Leman said, fearing the worst.

"I would like to discuss a matter of a most auspicious nature."

Leman frowned. "Raif Bey, please do not broach such matters with me. I am unable to entertain proposals of that nature."

"Leman Hanım, you misunderstand me. Are you open to discussing a proposal regarding your daughter?"

Leman went from being deeply uncomfortable at having to fend off a suitor to feeling absolutely furious that a middle-aged man had set his heart on her child. "A proposal?" she said.

"A colleague of mine is a young engineer. He is from Istanbul, cultured, of high moral character with an unblemished reputation, and has the added advantage of being handsome. He is a bachelor. I've dared to hope that Sitare would be permitted to make his acquaintance."

"Sitare is still a child."

"How old is she?"

"She is just . . . eighteen." In the context of their discussion, Leman could not believe what she had just said. Her daughter was eighteen! It seemed like only yesterday they were celebrating Sitare's fifteenth birthday, when Sitare wore a short dress and waltzed with her father. Leman bit her lip.

"Forgive me. I have distressed you. I will never raise the subject again."

"No, Raif Bey. Now it is you who misunderstands. I seem not to have noticed that Sitare is no longer a child, that she has become a young woman. Of course I know how old she is, but . . ." Leman regained her composure. "Raif Bey, please allow me to consult my brother-in-law and my sister. I also need to test the waters with my daughter. Is she ready to meet with a potential suitor? Is she open to a courtship? I had hoped she would return to school, but if the gentleman in question is a good match, perhaps . . ."

"We can arrange a chance encounter between these two young people whenever you like."

For the first time since her husband's death, Leman went to bed that night thinking not about Mahir, but about whether or not her daughter was ready to marry.

Suat brought Leman a cup of coffee. Sitare had been reading late into the night and had not yet come to breakfast.

"We need to talk about Sitare before she gets up," Suat said as she cleared their plates. "Raif Bey telephoned Hilmi yesterday. He proposed that we all join him for a walk on Sunday. I assume his engineer friend will be there as well. Shall we mention it to Sitare?"

"I'm not convinced she's ready," Leman said.

"We were both married long before we reached her age."

"The times have changed. And Sitare is quite childish for her age. I don't know . . ."

"You're making a mistake if you have any of the young men on Burgazada in mind. They've all become her friends. Sometimes I think it was a mistake to send our children to an American school. They've learned English, but they've also adopted strange customs. All this talk of friendship between boys and girls. As though one can ever be friends with a member of the opposite sex!"

"Suat, you're better at this sort of thing than I am. Find out how Sitare feels about marriage. Ask her what she would do if a gentleman came calling."

Suat held a finger to her lips. Leman turned around and saw Sitare in the doorway rubbing her eyes. Was that delicate girl with the bleary eyes, stretching and yawning in a poplin bathrobe, a child, or was she a young woman prepared to assume the responsibilities of matrimony?

"Come on in," Leman said to her daughter. "Would you like a cup of coffee?" Sitare was taken aback. She had never been offered coffee before.

"I'll have breakfast first."

"I'll make it for you," Suat said, rushing off to the kitchen, dirty plates in hand. Sitare sat down next to her mother.

"Sitare, you've had a chance to reconsider. Are you certain you don't want to go back to school?"

"Yes, I am."

"What are you planning on doing? Would you like to work, or get married? Have you thought about your future?"

"Most of my friends are in school. A few have married. There's Mualla, for example. None of them work. I guess I'll get married, too."

Leman remembered Mualla's wedding the previous summer. She was the daughter of a doctor friend of Mahir's. Back home after the ceremony, they had gossiped about the reason Mualla might have been married off at such a young age.

"If you'd like to get married, there are suitable candidates. You remember the Camcıoğullar twins out on the island, and there was Ahmet—"

Sitare cut her mother off. "They're boys, mother. I don't want to marry someone my age! Ahmet still has to go to medical school, and then he'll be an intern."

"If you love someone, you wait."

"Like Aunt Sabahat?"

"Never mind her for now. So from what I gather, you don't have feelings for any of the boys at school?"

"We're just friends."

Suat was right, Leman thought.

"I think a husband should be older, more settled, able to look after his wife."

"There aren't many men like your father, my dear," Leman said. When Suat came in with the breakfast tray, she found Leman and Sitare in tears.

"We were talking about marriage, and Sitare said she wanted a husband like Mahir," Leman said. She left the room to wash her face and dry her eyes. Suat decided to pursue the subject further. "Sitare, would you consider marriage?"

"Yes, Auntie. Father died so suddenly. Grandfather is quite old now, and if anything happened to him, what would happen to my mother, Grandma, and me? We need a man. Who would support and protect us?"

"Sitare! What about me and Hilmi? Don't marry for the wrong reasons, my dear. Even if, God forbid, something happened to Hilmi one day, we would still have our pensions and a few properties. Marry for love, not to support your family."

Leman came back into the room. "What were you talking about?" she asked.

"The same thing," Suat said.

"Even if I do marry for love, I want a husband who is more mature than I am."

"If someone were to mention they had found a good match for you, would you consider meeting him?"

"You can't be serious! Are you trying to arrange a marriage for me? Just try it! I'll spill a tray of coffee all over the guy. If I meet the right person, I'll get married. That's the only way!"

Sitare picked up her empty breakfast tray and took it to the kitchen. The second she left the room, Leman said, "I wonder how old this engineer is."

"If he's an engineer, he's done his military service. He must be going on thirty, at least."

52

The Matchmaker

Raif Bey, the confirmed—and by his own account, perfectly content—bachelor, had recently taken to lecturing Muhittin on the unbearable hardships of being a single man, which he always followed with yet another appeal for his friend to get married before it was too late. Muhittin had had enough. Finally, he snapped. "Are you trying to set me up with someone?"

"Yes," Raif Bey said, eyes sparkling.

"Raif Bey, I'm dead set against arranged marriages. Call me overly modern, if you wish, but I believe in kismet. If I meet a woman one day who makes my heart beat faster, I'll know she's the one."

"How do you know the girl I have in mind won't get your heart beating faster? And anyway, what's so modern about believing in fate?"

"I'm going to tell you a secret. I resigned from my job at the municipality because everyone, including the governor, was trying to get me married. You're wasting your time."

"The governor would be a terrible matchmaker. He has no appreciation for beauty and elegance."

"Fine then," Muhittin said. "I'll agree to look at this girl from a distance, just to put an end to this once and for all. If I don't like her, you'll never try anything like this again. Will you agree to stop hectoring me?"

"Yes, but I want you to know that I don't normally do this. It's only because I love you like a son and think this girl would make you happy that I keep insisting. She is from a good family, and pure and lovely as a mountain spring. She has attended high school and speaks English."

"I've met droves of girls with those same qualities. I don't know exactly what it is I'm looking for, but I'll know when I see it."

"Join me for a poker game this week at the house where she's staying with her relatives."

"No way! I don't want to be introduced to the girl or her family. Why raise anyone's hopes? Point her out to me from a distance."

"I'll arrange everything just as you wish, but we'll have to do it this weekend. She and her mother are returning to Istanbul soon."

"Okay. Enough. Now, can you get the latest file on the Çubuk Reservoir? It's urgent."

Muhittin heaved a sigh of relief when Raif Bey scurried out of the room. He was actually looking forward to seeing this girl if it meant his friend would stop badgering him.

When Raif Bey returned a short time later, he had a file under his arm and a plan on his lips. The girl was going for a walk with her family on Sunday, followed by tea and cake with Raif Bey at Özen Patisserie. Muhittin would just happen to be sitting at a table in the patisserie when she arrived there.

"All right, but listen to me: If I'm not interested in her, I'll have my slice of cake put in a box, make my farewells, and go home. No insisting. And don't get huffy if things don't go as you planned."

"Don't worry, you'll love her," Raif Bey said as he left the room on winged feet, lips pursed in a bow-shaped smirk of sheer delight.

53

Sabahat Writes to Aram

Dear Aram,

Don't imagine that my not having written for some time means I have forgotten you for even a moment. I had expected an easier time of it in an empty house, but the opposite has happened. It turns out everyone played a part in making this house the home I so loved, even Leman. Mother and Father are miserable. Father speaks to me only when he must, but he does not talk to anyone else, either. If it were not for his twice weekly visits to his friend, Ahmet Reşit Bey, I fear he would lose the faculty of speech altogether. Mother is suffering shortness of breath and finds it exhausting to talk for any length of time. Thank God my grandma is here, for hers is the only human voice I hear in this house.

I have begun looking for a job, Aram. I might be going back to school; that is, to the American High School for Girls. The board of education informed me that there is an opening. I have an interview next week.

I have some bad news and some good news. Mehpare says Saraylıhanım has not eaten anything for a week and is very frail. Father is upset about that, too. I fear she is coming to the end of her long life.

Now, here is the good news, which I have saved for last. You won't believe it! Our little Sitare has a suitor, but they haven't even told the poor thing about him. My sister wrote that she is afraid Sitare would make a fool of herself if she knew. There's a young engineer, a friend of my uncle's knows him from work. The plan is for the family to encounter the engineer by chance while they are out on a walk. Leman wants Sitare to wear her prettiest dress that day, but she doesn't know how to arrange it without telling her why. You know what Sitare is like. She's certain to do something comical that day.

Dearest Aram, I will make time today to go to Armine's and get your letter. How is your cough? Be sure to wear an undershirt. I should have some amusing stories for you next week. I'll also let you know how my job interview went.

With love,
Sabahat

54

Kismet

Muhittin was sitting at one of the two tables in Özen Patisserie, forcing down a hot cup of salep as he cursed himself for letting Raif Bey talk him into this. He asked the waiter to sprinkle a little more cinnamon on the salep. He was sitting in front of the glass door, watching people go by. As usual, he had arrived ten minutes early. Raif Bey, who was normally so punctual, had not yet arrived. *The girl must be making Raif Bey late,* Muhittin speculated. Well, that was another reason to keep his distance. The moment he saw Raif Bey, he would say, "What a coincidence! I was just leaving. Good day. See you at the office on Monday." Yes, that is what he would do.

Muhittin's frown was replaced by a smile when he saw a young lady peering in through the window. She had a lovely face, but an extremely flat and wide nose, squashed against the glass as it was. Their eyes met. She returned his smile, then she stepped inside, followed by a couple of boys. Her light auburn hair fell straight down her back, and her eyes . . . Muhittin had never seen a pair of eyes so lively and luminous, so oddly compelling, neither hazel nor brown, more like honey, and flecked with gold. She was slender and held herself straight. On her lips was a mischievous smile.

"Six tea cakes please," she said to the man behind the counter.

Muhittin couldn't take his eyes off her. She was wearing a light-beige coat over a dark-green sweater and a tartan skirt.

"Bülent, how many do you want?" she asked the freckled, skinny boy next to her.

"One is enough for me."

"I'll have two," said a plump little boy with enormous eyes.

"Rasin, you'd eat all six if we let you," the young lady said. Muhittin smiled again, but this time she didn't see him.

She was paying for the tea cakes, and in a moment she would walk out of the shop. How would Muhittin see her again? He felt like following her and finding out where she lived. He'd never done that, never followed a girl like a stray dog sniffing out a bone. And what about Raif Bey? How could he leave before Raif Bey came? *I'll say I got sick, that something urgent came up,* he told himself. He got up. He was going to follow her. He had to see more of her, see her face again and again, until he understood it, until he memorized it.

His heart was beating faster. He started to stand up.

"Oh! What a coincidence, Muhittin Bey! Fancy running into you here. It's a small city, isn't it?" Raif Bey smiled and held out his hand. She was leaving with the two boys!

"I . . . um . . . Raif Bey, please excuse me. I have to go."

"Let me introduce you to Hilmi Bey. This is Muhittin, the chief engineer at my office, and this is Suat Hanım, and her sister, Leman Hanım."

"Raif Bey, I . . ." The young lady was walking back inside. Muhittin tried not to stare.

"And this is Sitare, Leman Hanım's daughter."

The room was spinning. He was shaking hands, and there were names, but he had no idea who was who. Except for her. Sitare. It was the first time he had met anyone named Sitare. *Sitare.*

"What a nice name," he stammered.

"It means 'star' in Persian," Sitare explained, looking at Muhittin with eyes like starbursts.

"Muhittin Bey, we were planning to walk through Çankaya. Would you care to join us, or are you busy?" Raif Bey asked.

"No, no, I'm not busy at all," Muhittin said. "Yes."

55

Aram Writes to Sabahat

Dear Sabahat,

I just received your news of Saraylıhanım's death. My condolences, my dear. I can imagine how sad you are. There was nobody like her, and she'll be missed. May she rest in peace. You were right not to inform Leman and Sitare. It would have needlessly upset them to learn about a death in the family while they are still mourning Mahir. I'm eagerly awaiting any news you have of Sitare. Share every last detail with me!

As for your job, Sabahat, that is the best news I have heard in a long time. Stop worrying about the salary. What is important is that you are doing a job you love in a place you love. And what wonderful news that they will provide accommodation as well! It will be like living in a nest high in a tree above the Bosphorus. I'm so happy for you. Here, it's as cold as ever and I never manage to get warm. I'm grateful for the socks and undershirts you

sent. *My only complaint is the cold and not being able to see you. Give each of our friends my greetings.*
  Yours,
  Aram

56

Sitare's New Life

The walk on Sunday concluded with a light meal in a country coffee-house in the vineyards of Etlik. Leman and Suat bombarded Sitare with questions the moment they got home. What did she think of the young engineer? Did she like him? "He reminds me of Prince's master," Sitare said, confounding the sisters for a moment. Who was Prince? Finally, they realized what the girl was talking about: Prince was a black dog that was walked daily past the house on the island. The dog's master was a tall German with combed-back hair and a bearing so erect they joked that he looked as though he had swallowed his walking stick. The sisters had figured out the reference to Prince's master, yet they were no wiser on the question of how Sitare felt about Muhittin.

Muhittin joined Raif Bey that week for a poker game at the house, invited the entire family to lunch that weekend in Çiftlik, and took Sitare and Bülent to the cinema one weekday evening. Just a few days before mother and daughter were to return to Istanbul, he came to the house with Raif Bey and formally asked for Sitare's hand in marriage.

"Sitare will make her own decision," Hilmi Bey said. Muhittin and Sitare excused themselves and set off on a walk to Yenişehir. Leman was certain her daughter, who had never given the slightest indication she admired Muhittin, would refuse his proposal. "What a pity!" Hilmi kept saying. "She'll never find such a suitable candidate!"

About an hour later, Rasin announced, "They're coming!" from his post in front of the window.

"Are they smiling or frowning?" Hilmi asked.

"Neither."

"Are they arm in arm?"

"No."

"Are they walking close together or far apart?"

"Close."

"Well, that's something, at least!"

"We would like to announce some good news," Muhittin said as soon as he stepped inside. As Suat, Hilmi Bey, and the boys embraced Sitare, Leman looked at Muhittin and in a low voice said, "I wish you both every happiness."

That evening, Leman decided, she would sit down for a heart-to-heart talk with Sitare and explain the possible consequences of a sizable age difference. She herself had married a man many years her senior; now she found herself a young widow! If her daughter still wished to proceed with the marriage, then Leman would once again wish the couple every happiness, but mean it this time. "But Grandfather is still alive" was all Sitare said later that evening.

Sitare wished to marry Muhittin. The return to Istanbul was delayed. Muhittin was too busy at work to leave Ankara, so it was decided that the young couple would be engaged at once, with a wedding date to be decided later. Ah, but how could they proceed without obtaining Grandfather's consent?

***

In Istanbul, it was arranged that Gül Hanım, Nusret, and Saadet would visit Reşat Bey and Behice Hanım on behalf of Muhittin to formally request Sitare's hand. Nusret arrived at the mansion in Beyazit with a dozen white roses, and Saadet carried a box of chocolate-covered candied chestnuts from Markiz. Sabahat greeted the guests at the door and ushered them up to the freshly dusted and polished formal sitting room, outside of which Reşat Bey and Behice Hanım were waiting on the landing. Gül Hanım wore a navy-blue scarf over her hair and a dark coat that reached her ankles. With a leather bag draped on one arm, Saadet was stylish in a tailored gray jacket and matching calf-length skirt. Nusret kissed Behice Hanım's hand, as was customary for a woman of her age and status, but he then neglected to bring her hand to his forehead in the traditional show of respect. *How French! This family is not unlike ours,* Behice thought. *A mishmash of old traditions and new ones.* The families sat opposite each other in armchairs. The guests refrained from eying the room, even discreetly, not glancing even once at the large framed photograph of Sitare resting on the table. Gül Hanım spoke only to make the customary introductions and pleasantries.

Over coffee, they discussed the rapidly changing city of Istanbul. Once the empty cups were sent away, Nusret cleared his throat and came to the point. As his father was ailing and thus unable to join them, Nusret represented his wishes, and on behalf of his younger brother, Muhittin, he, Nusret, would like to request Sitare Hanım's hand from her grandfather, Reşat Bey. Nusret extolled Muhittin's virtues, assuring his listeners that Muhittin possessed a sterling character and was nothing like his elder brother. No, the younger brother had always abstained from alcohol and tobacco, gambling, and libertinism of any kind. Saadet stifled a giggle. Nusret masked his own chuckle with a cough. Sabahat decided on the spot that Sitare's prospective brother-in-law was an absolutely wonderful rake.

***

Once the engagement ceremony was set for the month of April, Leman and Suat went to the marketplace in Ulus, selected a length of dark-blue taffeta, and arranged for Sabiha Hanım, a tailor who was just beginning to make a name for herself in Ankara, to design a gown with a narrow skirt and puff sleeves. The ceremony was held at Hilmi and Suat's home and attended by about twenty relatives and Muhittin's close friends. Nusret and Sabahat were the only relatives able to come from Istanbul.

Sitare was strangely subdued. Leman wondered what had happened to her lively, impulsive daughter. However, once the ceremony was over and everyone had gone home, the old Sitare came back, imitating the guests with Bülent. "If Muhittin sees her like this," Leman said to herself, "he'll bring her straight back."

It was not until late summer that Muhittin was able to travel to Istanbul to meet Reşat Bey and Behice Hanım, who warmed to him at first sight: Muhittin was the kind of man to whom a daughter could be entrusted.

Muhittin presented Sitare with a choice: either they would host a wedding reception wherever she wished, or they would go on a honeymoon to Rome, Vienna, and Berlin. In their final destination, he would show his wife the university where he had studied and introduce her to the Germany family that had hosted him. Unfortunately, he did not have the financial resources for both a wedding and a honeymoon. So, which would it be?

Sitare chose a honeymoon without a second thought, thrilled at the idea of traveling with her husband. But Leman was a little crestfallen, as was Reşat Bey. Mahir would have found a way to hold a wedding reception for his daughter. Reşat decided to undertake the expense himself.

Muhittin visited the house on the island one evening, where they coordinated events with the holidays, when Muhittin would have time off work. The state-sanctioned exchange of vows would take place at the end of April at the Beyoğlu Registry Office, and a reception for close relatives and friends would be held that same evening at the mansion in Beyazit. Muhittin would go back to work the following day, returning to Istanbul in June for a wedding party at the Cercle d'Orient, in Beyoğlu, after which the couple would spend two nights at Cercle d'Orient's hotel in Tarabya before setting off for their honeymoon in Europe.

Sitare was beside herself with joy, Leman was able to indulge in the sort of pleasurable anxiety of fussing for fussing's sake, and Reşat Bey and Behice Hanım were satisfied that Mahir, if he was looking down on them, would be pleased. The one dark cloud in that period was the death of Neyir Hanım, who, true to form, passed from this world without being a burden on anyone or uttering a single complaint. Sabahat shed many tears for her grandmother and former roommate, but the other members of the family were either still in mourning for Mahir's much less timely death or too swept up in the excitement of the upcoming wedding to dwell on the loss.

57

The Wedding

Sitare buttoned her snug black tailored jacket, tilted her little hat toward her left eyebrow, and lowered her polka-dot veil over her eyes. The woman reflected in the mirror looked closer to twenty-nine than nineteen. She was ready.

It was taking Leman forever to powder her nose. No sooner did she achieve the desired effect then a tear would roll down her cheek, spoiling it. She dabbed at her face with some cotton, reapplied her mascara, and set to work again with her powder puff. If only Mahir was here at her side on this special day. He would have been so proud. Another tear, another streak of mascara! Reşat called out from downstairs: "Come on, we're going to be late." She grabbed her handbag and ran down to join her family in the entrance hall. She could hear the light clicking of Sitare's new high-heeled shoes.

Standing with her hand on the banister midway down the stairs as she waited for her dumbstruck family's comments was a poised young woman. Leman clasped her hands under her chin and gazed up at her daughter, oblivious now to the tears ruining her makeup.

Once the tedious signing of the marriage certificates and long line of well-wishers had been dispensed with, the family went home to receive their close relatives and friends for the wedding dinner. Hüviyet, Fazilet, Naci, Melek, school friends, and cousins gathered around Sitare, along with Muhittin's family members. Naci sang everything from German lieder to arias and tangos while Bülent, on the accordion, and Sabahat, on the violin, played a repertoire of classics and modern hits. Salih Bey and Gül Hanım grew wide-eyed at the unusual entertainment, and Reşat Bey suggested adjourning to the sitting room. But no, Salih Bey was simply waiting for the opportunity to dance a Bosnian *kolo* with his son. Nusret Bey joined in with Rumelian folk songs, dancing as he sang, and Saadet contributed a few favorites from the old country as well. Then it was Leman's turn to play some Istanbul classics on the piano. When the elderly members of the party retired to the sitting room, the young people fox-trotted and jitterbugged to gramophone records until Muhittin and Sitare led the final dance of the night, a waltz. Soon other couples joined in, spinning each other around the room and, unavoidably, bumping into each other, to the merriment of one and all. There was fun, laughter, and dancing. From a corner, Leman looked at the scene and dabbed at her eyes with a handkerchief.

58

The River of Life

Life is like an everflowing river. That's what Sitare was thinking as she looked at the wedding photographs in the hotel room. There was a photo of Azra and her fiancé, and kneeling in front of them she spotted Mualla and her husband Habib. Semiha, also in the photo, had been married awhile, and Vala had been married the previous week. The beauty in the corner was Siret, still single, but waiting for Mehmet Ali to finish his military service. Had she and the little women posing in that photograph really played beach volleyball together only a year or two earlier? Were they the same girls forming a human pyramid in another photograph, the ones who had tickled each other in the dormitory, tittering and screaming, until the headmistress scolded them?

When did we grow up? Sitare wondered. *How fast it happened! Was it in the space of a minute, or overnight? When did those round faces and pink cheeks become delicately sculpted, and when did real breasts* replace *balls of cotton?* Was there a precise moment when she'd officially become a grown-up? Had it been when she found out her father was dead, when she slipped into the tailored black jacket for her wedding ceremony, when she changed into a white gown for her wedding reception?

Life is like a flow of water. That was the first line of the poem her father had sometimes recited. And she would be carried, as though by a current, to a house where she had not been born, to a neighborhood where she had not grown up, to a brand-new city whose streets she could not name. She would flow with the current to Ankara. If Mahir had not died quietly in the night, how different her life would be. She never would have met Muhittin. She wouldn't have been wearing the long white gown in that photograph. Her father, even in death, had altered the course of her life. Muhittin was a good man, handsome and kind, and Mahir would have liked him. He was a serious man, more like Reşit Bey than the father-in-law he would never know. And he loved Sitare, loved her faults and her impulsiveness, loved her just as much—if in a different way—as her father had.

Sitare wished Mahir had seen Leman at the wedding reception in a black dress with lace at the bust and Grandmother's diamond bird brooch pinned to the collar, elegant and forbidding in her melancholy.

After the wedding, the brooch had been presented to Sitare, who would pass it along to her own daughter, if she had one, and if the girl married one day. Leman had not been impressed by the brooch Muhittin had pinned to Sitare's collar; it was too understated and modern.

"Are you still looking at those photos?" Muhittin said from the other side of the room. "Darling, the cab will be here soon."

Sitare slipped into her handbag a few of the wedding photographs Nusret had sent to their hotel. They would soon be catching a plane to Berlin. Sabahat and Nesime would be taking those items they wouldn't be traveling with to the mansion in Beyazit, but Sitare suspected that the rest of her family would be waiting at the airport in Yeşilköy to see them off.

There was a knock on the door, and Sabahat stepped into the room. "Are you both ready? Your cab is here. Go on, I'll take care of everything here."

Muhittin and Sitare embraced Sabahat. As they were walking through the door, Sitare ran back and hugged her aunt again. "Sabahat," she said, "you'll be getting married soon, too. I can feel it. Believe me."

59

Chocolates and Divorce

Gül Hanım pulled the unopened boxes of chocolates out of the trash can, wiped them with a damp cloth, and hid them in the bottom of the screen-covered cupboard in the kitchen. When Saadet was not looking, she would let the boys pop a few chocolates into their mouths. Why throw away perfectly good Swiss chocolates? Wastefulness was a terrible sin in the eyes of good Muslims, a tenet she had clearly failed to impress on any of her children except for Muhittin. The prodigality of the other two was both a sin and a shame, she clucked to herself. Their failure to perform their prayers would be recorded against them, but their wastefulness would be considered a far graver transgression come Judgment Day. For a moment, Gül Hanım considered sending the boxes of chocolate to Ecla, who would pass them around to her guests and say they were from her generous mother-in-law. No, no! Why not let Salih Bey enjoy them after the others had gone to their rooms after dinner?

Saadet had suffered terribly in the days after her husband left, crying in her room and seething in silence, until she finally seemed resigned to the estrangement. There had been no time for moping, not with all the shopping for her brother's engagement and wedding, ordering gifts for Sitare, meeting with seamstresses and tailors, selecting a brooch for Muhittin to pin on the bride, and furnishing a new flat for the young couple. Saadet had forgotten Ekrem completely, or at least that was what Gül Hanım thought. Her assumption was a reasonable one. The name Ekrem had not been mentioned in the house since the day they had asked for Sitare's hand. That is, until just last week, when Gül Hanım had sat her daughter down and said, "If you still love your husband, talk to him. Ask him to come home."

"I'd rather die."

"Do you want a divorce?"

Saadet had not answered. Divorce was so rare that nobody quite knew what it was, and if the word was pronounced at all, it was usually in a whisper. Saadet was not opposed to Ekrem moving into a house of his own. She would remain his wife in the eyes of the law, and one day, for the sake of the children only, they might agree to live together again. Gül Hanım thought her daughter's wishes were somewhat—if not wholly—justified. After all, Saadet had stood by her husband back when he was a poorly paid attorney. She had never complained or made unreasonable demands. Their sons had been born in Salih Bey's house and had been fed at his table, a fact Saadet had never flung in her husband's face. She had never asked him for money. When Ekrem had given up his legal practice and gone into business, she had stood by her husband yet again. Salih Bey's properties had even been mortgaged to secure bank loans for Ekrem. To be fair, he had repaid the family in full, but what other wife would have done that for her husband?

Ekrem had made a mistake. He was in the wrong. But by chasing her husband out of the house in front of everyone, Saadet brought shame upon herself. Naturally, Ekrem would return only if his wife asked him to. Gül Hanım knew Saadet secretly hoped that Ekrem would approach her on bended knee and beg to be allowed to return, just as she was absolutely certain that Ekrem was waiting for his wife to make the first overture. Saadet was so obstinate! Her Bosnian blood had turned her into a stubborn mountain goat!

The previous week, Ecvet and Erol had visited their father when he returned from a business trip abroad. He had brought them both school bags, caps, and two pairs each of fine woolen socks that went clear up to the knee. He'd also given them a few boxes of chocolates to give their mother and their Jijo.

Saadet had said nothing about the gifts for the boys, but she had rushed off to the kitchen with the chocolates. Unable to find them after dinner, Gül Hanım had asked where they were.

"I threw them out!"

"Mother, you could have at least left a box for Jijo," Erol had said.

"Jijo wouldn't touch them, and neither would your grandfather. You and your brother are the only ones in this house with a financial claim on Ekrem Bey."

Gül Hanım had bitten her tongue and soothed her daughter, whose hands were trembling in rage. The following day, Gül Hanım and Saadet visited a friend and learned that the other woman had accompanied Ekrem on his business trip and returned laden with presents. "Don't believe everything you hear," Gül Hanım had said. "Someone saw them at the department store," the gossip responded. "Why are you telling us?" Saadet snapped. "Ekrem Bey is a stranger to us now. What he does is none of our business."

Shortly afterward, Saadet and Gül Hanım bid their hostess a good day. On the way home, Gül Hanım pronounced the gossip an ill-mannered woman. Saadet responded, "It is your former son-in-law who is ill-mannered. He buys bags of presents for his mistress and socks for his sons! And for me he gets two boxes of chocolates!"

Perhaps I should have left those chocolates in the trash, Gül Hanım was thinking when she was startled by Saadet's voice.

"Mother! I've been calling you for half an hour."

Gül Hanım turned to her daughter. The elderly woman did not need her spectacles to see the shimmer of tears on Saadet's face. Saadet was holding a small, yellowish sheet of paper. Gül Hanım felt the churning in her stomach she always got at the sight of a legal document.

"What's that thing in your hand?" she asked in a low voice.

"Ekrem Bey has served papers." She spoke in a strangled whisper, one syllable at a time. "He's divorcing me, Mother. Incompatibility of temperament."

Gül Hanım rushed over and caught Saadet in her arms as she fainted, and screamed as loud as she could for Salih Bey and her grandsons to come and help. They stretched Saadet out on the divan in the living room, waved a bottle of cologne under her nose, and wiped the beads of sweat from her temples and forehead. When tears emerged from Saadet's closed eyes, Gül Hanım knew she had recovered. Excusing herself for a moment, Gül Hanım went into the kitchen, took the boxes of chocolate out of the cupboard, and threw them into the trash.

60

Beautiful Ankara

As Sitare dusted their small flat, she whistled along to the rousing strains of the "Ankara March" playing on the radio: "Ankara, Ankara, beautiful Ankara. First city created out of nothing." Sitare truly believed with all her heart that Ankara was the most beautiful city in the world. In the afternoon, she would look out the window at the pairs of lovers congregated below the clock tower in Kızılay Square, the political heart of the city. The entire town seemed to flow past her window. Right across from their apartment building, which was located on Ankara's broadest boulevard and in its most lively and modern neighborhood, was the heroic statuary of Güven Park and the ornamental pool of Kızılay Park. Their building also housed the hottest nightclub around, Süreyya, as well as the Ulus Cinema. To top it all off, Sosyal Apartments was one of the rare residential buildings to feature central heating. There were four main entrances, and the complex covered an entire city block. The landlord had converted the flat rooftop into a garden terrace with potted plants, flower beds, and an oval pool in which red fish circled. In the evenings, everyone would go up onto that rooftop terrace to drink and chat with their neighbors. Ankara's attractions were too numerous to list! Adding to Sitare's enjoyment of the city was the decision many of her friends had made to move there. There was Azra from high school, also married to an engineer, who had told her just yesterday that another former classmate, Ferruha, had moved into town. She wondered if Ferruha had a telephone. Muhittin, who was so often away, had had a phone installed so he could hear his wife's voice, and it also enabled Sitare to chat and make plans with her friends. In addition to making shopping expeditions and hosting bezique parties, she taught English twice a week to two little girls. Years later, Aram and Sabahat would laugh when they learned of it, but she didn't care and told them that she was applying the methods Aram had used with her. The one area of her new life Sitare had not immediately taken to was cooking. She had never been allowed to cook as a girl and had no experience. One evening, Muhittin came home to find the kitchen wall near the stove covered with pasta.

"Sitare! What is that?" he asked.

"You can find out if pasta is done by throwing it against the wall. If it sticks, it's done."

"Who told you that?"

"Azra."

"Sitare, you've thrown nearly the whole pot of pasta at the wall! There's not enough left for dinner. Get dressed, I'll take you out to Karpiç tonight for dinner."

Over time, Sitare had found yet another reason to be glad they had moved to Ankara. Had they stayed in Istanbul, she would never have learned anything. Here, she had slowly become a skilled housewife. If she burned the cake the first three times she baked it, it came out perfectly the fourth time. By her sixth attempt at stuffed grape leaves, Muhittin's compliments to the lovely chef were genuine—not that Muhittin ever complained. He ate anything and everything she cooked.

Still, Muhittin wished he and his wife shared more interests. Sometimes at dinner, for example, he would explain how fortunate it was that Russia supported Turkey's claims on the straits of the Bosphorus and the Dardanelles. "If it weren't for Moscow, Europe would never have allowed Turkey to gain full control," he would be saying, and then he would fall silent when he realized Sitare was not listening to him. There was so much happening, and he would have loved to discuss it: the new labor law; low-interest loans for farmers; efforts to stamp out poverty; the successes of the five-year development plan implemented in 1933; the new railways, factories, institutes, and power plants. Why, just in the year they were married, the state had nationalized the Istanbul Telephone Company; established the first power plant in Amasya; founded the chrome smelting plant in Elazığ; extended the railway lines so that they stretched more than four thousand miles; and opened plants to produce ethyl alcohol, cloth, and cardboard in Eskişehir, Malatya, and İzmit. Village schools and teacher training centers had been set up; Ankara University now had a School of Language, History, and Geography; and the Ankara State Conservatory and State Theater had been founded under the direction of Carl Ebert.

Muhittin wanted to share all of these successes with his wife. He so identified with the young republic that he was like a proud parent trying to show off his child's achievements. But Sitare clearly preferred reading Halide Edip Adıvar's novel *The Clown and His Daughter* to listening to her husband gush about their country.

Not to worry. She's still young, he'd tell himself at night as he buried his face in her hair and touched his lips to her smooth skin.

Sitare was not the only person too caught up in daily life to worry about the country's future. Muhittin found that very few of his colleagues were concerned by the possible ramifications of the months-long Dersim Rebellion suppressed in September 1937, or by the increasing militarism of Hitler's Germany and the ongoing Spanish Civil War. Worrisome, too, were the reports on Atatürk's health. The father of the country was said to be ailing, and Muhittin was both saddened and alarmed.

61

November 10, 1938

Muhittin's fears proved to be prophetic. The first intrusion of the outer world into the newlyweds' domestic bliss occurred near the end of 1938 and brought them closer together. It was announced on the morning of November 10 that Mustafa Kemal Atatürk was dead. Sitare learned of it only when her husband came home that evening. They sat in front of the radio, crying and talking all through the night. Their country had lost its founder and first president. Could it manage an orderly transition to new leadership, or would there be chaos? The following day, İsmet İnönü was elected by parliament to lead the nation.

A new era was dawning in Ankara.

As Atatürk's body was lying in repose in Dolmabahçe Palace, in Istanbul, it was decided that the Ethnography Museum in Ankara would be used as his temporary resting place. On the morning of November 19, after funeral prayers were said in the palace, Atatürk's casket was transferred to the battle cruiser TCG *Yavuz* and sent off with a hundred-gun salute to İzmit. A funeral train then carried the body to Ankara, stopping at each station along the way to allow the throngs of mourners to pay their respects. Atatürk, who had always been greeted with cheers when he arrived at the central train station in Ankara, was met this time by tears and funeral marches. His casket, wrapped in the Turkish flag, was placed on a catafalque in front of the Grand National Assembly, to be guarded by four officers wearing swords. Thousands flocked there, all through the day and night, to pay their respects. The following day, a horse-drawn caisson conveyed the father of the Turks to his temporary resting place. The cortege included Turkish statesmen and generals, as well as dignitaries and honor guards from numerous countries. Soldiers from foreign lands, some of which had been mortal enemies just nineteen years earlier, stood with their Turkish counterparts, their weapons pointed at the ground. Farther back walked students, teachers, workers, peasants, shopkeepers, and housewives.

Sitare watched the funeral procession with her newly retired Uncle Hilmi and Aunt Suat from a building on the route. Muhittin was marching with the state dignitaries, and Bülent and Rasin were there with their schools. When Sitare started crying, Hilmi Bey said, "When I first came to Ankara, the French, British, Italian, and Greek flags were flying over the train station. It is because of Atatürk that our flag waves there today. Look, even our former enemies are here to pay their respects. Don't cry. Be proud!"

Shortly after Atatürk's death came a dark period for Turkey and for all of Europe, which, having learned nothing from "the war to end all wars," was mobilizing for battle once again. On the morning of September 1, 1939, Germany invaded Poland. Turkey prepared for the worst. Sitare and a few of her friends began attending courses twice a week to learn how to prepare dressings, clean wounds, and stanch blood. Soon, every young civil servant in Ankara could say his wife had learned the fundamentals of nursing.

As Turkey tried to stay neutral in the war, food rationing began. The government was on edge, and the people were weary of the increasingly hard times. A black market was thriving. Blackouts were ordered. And then, on November 27, 1939, an earthquake shook Erzincan, killing thirty-three thousand and destroying forty-five thousand homes. Sent to the epicenter, Muhittin was away from Sitare for two months.

Somehow, Muhittin and Sitare managed to preserve their happy marriage. All they lacked was a child. In their first two years together, they had taken measures to avoid getting pregnant, but now they wanted a child, and still Sitare had not become pregnant. Leman advised them to consult with a doctor, who told them there was no medical reason in the way of their dream.

62

Narmanlı

Leman packed two nightgowns, two toothbrushes, and a bottle of cologne in her accordion travel bag. She placed a straw hat on her head and applied rouge to her lips. "Come on, Sitare," she called out. "If you don't hurry up, we'll miss the ferry." Her daughter was sitting on a divan in the entrance hall of the family summer house, paging through a fashion magazine. Sitare put down the magazine and gathered her things. She went out to the front garden, where her grandparents were sitting in wicker chairs under the arbor, and gave them each a kiss. Leman rushed after her, toting her own heavy bag.

"There's still half an hour before the ferry," Behice Hanım said.

"She can't walk very fast in her condition."

"Are you coming back this evening?"

"We might spend the night in Narmanlı. What do you say, Sitare?" Leman asked.

"I miss Bülent. I'm going to stay with my aunt. You can stay in Narmanlı if you like."

The family had rented a flat with a street view on the third floor of Narmanlı Apartments, situated on the corner across from the Teşvikiye Mosque. The mansion in Beyazit had been sold at the beginning of the summer, and the new owners would be moving in by the end of September. The plan was to move into the flat when they left the island for the season. Suat and Leman had found the family's new home together. It was close to Şakayık Street, where Suat now lived with her husband, and it was also within walking distance of the mansion where Reşat Bey's old friend, Ahmet Reşit Rey, lived. The family praised the spacious, bright rooms of the new apartment in an effort to take some of the sting out of having to leave their mansion. There were many sensible reasons for the move. The family had shrunk in size, the expense of maintaining and cleaning such a large house was prohibitive, and Beyazıt was no longer a desirable neighborhood. Most importantly, Leman's parents thought the time had come for Leman to leave her memories of Mahir in the old house.

While Sitare was being examined, Leman sat in the waiting room and read magazines. She, the wife of a doctor, still preferred to stay away from patients, even when it was her own daughter. She had once made the mistake of accompanying Sitare into the dentist's office, and the sight of her daughter in pain had made her nauseous for several hours. When the examination was over, Dr. Tevfik Remzi Kazancıgil called out, "Come on in, Leman Hanım. It's all over."

Leman stepped inside the exam room. Sitare was on her feet, and the nurse was helping her to collect herself.

"Everything is going well," the doctor said. "The baby should arrive no later than the beginning of October."

The mother and daughter slowly trudged up steep Kazancı Yokuşu to Taksim Square, where they boarded for the first time the

Maçka-Taksim-Tünel streetcar to their new neighborhood, sitting one behind the other in the single passenger seats of the red car.

"Shall we get off at Teşvikiye to look at the apartment?" Leman asked.

"I'd rather stop off at my aunt's," Sitare replied. "I need a cup of tea."

They got off at the stop in front of the police station and went into the two-story apartment building on the corner of Karakol and Şakayık Streets. There was no reason to ring the buzzer; Suat had seen them. "Come in," she said, waving them into a hallway smelling of freshly baked cake.

"Isn't Bülent here?" Sitare asked.

"He'll be coming home around six."

Bülent had graduated from the College of Business and Commerce and was currently employed by a German firm. A short time later, he returned home with his father. Rasin was hungry, so they sat down to dinner early. Suat described the new seating arrangement in the Narmanlı flat to Leman, who was anxious to go and see for herself. A bed was made up on the living room couch for Rasin so that Sitare and Bülent could stay in the same room, talking late into the night like they'd often done as kids. Hilmi Bey and Suat decided to walk with Leman over to Narmanlı. Bülent and Sitare were stretched out on their beds in Rasin's room talking about the old days and how Leman had made him translate Sabahat's letters, when Sitare cut him off. "Bülent! I think something's happening. I wonder if I'm about to have the baby."

"What's happening?"

"It's a weird churning feeling. Am I in labor, Bülent?"

"How I am supposed to know? I've never had a baby!" His eyes as big as saucers, Bülent ran to his parents' room, but they weren't back yet. He hesitated for a moment, not sure if he should leave Sitare alone as he looked for his parents. He had just changed out of his pajamas in the bathroom when he heard a key turning in the lock. They were home. Thank God!

"Sitare's having a baby! She's having a baby!" he yelled. In an instant, Suat was at Sitare's side. She was standing up, hands on her belly, as fluid flowed down her legs.

"Hilmi! Get a cab, quick," Suat shouted. "Bülent, run and tell your aunt!" Suat ran to the door and shouted down the staircase: "It's number two, on the third floor. Bülent! Don't forget. Number two, third floor."

Five minutes later, they were in a cab on their way to the hospital. Leman was cursing the good doctor who only that day had told them Sitare wasn't due for at least another fifteen days.

63

Delirious

Muhittin took another photograph of the chasm stretching out before him. In places, the rain-engorged Euphrates snaked along the riverbed below crags so sharp and bare it was as if they had been carved by a sword; and in other places, it meandered past tree-dotted bluffs. It was madness to attempt to plant electrical poles in the upper reaches of this valley, but there was no other way to bring water and electricity to the mountain villages. Muhittin had been struggling for almost three weeks to widen a rough track. He had done all he could, but it had not been enough. At their most recent meeting, the minister had told him to shift his focus to housing problems, to which he had retorted, "How can something that doesn't even exist have any problems?" Much of the local "housing" was in the form of caves lacking front doors. He could build simple two-room structures. The bottom floor would be used for livestock, as was the custom in these parts, but at least the local families would have indoor toilets and a kitchen. When he had suggested leaving water and power issues for later, Avni Bey had said, "Muhittin, you'd better watch your step. You've got a family now; your wife is expecting."

The ministers and bureaucrats in Ankara were absolutely clueless when it came to conditions in the field.

Yes, Avni Bey did have a point. He did have a family to support, and he had a wife whose face he had not seen in the two months he had been here, riding donkeys and horses in the mountains and traveling by kelek on the Euphrates. Sitare was in Istanbul, out on the island with her grandparents. He missed her and his little home. He missed turning a spigot for water, pushing a button to turn on a lamp, and striking a match to light the stove. He missed civilization, water, soap, clean white sheets; sitting on a winged chair with his feet up while he read the newspaper; having lunch at Karpiç with his wife; dancing at Süreyya.

For what seemed like years, Muhittin had been using the river as his toilet, washing his laundry in that same river, sleeping with the setting sun and rising with the dawn, and subsisting mostly on stale bread and powdered yogurt soup. His face, neck, and the exposed areas of his arms, from the elbows down, looked like tanned leather. What would Sitare say when she saw him? He looked nothing like Prince's master these days. With his mane of unkempt hair and his shaggy beard, he looked like a day laborer.

In three days, he would set off from the nearest village on the back of a donkey to see if he had any letters. He had heard nothing from his wife for fifteen days. In mid-September, when the road had been built and utility poles erected, he would head straight for Istanbul without stopping in Ankara. He had promised to make it back for the birth of their first child. Sitare had had such a difficult pregnancy that they had worried for a time about the baby's health. He had taken her to the Porsuk Reservoir one day, and she had been bitten by a mosquito. Who would have guessed that his wife would contract malaria in a place like Eskişehir? He'd lived near a swamp in Adana without getting ill even once. Her chills and fever had kept recurring, and her daily doses of quinine had side effects that complicated her pregnancy. At the beginning of the summer, a friend, Dr. Mim Kemal, had even warned that the pregnancy might have to be terminated for the sake of the mother's health. Thank God those days were behind them, and the baby had nearly been carried to term. He wrote encouraging letters to his wife whenever he could: "Hang in there, my dear, we're almost there."

Muhittin shivered in the wind. In the mountains, it had started to get cold in early September. He wished he had brought heavier clothing. He went over to the tent to get another shirt. Şamil was retethering the tent poles to the stakes.

"The wind's picking up, Engineer Efendi," Şamil said. "I'm making sure our tent doesn't blow away."

"Could you make us something hot to eat tonight?"

"All we've got left in the pack is powdered yogurt for soup."

Muhittin buttoned up a second shirt and cursed himself for not having brought a sweater. When he came out of the tent, he could see a small dust cloud on the horizon. Someone was riding up on a donkey. That was odd! They were supposed to be out here on their own for another three days. He went back into the tent and got a pair of binoculars.

"Şamil, is that Asaf riding up to us? Could you have a look?"

Şamil took the binoculars. "Yes, it's Asaf!"

"Why is he here?"

"How do I know? He's got an extra donkey with him."

"Something's happened at base camp. They must need my help. Good grief."

Fifteen minutes later, when Asaf was within earshot, Muhittin shouted, "What happened? What are you doing here?"

"I came to get you, sir."

"What happened? Spit it out, Asaf."

Asaf tethered the donkeys to a tree and came running up to the level ground where the tent was pitched. "The headman sent me, sir. Your baby has been born! A telegram came. Hey, sir, where are you going?"

His things hastily stuffed into his duffel bag, Muhittin came running out of the tent. He kissed Asaf on the cheeks. "You guys can take down the tent tomorrow and go back with one donkey. The jeep will come and get whatever you can't carry. See you." He ran down, untied one of the donkeys, and jumped on its back.

A baby! It had been born prematurely. He wondered if it was healthy. And how was Sitare? Had they made it to the hospital? Had she given birth on the island? Or, God forbid, in the street?

As he spurred on the donkey, he did some quick calculations. If he got to the village within two hours, he would be able to get a vehicle to the city, and from there a bus to Ankara. No, he would take a vehicle to Elazığ and catch the train to Ankara. It would take time, but there wouldn't be any surprise delays, like a flat tire or a landslide. He decided against going to the base camp. He could change and bathe when he got to Ankara. He had no time to lose.

In the village, he asked if there was a vehicle free to take him to Elazığ. Damn it! There was one only one, and it had just left to take the midwife to a neighboring district.

"You'll have to take the bus. There's one leaving this evening," the village chief told him.

Muhittin went to the dusty square where the buses departed. There was an empty seat in the very back. After three hours of traveling on a bumpy dirt road, they reached Elazığ. The driver got up and looked at the one passenger still on the bus.

"Aren't you getting out?"

"Was this your last trip?"

"Yes. My next one is early tomorrow morning."

The passenger was waving a ten-lira note. "I'm in a big hurry. Could you take me to the station? I've got to catch the train to Ankara."

"Is all that money in your hand for me?"

"If you get me there in time, yes."

"Hang on tight," the driver said as he stepped on the gas pedal.

***

Covered with a layer of white dust, Muhittin was sitting on a wooden bench in the train. He made a pillow out of the extra shirt he was wearing and fell asleep.

He didn't wake up until they were pulling into the station in Ankara. Stiffly leaping off the train, he ran over to the counter and bought a ticket for the sleeping car to Istanbul. The train wouldn't leave until later that day. There were cabs lined up in front of the station. *Bless you, civilization!* he thought. He got into one and told the driver his address.

"My wife just had a baby," he added.

"Congratulations. Boy or girl?"

"I don't know."

And he really didn't know. He got out at his apartment building and went into the empty flat. The curtains were closed, and it was dark. Dust danced in the sunlight filtering through a crack in the curtains. He left them closed and went into the bathroom to draw a bath. The water came out red with rust and cold—today wasn't one of the days the building got hot water. Never mind! He could still soak in a tub of water. He balled up the dusty, smelly clothes on his back and threw them into the hamper. He went into the kitchen naked and opened the wire-covered cupboard. Empty! Easing himself into the half-full tub, he sang the praises of civilization for the second time that day.

Setting the alarm clock, he stretched out in the bed he had missed and imagined being next to his wife. When the alarm sounded, he would shave, get dressed, and catch his train. He didn't want Sitare to see him looking haggard and exhausted. Nor his baby. *Who knows,* he thought, *perhaps babies understand and remember more than we give them credit for.* He would have a nap for the sake of his wife and his child. His child! A new life! He didn't know if it was a boy or a girl, healthy or unhealthy, disabled or not. All he knew was that he had a child. *This,* Muhittin thought as he was falling asleep, *is what it means to be delirious with happiness.*

64

A New Life

It was Suat who opened the door and welcomed Muhittin into the flat in Narmanlı. Beaming, she held a finger up to her lips and spoke in a whisper.

"We've been waiting for you, Muhittin. Welcome. Come in, dear. Try to keep it down. Your daughter didn't let any of us sleep until dawn. Everyone's in bed. Sitare just fell asleep, too; she was so exhausted. I'm looking after the little tyrant." Suat took Muhittin by the hand and led him into the living room. "Come on, we put the cradle in here. She's finally asleep. Keep quiet."

Muhittin tiptoed through the living room. Suat had said "your daughter." *It's a girl!* he thought. He had a daughter. He leaned over the cradle festooned with colorful ribbons. There, mewing in her sleep, a tuft of fine hair falling over her forehead, was the tiniest, most beautiful baby he had ever seen in his life.

"She arrived a little prematurely, but she's healthy as can be," Suat whispered. "Muhittin, I was there with Sitare the whole time. I prayed and prayed for a healthy baby. The birth was easy. The pregnancy was difficult, but the birth was no problem at all. After they swaddled her, they gave her to me first. I held her in my arms and whispered her middle name into her ear. Now that you're here, you can choose her name."

"What is her middle name?"

"The same as mine. Ayşe."

"You've done well. That one name is enough for her. She's so tiny I don't think she could carry two names."

Muhittin couldn't resist reaching into the cradle. "Wait, let me help you. I'll pick her up without waking her," Suat said, gently scooping up the baby with practiced hands and handing her, blanket and all, to Muhittin. "Support her head."

Muhittin looked down at the miracle in his arms. The baby made faint snorts and squeaks, an eye winking open and closing. Muhittin caught a glimpse of deep blue.

"She has blue eyes," he said.

"Just like her dad."

"My daughter."

The weeks he had spent in villages without roads, water, and light; under lice-infested quilts; eating rock-hard bread he had moistened in his mouth before swallowing; working with blockheads—oh, and they were many!—who fought progress and beauty every step of the way; sometimes succumbing to a deep pessimism: it all vanished. His ears filled with birdsong. His heart filled with light. Every cell in his tired body was reborn. He was, once again, full of hope; he was, once again, the idealistic and confident engineer who had set out for Anatolia ten years earlier. The world would be a better place for his daughter. He would help build a better country; he could do it. When Ayşe grew up, every town would have power and running water; there wouldn't be a single town without a school; there wouldn't be a single person who hadn't learned how to read and write.

Hope! Each new life is hope. Each new day is hope, he thought.

Muhittin buried his nose in Ayşe's neck, and as he breathed in that baby smell, milk mingled with soap, he knew that never again, not for the rest of his life, would he know a love so pure and so charged with meaning.

Epilogue

Novels come to an end but have no real ending. This one concludes with my birth, the beginning of a life that will end with my death.

A tidy ending is particularly elusive when the "loose ends" are cherished family members.

My father's father, Salih Kulin, passed away four months before I was born. Sadly, I would know the grandfather who was never happy in his adopted country and always yearned for his homeland only from photographs.

My father's mother, Gül Hanım, spent the rest of her days surrounded by Bosnian relatives and friends in the mansion in Sultanahmet, confined to her bed for the last seven years of her life following a stroke. I was fourteen when we lost her.

My great-grandfather on my mother's side, Ahmet Reşat, died after a prostate operation the summer I turned ten. It was my first encounter with the death of a loved one, and it shook me badly. My maternal grandfather, Doctor Mahir, had died six years before my birth, making Ahmet Reşat the only grandfather I had ever known. With his speech, clothing, and manners, he was an original, and I was devoted to him. Although I was still a young girl when we lost him, my relationship with my great-grandfather affected me greatly and would inspire me many years later to write the novel *Farewell: A Mansion in Occupied Istanbul*. I believe that it is partly because of me that my great-grandfather, who still appears in my dreams on occasion, left this world at peace with the new Republican regime. His wife, Behice Hanım—that is, my great-grandmother—lived for another six years, gazing out the window of the Narmanlı apartment and missing her husband.

Grandmother Leman, who was widowed at a young age, spent the rest of her life in Narmanlı, the apartment they moved into the year I was born. She never remarried, devoting herself entirely to her one and only granddaughter—that is, to me. When I arrived in Istanbul to begin junior high at Robert College, her life grew busy: when I married, she rejoiced; when I divorced, she grieved; when I remarried, she rejoiced again; and the fact that I brought four sons into the world made her nearly burst with pride. At ninety-seven, according to official records, but not a day under 102 according to family lore, Leman Hanım passed. Whenever I remember her, I always feel a pang that I was never able to show how much I loved her.

Bülent, the elder son of my grandmother's sister, Suat, and my great uncle, Hilmi, gave his parents two beautiful granddaughters. Suat and Hilmi, too, honored family tradition by devoting themselves to their grandchildren. Perhaps my great uncle, a fine painter, could have had a more colorful life. Had he had the opportunity, his paintings might today line the walls of an art museum, as well as my apartment. He opted instead to remain "the man of the house." While nothing would compare to the summer house on the island, our family enjoyed many splendid summer holidays in the 1950s in the garden of the villa they built on the Asian shore of Istanbul.

My grandmother's younger sister, Sabahat, and her great love, Aram, married six months after I was born, in 1942. I have related their marriage in detail in a biographical work entitled *Joy*. Although their daughter, Filiz, belongs to my mother's generation, she is six years younger than me and grew up to become like a sister to me. My great aunt Sabahat died before her husband. By that time, their daughter Filiz had moved to America, and bureaucratic hurdles prevented her from returning. I cared for my dear Uncle Aram, who loved me as a daughter. He breathed his last breath in my arms. Filiz still lives in New York with her husband and her cat.

I proved to be the most productive of my cousins. Currently, I have four sons, eight grandchildren, and twenty-nine published works.

Let me remind readers of this book that in two later biographies, *Joy and Sorrow*, and *Illusions* (not yet available in English), I write of my life, which began in September 1941, and the life of my family, and I explore Turkey's social and political evolution.

I would like to take this opportunity to thank Ledig House and D. W. Gibson for welcoming me to their writers' colony, where I worked on this novel in September and October of 2008.

About the Author

One of Turkey's most beloved authors, Ayşe Kulin is known for her captivating stories about human endurance. In addition to penning internationally bestselling novels, she has worked as a producer, cinematographer, and screenwriter for numerous television shows and films. Her novel *Last Train to Istanbul* won the European Council of Jewish Communities Best Novel Award and has been translated into twenty-three languages. *Farewell: A Mansion in Occupied Istanbul* was long-listed for the International IMPAC Dublin Literary Award in 2011.

About the Translator

Born in Salt Lake City, Utah, in 1964, Kenneth Dakan has spent the past twenty-five years working as a freelance writer, editor, voice-over artist, and translator in fields ranging from cinema and travel to banking and contemporary art. Currently, he lives in Istanbul, where his focus is on literary translation from Turkish to English. Among the many authors whose works of fiction and nonfiction he has translated are Perihan Mağden, Ayşe Kulin, Ece Temelkuran, Birgül Oğuz, and Buket Uzuner.